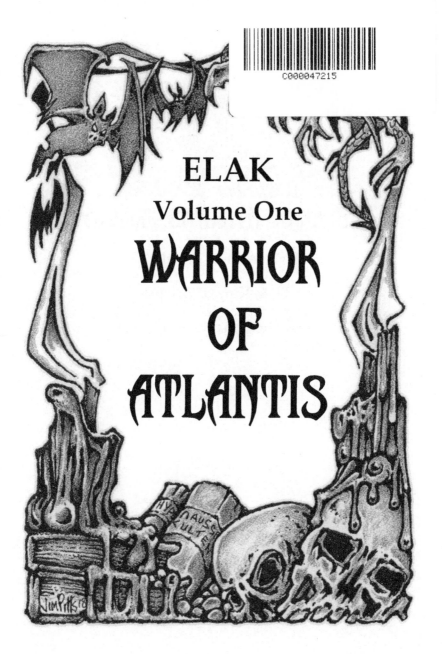

ELAK

Volume One

WARRIOR

OF

ATLANTIS

ELAK OF ATLANTIS TRILOGY

Elak, Warrior of Atlantis

Elak, King of Atlantis

Elak, Sea Hawks of Atlantis

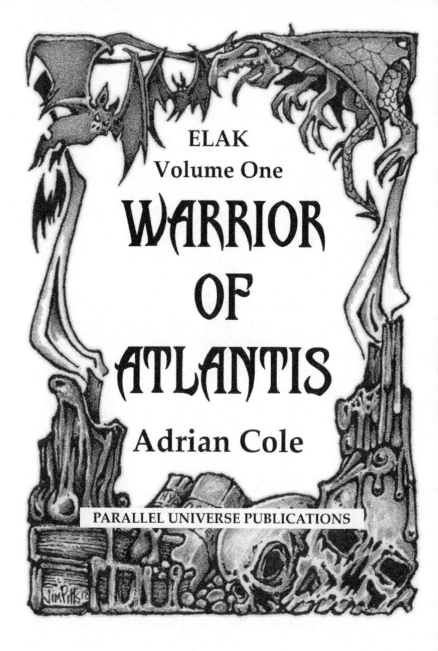

ELAK
Volume One

WARRIOR

OF

ATLANTIS

Adrian Cole

PARALLEL UNIVERSE PUBLICATIONS

A SONG OF PICTISH KINGS, first published in *Heroic Fantasy Quarterly Magazine*, no 49, 2021
DEMONS OF THE DEEP, first published in *Heroic Fantasy Quarterly Magazine*, no 40, 2019
ON DEATH SEED ISLAND, first published in *Tales from the Magician's Skull*, no 4, 2020
TOWER IN THE CRIMSON MIST, first published in *Savage Scrolls 1*, edited by Jason R Carney, Pulp Hero Press (USA) 2020
A DREAM OF LOST VALUSIA, first published (as **Dreams of a Sunken Realm**) in *Tales from the Magician's Skull,* no 5, 2020
SAILING ON THE THIEVES' TIDE, first published in *Swords & Sorceries: Tales of Heroic Fantasy* vol 3, edited by David A. Riley, Parallel Universe Publications (UK) 2021
THE SINGERS IN THE STONES Published here for the first time.

ISBN: 978-1-7393674-5-9

Parallel Universe Publications, 130 Union Road, Oswaldtwistle, Lancashire, BB5 3DR, UK

Dedication

To the memory of a good friend,
Dave Holmes, who died far too
young in February 2017, and who
will be so sadly missed by all
those who knew and loved him.

Lycon battling the sea creatures in *The Singers In The Stones*

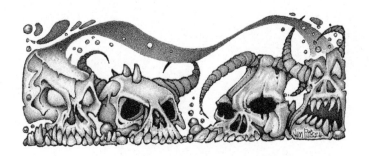

CONTENTS

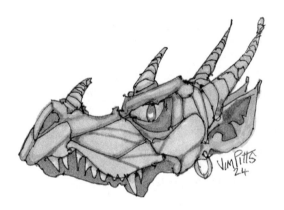

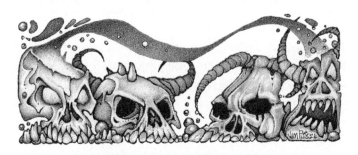

INTRODUCTION
David C. Smith

Sword-and-sorcery fiction is a versatile genre.

Writing for a living in the early 1930s, during the unforgiving worldwide Great Depression, Robert E. Howard fashioned the genre from equal parts adventure, historical, and weird and horror fiction, with some of the rough Texas frontier mixed in — tough, transgressive storytelling for a tough time. But because it draws inspiration from such diverse sources, sword-and-sorcery fiction can accommodate writers eager to fashion a variety of stories.

Following Howard's death, such writers as Henry Kuttner (author of the original Elak stories) and Clifford Ball wrote flat-out pulp fantasy-adventure, more concerned with plot and character heroics than the confrontational darkness that often was part of Howard's storytelling. The genre fell by the wayside during the 1940s and immediate postwar years but was successfully revived in the 1960s and 1970s by such artists as Fritz Leiber and Michael Moorcock and the defiant, rules-breaking Karl Edward Wagner.

The sword-and-sorcery boom of the 1970s, coming as it did after the resurgence of interest in (and sales of) Howard's Conan stories in the Lancer paperbacks, gave us everything from misogynistic sword-and-planet novels (on the paperback racks next to the sword-and-sorcery covers) to Brak the Barbarian and a seeming myriad of clones. Any originality during that time was apparently due to editorial oversight—publication of David Mason's books, for example. The really inventive work was being done in fanzines outside the commercial mainstream by a generation just then pushing the boundaries of the genre in new directions—Richard L. Tierney, Charles R. Saunders, Jessica Amanda Salmonson, David Madison, and a small host of other truly inventive writers.

Adrian Cole is one of that generation. He had his start in that decade of creative excitement and inventiveness, our 1930s. Post–Howard boom and pre–*Dungeons and Dragons*, the writers of that brief flowering published one another, engaged in lively discussions in the letters columns of their fanzines, and typed like crazy, drawing inspiration from the best of the early *Weird Tales* authors, ancient Roman history, medieval sagas, Victorian-era novelists, motion pictures both silent and sound, and, frequently, obscure sources found on rainy afternoons spent browsing in the library stacks.

Inspired is a good word to describe both Adrian's fiction as well as the glamor that possesses him when he is writing this fiction. Inventiveness is another. So is versatile. A British Fantasy Award winner, he has, with his growing list of stories featuring Elak of Atlantis, taken on the mantle of Kuttner and expanded the repertoire. We are again in the days of weird adventure, as in the classic mid-century pulp stories that took us next where we could not guess.

Weird adventures these stories are, but also heroic, for Elak is a hero in the best sense of those figures who have come down to us in the recountings of their grand exploits—King Arthur, Siegfried, Robin Hood, Sinbad the Sailor, and so many more. They are, in fiction, presented to us as living for a purpose greater than themselves—the mark of a true hero—while enjoying the somewhat selfish craving for the next episode that will provide them the thrill of a challenge to be overcome. This is certainly true of Elak, whose stories here follow his progression from young king of Cyrena to king of Atlantis.

Elak has a number of challenges to face before he ascends to the Dragon Throne. Assisting him are his true companions Lycon and Dalan. Lycon, with Pictish blood in him, is a fighter born. Dalan is High Druid in the Order of Cyrena, and he is a powerful sorcerer indeed. He also serves in a paternal or avuncular role for the headstrong Elak, sympathetic to the young royal's ambitions and abilities but providing a cautionary nod when needed to check Elak's very frequent desire to dive headlong into whatever he confronts, a trait that Dalan quite rightly sees as potentially being self-defeating if not outright fatal.

So we have a trio of powerful characters who each come alive by way of Adrian's keen writing, which serves us so well as we enjoy these weird adventures. And they are evocatively weird in the highest literary sense, echoing that characteristic of this enjoyable fiction from a century ago. When Elak, Lycon, and Dalan enter the strange domain of Death Seed Island, for example, Lycon, head still pounding from the previous night's debauch, says, "The island noises aren't right." And Dalan, on confronting what grows in that place, observes, "I know of many plants that drug their victims before absorbing them."

The island noises *aren't right*. Plants that don't just poison intruders, or even strangle them, but *absorb* them. Two examples of many displaying Adrian's prescient and artfully done, one-step-ahead inventiveness. We anticipate something weird because these are, after all, stories of weird adventure. But to have the weirdness presented, not with mundane language but with pointed word choices and phrases, adds to the frisson of strangeness, and Adrian gives us that.

His characters are strong and have depth; they are self-aware and follow codes of conduct to which we can be sympathetic, albeit they exist in a dangerous world with elements of the uncanny ready to intrude at any moment. They are large in the sense that all heroes must be, in their emotions and their actions, how they live and survive. Everything about these stories, in fact, is large: large emotions and ambitions, large gods, large settings, and everything is ancient, as well, the islands and monsters, citadels and fortresses, mountains and seas, all as we imagine the prehistoric world *must* have been—bigger than us, but peopled with figures equal to those enormities. As Elak declares, in *Tower in the Crimson Mist*, "If we are to die in this place, let's do so with fire in our bellies!"

We get to know these characters by the details and insights Adrian provides as we follow Elak and his companions on their adventures. In *Warriors from the West*, for example, Elak and his fighters enter a deep forest and make their way through nighttime gloom. Now, Elak is a sea-going Atlantean. He misses the waves, his natural habitat. All march inland, while

"the air grew colder, closing like fingers of frost, and *the sea seemed very remote.*"

Nicely put, that insight into the character's sensibilities. In *A Dream of Lost Valusia*, Elak exhibits a growing maturity and self-awareness that surely would please Dalan:

"A battle would be more than welcome. Elak gripped his arm, restraining his burly friend. Lycon could hardly suppress a grin: there had been a time when Elak would have been even more eager than he for conflict, and no one was more fearless and valorous in battle than the young king. But *time was refining him*, preparing him, if he survived, for a more subtle life."

What an excellent phrase to capture our awareness of ourselves, caught as we are in ongoing Time. We can at least gain some insight into ourselves, if not wisdom itself. So can the young king.

Then there are Elak's ruminations on kingship itself and empire in the face of unrelenting Time:

"…they halted briefly to look back for the final time at the forgotten bones of the last Valusian city. *Is this the fate of all great nations? Elak asked himself. Do all mighty empires crumble and fall? And is this to be the fate of my Atlantis, though I make of her a queen among empires, mistress of the world?"* (from *A Dream of Lost Valusia*)

The imaginative ideas and inventiveness don't stop there. Consider the *living sea* versus the Crawling Death in *A Song of Pictish Kings*. As for Adrian's turns of phrase and good writing that add to our enjoyment (the italics are mine):

"Above them the night sky was cloudless, sprinkled with a myriad of stars, *their glare as piercing as eyes,* and *the men sensed they were being evaluated by the old gods they were disturbing.* Elak felt the hairs at the nape of his neck stirring, expecting at any moment to see *spectral figures seeping out of the trees."* (from *A Song of Pictish Kings*)

"A shout from aloft sent the two men forward to join the captain at the prow. It dipped and rose, cutting into the foam, spraying the men with cold sheets of it, but through its salty curtain they could discern the sea mist, which had now become far more dense, rolling forward like a tidal wave. It would be impossible for the fleet to avoid it; the sea was like a live thing, dragging the ships into the embrace of the roiling murk. *Instinctively Elak drew his blade...*" (from *Towers in the Crimson Mist*)

"...figures who *wore the shadows like cloaks.*" (from *A Song of Pictish Kings*)

"Numenedzer realized if he fought here, he would doubtless die in this *maelstrom of blood.*" (from *Demons of the Deep*)

"Dalan *wore a look of thunder.*" (from *Demons of the Deep*)

"No sooner had he spoken than a ripple of movement across the beach, *like the shiver of a horse's flank,* made every man there gasp." (from *On Death Seed Island*)

Being evaluated by old gods. Spectral figures seeping out of the trees. The immediate instinct of a warrior to reach for his weapon. Looks of thunder. And that movement across the beach like the shiver of a horse's flank—perfect. It's an image suiting the story environment as well as one familiar to every character in the story.

This is good writing, very good writing, and a good reason to read and enjoy Adrian's fiction. But there is more, just as there is more awaiting those intruders on that dangerous, deadly island. With Adrian, it's not just inventive or colourful turns of phrases: it's the way he writes entire. For example, here is the second paragraph of chapter 8 of *Demons of the Deep*: cleanly done, with sentences of moderate length that march, taking us step by step through the vision described without our having to second-guess anything, and wrapping up with a potent symbol reiterating what we've just been told:

"Dalan began his working. He drove the end of his staff into a crack between two of the mighty harbour stones and gripped the head of the staff, shouting out words from the secret language of his brethren, the words of a sorcerer. His voice rose above the thunder of the waves and mingled with the tumultuous air, and as the company watched, that air seemed alive, an overhead whirlpool of spirits and demonic beings, the sound of their discordant screams directed by the Druid's power. Bolts of blue fire shot down from the pandemonium above, and Elak gasped, afraid that Dalan would be blasted apart. But instead the energy flowed down through the brilliantly lit figure and into the promontory."

Adrian excels at this type of imagery, just as he does in his passages that portray the quality of ancientness. This is the sensation of deep time, of deep antiquity, so familiar to us from Howard's own imagination, time so distant that merely to contemplate its reach is sufficient to frighten ourselves:

"A sense of a long-lost era somehow pervaded the drop, as if the warriors were going backward into prehistory, an age long past, an age, perhaps, when the old gods and terrible magics held sway, *like dust waiting to rise again if disturbed*." (from *Tower in the Crimson Mist*)

"It has risen from the deeps through sorcery and wild storm, the workings of old magic beyond the memory of Man, *from a time when other creatures ruled the oceans*." (from *The Singers in the Stones*)

"Here there were many weapons, swords hung singly

on the walls, javelins stacked in clusters, and there were shields, axes and maces, *as well as other ancient Valusian weapons that Elak was not familiar with.*" (from *A Deam of Lost Valusia*)

And there is the powerful sense of Lovecraftian doom, unsettling but pulling us in:

"It will take power, dark sorcery maybe. And of a dangerous nature. We must call upon gods whose price for aid would not be easy to meet. Cruath Morgas knows this. He would invoke the Lords of Midnight, and bring them to earthly form. I fear the consequences, Elak. *Our world is no place for such as them and the things that serve them.*" (from *The Singers in the Stones*)

Of course, I could go on with further examples, but you'll find your own to enjoy as you sit back with this collection. Adrian Cole has met Henry Kuttner more than halfway and presents these adventures of King Elak and his companions with gusto and sincerity. They are heroes all. Join them now in their ancient world where, even when they succeed in their quests and confrontations, such successes may be only momentary. Further adventures—and horrors—await. "We will need to be watchful, always," as Elak says.

Enjoy. I am going back now to join you—and Elak—and reread them all!

David C. Smith
Palatine, Illinois
January 2024

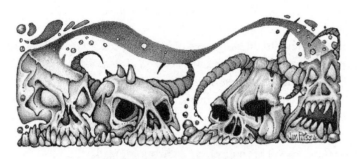

FOREWORD
THE RISE OF THE
DRAGON THRONE

Sword and Sorcery was arguably created by Robert E. Howard, when he wrote his Conan and King Kull stories, and certainly it was generally felt that his extraordinary characters were the blueprint for what readers thought of when anyone talked about Sword and Sorcery. Even today, when the genre has morphed and spawned other fabulous heroes and heroines, many people still think of Conan when Sword and Sorcery is mentioned. Henry Kuttner, as a young writer embarking on a career that would eventually propel him to the front ranks of science fiction writers of his day, was an ardent admirer of Robert E Howard, and in particular of Conan. So much so that, when REH died, the fledgling Kuttner wrote four pastiches, stirring yarns about his own hero, Elak of Atlantis, all of which were published in *Weird Tales* magazine. These were very much in the heroic barbarian mode (although the young Elak was born of royal Atlantean blood) and are undoubtedly Sword and Sorcery.

Some years ago, Robert M Price, himself a Sword and Sorcery writer and editor, asked me if I'd like to write a brand new Elak story for his magazine, *Strange Tales* (a reboot of a contemporary of *Weird Tales*, *Strange Stories*). Subsequently the first of my own Elak yarns was born, and over the last few years, quite a few more of my Elak stories have seen the light of day. The first of these have been collected herein, together with a brand-new novella, *Singers in the Stones*. This collection is chronologically the first in my Elak series, and will be followed by *Elak, King of Atlantis*, a reprint of the book that was first published in 2020 by Pulp Hero Press (US), and *Elak, Sea Hawks of Atlantis*.

When *Elak, King of Atlantis* first appeared, Sword and Sorcery scholar Morgan Holmes quite rightly pointed out to me that Kuttner's Elak became King of the country of Cyrena, in the north of the Atlantis continent, rather than king of the entire Atlantean continent. Although my Elak had made the jump from being monarch of one state to that of emperor of a continent, it was a perfectly natural development, but got me to thinking that there must be a lot of interesting ground for Elak to have covered to have reached his greater role. Hence I began penning yarns to fill in the intervening years and…well, these comprise this book: the gradual rise of his empire.

In Henry Kuttner's final Elak of Atlantis story, *Dragon Moon*, Elak and his companions Lycon and Dalan the Druid face their sternest test yet when they come up against the evil sorcerer Karkora, or the Pallid One. Karkora is the son of Mayana, herself a daughter of the sea god, Poseidon and the monstrous Karkora draws on ancient and terrible powers in a bid to rule Atlantis. In a clash of armies, Karkora's ally, King Sepher of Kiriath, a rival nation to Elak's Cyrena, the earth shakes to the unleashing of wizardry and flashing steel, until out of the chaos Elak's forces triumph and the servants of night are crushed. Elak slays Sepher and Karkora is destroyed.

Elak, Warrior of Atlantis is my version of what happened next. It is unashamedly inspired by Robert E. Howard's fiction, and part of the background I used as his *Hyborean Age*, which Kuttner also used. My Elak trilogy is a tribute and homage to the two great writers.

I am indebted to Robert M. Price for his initial suggestion that I take up the Elak reins and also to Morgan Holmes for his comment on Elak's kingship. Without either, these stories would never have seen the light of day!

Adrian Cole,
Devon, England, 2023

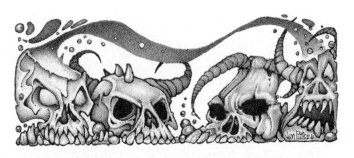

A SONG OF PICTISH KINGS

In those most turbulent of days, Elak reluctantly took upon himself the kingship of Cyrena, following the death of his brother Orander through the machinations of the sorcerer Karkora. After Elak's victory over the great darkness of the Pallid One's powers, he sat upon the Dragon Throne in its fortress castle, isolated in the secret mountains. The rebuilding of the state began and Elak strengthened his court in the city of Epharra, which was to become the capital and most illustrious city in all of the great continent of Atlantis. At this time, the continent was a loosely knit confederation of city states, some strongly allied to each other. Northern Cyrena was the most powerful, and had a strong ally in neighbouring Sarhaddon and its queen, Esarra. Another ally was the city state ruled from Poseidonis, under the young monarch, Kellotris. After the war with Karkora, Kiriath was quick to come under the golden dragon banner, and other city states soon followed as the Cyrenian Councillors persuaded their young monarch to grasp the bull by the horns and unify the chaotic states of Atlantis into one, powerful nation. These were troubled times where revolution brewed like a constantly seething storm, and in such days strange and unlikely alliances were forged.

- Helvas Ravanniol

Annals of the Third Atlantean Empire

1: Warriors from the West

Dawn had barely broken, streaking the eastern clouds with fire and crimson banners beyond the crooked arm of headland. Below rocky coastal cliffs, hidden in deep shadow, the narrow cove whispered with life, waves pushing sleepily across its sand, stirring low banks of accumulated weed. A solitary ship had been beached, its lamps doused: it had the appearance of a spectre, or sea beast risen silently from the surf combers. Men disembarked: a swarthy, sea-going crew, bronzed by the sun, muscular bodies short, arms wreathed in tattoos, ringed with gold. Their blades gleamed, their hunters' eyes alert, yet for all their latent power, they crossed the sand as noiselessly as a sea breeze.

Beyond, at the edge of the rocks, another handful of men slipped from cover. The two groups converged. This second group were led by a figure garbed in a long, flowing robe of neutral grey, who carried a tall staff, identifying him as a Druid, a man of importance in these lands. The men with him were armed guards wearing the retinue of Cyrena, where the newly crowned Elak was beginning to stretch wings of power.

The leaders of the two groups met and greeted each other gruffly.

"I am Dalan," said the Druid. "High Druid in the Order of Cyrena, and I act as the voice of the king, Elak. My words are his words."

The shorter, stockier man grinned like a tiger. His hair was dark as raven's feathers, long and thick, silver strands woven into it; from his ear lobes dangled beautifully crafted silver skulls. His sword was likewise superbly made, its length lavishly filigreed. "I am Borga, king of the Pictish Wolf Clan."

"You are welcome to our shores." The Druid had never expected to utter such a welcome to this notorious hunter from the west, whose reputation as a conqueror of the many islands there stirred terror in the hearts of Atlantean citizens, on land and sea. The Pictish empire was growing, and greatly feared. Dalan knew the day would come when it would clash with Atlantis – such things were in the stars. Thus the request for a peaceful meeting was unusual. Picts commonly let their cold steel do their talking.

Three of Dalan's warriors set a cask down on the sand. Moments later it had been opened. The Druid drew off a fat beaker of mead, took a long draught, and nodded in appreciation. He gave Borga and others of his sailors beakers which were soon filled and quaffed in an understanding of peace, at least temporarily.

"Atlantean mead is strong and sweet," said Borga. "I confess we've plundered your ships in northwestern waters and tasted it before." His eyes gleamed, feral, and he grinned, as if challenging the Druid.

Dalan smiled wryly. "Our nations have not enjoyed the best of relations, Borga of the Wolves. Yet you seek an alliance."

"I hear your young king desires to bring all of Atlantis under his sway." He refilled his beaker and drank eagerly. "It will take a heroic effort, and many, many warriors. We know your western seaboard well. Some of its people will rush to the golden dragon banner, but others will resist. The wars will be long and bloody—many lives will be lost."

Dalan grunted in agreement. Borga spoke truly enough. The Pict's secret messages to Elak's court suggested a potential alliance, and although the Atlanteans found this highly desirable – the conflicts with the Pictish Isles had raged across many decades, damaging trade and progress – fear of treachery would always guide their response.

Borga's grin widened. "I'm sure your trust in my proposal is fragile. Why should my nation, free and unfettered by Atlantean kings and laws, come to you for aid?"

Dalan again nodded.

"We have a mutual enemy," said Borga, his grin blurring into a grimace as deep anger clearly fuelled his mood. "Sorcery of the blackest, vilest kind! Our shamans have deflected it, but our powers alone are not enough. Slowly we are being bled, our islands threatened with extinction. Don't think to benefit from this, Druid! Once we are crushed, Atlantis will be next. forced out of our islands, we will seek new homes on Atlantean shores, likely through a fresh war that none of us desires."

Dalan was deeply shocked by the Pict's words. They were so unlike the usual bravado and loud boasting of the western warrior clans. Even facing defeat they would scream out their wild defiance until the last man fell. To hear talk of utter defeat from one of their great war chiefs was unheard of. Borga's men were silent, eyes cast down, strange for men normally so belligerent.

Borga read Dalan's muted incredulity. "Many of us have lost family and loved ones. We fight hard, but the tide is against us."

"What is this enemy you speak of?"

"We call it the Crawling Death. Earth and sea risen up as though the gates of all the hells have opened. No man is safe from its insatiable hunger."

2: The Crawling Death

Elak and Lycon stood silently among the small group of warriors guarding Dalan's back, both wearing Cyrenian livery, disguised as ordinary fighting men. Dalan had raged against the idea of the young king and his right-hand man joining him for this dangerous meeting with Borga, but Elak would brook no dissent. His face was not known to the Picts. He wanted to hear for himself what the legendary wolf warrior had to say. Listening to Borga now, he felt the stirring of horror.

"Our mainland, Krannach, is a large land mass surrounded by scores of lesser islands," the Pictish chief continued. "Many have been swamped by the Crawling Death and the creatures serving it. Krannach is well defended, but our strength is not enough. Our shamans have flung Pictish sorcery at the enemy, but there is something at its heart, ancient powers from beyond time, monstrous and warped. You, Druid, are said to have power—there are known to be great sources of high magic in Atlantis. We would have you and those powers at our side."

"This is no small thing that you ask, Borga."

"No, but aid us, and you will benefit doubly. The Crawling Death can be cast back into the pits that spawned it and Atlantis, too, will be safe. For this help, we will come to Elak's support when he rides out to win his empire. With Picts for allies, he will overrun this continent. It will be the beginning of a lasting peace between us."

Elak looked discreetly down at the full-bodied Lycon beside him, whose face was less inscrutable than his king's. Elak knew Lycon burned to shout his distrust. Lasting peace with the Picts? The Atlantean courts would have laughed at the suggestion. Yet Borga's fear of Atlantean sorcery he'd faced was undeniable. There was an element of desperation in his plea.

"Elak will be told of this," said Dalan. "You will have an answer before the sun sets." He pointed into the mist banks the dawn light was slowly revealing, and the vague shapes glimpsed in their greyness. Dalan's sensed the

Pictish fleet's numbers, enough for a major raid, if there was to be treachery, though his instincts told him Borna was genuine. "Meanwhile, your ships are under our protection."

"If your king accepts," said Borga, "I invite Atlantean ships to return to Krannach with me, to be your king's eyes. When they see the Crawling Death, perhaps Elak will fight beside us." He waved one of his men forward, a young warrior, muscular and already battle-scarred, with harsh features and a withering gaze. "This is my son, Kaa Mag Borga. He will stay as hostage at your court, if you come back to the Isles with me."

"I will have food and more mead sent to you while you await our king's reply," said Dalan, ending the meeting. Wordlessly Borga led his men back to their ship to await Atlantis's answer.

*

"Preposterous!"

The word cut the taut atmosphere like a knife in the Council chamber. Zerrahydris, most prominent member of the City Council, looked apoplectic. The small, circular room adjoining the main Council hall, was humming. All the principal Councillors had been summoned, while Dalan and Elak sat patiently before them. Dalan had barely finished his report, delivering Borga's proposal.

"The western wolves have failed to break our resistance for so long, they grow desperate," said Zerrahydris. He was a highly respected member of the Council, second in power, many knew, to the throne itself, though loved and respected for his intense loyalty to it. "This is a plot to weaken us before they come for the kill. I know these savages of old!"

Elak listened attentively. Dalan had warned him Zerrahydris would oppose any alliance. The

Councillor's father had died fighting Picts, when Zerrahydris had been a young boy. In all his years on the Council, he had raged against the westerners and always urged suppression of them. Elak stood up and the murmuring in the chamber quickly died. The king was young, but he was a tall, imposing figure, and in the defeating overthrow of the demonic alien Karkora and Erykion the sorcerer, he had proved himself a remarkable and dependable champion.

"If Borga speaks the truth," said Elak, "all of Atlantis is in peril. We dare not risk dismissing the Pict's words."

"Sire, you simply cannot trust the serpent tongue of a Pict!" persisted Zerrahydris. A number of the Councillors stood with him, but it was noticeable that more of them wanted to hear Elak out.

"He's prepared to leave his son, his heir, with us as a hostage, as a mark of his sincerity. I accept that. We must learn the truth," said Elak. "I will send a ship back with Borga. Dalan will be aboard. If this Crawling Death is real, and the sorcery unleashed by its masters reaches out into Atlantean waters, Dalan will know. So—I will have my finest ship prepared. Meanwhile we must fortify Epharra, strengthening it in readiness for our next campaigns. There is much to be done."

Zerrahydris and his supporters realized there would be no further discussion, and as the king had the final word, the meeting dispersed. Afterwards, in his private chambers, Elak spoke to Dalan and Lycon. "I'll lead this expedition myself. Both of you will be with me. No one must be told, and I'll travel disguised as a warrior."

"You!" cried Dalan, appalled. "That is madness!"

"If Atlanteans are to believe the Picts, it will take our word to sway them. Get word to Borga with all haste. The *Wavecutter* will meet with him out at sea, under tonight's stars."

3: The King's Spy

Olvaros slid across the roof, silent as smoke, belly to the tiles, ears straining for any hint of sound. Beyond him, etched by stark moonlight, row upon row of ships, from Atlantean battle galleys to smaller fishing craft stretched out at their moorings across the Bay of Gold. Around its rim, a few harbour lights gleamed; the silhouettes of Epharra stood out like sentinels. Behind them, smudged by night, the growing city reared up into the surrounding hills. Since Elak's rise, Epharra had burgeoned quickly, with new warehouses, temples, markets and an extension to the docks which included the largest military barracks in Cyrena. There were rumours the young king even intended to have the Dragon Throne brought here from its mountain castle, to be the core of his new empire.

At the roof's edge, Olvaros peered down into a courtyard. A man crossed it furtively—two armed warriors followed him, evidently protecting his back. Olvaros recognized the man as Kranaldis, a city Councillor, who quickly entered a low door into the building. His guards stationed themselves outside it. Olvaros grinned. He had no intention of entering that way. Hours before, in daylight, he'd reconnoitred the roofs hereabouts. There was another way in and now he slipped down to the tiny window. It was a simple opening in the building's upper wall—inside was a small, neglected storeroom.

Olvaros continued to move stealthily, well-practiced as a spy for the royal household. He opened the door gently and moved out and along a dusty corridor, until he came to a balcony, partially blocked with abandoned furniture. Below was a chamber, once a hall, now long neglected. A few narrow candles lit the drab surroundings: drapes were torn, thick with dust and cobwebs, and the walls were flaking. A table had been set in the hall's centre, with a few chairs, the floor devoid of carpets, bare boards exposed and in places wormy. No doubt, Olvaros mused, its current visitors had chosen it precisely because of its insalubrious condition.

Two men sat at the table and were joined by Kranaldis. Olvaros recognized both. One was Mittrubos, another Councillor, and with him was Scuvular, a cousin to Elak. The Councillors were in late middle age, while Scuvular was younger, less than thirty, a man in wasted physical condition, corpulent and pasty-faced. He was notorious for self-indulgence at court, preferring its confines to the field of battle.

"You're certain you were not seen?" said Mittrubos, whose nervousness was evident in his visible restlessness, his head turning to catch the slightest sound.

"Yes," said Kranaldis. "The city sleeps. So – what have you to report?" He directed this at Scuvular.

"I spoke to my brother, Vannadas, late in the day. The king will leave the city before dawn, on another of his private engagements." Scuvular spoke with a rasping voice, edged with contempt: Olvaros heard each word clearly.

Kranaldis growled with suppressed anger. "It underlines our concerns about his suitability to reign. Ever putting himself at risk. Zerrahydris and the others try to control him, but they are not strong-willed enough. No good will come of it. Sooner or later, Elak will fall foul of our many enemies. A king should rule with an army at his back, always!"

"This time he goes too far," said Scuvular. "He's sailing westward."

"Into Pictish seas?" said Mittrubos, horrified.

"Vannadas has been put in command here again. He says Elak sails with a Pictish escort. An *alliance*." Scuvular laced his words with scorn.

"By the gods," murmured Mittrubos, "that's a dangerous game. Elak *trusts* the Picts? Is he insane!"

"If the king falls during this mission, your brother, as first in line to succession, will take the Dragon Throne."

Scuvular's grin sent a chill through the Councillors, and above them, Olvaros also experienced deep unease.

"It brings me one step closer to the throne," said Scuvular. "Vannadas does not enjoy the best of health. His wounds in service of Cyrena over the years have weakened him. His days are numbered."

Mittrubos grimaced, but Kranaldis nodded. "Soon we must take drastic action, for the good of Cyrena."

"For all Atlantis," added Scuvular, whose ambitions were ill-concealed. For a while the men discussed their intentions, coldly plotting a course that would bring grim changes to the ruling of the state.

Olvaros had heard enough. It had been a close ally of Vannadas who'd employed him on this mission, for there'd been more than a little suspicion in the royal court that treachery was brewing. When was there not? Olvaros mused as he slipped back to the roof, leaving as discreetly as he had come. As he prepared to drop down to the alleyway and back towards the royal courts, something struck him hard under his ribs, and a sudden fire burned sharply in his gut. He sank down, gasping in agony.

An arrow was lodged in him, and he knew instinctively it was a fatal strike. Already blood trickled from his mouth. As he fell over the edge of the roof into the darkness below, he heard a voice, something from a bad dream.

"Take him out to sea and let the sharks finish him."

4: In Troubled Waters

"Dalan is much angered," said Lycon softly. He stood

beside Elak, both accoutred in the uniforms of Cyrena's royal household guards. The deck of the *Wavecutter*, fleetest of Atlantean war galleys, swayed as the sleek craft sped through the western seas, great sails billowing in a light gale. Elak stood a head taller than his stocky companion, looking ahead to the prow, where the lone Druid leaned out and studied the seas and accompanying Pictish fleet. Elak and Lycon had taken on aliases for this mission. If the Pictish sea wolf had known that the Cyrenian king sailed in this company, the gods alone knew what advantage he'd make of it.

"Dalan's anger is directed partly at me, for taking such a risk,," Elak said with a wry grin. "Yet I sense in him a deeper anxiety. He sees things, Lycon, from the remote past, but also the paths of the future. It is the latter which so disturbs him."

"Our fate?"

"Possibly. There's something in the future of Atlantis hanging like the threat of a great storm in Dalan's mind. He spoke to me of a crossroads in our fortunes and those of the Picts. What transpires now could affect the balance – stabilize it or plunge us all into catastrophic wars. The misery they would cause across generations is what angers him. It's why he's come on this mission. To keep that balance."

"Borga won't betray us," said Lycon, with conviction. "Not while his son is hostage in Epharra. They are Picts. Their blood is their bond."

Elak nodded, though his face remained clouded. He knew little of his companion's early life and had never sought to pry personal knowledge from him, but he recognized there was a degree of Pictish blood in him. Perhaps it accounted for his ferocity and dependability in battle. Many had mistaken Lycon for a drunken sot, bloated and unfit, but Elak knew well enough Lycon could match any man in combat. Certainly there was no one else he would rather have beside him in a tight corner – and they'd shared many of them, especially in the last year, when Elak's dragon banner had been carried far and wide across Atlantis, bringing ever more states under the new empire's control.

"Dalan is also concerned about Epharra," said Elak. "My cousin, Vannadas, has done well for me, holding my throne while I've led our armies in the field. Some think he should be king in my place. Vannadas is loyal, though."

"He would die rather than betray you," said Lycon. "As would the vast majority of your people."

Elak frowned. It had been Lycon's way of gently reminding him that now was the time to be the king, to let go the wayward past of an adventurer with its independence and complete freedom of will. "I'm sure Vannadas will honour us. There are others, though, who might not. The Council is largely behind me, and as long as Zerrahydris is at its helm, they will support me."

"He'll be incensed when he discovers you're on this voyage," Lycon said with a low chuckle. "He's an old woman at times. But in fairness, his advice is always sound."

"There are those among the Councillors who might not be so loyal. Vannadas does not enjoy the best of health. If anything should happen to him, his younger brother Scuvular will succeed him."

Lycon spat over the rail. "That devious rat! A man you should never trust. I've seen the naked envy in his eyes when he looks your way, Elak. He lusts for power – for the Dragon Throne itself."

"Aye. He is watched. Vannadas, too, has doubts."

"While the cat's away, the vermin play."

Elak was about to respond, when a shout from the

ship's mainmast snared his attention. The lookout had seen something in the surrounding waters.

Dalan approached. "We near the outer Pictish islands. Can you smell the air? Something has died here—a miasma hangs over the sea."

At the rail, Elak and others of the crew stared at the rise and fall of the waves. In a moment they saw a mass of forms, tangled together like a long raft of weed, countless bodies, twisted and broken, and with them the bulbous, fat tendrils of some deep, oceanic creature, ripped and leaking. As the *Wavecutter* ploughed on through the murky waters there were more of these dreadful conglomerations. They were all Pictish.

"The Crawling Death!" said Lycon.

Dalan shook his head. "Front runners of its army."

"A war canoe approaches," said Lycon, watching the Pict fleet, which had sent the oncoming craft. Moments later Borga came aboard. Elak and Lycon slipped back into the ranks while Dalan met the Pictish king.

"Our easternmost island, Skaafelda, lies ahead," said Borga. "We'll land there. Have your men prepared. We may be attacked, though I believe Skaafelda to be a dead place now." He spoke with barely suppressed fury. "We'll go there in our war canoes."

Lycon scowled, whispering to Elak, "Their canoes! We'll be completely at their mercy."

"I understand your concern. But I cannot believe Borga has brought us thus far to murder us. And he did not lie about the Crawling Death."

An hour later several war canoes alighted on the pale beach of the island. Elak and Lycon were among the warriors Dalan selected to accompany him, and as they walked up towards the lush undergrowth and spreading jungle, the entire party was conscious of an unnatural atmosphere, the air heavy, as if something had been badly burned. Among the mottled greenery, there was an alien pall of decay.

Dalan clutched his staff tightly. It vibrated, like a tuning fork reacting to sorcery of the darkest kind. Instinctively he knew that horror lay beyond those trees.

5: Island of Death

Scuvular sipped his wine slowly, pushing away the remains of the large meal he'd just gorged. He studied his brother, Vannadas. Although the latter was his elder by four years, he looked far older, his shoulders sagging, the weight of his temporary office heavy. "No wonder you look so haggard," Scuvular laughed mirthlessly. "These deceits will not suit the Council when they come to light."

"Elak knows best how to serve Cyrena," Vannadas snapped, breaking off in a fit of coughing.

"Such risks, though! Elak is younger than I am, hardly out of boyhood. Statesmanship is learned over many years. Elak is at times a hothead. I grant you he's a wonderful warrior, always prominent in battle, leading by example. But he'd be no good to Atlantis dead!"

"He is well protected."

"By that drunken sot, Lycon!"

"Lycon's nobody's fool. And Dalan wields the great power of the ages."

Scuvular nodded, though his whole mien suggested scorn. "He'll need it against Pictish savagery. If Borga discovers our king is there in his clutches –"

"He dare not act against him."

"You mean we have his son, Kaa Mag Borga? Oh yes, I know about him. Shut away here in Epharra with two of his own guards, brooding in his seclusion."

"Borga would never do anything to risk his son's life."

"If it is his son."

Vannadas's face clouded. "What are you talking about?"

"We've only his word for it. The Pict calling himself Kaa Mag Borga may be a fraud. A sacrifice. Let my men interrogate him –"

"No! Dalan was satisfied. We do as we have been ordered by the king."

Scuvular sat back, waving his arms in a gesture of acceptance. "Of course. But be aware the Council is divided on this, brother. It is only reasonable of them. We are entering a new era. Once the southern states of Atlantis are brought under our banners, we will rule the entire continent. Something which will be very evident to Borga and his wolves. A united Atlantis would hardly sit well with his ambitions."

"For now, we wait," said Vannadas.

Scuvular knew his brother well. He'd been chosen for his obdurate loyalty to the young king. Well, there was one way to eliminate Elak. If Kaa Mag Borga and his guards should be found murdered, and if word of such Atlantean perfidy got back to the Pictish king, Elak wouldn't survive another day. *And if Borga invaded,* Scuvular thought, *an outraged and unified Atlantis would be ready for him.* He poured himself more wine. *So—if Borga's son is killed and one of the guards escapes and flees back to the west with word of the betrayal...*

*

On Skaafelda the Picts and Atlanteans broke through the overgrown trail and came upon the mangled ruins of a former stronghold. Dalan surveyed the broken remains with a deep frown, and among the guards behind him, Elak and Lycon suppressed gasps of horror. The Pictish buildings were not as elaborate or advanced as Atlantean architecture, most having been hewn from the rock faces and cliffs of the area, roofs constructed from beams and thick leaves. Devastation was in evidence everywhere. Stone had been calcified and in the bright light of midday its bleached whiteness was like soiled snow, every wall tainted by whatever had touched it, as if an unnatural canker had been let loose. Trees had also been contaminated, and a closer inspection revealed numerous bodies, many tangled together like roots, all morphed to chalk-like stone.

Borga stood beside the Druid. "The Crawling Death. No one here survived it."

"It came from the sea," said Dalan. "I have read of such things in ancient manuscripts, a curse almost beyond living memory."

Elak and his warriors studied the calcified dead, whose faces were like those of crude, primitive statues, features crumbling, sloughed off, or sucked from them. Limbs were cracked and broken, most knotted together horribly, as if fused in a firestorm. Among all the debris there were great coils, also transmogrified into flaking stone. Serpents, perhaps, or the once undulating arms of whatever had come up from the ocean deeps. Over everything hung the stifling reek of sorcery.

"Where else has this happened?" Dalan asked Borga.

"The source is in the northernmost of our islands, Brae Calaadas. We've been hearing rumours of a secret sect there for years. Whenever we've sent men to investigate, they've returned with tales of the Crawling Death and the stone curse it brings. Until recently, it kept to itself, seeming to have no interest in the rest of the isles. So we shunned it and kept watch. Now this has happened here and on other of our smaller, eastern islands at the rim. It cannot be resisted."

Dalan shook his head. "Not without a counterbalancing sorcery."

"Can you provide it?"

"Not alone. There are powers I can call upon, but I can be no more than a focal point. You have many shamans? What are their numbers?"

For a moment Borga's face clouded, clearly reluctant to release such knowledge, but he managed an evasive reply. "Every major island has one, though many guard their powers jealously. I've spoken to other Pictish kings. We have fought each other for many years, though in recent times there is an uneasy peace in place."

Which is one reason you've never crossed the ocean in vast numbers to invade Atlantis, Dalan thought.

Borga may have read his thoughts, for he smiled wryly. "The shamans enjoy individual power, under their kings. To combine strengths might lessen their individual standings."

"The Crawling Death, and more specifically, whoever is controlling it, will know that. They'll do as they have done here, cut you down, one by one. Only in unity can you defeat this enemy."

"Which is why I have called upon you and your young king for aid. Not all my fellow kings think well of me for that. Doubtless some have called for my head on a spear." Borga laughed, spitting into the white dust.

"Who controls these dark powers?"

"We hear whispers of a sect, several sorcerers from the far north, almost in the ice regions of the Vaarfrost. A place of mysteries and terrors from the underworld, where a pit gapes on a realm inhabited by shunned gods. It is how our myth-makers speak of it. Until now, no more than a legendary, sleeping realm." He pointed at the grim chaos around them. "But sleeping no more."

6: A Gathering of Kings

Elak spoke softly in the confines of the small cabin

where he, Lycon and Dalan had retired for the night on the *Wavecutter*, away from Pictish ears. "What can we achieve, Dalan? What Borga has described is a danger far beyond what I expected. What can one Atlantean ship and your high magic do against this monstrous invader? Should we turn back and gather a fleet, if we are to assist Borga?"

Dalan looked nonplussed, something rare for the Druid. "We are committed to visiting the Pictish council. To slip away now would be seen as cowardly, and there could be dire repercussions."

"I did not mean flight!" said Elak. "I spoke of a tactical withdrawal, with Borga's understanding –"

Dalan knew that, however brash and impulsive Elak could be at times, he was no coward. And the young man was already showing signs of diplomacy. "I think we should learn more of this northern threat. Hear their council then choose our path."

Lycon scowled grimly. "They're infamous for their treachery," he said. "If we bring a fleet to their waters, we need to be very sure of Borga. How far can we trust him?"

Not for the first time, Elak wondered about his friend's attitude towards the Picts. The two nations had warred periodically for many years. Some deep grudge was locked inside Lycon, something that fuelled his animosity. He never talked about it, and Elak was too fond of him to try and pry it from him.

Several more days passed. The sea remained calm, its fogs clearing to reveal the main land mass of the Pictish islands, the huge Krannach, looming on the horizon. Its outer archipelago soon enfolded the fleet. The sun blazed and seabirds whirled in great clouds – the evil atmosphere at Skaafelda appeared to be a distant nightmare, and as the *Wavecutter* eased into the harbour berth prepared for it at Krannach's main port, the world seemed a calmer place.

*

Elak studied the faces around him in the huge Pictish council room. Several kings were present, their tribes coming from far and wide, their many islands stretching across a great expanse of the western ocean. Each tribal king, like Borga, was battle-hardened, a fierce warrior used to the rigors of local wars and sea-faring raids across the world. In recent times Atlantis had become less of a target for them, but Elak knew a day might come when old rivalries would flare anew. Here, in this seething council, where scores of warriors lined the circular hall, all fully armed, some even painted for war, the young king felt a little intimidated and for once questioned his decision to risk himself in this venture. He sensed, too, other figures who wore the shadows like cloaks.

Borga addressed the gathering, his voice rising above and silencing the clamour. He spoke of his voyage to Cyrena's shore and of his appeal to the Atlanteans. He introduced Dalan, and although Borga made much of the Druid's powers and willingness to combat the Crawling Death and its masters, there remained a degree of suspicion and hostility among the Pictish ranks. There were kings here who visibly disapproved of Borga's actions, though for now they had set these aside, listening. The terrors that had been unleashed on their nation had temporarily subdued their belligerence.

When Borga concluded, one of the kings stepped forward, muscular arms folded across a huge chest in a clear gesture of defiance. "Will this high and mighty Druid tell us how he intends to stem the black tide from the north?" There was a chorus of wolf-like growls behind him and several blades and spears gleamed in the filtered daylight. "What powers does he have?"

Dalan remained outwardly calm. He stood tall on the

dais where he and Borga addressed the warriors. He raised his staff. "Powers have been given to me," he said calmly. "My staff embodies ancient magic, handed down for many generations. What lies herein is said to have originated in the stars. Yet it will not be enough to crush your tormentors. Where are your shamans?"

From the closely ranked audience, several of the figures who had kept in shadow now revealed themselves, men unlike other Picts, much older men, their hunched bodies wrapped in furs and pelts, their arms circled with gold and silver, numerous tokens hanging from their necks, carved bones and brilliant gems. Each shaman held a long, elaborately carved staff, from which feathers and more bones hung. Their faces, daubed with garish paint, fixed doubting gazes upon Dalan: their eyes were filled with challenge, for in this realm, only they were holders of the ancient powers, the wielders of sorcery.

The air about Dalan's staff hummed as though a swarm of hornets flew around it. "My staff alone will not be enough. It will need the combined strength of yours. A mixture of spells and sorcery that can break the power from the north. I have seen it!" he said, his voice suddenly raised like a strong wind, so that for a moment the entire company felt that vibration of power.

One of the shamans spoke. He was the eldest of them, gnarled and contorted, though his ancient frame yet throbbed with supernatural energy that made the others fall back in respect. "I am Cruath Morgas, servant of the Pictish Lords of Midnight."

Dalan and his companions saw the blind, white eyes, although they understood that here was a man of vision, a man who had looked beyond normal human realms, his power unquestionable. "I read the power you bring, Druid. Let no man here doubt it! Yet I ask – why are you here? Why should you aid your ancestral enemies? You and your Atlanteans, whose hands are red with Pictish blood. I smell it upon you!"

This brought a great howl from the massed warriors. The blind eyes of Cruath Morgas turned upwards to the daylight seeping in through the high rafters. "The Lords of Midnight are vengeful gods. Blood for blood is their way."

Again the Picts howled, now like a vast wolf pack, baying for the blood that the shaman spoke of, blood they were eager to spill.

Elak's hand tightened on the hilt of his rapier. If this came to a fight, he and his men would surely be overwhelmed.

7: The Eyes of the Shaman

Cruath Morgas stilled the mob by raising a withered hand. His dead eyes fixed on Dalan; lips twisted in a grim smile.

The Druid remained calm, his voice level. "I have seen the workings of the enemy, and the chaos that is the Crawling Death. If it brings ruin to the Pictish nation, it will not stop at that. It will cross the ocean to Atlantis and all the world. The darkest of gods are stirring—their work must be undone, whatever strange pacts it takes. Pictish and Atlantean power, fused into a mighty weapon of resistance, will rise above the darkness. All else must be set aside. Pict and Atlantean must stand shoulder to shoulder. Divided, we will all be drowned in the coming madness."

Silence gripped the huge chamber, the Picts hanging on the reply of Cruath Morgas, whose shrivelled body ironically held the balance of power. The shaman was slowly nodding, as if his inner eye could view the visions conjured by the Druid's powerful speech. His head turned so it seemed he was studying the Atlantean warriors behind and below Dalan. Elak had been permitted to bring a score of them with him to this council. Like the Picts, they had retained their weapons, though they stood as a solid unit, silent and unblinking. The shaman moved awkwardly toward their front rank.

"These are your finest," he said. "Every man here has distinguished himself in your recent wars, your young king's rise to becoming overlord of Atlantis. You would have Pictish warriors beside them in your annexation of total eastern power. This is the price we must pay for borrowing your sorcery."

Dalan said nothing, but watched the old shaman closely as he stood under the very gaze of the Atlanteans, sniffing like a hound. Cruath Morgas gently pushed aside two of the unresistant warriors and then two more behind them, creating an opening in their ranks as they shrank from his touch. "Come forward," he called, indicating Lycon, with a grin of triumph.

Beside Lycon, Elak tensed. He knew well enough these moments were to be a trial. Lycon would have to obey. To Elak's relief, he did so, stepping out to face the shaman.

Cruath Morgas touched Lycon's arm gently. "As I thought," he said. "Here is a man with Pictish blood in his veins. Do you deny it?"

Elak could see the anger rising in his companion. If it gave way to temper –

"No," said Lycon.

"Your mother," said the shaman. "She was a Pict."

Lycon nodded.

"And you are Lycon, the closest of King Elak's warriors, are you not?"

There was a unified gasp from the ranks of the Picts, for word of Lycon's prowess had reached these shores, carried home by raiders who had studied the rise of Cyrena like hawks.

"It is said," Cruath Morgas went on, "that you once swore a blood vow that you would bring the Pictish clans to their knees if ever your king brought war to us. Many of our warriors would put that proud boast to the test – here and now."

Before Lycon could respond, Elak pushed through his guards and stood beside his companion, pulling free his rapier.

"It is also said that the king's servant never ventures far from his side," said the shaman, his blind eyes turned to Elak as though he could see him plainly. "Is that not so – *Elak of Atlantis*?"

At this, pandemonium broke out among the Picts, and several of the kings stepped forward, swords drawn, holding back what was now an angry mob.

"I am Elak, yes, but know this. I will defend Lycon with my life. As will the Druid. You may think to kill us now, but we will take many of you with us –"

"Wait!" Dalan's voice was imperious and sounded around the hall like a peal of thunder. "This is not the time for killing!"

Beside him on the dais, Borga raised his own blade. "Be silent!" he roared to the masses. "I have not bargained with Atlantis to have her king brought here and betrayed! My son stands as surety for my bond. He is in Epharra. Atlantis has acted in good faith. And Elak has seen for himself what we face."

Elak wondered if Borga had known his identity all along. If he had, the Pictish king hid it well.

One of the kings towered over Cruath Morgas. He was unusually big of stature for a Pict, whose men were generally far shorter. Like Borga, he was in his prime, and his bronzed body rippled with muscle, shining like polished hardwood. Tattoos wound around his arms and across his chest, serpents and dragons, mouths open to reveal fangs coloured with blood. He held a huge war axe and two swords jutted from his thick leather belt. "You know me," he called to the warriors. "I am Slaath Mag Barrin, king of the western shores of Pictdom. I bow the knee to no man." He gazed meaningfully at Borga as he spoke.

Elak read the enmity between them, guessing that here was the main threat to Borga's ambitions to rule all Pictish clans.

"I will never fight beside an Atlantean, even in an alliance!" Barrin roared like a bull, huge frame quivering with emotion. "My family have fought Atlanteans since the dawn of days. Some fell into slavery at their hands!"

Borga raised his hand and the hubbub among the warriors slowly subsided. "We have a history of death and bloodshed. But that ends if the Crawling Death takes us down to hell. Without Atlantean steel beside us, we are damned."

Barrin spat. "That for Atlantean steel." He glared at Elak. "Each of my warriors are worth ten of yours. You are not fit to stand at our side."

Borga would have roared back angrily, but Elak was not intimidated. Tall as he was, Barrin was a head taller. "If you doubt my mettle, then put it to the test. Call out your finest warrior." Elak held up his rapier. "Let us see if he can match me."

Barrin laughed and rammed his axe haft into the earthen floor, stepping back. "I accept your challenge. As for your opponent, why, what Pict here would deny *me* that pleasure?"

8: A Clash of Steel

A space was quickly cleared at the foot of the dais, allowing Elak and the huge Pict to circle each other, eyes locked, teeth barred in grim smiles. Lycon and Dalan knew they dared not interfere, both cursing under their breaths at Elak's impetuosity. If he lost this fight, he'd forfeit his life and if that happened the Cyrenian cause would be in ruins. It was one roll of the dice too many. Dalan put his hand gently on Lycon's shoulder, feeling the smouldering frustration in the man, but they remained still and silent.

Slaath Mag Barrin fought with a sword in each hand, both short, stabbing weapons, ideal for close-in fighting. The air hissed as he swung the blades in a few initial passes, his face the face of a wolf scenting blood. Around him the Picts growled encouragement. All the ancient enmity between them and the easterners boiled. Borga looked on with a deep scowl, though this affair had gone beyond his intervention.

Elak was fast, ducking and weaving with deceptive speed for his height, and Barrin's blades chopped at his shadow. Elak used his rapier like a serpent's tongue, prodding and probing inside the Pict's guard, but Barrin, for all his size, was also nimble, a veteran of numerous fights, as the countless scars on his hide attested. The blades met and a shower of sparks sizzled like a halo around the two men, the air shimmering. Barrin feinted with his left blade, then struck upward with his right. The sword point traced a thin line from Elak's midriff to his upper chest, parting the cloth and nicking flesh. It brought a great roar from the watchers in the hall, but Elak's immediate riposte turned this into a gasp as the rapier's point tore across Barrin's left shoulder, also drawing blood. It ran freely down his upper arm. If it had pained him, he made no show of it, simply grunting dismissively, redoubling his efforts.

For a long time they tested each other. Barrin was no fool, and would not be tempted to any rash flurry. He was a natural swordsman and Elak knew that if the Pict had been trained by one of his own master guardsmen, he would have been even more formidable. It took all Elak's skill to keep him at bay, parrying first the left blade, then the right. The circling continued, both men's chests heaving with effort. It began to seem that the man who tired first would be the one to fall. And yet neither flagged.

Barrin broke the pattern and made a rush, using his swords in sweeps, eschewing finesse and opting for power. It seemed that he would overcome Elak with sheer animal strength, but again the young king slipped aside and drove his blade in at his opponent, ripping flesh from his upper arm. This time Barrin was angered, and he roared with fury. He swung round and flew at Elak like a maddened bull, chopping relentlessly. Elak's thinner blade took the blows and withstood them, deflecting them without snapping, as many blades would have. Elak, however, was driven back.

They broke apart, breath rasping. Barrin's bloodied left arm leaked so much blood to his hand, that the sword hilt had grown slippery. With a snarl he tossed the weapon aside and fought on with one blade. He was no less dangerous and soon had dealt Elak a cut to the ribs, though the wound was slight. It served, however, to bring more howls of glee from the audience, who sensed a swing of power Barrin's way. The Pict aimed a kick at his opponent from close quarters, but Elak remained agile and evaded it. He closed in and Barrin defended his upper torso from another thrust of the rapier.

It never came. Instead Elak went low and ran the point of the rapier into Barrin's left thigh, going in deep and drawing a shriek of pain from the huge warrior. Elak leapt back in time to avoid a slicing cut of Pictish steel and although Barrin made to follow up, his wounded leg could not take the strain and he went down, falling to his knees, his sword knocked from his grip by the impact. He scrambled to retrieve it, but Elak had moved with the speed of a striking serpent and trod hard on the blade. Barrin swore, making to rise, but Elak's rapier point snaked out and touched the flesh under his chin.

Silence gripped the entire hall. No one moved. It was over, and Barrin was about to be dispatched. He lifted his head high, exposing his neck. It would be a proud death, one that his people would remember.

Elak paused, and something in his eyes relayed to Barrin that he would not administer the kill.

"The victory is yours, eastern vermin!" Barrin snarled. "Take your prize. End it!"

Still Elak hesitated. It was enough that he'd triumphed. There was no need to waste the life of this powerful warrior.

Mercy was not the Pictish way, however. Barrin scorned it and, before Elak could react, thrust his head forward, so that the point of Elak's rapier was driven through his neck and out the other side, spilling more blood. The huge Pict's eyes widened as he tried to shout out one last defiant appeal to his dark gods, then clouded over as he toppled sideways. Elak glared at his blade as though it had betrayed him. He was conscious of the shouts of the Picts and swung round, ready to defend himself against the expected tide of fury.

However, they held back, their voices subsiding. One man stepped forward. He was a young warrior in his prime. He pulled Barrin's great axe from the ground and kissed its wide blade. He stood before Elak, and for all his latent ferocity the young king saw tears in his eyes.

"I am Kurrach Mag Barrin, son of the fallen."

Elak wiped the streaming sweat from his face. If he must fight again, it would be an unequal contest, this time one he was certain he could not win.

9: The Twisted Plan

Scuvular leaned back lazily in the padded chair. In this cramped room, above the drinking hall of a dockside inn, the sounds of laughter and singing from below were muted. The Councillors Kranaldis and Mittrubos sat with Scuvular, Mittrubos as nervous as a cat, twitching each time a louder burst of noise welled up from under the floor. This was a vile den, frequented by thieves and pirates, barely tolerated by Epharra's officials. However, Scuvular had insisted on its use as a precaution against any more of Vannadas's spies, since his own had killed Olvaros. To be found plotting together now would undo everything.

"It's all a matter of timing," said Scuvular, thick features grotesque in the candle-light.

"How much longer?" said Mittrubos.

Kranaldis was less tense, but nevertheless frowned uneasily. "Elak has been gone for several weeks, and may be away for more."

"It's a long voyage to the Pictish isles. The longer he's away, the more restless the people get. And you know how uncomfortable the Council is."

Kranaldis nodded. "Zerrahydris frets like an old maid."

"Concerned about the Pictish guests, no doubt. They're restless, too. Their confinement is like imprisonment. Picts like the outdoor life."

"So what is your proposal?" said Mittrubos.

"As you know, I have a small fleet of trading vessels. It's due back in Epharra from the western port of San-Mu in a matter of days. The fleet's captain, Theorron, is used to carrying out special missions for me."

Both Councillors had heard more than a few rumours that Scuvular engaged in illegal trade. They had deflected the inquiries into it occasionally set up by their colleagues, as it played to their advantage, but they found Scuvular's operations distasteful.

Scuvular smiled with self-satisfaction. "I have men involved in the guarding of the Picts, rotated with other guards. When the moment is ripe, my guards will slay Kaa Mag Borga and one of his protectors. The other will be, ah, rescued, and smuggled away before he can be interrogated by Vannadas. His story at home will be it was on the orders of Vannadas that the Pictish king's son was murdered. My men will bring the Pict secretly to me and I will profess my horror at the outrage and offer to get the Pict to safety."

"At a price," said Kranaldis, and for once his grim features broke in a smile.

Scuvular gave a low laugh. "Of course. I will offer Borga assistance in his vengeance. Captain Theorron will ship the Pict back to his homeland, leaving Epharra at night, under cover of another trading mission. Once there, the Pict will expose Elak's treachery and we'll be rid of him, the arrogant High Druid and that accursed Lycon."

Mittrubos shuddered. "Surely Borga will launch a war fleet upon us!"

"For certain. And its victory will be assured, for he'll have allies here. I'll have groomed the Pict accordingly. He'll believe I sought to resist the killing of Kaa Mag Borga and that I have supporters who'll help Borga's invaders get into Epharra and bring down the remainder of Elak's supporters, including Zerrahydris and all Councillors who are not with us."

Kranaldis nodded slowly. "It is well reasoned. Dangerous, but Borga will know an invasion of Epharra would be risky without inside help. He couldn't be sure of taking the city."

"Once the victory is his, he'll not want to set up a base here," said Scuvular. "He'll have to make me his satrap."

Mittrubos paled. "Gods, but we'll be an annex of the Pictish empire."

Scuvular laughed. "I don't think so. Elak has almost completed the subjugation of all Atlantis. Once I sit upon the Dragon Throne, I'll be satrap in name only. I'll have the entire continent at my disposal—I'll kick the Picts back into the ocean and harry them well clear of our shores. As I said, timing is of the essence. And patience. For now, we await the return of my trading fleet. Once Theorron arrives, we'll set events in motion. Shall I order us some wine? This inn may be a dung hole, but I promise you, the vintage here is excellent."

*

Elak was aware of the intense silence gripping the hall. He was prepared for Kurrach Mag Barrin's attack, as the great axe rose before him. However, the young warrior turned its gleaming blade and proffered it to the Atlantean, dropping to one knee as he did so.

"The victory was fairly won," he said, eyes fixed on the still form of his fallen father. "The House of Barrin will stand with you."

"And Atlantis will stand beside you," said Elak, hugely relieved. "Together we'll oppose the Crawling Death."

Cruath Morgas turned to the gathered Picts. "You have heard King Elak. See, his blood mixes with that of the Picts! Now it begins. Now we call upon the Lords of Midnight to aid us."

10: The Teeth of the Island

The *Wavecutter* rode the sea effortlessly, spume flying back across its deck, where Elak's warriors waited patiently, watching the waters ahead as the ship passed through the islands' labyrinthine passages. Dalan stood impassively with Elak and Lycon. On either side of the ship, the leading Pictish craft also surged northward. These vessels were less sleek, heavier in the beam, their billowing sails less trim, and Elak knew that he could outrun them easily if it came to a race. He also knew Borga had allowed him to sail in the *Wavecutter* rather than in a Pictish craft so neither he nor his companions, especially Dalan, would be able to study it in detail.

With a strong gale blustering behind it, the fleet sped northwards swiftly and arrived at the outer islands in less than a week. Evening was waning, the sun's crimson ball slipping into the western ocean as the lookouts sighted the remote Brae Calaadas, outpost of the Pictish isles. It was a large island, many scores of miles across, its southern coast sheltered from the blasts of the northern weather, strung with inlets, small beaches and coves. The fleet eased into one of the wider coves, beaching in twilight. Above it, hanging like a dark fist, the packed trees were as silent a wall.

Elak and his companions alighted and in moments Borga, Kurrach Mag Barrin and other Pict warriors and their shamans joined them in the shifting sands. Borga indicated the dense forest. "We camp there for the night."

Elak would have preferred to remain on his ship, but knew the Picts were primarily landsmen. They had taken to the seas through necessity, but unlike the Atlanteans were not natural sailors. Elak nodded to Borga, and the King led the war party, several hundred men strong, up the beach to an almost invisible path into the first thicket.

*

Long before dawn, Borga and a few picked warriors and Cruath Morgas came to Dalan, who had slept lightly. "Across the valley, cut into the low hills, lies the ancient

51

citadel of Tergarroc. It is a place of legends and ghosts, and at its heart lies a system of caves that are said to plunge into the underworld, the spirit regions."

Dalan, Elak and Lycon nodded in silence. The Picts were a superstitious race, but here in this region, who knew what dark gods and spirits roamed?

"We must learn the strength of this sect," Borga went on. "Will you spy on them with me?"

Elak nodded, glad to be active. The party, including fifty Pict warriors and as many of Elak's, merged once more with the forest and wove its way through the nocturnal gloom. Above them the night sky was cloudless, sprinkled with a myriad stars, their glare as piercing as eyes, and the men sensed they were being evaluated by the old gods they were disturbing. Elak felt the hairs at the nape of his neck stirring, expecting at any moment to see spectral figures seeping out of the trees. This was a strange, alien terrain, its air like no other he had experienced, as if he had crossed into another world, a place of the dead and unknown powers. The air grew colder, closing like fingers of frost, and the sea seemed very remote.

They cut through a deep ravine and climbed its far end until at length they broke through the trees and stood high up on the rim of a huge depression, crater-like, the far side of which rose even higher. The brilliant starlight, pulsing with strange energies, picked out the buildings and caves of the city, Tergarroc. It seemed to hang, suspended from the vertiginous cliffs, huge tangles of forest interwoven about its angled streets and walkways like something from a disturbed dream. Indistinct shapes flapped around the towers and crooked knots of immense trunk, creatures of the night that swooped and dipped like huge bats, guardians perhaps of the bizarre city.

"The masters of the Crawling Death are within those

walls," said Borga softly to Elak.

Dalan studied the lower slopes of the city, where several wide steps and ramps dropped into a large, circular lake whose black waters were as smooth as oil, redolent with evil airs, streamers of curling mist rising like an evil breath. The water began to swirl slowly, as if stirred by a mighty, unseen hand. "Whatever powers lie here, they have sensed us," Dalan said, gripping his staff. Behind him a group of the Pictish shamans moved cautiously to the lip of the drop, studying the waters as thicker mist tendrils rose.

There came a loud *crack!* across the lake, high up along the rock rim, and all eyes focused on the stone. An indefinable shape moved as an immense slab of rock and massive root broke free of the cliff and slid towards the water. Other such shapes burst from the walls and slipped down. There was something *deliberate* about the slow fall. The waters boiled as the monstrous things plunged in, clouds of steam rising. Behind them, the rockfalls had left vast gashes in the cliff face and as Elak and his companions watched, they saw the stone ridge morphing until a dreadful, spectacular image presented itself. The scarp now had the look of a row of colossal, cracked teeth.

"They watch," said Dalan, pointing to the city. "The sorcerers who control the elements in this place see us." He raised his staff and called to the shamans. "With me! Pour what powers you have in your staffs into mine. Quickly!"

Fear overcame their reluctance to serve the Druid's will, and in moments a dozen shamans had directed the energy of their staffs into Dalan's. He pointed it at the seething lake, and a stream of white light beamed down like molten fire. For long moments the sound of that power and the roar of the collapsing stone clashed, a raging, elemental fury, until at last things fell eerily silent. As the waters churned anew, serpentine shapes burst up from the deeps, coils of some dread undersea nightmare. Elak had seen these before – floating in the ocean, twined with mounds of the dead, and at Skaafelda, where the white stone had calcified even more fallen.

"The Crawling Death is come!" cried Borga, about to flee.

"Wait!" shouted Dalan. As the writhing shadows of horror thrashed ashore below them, snaking up this side of the cliff, the waters of the lake again boiled, then abruptly subsided, sucked downwards into the depths of the earth, driven there by the power of Dalan's sorcery. There was a final moment of stillness, as though all the powers at play here were waiting.

"Do you hear it!" said Lycon. "From below. Dalan, you have woken another power! Can you not feel the island move? Whatever is rising, it will tear the land apart – and us with it!"

"Lords of Midnight, come to our aid!" roared Borga, raising his war axe high, as the entire company felt the grotesque shifting of the island, like an impossibly huge beast rousing itself. Overhead the clouds boiled, as though the ancient Pict gods had answered the king's shout.

11: A Bloody Night in Epharra.

A small group of men passed through shadowy, narrow alleyways and side streets, where curious moonlight could not reach down and reveal who these silent creatures were. They were armed, all but one wearing the livery of the royal guards, closest to the throne. The leader wore a single, thick robe, cowled to make his identity even more secret. With Scuvular were a dozen of his most trusted warriors, greedy men who had been promised much when their master achieved his ambitions. Tonight would play a pivotal part in them. They made their way to a small temple, some distance from the city's heart, within whose high walled, secure gardens and inner retreat, the three Picts had been housed while the king and Borga undertook their business in the west.

Scuvular led his men to a side gate, unlocking it and admitting them. Quietly they padded to the inner gardens. "You have your instructions," said Scuvular, his men nodding. They were ruthless and ambitious and would not balk at the bloody work in hand. Scuvular watched them depart, turning to the one who remained.

"Now, we watch, Azarvis." Scuvular led the soldier around the garden to a narrow window, through which they could study unfolding events.

They saw the warriors crossing a lawn, limned in moonlight. Scuvular knew there was no one else here. The Picts had been left in peace, doubtless bored with their weeks-long confinement, but they were a stoic race and obeyed whatever orders their kings gave them. From the inner chamber, three men stepped into the light. This was Kaa Mag Borga and his two personal guards. They were not armed, though they had protested this, nor did they wear much protective clothing. The Pictish king's son did not trust the Atlanteans, but his father had warned him that without their aid, the fate of the islands hung by a thread.

Scuvular's assassins wasted no time. They drew their blades and advanced on the Picts with clear intent. The first of them rushed at Kaa Mag Borga, but the young Pict was wide awake, his distrust of the intruders firing up his own blood-lust. As the warrior drove at him, the Pict ducked and ran forward, his wide shoulders crashing into the lower abdomen of his assailant and then tossing him up and over as a bull tosses a man. The warrior hit the ground hard and before he could rise, the fist of the first bodyguard smashed into the side of his head, laying him out cold. His sword was immediately snatched up.

Kaa Mag Borga stepped aside as his companion used the sword to deflect the blade of the second and third attackers, and with deft but brutal hacking strokes, cut into flesh and bone, disarming both of them. In a matter of fierce moments the three Picts were armed. The remainder of the warriors closed in, trying to circle the Picts, but the three intended victims formed a close circle that afforded a tight defence.

From the hidden window, Scuvular cursed softly. It was essential that the Picts were killed. He cursed further when another of his warriors was gutted, and as the man fell, spewing blood, he tangled with the soldier behind him, and had no time to adjust his balance before one of the Picts drove his blade into his exposed throat. Though outnumbered, it was evident that the Picts, armed as they were, would not be cut down. Instead they took the offensive. A vicious fight ensued, blades clashing, bones breaking, and blood dripping.

Scuvular was quick to re-think his plans. "Stay here, Azarvis. Above all, do not be seen in that livery." Scuvular went round to the garden's gate and entered, holding a short stabbing sword of his own. When he reached the fight, he allowed himself to be seen by the Picts, who were about to chop down the last of their opponents, and feigned horror at what he saw.

"Traitorous vermin!" Scuvular cried, and drove his blade into the gut of the startled Atlantean warrior before him. As the man slid to the ground, Scuvular watched the others die in a last violent press by the Picts.

"Royal guards!" said Scuvular. "By their livery! They serve the Council. I know who is behind this."

Kaa Mag Borga came close to him, the bloody sword rising as if it would finish its savage work with Scuvular's death. "My father will burn your city to the ground for this."

"Wait! This is not the work of the ruling Council.

Renegades are behind this. You must stay here. I will expose them. You will be safe. Your mission will not be compromised." His heart pounded as he could see the uncertainty in the Pict's eyes, but at last the warrior nodded.

"Do what you must. But we keep the swords."

Scuvular nodded and quickly left, locking the gate behind him. Azarvis, who had seen the entire debacle, gaped at his master and the blood splashed liberally across his robe.

"Wait awhile in the shadows until I call on you. Do not leave until I come to you again."

Azarvis did as bidden, and the night swallowed his master. Scuvular made his way as swiftly as he could through more cramped alleys until he reached the back of an inn. He went upstairs to private chambers he had hired. Mittrubos and Kranaldis awaited him. They saw the blood and their faces were white with apprehension.

"It is done," said Scuvular. "Kaa Mag Borga is slain, with one of his guards. It but remains to get the other away, back to his lands, to report. Come, you must help me."

He led the Councillors to the temple's garden, although they were both reluctant to enter, especially Mittrubos, who shook with terror. Inside, they found the slaughtered guards and stood over them, horrified.

"Gods," said Kranaldis. "Must we dispose of these?"

From the shadows, the three wraith-like Picts stepped forward, their blades raised.

Scuvular pulled out his own weapon once more and rushed upon Mittrubos. "Strike!" he cried to the Picts. "These are the men who betrayed you. False Councillors! They want no part of a Pictish alliance!"

Mittrubos fell, his face a mask of shock, dying as the Picts combined to cut down Kranaldis.

"I will bring Vannadas, the king's regent, to see this

perfidy. He will reassure you that it was no more than a small group of dissidents."

Kaa Mag Borga and his men looked slightly bemused, but again they allowed Scuvular to leave them. Outside the garden once more, Scuvular called on Azarvis.

"Make a small cut across my face," said Scuvular. "And my arm – open the flesh, though carefully. I would not bleed to death." He could see Azarvis looked bewildered. "Do it, man! Our plan has failed. I have to convince the Council that I had no part in this conspiracy. It must be made to look as though Mittrubos and Kranaldis were to blame and tried to kill me. I aided the Picts in thwarting them, but took the cuts for my trouble. Do this for me, Azarvis, and say nothing. With the death of the men in the garden, you are now promoted to be my prime captain. There will be another time for rebellion."

Azarvis nodded, his face sombre. His eyes, however, attested to his delight. One man's misfortune was another man's gold.

12: The Ocean's Fury

A remote, dreadful roaring rose from the bowels of the emptied lake. Elak and his companions watched as the shapes that had been clambering up towards them like mutated ogres paused as though confused by the tumultuous din below.

"We stand firm!" Dalan shouted and around him the warriors and shamans were like statues, rooted by their dread of what must be rising, a slumbering god free of the shackles of ancient sleep. Borga's face was set, the fear locked inside him held under control as he gripped his war axe and prepared to die before giving ground, even though the temptation to flee was almost overpowering. His men were with him. It was not the Pictish way to abandon a leader.

Abruptly there was an explosion from the drained lake as a huge fountain burst skyward, a concentrated column of water, within it a distorted visage, a screaming face, an elemental god, formed from its own fury. White spume cascaded over the rocks. The column and face within it collapsed but rose again, as if huge oceanic waves were pounding a shore at the height of a storm. The earth shook and more chunks of white cliff crumbled into the thundering waters, dragging masses of trailing vegetation into the maelstrom.

"The ocean below the island," said Elak. "I can smell the salt. See – where it strikes the rocks, the surf breaks as if on a beach. Dalan has tapped the ocean."

Lycon nodded in horror. "We cannot remain here. We'll be engulfed." He pointed to the rising waters. Already the living sea had reached the Crawling Death and the monstrous figures, tearing at them with saline fingers, dragging them down into the deeps. The swirling waters thrashed as though huge sea leviathans were writhing in their death throes. The quays and ramps at the foot of Tergarroc began to twist and tumble like rotting logs battered by a rising flood and presently the lower buildings of the city tumbled away, instantly churned to mud.

"The sorcerers flee!" called Dalan. "I sense their terror. They are no match for the ocean gods."

"What have you unleashed?" said Elak. "Can you control it?"

"I have merely directed its power. The evil that rooted here on Brae Calaadas was an affront to the deep dwellers. Sorcery protected it, but our own was the key to unlocking the barriers. The sea will do the work of the gods."

Elak would have replied, but a wall of water rose up before them—there could be no possible escape from its battering embrace as it collapsed and poured down the outer slopes of the rim. However, as it crashed down like the fist of an angry deity, neither Elak nor any of the others on the ridge felt its grip. Water roared around them with the ferocity of a hurricane, but other than a few drops, it surged between or over the men, as if they existed in a bubble of air. They were knocked to their knees by the immense power of the waters and saw through the tumultuous cascades the broken shapes of white stone, chunks of rock that cracked and dissolved as they whirled past and downward to the outer ocean.

Elak's senses were rocked; he could not move, but the air became calmer. Gradually he was able to look up, not through a torrential flow of waves but at the night sky, where the glittering stars yet gazed down, their courses unchanged by the petty earthly stirrings below. Dalan was on his feet and pulled Elak to his. Presently the entire company had recovered, with no one lost. Below on the landward side, the lake had been restored, though its now placid surface was strewn with shattered trunks and twisted boughs. The entire lower half of Tergarroc had gone, the remainder hanging precariously from a cliff face that was riddled with huge cracks. On the seaward side, the jungle had been flattened, every tree down to the coves pressed into the earth and stone as if a landslide had swept down through them. The ships were safe, though, bobbing silently on the now calm ocean surface.

*

As the small fleet left Tergarroc, Dalan studied the waters, as though he could see deep down into their depths and weigh their secrets.

"The sorcerers," said Borga. "Have we destroyed them?"

"We have severely bruised their powers," said the Druid. "The ocean dwellers have cleansed Tergarroc of them. It is now but a shell, and it will slide into the silt at the bottom of the sea. Yet the cult that rose here has fled, scotched but not destroyed. As a wounded serpent grows a new tail, so will they reform."

"In the far north?" said Elak. "In the Vaarfrost ice realms?"

Dalan nodded. "A most dangerous place for any ships to follow."

Borga swore. "Even so, we must find them and strike while they are hurt."

"As we are now," said Dalan, "we are ill prepared for such a pursuit. They would evade us in those interminable ice caverns and floes. If we go back and gather all our powers, then we could begin the hunt. For now, let us be content that we have delivered them a shattering blow. I doubt that the Crawling Death will trouble your islands again."

Borga grunted, but he could see the battle had taken a toll on his men and indeed, the powers of the shamans. He forced a smile, though, and raised his spear. "We go back to our islands," he roared. "We have feasts to prepare."

"A new alliance to celebrate," said Elak.

Borga scowled at him, but only for a moment before his face split wide in another grin. "Aye, Atlantean. And we'll seal it with our best mead."

Epilogue: Return of the Warriors

Vannadas coughed, his body badly wracked, but he forced himself to stand and study the group of men before him. His brother, Scuvular, was beside him, attended by Azarvis, commander of Scuvular's personal guards, and Theorron, captain of Scuvular's fleet of traders, lately returned from a voyage to San-Mu. The room in which the meeting had been convened, in a remote part of the city, far from prying eyes, was a low, dingy chamber, with a dozen or more crude wooden biers lined up by the walls, each bearing a bloodied corpse.

"Kranaldis!" Vannadas gasped, seeing the dead men's faces. "And Mittrubos! Two city Councillors. How has this happened? Who is responsible?"

"Treason," said Scuvular. "They plotted against Elak and intended to have Kaa Mag Borga and his warriors murdered, with word sent to the Pictish king. Elak, who is with the Picts, would have been torn to shreds."

Vannadas nodded solemnly. "Olvaros suspected as much."

"Olvaros?"

"A spy for the royal household. He had been following a number of suspects."

"Where is he now? Can we question him?"

Vannadas grunted. "I fear he has been discovered in his work. I have heard nothing from him."

"You mean he's been killed?"

"Yes." Vannadas moved slowly among the biers, looking again at the faces of the dead. "Who are these soldiers?"

"As you can see," said Scuvular, "they wear the livery of the two Councillors. The Picts were too powerful for them. I saw some of the skirmish and had to defend myself." He held up his bandaged arm. "I got this for my pains. Fortunately Azarvis and his men were able to put an end to things, but not before the two Councillors were killed."

Scuvular indicated Theorron, his burly sea captain. "Tell my brother what you learned."

Theorron turned to Vannadas, speaking his carefully rehearsed words. "Sire, there are always whispers among crewmen, talk of plots. I don't always pay attention. But I caught whiff of something disturbing, talk of messages being relayed from here in Epharra to the Pictish Isles. Kranaldis was behind it. I have only been returned for a short while. I came to Scuvular as soon as I was able with the news. The plot, I found, had already been thwarted."

Vannadas nodded again. "The question is – who did these traitors intend to put on the Dragon Throne?" His anger, barely concealed, prompted a fresh bout of coughing.

Scuvular took his arm and supported him. "You're in no fit state to conduct an inquiry, brother. Leave that to me. I'll get to the bottom of it. If there are any others involved, I will root them out. In the meantime, I'll see that Kaa Mag Borga is properly protected."

"I am grateful. Elak will return soon. You will be well rewarded for your part in this, brother. We need to keep King Borga sweet."

*

Borga and his Picts came again to the western shores of the Atlantean continent, to the small bay where they had first met with Dalan and his young king. The sun had barely risen as the small party of Picts gathered on the beach. Elak pointed to the shadows where the trees met the sand.

"They come," he said. He had sent a fleet craft ahead of the *Wavecutter* to let Vannadas in Epharra know he was returning. And it was Vannadas now who stepped out into the post dawn light. In the party of men with him were Kaa Mag Borga and his two Pictish guards. Borga met his son and hugged him openly in front of the company.

"The price of your patience," said the Pictish king, "is a victory. A Pictish and Atlantean alliance." He turned to Elak, who grinned. "Perhaps the beginning of a new era."

"I would be glad of that," said Elak.

"When you need us," said Borga. "You have only to call." Then, with a brief, courteous nod to the Druid and Lycon, Borga led his son and the rest of the party back to his ship.

"I am relieved to see you safe, sire," Vannadas said to Elak. "Can I assume you will be taking up residence in Epharra for the foreseeable future? The burden of leadership is not something I'd wish to bear for long."

Elak clapped an arm around his shoulder. "Of course!" he laughed.

Behind him, watching the western ocean quietly, Dalan kept silent. It had been a small triumph, a battle, not a war. The invisible sorcerers they had defeated on Brae Calaadas would be licking their wounds, healing themselves. It may take them some time, a year, five, ten? No it would not be that long. Undoubtedly they would already be preparing for the next wave in their thirst for conquest.

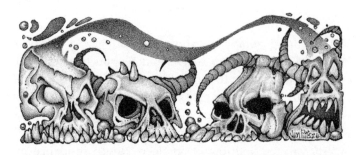

DEMONS OF THE DEEP

Encouraged by his successes in the military campaigns to begin the unification of Atlantis, and by the willingness of many of the city state monarchs to come under his dragon banner, Elak led his army further south to where their remoter states were in political turmoil, run mostly by ambitious nobles and independent monarchs, constantly hovering on the brink of internecine strife. It would take a civil war to settle the disputes, and for a year after his triumph in Pictish lands Elak's banners were seen across the lands, gradually restoring order and an uneasy peace.

- Helvas Ravanniol

Annals of the Third Atlantean Empire

1: Crawlers from the Deep

The southern port of Zangarza slept deeply under a swollen moon, its docks and buildings silent, seemingly devoid of life. Here, at the southeastern end of the huge Atlantean continent, the city was isolated, almost impregnable, carved as by legendary giant hands into the lower slopes of soaring cliffs, nestled in the sweep of a tight bay. A long, curling promontory prodded like a monstrous finger out at the southern ocean, its lone palace separated from the main harbour. The recent northern wars had not touched this remote area, where most people went about their lives as they had for generations, fishing and trading. Conflict on a large scale was uncommon here, and people were generally contented and not a little complacent.

On the high walls of the promontory palace and its watchtowers, the guards, who had been secretly imbibing wine brought to them by certain serving girls from a local tavern, yawned and fought off sleep. None of them could recall the last time anything had threatened the city, from either the land or the tempestuous sea, although an occasional southern blow had rocked the stones with its fury. Not tonight, however, for the air was still, the skies empty of clouds and the waters lapping in the gentlest of tides against the beach and rock pools.

Kraddus, a lone guard, had left his companions on the wall and descended narrow stone steps to a curve of sand under its shadow, where he relieved himself, humming tonelessly as he did so. Preoccupied, he neither heard nor saw what rose out of the shallows and scuttled up the narrow beach towards him. It was vaguely man-like, its hunched shape blotched with moonlight, its curved back a carapace, its elongated arms ending in fat claws resembling those of a deep-water crustacean. As Kraddus turned to face it, a scream died in his throat as one of those claws choked it off. The guard's head sprang from his shoulders, the neck pumping blood, the body toppling.

The waters of the ocean suddenly boiled with life as more of the water beings rose up: soon hundreds of them crossed the beach, an army of monstrous intent. They climbed the near vertical wall easily, like huge crabs, their claws clattering on stone. Beyond the rim, the other guards dozed, oblivious to the rising nightmare. Too late they saw the doom close in. Along the promontory wall, the entire night watch was taken. One by one the warriors succumbed to the horrible embrace of the sea beasts, falling to their knees, feeling the cold clutch of the ocean. Their veins pulsed with something new, a freezing new marrow entered their bones and the transformations began.

Soon after the invaders had snared their victims, the guards stood upright once more, faces twisted in a bizarre mixture of pain and frightful glee. Already their arms were lengthening, their hands turned, contorted into the lobster-like claws of their assailants until, even in the brightest wash of moonlight, they were indistinguishable from them. And a score more warriors were added to the host as it turned its attention to the unguarded streets of Zangarza, where the blood feast would soon begin.

*

Not all of the city slept. In the great palace of Numenedzer, the monarch himself sat with several of his most trusted counsellors, among them the High Sorcerer of the city, Querram Urgol. They had been deep in discussion for many hours, plotting and arguing over ambitious plans. The world beyond their lands was in turmoil, and they hungered for an advantage, for new powers that would strengthen Zangarza's standing in Atlantis.

"When does King Thotmes arrive?" asked Grannodor, commander of the city's navy. He referred to the strongest of the monarchs of the southern kingdoms that had pledged service under Numenedzer's banner. The two kings were now by far the most influential in these southern regions. A war between them had seemed almost inevitable, until Numenedzer had recently devised a daring alternative plan. Not all his subjects, however, approved of it.

"In two days," Numenedzer answered. "His entourage is under my sworn protection, so there will be no aggression towards him or his men, on pain of death. I will not move from that." *But if he doesn't have the guts to see my plans through,* thought the king, *he will forego any protection from me.*

"You trust him?" said the High Sorcerer, not for the first time. "You are sure he will agree your proposed alliance?"

"He and I are well matched in the strength of our armies. An open war between us would impoverish us both, and leave the way open for the northern dog, Elak." There were murmurs of agreement. The rise of Elak's empire was of real concern to those gathered here.

The High Sorcerer nodded, but his face was a cold mask. His inner thoughts were ever unreadable. Many believed his ambitions were his own, though none dared say as much. There were rumours that he had once served under Karkora, the monstrous power who had sought to control all of the lands of men before his destruction by Elak of Cyrena. "You should place your faith in the ancient powers, my lord," he told Numenedzer. "With them you could scourge all of Atlantis and rule as a god."

"We've been over that a dozen times, Querram Urgol," snapped the king. "Those powers are far too dangerous. In time gone by they almost brought annihilation to our world. I would rather use the power of the sword!" *And I'd also rather maintain control, not surrender it to a sorcerer who would likely look to establish himself as ruler of my lands – and more besides. My daughter, Hamniri is a woman now, wise for her age, and she will rule Zangarza after me.* He would go to any length to protect her legacy. If that meant swatting King Thotmes aside, so be it.

Commander Grannodor, a veteran, gazed disapprovingly at Querram Urgol. "A strike in the dark with a good, clean sword, however treacherous, is preferable to sorcery."

The king did not flinch. "War is war. King Elak has

agreed to come to our peace talks, and to look for a way to bind all of the smaller kingdoms. But we know it will be under his banner. My spies in Cyrena tell me his Council wants to see him crowned over us all, even if the fledgling king has no real desire to be a conqueror."

"Which is why we must ally ourselves with Thotmes and assassinate Elak," said Querram Urgol. "However, without sorcery to help you after Elak's removal, we will all be at risk. The northern armies are growing stronger by the day. Cyrena has them all under its sway. They are savouring their new union."

"One step at a time," said the king. "We will formalize our plans with King Thotmes before Elak arrives. Then, together, we will remove Elak, here in Zangarza."

Querram Urgol inclined his head respectfully. "As you wish, sire."

Yes, mused Numenedzer. *Your lust for power grows harder for you to conceal. Once you've served your purpose, I'll set your head on a spike along with the others.*

2: Treachery by Moonlight

While the monarch and his associates brought their night's plotting to an end, the crawlers from the deep swarmed into the city like a plague of locusts through fields of wheat. They were merciless, breaking into homes and killing the occupants without a shred of pity or compromise. Up through the tiered streets they raced, and though there were barracks and watchtowers, well-staffed with Zangarza's warriors, nothing could halt the remorseless surge of the ocean horrors. And still the abominations came from the ocean, wave after wave.

King Numenedzer had barely taken to his night chamber in the opulent palace that spanned the uppermost heights of the city, when he heard strange sounds out in the night. Drawing a thick robe around himself, he went on to the curved balcony that afforded him a sweeping view of the harbour and city spread below him in the vivid moonlight. Again he heard the sounds – now he recognized them. Screams! From all directions. And the clash of arms. Shouts. A battle? Gods of the Deep, here, in his city? How could such a thing be?

Behind him the doors to his bedchamber flew open. He had no time to be outraged, snatching up a sword, one of several he always had to hand, even here in his inner sanctum. He was a big man and had always excelled in the use of a sword, his stamina and strength legendary among his people. He scowled at the guards who had burst in on him, prepared to defend himself, if this was to be a betrayal.

"Sire!" cried the first of them, Thraxus, captain of the palace guard. He carried a sword, but clearly not for an attack on his monarch. A dozen of his elite guards were with him, all armed and prepared for conflict. "Forgive this rude intrusion, but the city is under assault! The sea has disgorged an army. Half of Zangarza has already fallen."

"Who is behind this perfidy?" the king fumed, quickly dressing himself. Beyond the doors he could hear a tumult and the ring of steel on steel, more frightful screams as men died.

Thraxus and his loyal guards ringed the king, pulling the doors closed and ramming the thick bolts home to secure them.

"I will fight!" snarled Numenedzer. "I am no coward. If my people stand against the foe, I will lead them!"

"You cannot, sire," said Thraxus, though he looked appalled, uneasy at correcting the king. "We are vastly outnumbered. We must get you away, sire. You must flee the city. That or die with us."

The doors burst open as if smitten by a landslide, the

thick wood disintegrating. From the shadows beyond rushed a wave of the creatures from the ocean, the hunched, clawed beings, bloodied and hissing with the lust for destruction. The king saw with utter horror those snapping claws, and the teeth of these fiends, long and sharp, like the fangs of jungle predators. What terrible hybrids were these, and what dark art had spawned them?

A ferocious battle began as Thraxus and his men tore into the devils, chopping many aside, holding back the onslaught, but only momentarily. There were far too many of the intruders. Numenedzer realized if he fought here, he would doubtless die in this maelstrom of blood. Better to let his men buy his life while he took the secret stair out of his chambers and flee into the heart of the mountain, where he could affect an escape from the city.

He was about to escape, when a tall figure emerged from behind the velvet curtains that disguised the stair to freedom. It was the High Sorcerer, Querram Urgol. A cruel smiled played upon his lips as he faced his monarch.

Numenedzer understood the truth at once. As he suspected, here was the betrayer! "You have done this!" he cried, raising his sword, intent on spitting the skull of the sorcerer. Querram Urgol swung his long staff, a black rod, carved ornately with ancient glyphs and sigils, and a bolt of blue light exploded as the weapons clashed. Numenedzer was flung aside like a rag doll, fetching up on the stone floor of the balcony. Behind him the moon blazed like the eye of a hungry god, eager to see a sacrifice.

"Unworthy dog!" gasped the king. "I spit on your treachery!"

Querram Urgol pushed the tip of his staff down at the chest of the king. "The time of change has come," he said coldly. "A new power rises from the ocean. Xeraph-Hizer, the Leviathan Lord, is awakened. Sorcery will rule Atlantis now. From this place, it will spread and Man will fall."

Numenedzer gazed in mute horror as the High Sorcerer raised his arms, and in the moonlight, his claws gleamed, and his face altered, testament to his transformation. He was no longer a man. Nor were the guards who had rallied to him. All of them, chopped down in a bloody rain, rose again, their bodies contorted, their limbs transmuted. Down in the city, the last of the screams had ended, replaced by a new sound, a discordant, alien shriek of victory as the massed crawlers from the deeps gave voice to their triumph.

The last thing the king thought of as the sorcerer's staff again dug into him, parting his flesh with searing heat and agony, was his daughter, Hamniri. She and her entourage were in the palace along the harbour side. It had always been a secure place, but against these things, could it possibly have stood unscathed? And if so, for how long? He was spared the misery of dwelling on this, as darkness closed over him and he collapsed.

Querram Urgol turned to the victorious clawed ones. They were silent now, misshapen heads bowed as they awaited new commands. The city was theirs. Already many of the fallen outside were rising, newly shaped, obedient to a fresh cause.

*

The early morning sun beat down, already bathing the land in a dry, wearing heat. Slowly the large body of men rode across an open terrain, watching the rocky slopes ahead of them where the road wound to the uppermost watchtowers of the city.

Scouts galloped back to the company of guards who rode with the young king, Thotmes. He was clad in war gear and well-armed, though this was a peaceful mission.

Numenedzer, the king of Zangarza had sworn an oath, claiming a deep desire to form a union. Thotmes had enjoyed banding his city-states into a kingdom since taking its throne at sword-point almost a year since. A war with Numenedzer had its appeal, but there was always the danger of losing the campaign and becoming thrall to Zangarza. Whereas unification could lead on to greater conquests to the north, perhaps even the Dragon Throne of Cyrena. Often had Thotmes thought of that.

"Zangarza, sire," said the first of the scouts. "It lies beyond the cliffs. It is strangely silent. They have sent no ambassadors to greet you."

Thotmes scowled. Why should Numenedzer insult him at this stage in the negotiations?

3: Carnage in the Streets

Thotmes studied the winding road carefully, his unease mounting. There were low walls along the ridge; the road fed into an open gateway. Up on the walls, a number of figures waited, draped in hooded cloaks, black and motionless in the sunlight's glare. These guards resembled huge crows, not men, though there were no birds visible. The oncoming army had startled them into flight. A lone rider galloped to the warriors at the young king's side.

"The way ahead is clear, sire. Zangarza's watch has waved us forward."

Thotmes nodded and his guards formed a shield in front of him, leading the way to the gates. The king had brought a strong force with him, taking no chances with his potential allies. If there were to be treachery, his army would waste no time in attacking, though his ambassadors had told him the city was built into the cliffs and would not be a good place for either an ambush or an open conflict. The outcome of any such battle would be completely in the lap of the gods. Numenedzer would hardly risk success in such a way.

Inside the gates the road curved downward and back on itself as it threaded the vertiginous buildings. Everywhere remained silent, as though this uppermost part of Zangarza consisted of nothing more than tombs, a necropolis looming high over the city's suburbs and temples.

Where are the inhabitants? Thotmes asked himself. The place seemed dead, abandoned. Far below, the restless waves of the great ocean curled into the sickle-shaped bay, but there were no ships berthed. That seemed extraordinary for a port that was famed in these southern lands for its sea-trade, its mariners respected the length of the southern coasts and beyond.

Further down the road, a group of men at last appeared, on foot and waiting to receive Thotmes and his entourage. Like the guardians on the wall, these men were hooded and cloaked, their faces shielded from the fierce heat, their arms held beneath their cloaks. They had the appearance of priests. Zangarza was known to worship strange sea gods, with a secret sect running the priesthood. There had even been rumours of sorcery, though this was not uncommon here in the southlands. Thotmes had quashed the powers of the sorcerers in his own city and revived the cult of sun worship, much to the delight of his people.

A spokesman for the hooded men stood before the king, but his face remained invisible. His voice came clearly on the still air. "Greetings, o king, from Numenedzer, our ruler. He awaits you in his palace. We will escort you."

Thotmes masked his reaction to the strange voice, which seemed flat and lacking in emotion. His commanders turned to him, equally surprised. It was obvious they feared a trap. Did Numenedzer, after all, plan to eliminate his main rival? Zangarza's king was reputed to be a devious man.

Was the suggested alliance to topple Elak of Cyrena a trick? Thotmes spoke quietly to his warriors.

"Be prepared for bloodshed. Send scouts out into the side streets. At the slightest hint of betrayal, form ranks and pull back. If it is to be a contest, we'll burn this city to ash!"

His men were deployed as he asked, slipping unseen by the hooded escort into several of the side streets. The first group were assailed by a pungent smell, a mixture of the sea and something else, a foul aroma. As fighting men, they knew that stench as spilled blood, and worse. Shadows clung to the buildings, deep in the alleys, where shapes appeared fleetingly in windows and doorways before withdrawing, like huge spiders scuttling to safety.

One of the groups entered a wider doorway which opened onto an enclosed square, heaped with what at first appeared to be rubble, but as a shaft of sunlight moved across it, shapes emerged, and the soldiers gaped in horror. These were bodies, scores of them. And among them, something scavenged. Bulbous, misshapen heads looked up, mouths crammed with dripping red meat. Scavengers, they fed on the mound of bodies. Cannibals! These creatures seemed less than human, their elongated arms raised to display horrific claws, crimson with the blood of the fallen.

"Back!" cried the leader, Immuz. "We must warn King Thotmes." It was already too late. A host of the clawed beings burst up through the carpet of dead and surrounded the soldiers. Without warning these horrors flung themselves forward. Swords hacked at their chitinous bodies and clashed with the massive claws, but to no avail. There were too many of the mutated beings and their bloody work was soon over as they overwhelmed the intruders.

In the street outside, other warriors were looking into buildings and outhouses. They heard the sound of battle and rallied, approaching the wide doorway to the square, preparing for an assault. Before they could go through to the square, several shapes emerged into the sunlit street, led by Immuz. He was splattered with blood, his beard and hair thick with it. His short cape was twisted around him, covering his arms for a moment. He approached his second line of men and they read something alien in his eyes, and in those of the soldiers who had emerged with him.

Immuz flung back his cape and revealed a thick, ridged claw. With one terrible sweep he used it to partially decapitate the first of his men. A fresh fight broke out in the crowded street, as terrible as the one fought in the inner square. Immuz and his first wave of men were all changed, possessed by creatures from some other realm, the sea perhaps: the saline smell and the hardening of their new skin testified to a grim transmogrification.

This grim fate befell all of those sent by Thotmes to reconnoitre the streets and alleyways, although the king had no inkling of what was happening. The city walls muffled the sounds of bloodletting and slaughter. Protected by his senior guards, he rode slowly down into the city. He was still high above the harbour when the hooded guides led his company along the wider slope to the palace gates. Another group awaited them. One of its members stepped forward. He wore a long robe and headgear that marked him as either a priest or sorcerer, and he bowed to Thotmes.

"Welcome, lord of Kanda Kara. I am Querram Urgol, High Sorcerer of Zangarza. My king, Numenedzer, awaits you within." He raised a long staff in salutation. "I am at your mercy, Thotmes. Please use me as an insurance for your safe passage."

Thotmes nodded, though he knew how dangerous these sorcerers were. It had not been easy ridding his own city of them. Querram Urgol exuded power, and the young king felt it as surely as he felt the hot sunlight.

Inside the palace, Thotmes and his guards were taken to the throne room, an opulent place, lit by the sun from openings in its curved dome, its statues and carvings no less regal and impressive than those of Thotmes' own city. He stood before the throne, which had been cut from a single huge stone of marble, its striated colours dazzling. The man seated upon it was heavily cloaked, in spite of the clammy heat. His thick black hair obscured most of his face, his arms resting on the sides of the throne, hands inside long sleeves.

"Welcome, Thotmes," he said.

The younger king bowed, though Numenedzer's voice seemed unduly cold and hollow. An overpowering smell of the sea permeated everything.

4: The God from the Ocean

Numenedzer's soulless voice rang out in the great hall. The king remained as immobile as the many statues behind the throne and lining the sides of the temple. "This is a momentous occasion for our cities, this coming together in preparation for greatness. Our ocean lord, Xeraph-Hizer, will soon rise from his deep cradle and pour his energies into his servants! Between us we will sweep his enemies from all of Atlantis!"

Thotmes, the visiting king, scowled. He looked around him, seeing the details of the statues properly, realizing they were not sculptures of gods or demi-gods that he knew or worshiped. All represented beings of an aquatic nature, finned and gilled, with long spines more commonly seen on the larger fish of the seas. And who was Xeraph-Hizer? Some dark, oceanic monster, summoned from the ocean bed by the sorcery of this robed devil, Querram Urgol? Thotmes glanced at the High Sorcerer, who stood close to the throne, his face serene, a hint of mockery in those brooding eyes. He had the appearance of a man, though his robes hid much of his shape, and Thotmes had a deeply uneasy feeling about him.

"I worship no such god," said Thotmes. "I came here to discuss an alliance, a combined force to overthrow Elak of the north."

"And we shall have one! Your army is here. Already your men are being shown to their new barracks. Tonight we shall celebrate with a feast to end all feasts! Tomorrow the northern dog arrives. Xeraph-Hizer's children will overwhelm him."

"Who is this god of the sea?"

Behind Numenedzer there were two huge columns rising up to the dome. Between them hung thick curtains of very dark material, woven with bright green symbols, suggestive of the ocean. Thotmes' question was answered as the curtains were drawn aside by invisible hands, revealing yet another statue. It was twenty-five feet high, and at sight of it Thotmes and his retinue drew back, shocked by the bizarre nature of the thing towering over them. It was cut from deep green stone, gleaming as if it had been oiled, giving it the impression of having just risen from the sea, which made it disturbingly life-like. Its arms were like the long appendages of a giant squid, its head long and bulbous, with a curved beak of a mouth. The eyes, immense jewels, reflected the sunlight in a way which suggested they were alive, studying the company.

"Behold, the great ocean lord, Xeraph-Hizer! Gaze upon his likeness and bow down. Soon he will rise from his deep city and come to us. He will bestow upon us all we need to overrun the continent – and beyond!"

Thotmes spoke softly to his men. "We are finished here. This is sorcery of the darkest kind. I'll swap blood for blood with any warrior, Elak included, in an honest fight. But I'll not sell my soul to this dweller in the deepest hells. Prepare to fight your way out."

The High Sorcerer, Querram Urgol, stirred, as though he had caught the whispered words. He held his staff aloft and light speared down from above, striking along its length and reflecting across to the huge statue. The monstrous thing seemed to quiver, its eyes even more fixed on Thotmes and his men. "It is written in your fate," said the sorcerer. "You cannot avoid a union with us now. Tonight, the conjunction of the stars will be mirrored here in Zangarza as your men and ours become one unit, children of the god. Revel in the power, Thotmes. You will be a god among men."

"We have our own gods," Thotmes replied, drawing his sword. His men did likewise. "And we will have none of this bowing to an alien. It belongs in the deep ocean. Let it remain there. We will leave. I will take my army and return to Kanda Kara."

A hollow laugh rang out from the enthroned monarch, or whatever being sat on his throne. "It is too late for that, Thotmes. Put away your swords and embrace your fate." Numenedzer had spoken as though his body was wracked by severe pain, that or held in a rigid grip.

Thotmes heard the rattle of arms behind him. Scores of warriors were entering the palace and lining its walls. Their numbers swelled, blocking off the young king's retreat. It would be suicidal to engage them, Thotmes knew. Instead he barked a command to his warriors and as one they launched themselves at the steps to the throne.

Querram Urgol struck the paving slabs with his staff and the ground shook as though an earth tremor ran through it. Thotmes and his men were thrown aside, some losing their swords as they fell. Numenedzer still had not moved, gazing down at the fallen men impotently. Thotmes rose and made a renewed attempt to challenge the king, but a deep dizziness shook him and he stumbled, darkness swirling about him. One by one, his men subsided, unconscious. The last thing Thotmes saw before he succumbed to the churning night was the triumphant rush of Numenedzer's transformed warriors and the claws they raised in murderous intent.

*

Elak, young King of Cyrena, rubbed his jaw thoughtfully, studying the scrolled map. Here in his tent, Lycon, his most trusted companion, had joined the Cyrenian king with Dalan, the Druid, and Arborax, commander of the royal army. Dawn had not long departed and today Elak and the not insignificant armed force he had brought with him would reach Zangarza, where a potential alliance awaited them. Elak had recently been elevated to the throne, and already he was bored with the strictures of his administration. How he longed to swim out to a ship and sail off to adventure among remote islands. Those days, he thought ruefully, were probably behind him.

"I'm surprised we haven't been met, as we are so close to our destination," said Lycon, yawning, and stretching his considerable bulk. He'd spent a restless night, not having had an opportunity to imbibe his usual daily quota of wine. Life on the road, marching with the army, was not his idea of fun. Dalan and Arborax remained more stolid.

"My forward scouts have reported very little," said Arborax. He was no more than a year or two older than his young king, but already his remarkable skills as a warrior and commendable bravery in the recent conflict with Karkora had won him promotion to the demanding role of commander of the army. He was loyal to Elak, and the two men were good friends.

Dalan, an introverted, sombre man, seemed unduly thoughtful. "It's an uneasy calm," he said. "If we were at sea, it would presage a storm."

A cry from outside made the four men all look up. Dalan's brows contracted in an even deeper scowl. "The way ahead is cloaked in darkness. Bad news approaches."

5: A Council by Night

Two heavily armoured guards entered the tent, bowing low before Elak. "Sire, news from Zangarza. One of its citizens has come."

"Bring him in," said Dalan, as though the Druid already knew what the southerner would say.

When the man entered, carefully watched by the guards, his appearance was a shock to Elak and his companions. The man was badly dishevelled, his clothes torn and bloody, his hair matted. He wore a look of horror, falling to his knees, gabbling so quickly he had to be stopped.

Dalan put a hand on the man's head, instilling a little calm into the shaking body. "Slowly. Give us your news. You will not be harmed here."

"They came!" cried the man. "From the ocean. Hundreds of them, as countless as the stars. Men, yet not men. And they struck. Zangarza's people fell, cut to pieces. Those claws – those frightful claws!"

Elak and his companions exchanged puzzled glances. The man gabbled on.

"I hid with a few of my closest companions. By dawn, when all had gone quiet we slipped like ghosts up into the city, where the streets were strangely abandoned. And we saw the coming of Thotmes, king of Kanda Kara. He and his warriors rode down into a trap! The creatures from the deeps. And worse! Many of our people who had fallen in the night, rose again, imbued with strange powers, transformed into the likenesses of these sea horrors! Their hands were – claws!"

"What of Numenedzer?" said Elak.

The man shook his head, tears streaming down his agonized face. "Who can say? He and his new ally may have fallen. One of my fellow guards, fatally wounded, told me with his last breath that, Hamniri, daughter of King Numenedzer, has locked herself in the lower palace with a handful of guards. The sorcerer wants her alive for some reason. He must have some vile plan for her."

"How do you know these things?" Dalan challenged him.

"I was with the king when Querram Urgol betrayed him and I was beaten senseless and left for dead. Somehow I managed to escape, along with two others. My companions took to the sea, but I fear for them. The sea devils must have taken them. Am I all that is left of Zangarza?"

"Where are these sea creatures now?" said Lycon, towering over the man.

"As I crept from the city, I saw they have made a new home there, killing or horribly converting the people! And they wait. If you take your army there, they will trick you and draw you in. Beware of sorcery! Querram Urgol has called up the powers of the deep night. His treachery has unleashed living nightmare upon the world." The man could say no more. He broke down, sobbing as he was gently led away.

Dalan wore a look of thunder. "The High Sorcerer," he growled.

"You know him?" said Elak.

"I do. He was banished from the northern cities where he once sought power, drawing on ancient rituals long denied to his fellows, for fear of bringing the fell spirits of outer regions into our world. Doubtless he played a part in Karkora's rise. He may have been banished and broken, but it seems he has mended himself. If he is behind this perfidy, it will take sorcery to crush him."

Arborax looked again at the map on the table. "Our scouts say the army of the visiting king, Thotmes, was substantial. It seems incredible it entered the city and was absorbed by these ocean invaders."

"Thotmes has scourged his city and lands of sorcery," said Dalan. "He'll not allow such things, and I doubt if he would have tolerated me, or my Druidic followers. He and his men would have been susceptible to the workings of Querram Urgol. We are better protected. When we enter the city, we will be shielded from sorcery. We will meet it on level terms, aye, and better!"

Elak nodded. "Certainly that must be what this sorcerer expects. A confident new king in me and a strong force, fresh from triumph in another series of battles in the north. Why wouldn't I attack, driving straight into the teeth of the enemy?"

Lycon was chuckling. "Oh-ho, I smell something devious. Our young ruler may be confident and arrogant, but he is not without guile."

Arborax shot the king's huge companion a glare. Lycon was the only man who would dare speak of Elak this way.

Elak, however, was laughing softly. "It must have rubbed off from the company I keep," he said.

"You have a different strategy?" said Dalan.

"We must give the sorcerer the impression we are walking into his trap. Thus a slow march forward to Zangarza, though we'll camp the army some distance from its gates. We should be there well before nightfall, but we camp overnight. That will give me time to effect a clandestine entry into the city."

Dalan's face clouded anew. "You, sire? If you wish to send spies into the city, by all means do it. But it is work for others. You cannot risk yourself. Not as king."

Elak again laughed gently. "I won't be alone. Arborax will lead the pick of his warriors, and Lycon will, as ever, be my right arm."

Dalan shook his head. "Your skill with a sword and your athleticism has become a talking point across the whole of the north, Elak, but you are facing sorcery of the darkest hue. Your steel will not be enough."

"I'm sure you're right, Dalan. Which is why you will also accompany us."

There followed a brief, candid argument, but Elak, as king, had the last word. In spite of Dalan's objections, the plan to enter the city secretly was agreed.

Arborax tapped the map. "The cliffs at the city's northern boundary are the way in. Steep and dangerous, especially by night. But unlikely to be guarded."

Lycon had paled. "By Ishtar, those cliffs will be vertical! Exposed to the blasts of the eastern ocean. They are wide open, unprotected."

Elak nodded. "A challenge, yes. But we've all been grumbling about the monotony and boredom of the ride across the land to get here. This little adventure will make our blood sing!"

Lycon gaped. It was bad enough having no wine among the supplies, but this! By the Nine Hells!

*

The full moon daubed brilliant light across the cliffs and the narrow path winding across their crumbling face. Elak and his picked company of a score, gritted their teeth against the stiff ocean breezes and occasional buffets of the night winds. Elak insisted that he and his commander took the lead as they began the difficult horizontal climb, finding the vital footholds that enabled them to traverse the cliffs and round the jutting headland that gave on to the outer structures of Zangarza. Dalan cloaked the company in such magics as he possessed, though there were no guards set here in such a dangerous approach. Lycon made much of the journey with his eyes almost closed in terror, but he masked his discomfort well. As a younger man he had happily shinned up a ship's mast, but these days his great weight hampered him.

Slowly the company eased its way downwards towards the foot of the cliffs and the spume that scattered over the lower rocks. Beyond the headland, the promontory on which the lower palace of the city squatted like a huge beast ran like an arm into the churning waters. The palace was dark, not a single light visible in its upper windows. The man who had escaped the city and spoken of the coming of the horrors from the sea had said the lower palace had sealed itself against the attack. And within its thick walls, Hamniri, daughter of the king, had locked herself away with her guards. If the gods willed it, she would yet be unharmed, a possible key to the city.

6: Lair of the Sea Beast

Elak's small company slipped silently across the last of the rocks to the base of the long promontory. The sheer walls of the palace rose over them, blotting out the moon, their few windows high up, no more than dark smears. Two of Arborax's nimblest climbers, men who had been weaned on the precipitous northern cliffs of the continent, climbed upwards like spiders, ropes wrapped around them. Inch by inch they braved the buffeting sea winds and melted into the mass of shadows. Eventually the trailing ropes were secured. Elak was the first to grip one and begin his own ascent. One by one the party climbed, even Lycon managing to find footholds in the stonework, though he cursed and spluttered with the effort.

There were no guards on the higher battlements. Doubtless the invaders had seen no point in setting any. The windows above were simple openings and had not been shuttered or barred against the elements or intruders—none were expected. Thus Elak and the company entered the palace's main watchtower, its narrow upper corridors shrouded in darkness, apparently empty. Dalan carried a short staff, its bulbous head glowing a dull blue, enough for the company to see by.

Elak, rapier in hand, moved down the first flight of stairs. Still he met no opposition. Everything was still, utterly silent. Down they went, coming at length into a hall. It, too, had been abandoned. Elak wondered if anyone was in this eerie palace. Had the enemy captured the king's daughter and gone up into the city? It seemed probable. Why did Querram Urgol want her? Surely the sorcerer did not intent some ungodly marriage with her, to cement his plans for dominion?

Elak sent his scouts out into the hall, looking for any signs of life, or clues to Hamniri's whereabouts.

Dalan sniffed the air like a wolfhound, nodding to himself and muttering curses. The Druid held his staff aloft and its head flared, the shadows in the hall leaping back like startled ghosts. There had been furnishings in here, and small statues, bowls and fat candles, but in the blue glow all could now be seen to have been overturned and flung aside, as though a great brawl had taken place here. In the centre of the hall, a dark pit gaped, a black maw which emitted a strong smell of the sea. Dalan stood on the edge and gazed into the silent depths.

"What has caused this?" said Elak. "It is not natural."

Dalan pointed to a slick substance, globules smeared around the sides of the huge, angled hole. "Something from the sea," he said. "A creature large enough to burrow through rock and soil. Summoned by more sorcery." He leaned forward and cursed anew. "See! Is that an item of clothing, stuck to the rocks?"

One of the warriors swung down lithely and retrieved the cloth.

"The king's daughter," said Arborax. "Could it be hers?"

"Ishtar!" said Lycon. "If so, she must have been taken below, into that dark hell."

Elak nodded slowly. "We have no choice. We must follow."

Dalan's face was clouded with unease. "There's great danger here. It was not men who tore that hole from the rock below. Some creature, and not a small thing."

"Yes, I know," replied Elak. "It will be at great risk, but at least we will not be expected. If Hamniri is alive, we must attempt her rescue."

"What is it you fear, Elak?" said Dalan. "The girl's life, of course. But there is more?"

"I wonder if she has become a pawn in Querram Urgol's game. If her father, Numenedzer is killed and she becomes queen of Zangarza, she could wed Thotmes and secure the union against me. Or worse, the sorcerer might wed her himself! Either way, we cannot leave her to her fate."

"I gather she's a handsome lass," said Lycon, beaming. "She'd make a good bride for any king. Not least of all yourself, Elak."

"This is hardly the time to make such plans!" Elak

snapped. "I'll take a bride in my own good time." He covered his evident embarrassment with difficulty. "Meanwhile we need to see to Hamniri's safety."

Dalan and Lycon knew it would be pointless trying to dissuade Elak from such a reckless course. He had a unique sense of honour, one of the reasons men were glad to stand beside him in a crisis. Soon the company was once again using the ropes they had brought, this time to descend the sharp incline. It was impossible to tell how deep the hole would be, though the sounds of the sea could be heard far below, drifting up on a breeze that also carried a carrion stench, that and an indefinable miasma that made them all pause.

It was a long, nerve-shredding climb, but at last it ended as the tunnel curved and levelled out to become a long, fat area resembling a burrow. Water dripped from the walls and the floor was a foot deep in brine. Slowly the party made its way along until it came to a wider, cave-like area. Dalan's staff lit up the immediate surroundings. Twisted stone columns had been chopped into the cave's sides, and long stones had been set out like altars. There were bones scattered about, and skulls that identified the remains as human. Dalan studied the walls, where narrow cracks led back into the bedrock. As his light shone into them, there were movements. The attack was sudden.

Scores of creatures squirmed out of the crevices, as large as horses, curved and slippery as jellyfish, many floating in the air, their numerous filaments of cilia waving beneath them like myriads of feet. Each creature had two long antennae that served both as sensors and as weapons. They struck out at Elak's company. Swords cut back at them as the men defended themselves, hemmed in on all sides, in danger of being engulfed by the sheer number of these horrors. The aerial advantage of the floating monsters almost won them the conflict, as they dived down on the already occupied warriors. As the assailants were cut from the air, they fell, a further danger, their gelatinous bodies like bloated sacks, threatening to smother Elak and his fighting companions.

The young king roared with youthful defiance, his blade a blur of light, an inspiration to the warriors around him. Dalan used his staff to blast many aside, the damaged creatures bursting into vivid flames. It held back the tide and enabled the company to cross the cavern and exit at another, low-ceilinged tunnel, barely in time to escape being choked under the massed sea-beasts.

The pursuit stopped as suddenly as it had begun, for the aerial creatures avoided this secondary tunnel, unable to press an assault other than at ground level. Elak led the way onward, pausing some distance in. "Do you hear anything?" he asked.

"Cries," said Arborax. "Someone's in trouble."

The place was a maze, but the sounds of distress, coupled now with the ring of clashing steel, led Elak's party to another chamber that opened on to a stunning vista of green, crystallized buildings, spread far below under a vast dome, also made of crystal, pure as glass. On the ledge that overlooked this alien city-scape, there was a melee, as a group of people, apparently human, were fighting off a small crowd of robed, priest-like figures. By the light of a few blazing brands, Elak discerned the assailants and their claws – beings who had once been men but who had mutated into quasi-human things, snared by the sorcery of whatever powers lurked in this deep ocean realm.

Elak and his company quickly flung themselves into the affray, chopping at the rear of the crab-men, cutting them down mercilessly, for they expected no quarter. Encouraged by fresh hope, the people who had been ringed in found renewed strength and between the two parties, the sea beings were beaten down, the last of them quickly scurrying away like broken crabs, absorbed by the darkness of the tunnels. Elak noticed that some of them carried manacles and chains. They had intended to take captives.

Arborax was first to the rescued party and found himself standing before a tall warrior woman, her tunic splattered in gore, her sword dripping with the blood of her fallen assailants. Her eyes met his and for a brief moment both figures were very still. Then she laughed, the sound ringing back from the low ceiling.

"Well met," she said. "I am Hamniri, daughter of Numenedzer."

7: Dark God of the Ocean

Arborax bowed. "We are from Cyrena. This is our king, Elak."

Elak also bowed, a knowing smile on his lips. "It is a pleasure to be of service," he said. "This is the commander of my armies, Arborax. Consider him your protector."

Hamniri frowned. "I am perfectly capable of protecting myself," she said, but then smiled.

Elak glanced at Arborax. The king could see his commander was clearly smitten by the girl. "What place is this?" Elak asked her.

"The evil outlying city of Xeraph-Hizer's servants. They plan to exercise numerous human sacrifices to raise up their ocean god. See, outside the dome! Those shapes – they are the sea guardians of the Leviathan Lord."

They all looked in consternation at the horrific things, wrapped in shadow, swimming in the ocean murk like gigantic flying beasts, long, distorted heads studded with countless eyes, scarlet jewels that exuded a terrible menace.

"Once Xeraph-Hizer is awake, they will rise up through

the waters to the surface and absorb all those who live in Zangarza. I was to be chained and possessed by their powers and used to deceive their enemies, such as you, Elak. The last of my warriors defended me." Hamniri held up the dripping sword. "I will defy them to the last drop of my blood!"

Elak grinned. "We are with you, princess. We must get back to your city. I have an army poised at its gates."

"Quickly!" called Dalan urgently. He had seen the shadows down in the crystal city rising up, an obscene tide, clearly intent on finishing the work their priest-things had failed to accomplish. As the Druid watched, he realized with deepening horror those shadows were part of one vast whole, a leviathan, Xeraph-Hizer. "The monstrous demi-god has been partially awakened. The more lives that are sacrificed, the quicker it will rise up. That must not happen!"

Elak led the way back into the tunnels. There were no signs of the aerial horrors they had met on the way down, and they reached the huge cavern, the sloping tunnel at its far end. It would be a difficult climb.

"The creature that carved this tunnel," said Hamniri, "it has been held back, while the people of the ocean city tried to capture me. I cannot say how long it will hide in its lair."

As they crossed the cavern, something vast shifted in the tunnel ahead—the huge globular beast was blocking their retreat. It filled the tunnel, its gaping maw a crimson cavern, ringed with a thousand teeth, its long, serpent-like tongue lashing the air.

Dalan stepped forward, raising his staff. "Gather brands," he called, indicating several cressets in the walls, where dry brands had been set. Elak's men grabbed a dozen of them as Dalan ignited his staff. Each of the men with a brand plunged it into the white light and immediately all the brands were flaring. "Come!" shouted Dalan, striding forward. The men moved in a line with him, driving straight at the monster in the tunnel. Dalan used his staff to toss a fireball at the beast and it exploded in the heart of that gaping mouth. The men rushed in, tossing their firebrands until a wall of flame rose up. Hideous sounds beyond it attested to the distress of the creature, and thick, black clouds of smoke billowed outwards, forcing Dalan and the men back.

Elak saw the smoke clear—the huge worm-like thing had slithered back up the tunnel. Dalan led the pursuit, his staff-light held high, as the pursuer became the pursued. The company waded through the rank waters of the tunnel to the place where it sloped more steeply upward. High up in its choking shadows, something moved, wrapped in flames.

"It will emerge in the palace," said Dalan. "We must kill it there, before it gets into the city."

"Sire!" called one of the vanguard. "We are followed." In the pitch darkness behind them, sounds suggested a living tide. More forces from the crystal city had boiled up into the tunnels, a mass of serpent-like horrors and was flowing forward with only one intention – to smother Elak and the escaping company.

"Climb!" shouted Elak. At once the company sprang forward, eager to ascend, though the rocks were slippery and sharp. Again Dalan used the fires of sorcery to delay the assailants below, where a black flood filled the floor of the pit, long, snaking tendrils of darkness probing upwards, mere yards from the lowest of the warriors. Yet the swirling, pitch mass did not boil upwards, seemingly fixed at one level. Dalan fought off the grasping tendrils and from his staff sparks fizzed and crackled, showering the entity below.

It was a gradual, tortuous climb, but the company at last reached the rim of the pit, clambering out into the hall of the palace. Many of its columns had been shattered, smashed aside, and one wall had partially collapsed. Elak watched as moonlight slanted in through a gaping hole high above, the silver glow limning the far end of the hall. The darkness abruptly flew apart as the great worm-thing boiled out from the detritus of shattered statues.

Dalan stood firm, casting yet another white bolt of light at the gelatinous spawn of the sea. Fire terrified it, ripping into it like a mighty, searing blade, and once again it swung about and sought escape, battering another wall until it crumbled.

"Will nothing kill it?" Lycon shouted.

"See, it is aflame," said Arborax. He was right, for the Druid's fire had ignited the monster and now white flames licked up one side of its vast, barrel-shaped trunk. The thing thundered out into the night, but its destruction was not complete. It could have plunged into the waters of the adjacent ocean, but instead, maddened by the fire, rose up and drove hard into the warehouses and lower buildings of Zangarza. From the upper parapets of the palace, Elak and the company watched its frenzied flight.

"It is beyond control," said Dalan.

"My father!" cried Hamniri. "And the people! We must help them."

"They have been changed," Elak told her. "The sorcerer, Querram Urgol conspired with the god from that undersea city. Your people, and the army of Thotmes, are no longer human. Unless this sorcery can be reversed. Dalan – is that possible?"

The Druid scowled. "Once the beast is dead, perhaps. And there will be worse to come." He pointed to the waters of the wide bay below them. "The things we saw beyond the sea dome – I sense them rising. And beneath us, something much more vast and terrible. It will feed on those who die. That worm-thing will kill to quench its thirst for human blood."

"Xeraph-Hizer," said Hamniri. "Once he is loose here, everything will be lost to him."

As if in response to his words, the sea exploded in a mountainous welter of spray and spume, the waves churning and rolling landward, engulfing the lower city and shattering buildings, ships and docks alike. In the bay, several gargantuan shapes burst from the water, long tendrils flicking the air, testing it as though in preparation for a new life, a life within the city, where they would feast on all that lived there.

Elak gripped Dalan's arm. "Is there nothing to be done?"

Dalan's face was a ghastly mask, his jaw set. "There is one working, but it is dangerous beyond words. The gods alone know what catastrophe it would unleash. I fear the consequences."

Elak pointed to the horrors in the bay. "Could it be any worse than what these nightmares will bring, to us and all the world?"

8: Molten Fire

The company crossed to the mid-point of the promontory and grouped together around Dalan, looking down at the waves as they crashed on the lower walls, almost powerful enough to sweep the construction away. Yet it had endured the most savage storms of the southern ocean for many years and it held yet. In the bay the seas still thrashed as the things from deep below drew closer to the lower city. Elak looked up at the buildings cut so dramatically into the cliffs, towering up to the starlit sky. Zangarza was normally well-disguised by moonlight, but this night its shadows and vague outlines, its blurred buildings and walls were garishly lit in places by the light from the blazing worm-thing. Fires had broken out in the tortuous streets as the great worm continued its frantic rise, away from the blazing white light Dalan had hurled at it. The creature left a trail of streaming fire and thick, stinking smoke. Buildings crumbled and slid downwards in its wake as it made for the upper palace. Zangarza had become an inferno as grim as any vision Elak had imagined in the Nine Hells.

Dalan began his working. He drove the end of his staff into a crack between two of the mighty harbour stones and gripped the head of the staff, shouting out words from the secret language of his brethren, the words of a sorcerer. His voice rose above the thunder of the waves and mingled with the tumultuous air, and as the company watched, that air seemed alive, an overhead whirlpool of spirits and demonic beings, the sound of their discordant screams directed by the Druid's power. Bolts of blue fire shot down from the pandemonium above, and Elak gasped, afraid that Dalan would be blasted apart. But instead the energy flowed down through the brilliantly-lit figure and into the promontory.

The great stones shook, but this was not the sea. This was deep below, far down in the hidden caverns, the roots of the city and the mountainous cliffs. Elak and his companions felt the earth shift, their ears filled with a terrible roaring. The sea rolled back to expose its bed, a tangled mass of weed and jagged rocks, where shapes slithered and scuttled away, a frightful army, dredged up from the deeps. Great gouts of steam blew upward and the seabed began to glow, a deep, rich red. Molten lava belched out of it and out in the bay the huge beings twisted and turned in agony, forced back under the waves, away from the coast.

Elak and the others turned to watch the city. Its southern section had been cut into the cliffs before they curved around a high headland. An entire slice of the city crumbled like sun-baked soil and fell in a gigantic landslide, revealing tongues of liquid lava. They poured down after the fallen buildings and into the sea, boiling it and giving rise to a great bank of steam.

"Zangarza!" cried Hamniri. "No one will survive!"

They could only watch as another huge slab of rock and buildings slipped down into the pounding waves, more banks of steam hissing and spreading. Elak turned to Dalan, but the Druid had dropped to his knees, his eyes tightly closed, his energy and magic almost spent. It was impossible to rouse him. The destruction could not be halted.

"Come!" shouted the king, as he and Lycon dragged Dalan to his feet. The Druid still clung to his staff and it pulled free as they tugged him away, moving along the shuddering promontory as quickly as they could. It felt as though an earthquake would soon strike the land, a deeper roaring underground presaging its coming. The sea beasts were gone, and with them all signs of life beyond the promontory.

Elak watched Zangarza. For the moment the dreadful landslides that had plunged a portion of the city into the boiling waters had ceased, although red hot lava still poured from the wide fissure near to the fallen headland.

"If we are to get away from this hell," said Lycon, "we must go up through the city. There's no other way."

Elak nodded. They reached the harbour and wormed their way up through the narrow, steep-sided streets beyond. Dalan began to come around, shaking his head dazedly. "We must go up. The gods alone know what chaos has broken out up there."

"My father," said Hamniri. "Is he alive? Can he be saved?"

Arborax glanced at his king. "A few of us can enter the palace –" he began, but Elak stopped him.

"We'll do this together," he said. "But be warned," he told the warriors, "the worst is yet to come."

As one, they climbed the streets, conscious of the enormous damage inflicted by the fleeing worm-thing, and the many fires it had left in its wake. If Zangarza did not slide into the sea this night, its remains would take years to rebuild. When they reached the lower area of the palace, they saw its main buildings had been broken open like shells. Smoke poured from numerous gaping holes in its walls and a sickening stench wafted over them in a cloud. The worm-beast had battered its way here, under the spells of the High Sorcerer, Querram Urgol, but it was no longer his, or anyone's servant. Its charred and disintegrating corpse had burst, spilling a mass of internal organs and thick, viscous ichor across the lower steps. Hundreds of corpses littered the area, people that had been transformed by the powers unleashed by Querram Urgol. What few were left to defend the palace cowered back as Elak and his company entered the final chamber.

Behind the throne, the statue of Xeraph-Hizer had split in two and each half leaned to one side, irreparably broken. Numenedzer sat yet upon his throne, motionless as stone, his glazed eyes fixed on a point far out in the bay. Beside him, only Querram Urgol remained defiant.

"Fools!" he snarled. "You cannot prevent the coming of the Leviathan Lord!"

Dalan managed to pull himself upright, summoning his last reserves of strength. "You have failed, traitorous vermin!" he said, raising his staff. Light poured from it, though not as fiercely as it had down on the promontory. Querram Urgol shrieked with the laughter of a madman and hurled sparks from his own staff of power. The energies smashed into each other like oceanic waves, filling the immediate air with thunder. Elak and his men were thrown off their feet, and could only watch as the two magicians clashed, rocking back on their heels, the fate of both held in a cosmic balance.

Elak saw a blur of movement. Before he could react, Hamniri had rushed forward, her sword raised. She looked like some manic demon from hell itself, hair streaming out behind her, lips drawn back in a feral scream of fury. She reached Querram Urgol, who could do nothing to stay her hand, his power snarled up in the mesh of Dalan's magic. Hamniri brought her blade down with horrific force and it sliced through the Sorcerer's head, neck and upper chest. His staff exploded in a flash of blinding light.

When Elak and his companions at last staggered to their feet, the air around them was thick with smoke. Elak broke through it and saw two figures beside the throne. Arborax had lifted Hamniri to her feet, his arms around her. In a moment she came out of her daze and smiled up at the commander. Elak heard a laugh behind him, where Lycon staggered out of the pulsing air.

"If Hamniri is to become the new monarch, how better to seal an alliance than with a royal marriage?" he said. "I'd certainly drink to that."

Elak grinned. "Arborax will have his hands full." However, he sounded more than pleased.

Their laughter was curtailed as yet another shape manifested itself. King Numenedzer stood up, drawing on last reserves of power. His body had seemingly grown in girth, his face a mask of anger and fury. Around him and up in the skies, the elements poured the last of their energies into the warrior king and he roared his defiance at the intruders who had wrought so much havoc on his kingdom and people. Hamniri would have rushed to him, but Arborax held her back, seeing the potent sorcery yet writhing in her father.

Numenedzer's blazing eyes fixed upon his daughter. "I have done this for you!" he roared, his blade flashing in the bizarre light, coruscating with undoubted magics yet to be quashed. "Xeraph-Hizer will fill you with his power and all Atlantis will sit at your feet!"

Hamniri broke free of the commander's grip and ran to stand before her father. "No!" she cried. "You are king, and will be cleansed of this foulness. You will make Zangarza a great ally of Atlantis, not its conqueror."

Elak and the others watched in trepidation as Numenedzer's flickering blade hovered over the girl, as if the king would kill her rather than concede. Suddenly a pain wracked him, deep in his chest and upper body. The sword fell from his now nerveless fingers and clattered away down the steps. He dropped to his knees, his face contorted in agony.

"Father!" cried Hamniri, rushing to him.

"You are right," he gasped. "I am indeed gripped by a foulness, a cankerous disease. This last year it has gnawed at me, my death inevitable. It is what drove me to elevate you. Querram Urgol's sorcery subdued it, but now he is no more, it surges anew in my blood and bones." His voice was a rasp, blood frothing at his lips. "I put off my death long enough to give you dominion over these foreign kings."

"There are better ways than war to make our world stronger," said Hamniri. She glanced back at Arborax. "Father, there are no more enemies here."

Numenedzer had shrunk down, seemingly half his former size. He nodded, exhausted, no fight left in him.

Among the scattered bodies in the palace, others were stirring. Many warriors had died, including men from Thotmes' kingdom, but not all, and as the dawn light began to pierce the chamber, those that lived stumbled to their feet, waking, as the king had, from their private nightmares.

Where their bodies had been contorted and monstrously re-shaped, they were now restored. Thotmes himself was one such survivor. Elak greeted him warmly as he came through a crowd of dazed survivors. The two men approached the throne and bowed before Numenedzer.

"I came to Zangarza in search of allies," said Thotmes. "I came to stand against sorcery and the dark gods of the ocean. For now, they have been bested and have withdrawn."

"Well met," Elak said to the ailing monarch. "Cyrena and all Atlantis would be your friend. Between us we'll rebuild the city, if Numenedzer will accept our aid."

Numenedzer hugged his daughter and managed a smile. "My daughter will rule Zangarza now. It is to her you must address your plans. I am spent. The darkness waits for me, but for you, a greater dawn is coming." He said no more, and soon after his daughter set him down for the last time upon his throne, where a deep peace claimed him.

Epilogue

Dalan stood high on the palace wall and studied the wide bay spread out below him, where the southern ocean now lapped calmly at the lower city walls. Beside him, Elak and Lycon also watched.

"The gods favoured us this time," said the Druid. "Though we have wounded the serpent, not killed it. Xeraph-Hizer lives yet, and there will come a day when the Leviathan Lord seeks to rise again."

Elak raised his fist to the heavens. "We'll be ready for him! Our new allies will give our Empire more power, and the people of Atlantis will be united under one banner, one throne."

Lycon grunted. "Then you'll accede to the Council in

Cyrena and be king of this new empire?"

Elak scowled. He was on the point of scoffing, preferring to stand aside and let another rule the continent, but even he had come to realize the will of the gods seemed to be that the mantle must fall across his shoulders.

Dalan, meanwhile, was deep in thought. The working that had caused the movement of the earth and the setting free of the molten fires had won them the day. But at what price? What damage had been done to the foundations of the continent? And when would it manifest itself?

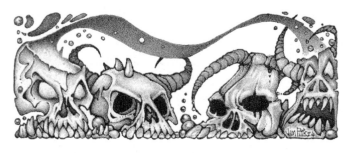

ON DEATH SEED ISLAND

*Thus King Elak left the southern city of Zangarza and its kingdom
in the hands of his new allies, Hamniri and her new husband,
Arborax. Rather than return to his homeland by land, Elak sailed
for distant Cyrena in the ship the queen had gifted to him, the
Windrider. Yet in all the oceans surrounding the great continent
of Atlantis there were many mysteries and places unmapped and
undreamed of, where powers beyond the knowledge of men stirred
and nurtured their own plans of conquest.*

- Helvas Ravanniol,
Annals of the Third Atlantean Empire

Prologue

Melshassar tossed and turned in his bunk, twisting the thin
sheets around himself like a shroud, his body bathed in
sweat. The sea captain had retired late, deep into the airless
night, satisfied his voyage had brought a welcome bounty,
trading metal with the city states of the eastern seaboard. Yet
for some reason his sleep was plagued with bad dreams,
though his ship moved slickly across calm ocean waters. The
skies gleamed above the lone craft, and moonlight shivered
on the gentle swell.

The captain's dreaming eyes studied those stars, a

veritable blizzard of them. In his dreams they were unfamiliar, their lights blurring into yellow and then a dull crimson glow. They swirled, clouds of them drifting down to the surface of the world, and with them came the sounds, a dreadful wind, presaging horror. The sudden grip of the nightmare intensified as Melshassar felt himself snared by the stellar current, drawn from his body on an astral tide where the stars were like seeds released by a burgeoning jungle.

Sea and stars mingled in a frantic vortex until the captain saw beneath his suspended body an island, a conglomerate of the stars, packed together and lit from within by hellish fires. Something was alive at the island's heart, a being of power, and that power, redolent with sorcery, dragged at Melshassar, pulling him to the core of his nightmare. In the air around it, all over the island, seeds whirled and danced, suddenly bursting and giving birth to repulsive, floating shapes, creatures of the ocean, bell-shaped, trailing long fronds, poisonous and deadly.

Melshassar saw men stumbling through the deep shadows of the island, mouths open in silent screams as the seed-creatures floated down and attached themselves to heads and shoulders, glowing intensely before collapsing the seamen into the undergrowth. At the heart of the island that monstrous creature opened its own maw, drawing in its servants and giving vent to a horrible, unearthly laughter. Blackness swamped Melshassar, his senses snuffed out like candles in that sudden emptiness: he plunged into a deep, alien sleep.

Well after dawn, he woke to the sound of his cabin door being thumped by one of his sailors. He rose, still partially numbed by his profound slumber, and went with the seaman up on to the deck.

"Land, sire," said the man with a grin. "We didn't want

to disturb you. See, we've already sent a party ashore."

Melshassar stood at the rail of the anchored ship and gasped. The island before him may have been bathed in brilliant sunlight, its verdant shore, so close, enticing to men who had spent so long at sea, but it was the island of his nightmare. Already the party that had gone ashore had been swallowed by the trees.

1: Infestation

"Every single accursed cask!" Ormaluc, Master of Provisions for the small fleet, spat the words out angrily to his captain, Balazaar, referring to the several large barrels of clean drinking water down in the ship's hold. "Full of worm and leaking copiously."

Balazaar grimaced. "All of them? So how much water do we have?"

"I estimate we've salvaged enough for two days at most."

"Barely enough to make landfall." Balazaar looked at their western horizon, where there was no sign of the Atlantean continent's coastline. The fleet, a dozen ships in all, had set sail from the southernmost port of Zangarza five days since, at the command of the young Elak, king of the northern city-state, Cyrena, but now speeding homeward to cement the greatest alliance the continent had yet seen. Once the niceties had been finalized, there would be a union of all states, with Elak its king. This following his latest triumph in Zangarza, where the despotic Numenedzer had been deposed and replaced by his daughter, Hamniri, a strong supporter of the young monarch.

Balazaar's ship, *Windrider*, had been a gift from Hamniri to Elak after their successful alliance. She had supplied the ships that would take Elak back to his capital. Balazaar was loath to wake his king, sleeping in his quarters. The young monarch and his aide, Lycon, were both fond of the revels, and last night had quaffed more wine between them than most men could handle in a week. And why not? Balazaar thought. They'd fought so heroically at Zangarza and earned their respite from the horrors of this world. And back in Cyrena, the young king would find his new role would give him little time for the dubious pleasures of the flesh.

The Druid, Dalan, mentor and adviser to the king, was berthed on another of the ships, which was just as well, Balazaar thought, smiling. The Druid was typically stoic and would not have approved of Elak's behaviour. The young king's wild days would have to end soon, once he took up the new office of supreme command. The Council in Cyrena would never tolerate his exuberance.

"We'll have to take casks from some of the other ships," said Balazaar. "Enough to get us further north."

Ormaluc nodded, relieved that the situation would seem to be under control. To be serving Elak himself was a great honour and the last thing he wanted was to be held responsible for this disaster. It would mean demotion to some third-rate galley in a remote part of the new empire. However, the solution was not to be so simple. Even before Balazaar was ready to send messages to his closest ships, he received several himself.

"Fires of Ishtar!" he growled angrily.

Ormaluc had not yet left the deck. He waited anxiously to hear his captain's news.

"Evidently our water casks are not the only ones affected by this worm plague. The other ships are all sending messages declaring themselves in the same predicament as us. Where were the casks from, Ormaluc? You provided them all for us at Zangarza?"

"Yes, sire. Every cask was clean, unmarked. I checked

them myself, for every ship. There was no reason to suppose treachery."

"Very well. Go below and salvage what you can. I'll turn the fleet westward. We'll have to find a port and take on new supplies." Balazaar left the deck and went below. Two armed sailors stood outside the door to Elak's cabin.

"I need to see the king," said Balazaar, handing over his sword and dirk to one of the men, though he was well known to them. The king's aide, Lycon, however, had insisted that no arms were brought into the cabin, other than his own and the king's.

Lycon was buried in the linen of one of the bunks within, his snores stertorous. Elak, however, was awake and washing in a bowl of cold water, attempting to sluice away a hangover that would have downed a large bull.

"Your pardon, Elak." Balazaar explained the fleet's dilemma. "I'm about to take us west, as we'll not make it home with what water we have left."

Elak dried himself. He was tall and lithe, his muscles bronzed by the southern sun, his chest and abdomen scarred already with the cuts of battle. He was famed among his men for leading by example, almost to the point of recklessness. "What has caused this worm plague? Has Dalan been informed?"

"I've sent word. As for the casks, our Master of Provisions is no slouch. He's clearly surprised by their condition. I know he's a man who takes pains over his work. If those casks had been rotten before we sailed, he'd have flung them out."

"Is it only the casks? What about the ship? No other wood is infected?"

Balazaar stiffened. "I'll have an immediate inspection undertaken." As he went back up on deck and sent men to carry out the inspection, the captain was met by another of the sailors, who pointed up at the tall mast and its lookout.

"Word from the perch, sir. There's an island to the east, no more than a few hours' sail away."

Balazaar went to the rail and gazed eastwards, but saw only water. He was not familiar with this part of the ocean, it being off the usual sea lanes used by the ships of Cyrena. However, with the new empire growing and expanding, there would be more time for exploration.

Shortly afterwards, Elak came on deck, followed by the surly Lycon, who had clearly not recovered from his drinking bout as sweetly as the monarch. He was not as tall as Elak, and was round-shouldered and of significant girth. Unshaven and with his thinning hair tangled about his bear-like head, he looked pale and shaky on his feet. Yet Balazaar knew him for a ferocious fighter, a good man to have beside you in battle, at which time he drew on remarkable reserves of energy.

"An island, sir," said the captain. "Not charted, but perhaps worth sending a small landing party."

"I gather we need water," said Elak. "Anchor the fleet here. It's calm enough and I don't smell any storms abroad. Take *Windrider* closer in and send a boat across to the island."

Not long after, Dalan had been ferried across from his ship and joined his king on *Windrider's* deck. "I've seen the worm plague," the Druid told Elak. "It's virulent, but so far has only attacked the casks. Their wood is not the same as the planking of the ships, which might explain it."

Elak studied the Druid's lined face. Dalan was far older and well versed in sorcery, with an understanding of high magic and its dubious qualities; they had marked him. Cool and sombre, he rarely smiled, seeing danger in every shadow.

"You think sorcery is at work?" said Elak.

"Until I know otherwise."

2: Landfall

Once the scouts had completed an initial survey of the island's nearest bay, Elak prepared to head a party of explorers, although Dalan was uneasy about the king leaving his ship. However, the Druid knew well enough the young man's predilection for adventure and stubborn determination never to send his men into a situation he would not himself enter. Dalan had been studying the island from *Windrider's* rail. It seemed typical of islands in this eastern ocean: many were volcanic cones, with a central mountain, lushly covered in dense green jungle, probably no more than a few miles in diameter. That mountain implied there would be running water. The chances were good that it would also yield fruit and large gourds, which could be cut and used to carry enough water to suit their needs.

The fleet anchored within a bay, and Elak's party of fifty went ashore, landing their small craft on the beach. It was not the expected expanse of hot sand. What seemed at first to be flattish, abrasive rock was identified by Dalan as hard, knotted roots, packed tightly together like an immense mat, interwoven with deep green weed. The men were glad to cross it and enter the fringe of the jungle. Its trees were unfamiliar, even to the most travelled of the sailors. Their trunks were almost hidden by the ivy-like growths that festooned them, and overhead the upper leaves of the trees fanned out in a vivid green canopy. The air was humid, clear but heavy as sea fog.

Elak, Lycon and Dalan stood together, studying the dense undergrowth. There was a narrow stream emerging from it into the bay, its banks wide enough to serve as a crude path to the interior.

Lycon squinted in the brilliant sunlight, his head still

throbbing from the night's debauch. "A strange place," he grunted. "I can't say why. The island noises aren't right. Making my headache worse."

Elak grinned. "Perhaps your head is contorting the sounds. You should go and duck it in that stream and clear it."

Dalan, who held his staff tightly, shook his head. "No. Not until we understand this place better."

They moved inland, watching the trees, alert for signs of movement. There were occasional aerial sounds, and the muffled growl of something beyond vision, the drone of insects. Elak marvelled at their clarity. This place had a unique, mysterious air to it, an atmosphere that was vibrant, pulsing with energy. He felt himself attuning to it, a not unpleasant experience. He sensed his men relaxing, shaking off the initial tension that always accompanied the first steps on new land, though he knew he could rely on them in a time of crisis.

Dalan, Elak could see, was less comfortable. "You sense danger?" Elak asked him.

"This place is soporific. The air is well perfumed. I know of many plants that drug their victims before absorbing them. We should take what water we need and go back. Find gourds."

Elak dispatched several groups of his men, who entered the jungle. It was soon apparent that there were entire groves of trees with sizable gourds, and the work began to cut and prepare them. The sailors laboured cheerfully, though they kept their attention focused on the surrounding walls of jungle, ready to defend themselves at once if need arose.

Dalan's expression remained grim. He had thrust the butt of his staff into the ground, where there was no soil, just an extension of the thick, root matting of the beach. The

Druid felt the ground under him shifting slowly, aware of its tremors as the men cut the gourds from the trees and chopped away some of the undergrowth to widen their working area. It had the same effect as that of dropping a large stone into a pond. Ripples spread outward from the grove, along the roots and fibres of the plants. The jungle was focused on the grove, seemingly crowding in.

When each of the sailors had cut and prepared a gourd, the party readied to return to the stream, but as Dalan made to lead them, he realized the way back had shifted, closed. There was a path, but the Druid felt certain it led in another direction. The jungle was playing tricks.

"Cut through there," he told the first group of sailors, indicating what he felt sure was the correct way. They obliged at once, several of them hacking at the thicket, chopping aside the tangled vegetation. However, they made little impact, for all their muscular efforts, the jungle closing up even more tightly. Some of their companions taunted them, but Dalan's withering gaze silenced the banter.

"What is it?" said Elak.

"The way we came has been closed. There is another path, but I think it leads inland, away from the bay."

Lycon heard the Druid's words and snorted irritably. "Surely we're not going to let a vegetable mass bar our way! Step aside. I need exercise." He used his sword energetically, cutting and chopping furiously, and for a while the path he was making opened up, its leaves and branches tossed this way and that by the ferocious efforts of the big man. Even so, it was in vain, for the more effort Lycon put in to the work, the resistance of the jungle grew stronger. Lycon stood back, chest heaving, face dropping.

"By the Nine Hells!" he cursed. "What is this weed?"

"There is an intelligence here," said Dalan. "We may have angered it."

Lycon's eyes widened incredulously.

"Perhaps we'd better take the path as offered," said Elak.

"Yes, we cannot remain here. Let me lead," said Dalan. "Have the men close ranks behind us." They formed a line of pairs, all swords drawn. Above them the sun rose. It was yet mid-morning. Dalan said nothing, but he feared being caught on this island at night, where sleep would for certain be a dangerous threat.

3: The Things in the Grove

As they wove their way along the path, Dalan felt something stir within his staff, a negative reaction to the jungle and the crowding trees. Above the men, huge branches bent over them, hung with lianas and other thick vines, though they were strange and unfamiliar, like the thick weed of an underwater kingdom. Dalan paused to study the trees, realizing they were not all what they seemed. He commented on this to Elak and Lycon.

"There is a geometrical shape to them," said the young king. "Almost as if they were –"

"Beams!" said Lycon. "By the stars! Are they from *ships?*"

"Wrecks," said Dalan, nodding. "See, there's another." It had become apparent that there were many of these strange beams, curved and poking upward like the broken ribs of ships' skeletons. Closer examination revealed other carved wooden shapes, smaller beams, spars, thick planks, all tangled together incredibly to form the dense matted jungle floor. It was also evident that most of the wreckage was very old, worm-ridden and blackened by time.

"They are beneath our feet," said Dalan. "They go so deep I cannot count them. This island must have been a trap for ships for years without number. And the wrecks are packed, far inland."

"We must go back," said Elak. "We will have to burn our way through."

"Too dangerous," said Dalan. "We'd not survive the conflagration. Something wants us here. Whatever it is, it will show itself."

Lycon held up his sword. "Then we'll give it a taste of honest steel!"

Dalan frowned uneasily. It was unusual to see him so uncomfortable. "I fear steel will be of no use. I sense something beyond. Life, of a kind unfamiliar to us."

The party moved further into the bizarre complex of tree and beam. Some of the wrecked ships must have been huge, hewn from monstrous arboreal giants, from an age long gone and in a style of craft unknown to the Atlanteans. They spoke of a remote history, a dark period of ancient sorcery and legend, and with each step, the men shuddered at the oppressive atmosphere. In time they came to a grove: the trees and beams curved away from it, as if it could be a shrine, or a place of sanctuary. Fat logs were lying, tumbled and rotting, at its heart, like fallen menhirs, though no one had yet seen stone – or earth – on this island. If this was once a shrine, it had been pulled apart.

Elak's company fanned out around him along one curve of the grove, their swords readied, in spite of Dalan's earlier comment. Dalan pointed with his staff to the great logs. "These are the source of immediate power."

His staff again stirred in his hand like a live thing, reacting to the logs. As the company watched, a thin cloud rose from the central log, pale green, like a disturbed swarm of tiny insects. However, the cloud writhed gently, as if shifting in a breeze, though the air in the grove was very still. In a moment it had formed itself into a distinctive shape and the men drew back in alarm. It was a human figure, crippled, its face a blur, save for the eyes and mouth.

It whispered and every man present heard the voice in his head, clear, its words spoken in their own language.

"Men of Atlantis," said the voice, "you are in danger. You must leave this island with all haste. The dark god of the island will absorb you, as it has done so many times before. The wrecks of the ages lie all about you. Flee, before you join them!"

"Who are you?" demanded Dalan, his staff thrust forward, its humming power apparently binding the ghost to its will.

"I am Melshassar, once of northern lands, an adventurer who sailed into these eastern waters. My ships and my men all succumbed to the horror that lies on this island, the god from the stars, he who feasts on our kind, and who would expand his empire through others like me." Around him, rising from the crumbling logs, other shapes rose up, pale and insubstantial, a small retinue, former sailors perhaps, the last men of Melshassar's company.

"Where is this god?" said Elak. "What form does he take?"

"On the mountainside, there is a way into his sanctuary. His shape can shift, though he is bound by his surroundings. He is the energy that threads through the island and gives it its life. He takes the life of mortals and uses it to fuel himself, as he will drain the life from you and all who have come here with you. When night comes, the starlight bathes him and nothing can withstand him. You must leave this island before the sun sinks into the western waters."

"And by day?" said Dalan.

"He stays out of the sunlight. Its heat and energy are the only thing he avoids. For you it is an opportunity to escape, though the jungle will deceive you, and try to lead you to his lair. The paths will inevitably twist you back that way."

Elak leaned close to Dalan. "If we are to meet this accursed god, perhaps we can confuse his plans. I'll hear more of him and his nature."

"Can you lead us to the god's sanctuary?" Dalan asked the wraith.

It nodded, though its smear of a face contorted in pain that spoke of hopelessness.

4: Seeds from the Stars

The company climbed the gradual incline of the low mountain, the path narrow but passable. On either side, life of a kind stirred, but never showed itself, as though the trees were filled with hidden serpents, the air with invisible flocking jungle birds. Dalan watched and listened, his body taut as a bowstring, his mental defences drawn up: he knew he dare not let them slip. Elak and Lycon, usually buoyant and cheery on such ventures, were subdued, almost solemn. Something in the atmosphere of this place weighed heavily on them like a pall.

Melshassar and the other ghostly figures, rose up above a gnarled tangle of branches resembling a huge knuckle of stone and the men climbed up on to it. From this vantage point, much of the island's jungle terrain could be surveyed below the party, deep green and packed, resembling a sea bottom more than a landscape. Dalan and the others studied the view and now they could see the true nature of time's damage to the countless ships that had foundered here. The entire island seemed to be composed not of land but of ships, mangled together, their beams poking skyward like huge claws, snapped and rotted. The growths that bound them were like a vast raft of kelp, the product of the ocean, heaped up by swirling tides and storms over the ages.

"Man was at his most primitive when Xumatoq drifted down from the stars and gave himself physical form," said Melshassar, his voice a whisper on the still air, though every man there heard it clearly. "Time is nothing to Xumatoq and the terrible masters he serves. His star seeds drifted with him and began their frightful work, drawing together their victims here, using the body of the god to mould and shape this island out of his flesh and bones. Ship after ship has been woven into it, and all their crews over the long ages absorbed, fuel for Xumatoq."

"The worm infestation!" said Elak. "Our ship's water barrels – the seeds came from the island."

"No sailors can go long without water," said Melshassar. "Thus were you lured here by the powers of Xumatoq."

"What is his purpose?" said Dalan.

"Conquest! Soon it will begin. The island will cross the remaining ocean between itself and Atlantis. Once close to the shores of the continent, all the seeds will erupt. A vast cloud of them will drift over the ports and cities, travelling up the rivers and over the land, until everything is infected. Man will be enslaved, and at the end, Xumatoq will open the gate and bring his masters through. A new age will begin, and mankind will become a memory, as you see us now – ghosts!"

"How far to the secret place of this god?" said Elak. "I've a mind to test his powers before night falls."

"It is close," said Melshassar. "You must avoid shadow and darkness. They are allies of the star god."

"Let us take fire with us," said Lycon.

"No man has ever raised fire on this island," came the voice of the ghost. "The wood has been poisoned by the star seeds, just as your ship's barrels were infected."

Dalan held up his staff. It glowed faintly with an inner light. "It may be true that no ordinary fire will burn here, but what I bring has a unique power. Lycon, bring me a branch."

Lycon used his blade to hack through a narrow twist of wood. It resisted the heavy strokes but eventually Lycon cut through it and gave the severed branch to the Druid.

Dalan held it close to his staff, which had begun to glow more vividly. The severed branch squirmed like a live thing, twisting away from the staff, as if in pain. Dalan's face gleamed with sweat as he forced his staff closer to the branch. After a long moment, he succeeded in igniting it and held it aloft, a blazing torch, its heat fierce. Black plumes of smoke rose from it, and the company guessed that to inhale these fumes would poison them. Melshassar and the ghosts wafted back, as though the heat seared what was left of them, a threat of evaporation.

The climb went on, slow and laborious, though not steep. It became more evident here there were no trees, no undergrowth, only the mangled carcasses of old, old ships woven together like giant briers, their sharp edges dangerous as any thorn. As the company moved upward, the beams rose higher, forming a canopy that slowly blotted out the sky and sunlight, thickening the shadows, making the way underfoot even more treacherous.

"My senses tell me this roof is closing over us," said Lycon to Elak. "Should we trust this mariner and his slinking followers? Perhaps they serve the island god."

Elak nodded. "Our course is set. I doubt we'd flee the place without a fight. Yet I'd rather conduct it in good, clean daylight. This place is becoming like a tomb."

The king's words proved prophetic, for soon thereafter the way ahead became a deep declivity, a gash in the piled debris, and the highest of the beams met and formed a series of twisted arches that became a roof. To go on meant to go underground, into a space that opened out like a cavern. Light of a kind seeped in from high above, a sickly yellow glow, with no warmth, like the phosphorescence of deep subterranean fungi. Only the faint glow of Dalan's staff provided better light and a nimbus of heat. By its glow the company could see the path run out like a gallery on both sides of the vast space, overlooking its depths.

Melshassar and his fellow spirits floated out over the chasm. "The god sleeps," came his whisper. "But when the day ends, he will wake and you will quit the mortal world. I must leave you here. For me to go beyond would be to court oblivion."

Elak followed Dalan out on to the lofty gallery. The two men looked down into the blackness as Dalan lifted his staff. By its light the secrets of those hidden depths were gradually revealed like the slow onset of utter madness.

5: The Waking God

They saw a vague central mass some distance below them, its details fogged in shadows. It appeared to be suspended over the fathomless vault, held in place by countless strands of varying thickness, all resembling either cables or roots, or a combination of both, stretching from the shapeless mass to the walls of the chamber, where they were attached like hungry vines to the jutting beams and wooden outcrops. A ferocious stench arose, that of rotting vegetation, combined with something else, like carrion left to decay: the company reeled back.

Elak gripped Dalan's arm. "That thing is alive," he said through gritted teeth. "I can feel its power."

The Druid's doubt and uncertainty were easily readable, rare emotions for one usually so resolute and dependable. He shook his head, as if to clear it of pain and confusion. "Though it is dormant, this power is beyond anything I have yet faced in this world. I think you should take flight, Elak. Save yourselves. Let me hold this monstrous presence here."

Elak's grin was wolf-like. "Fool's talk, Dalan. We'll –"

His words were cut short as a sudden surge of energy, a mental bolt, cuffed him like a strong wind. Everyone in the company also felt the change in the atmosphere. To a man they knew what had caused it. The god stirred in his slumber.

They fell back against the slick walls of the gallery, momentarily snared by its dark wood. Elak heard a rushing sound inside his head and closed his eyes against a blast of cold air. Immediately the visions began, and he sagged down, along with his fellows, to endure the revelations.

On his inner eye he saw the limitless expanse of space, initially nothing more than an impenetrable void, starless and frozen, but slowly lights emerged from its depths, stars like clouds of dust, embers from cosmic explosions far out beyond the rim of the universe, the hot breath of gods outside the narrow bounds of human comprehension. These stars were live things, fuelled with energy, voyaging across the void, envoys of something far more terrible, a great shadow across the light of seething nebulae. Xumatoq, servant of the omnipotent powers.

Earth was young, little more than a molten ember whirling around its star when the space-born stars burst and released their rain, their spawn. Breath of Xumatoq, they drifted down and sank into the primal seas, making a place for the seeking god. He fed on darkness and shadow, far from the light, consuming it and with it, potentially all the life force of the world, the energy alien to his own nature and that of the cosmic powers that had brought him into being. He was at war with the sun of this world, for the sun created more life, accelerated its growth and expansion. Xumatoq hungered for its extinction, and worked to drain it and make of it a cold, sterile stone. It was to be the work of millennia.

Countless centuries after the god's aquatic entombment, it shaped itself into a life form capable of floating in the churning soup of primal oceans and sent out spores that sought landfall and things that crawled or walked upon it. Early cities, primitive arrangements of stone, partially underwater, where early hominids struggled to become human, were infected by these spores, their hybrid progeny colonizing a few isolated coastal regions. These were hunted by more powerful beings, as Man raised himself from the slime, until they slithered back into the sea, spiralling back down a retrogressive evolutionary path.

Elak saw their remnants cluster around the oceanic god, who had become a floating mass, a drifting entity, dragging to itself the passing ships and sailors of the emerging nations, bound to a rudderless existence by its own monumental patience. The spores fed on the men whose ships they plundered to create the vast, artificial body of the god. Their ghosts became sirens, chained by the will of Xumatoq.

Elak exerted every fibre of energy within him, mentally tearing at the chains that threatened to bind him too thoroughly for him to move. He knew if he could not break free, the will of the god would enter him and make him its fodder, as it would his companions. The young king staggered groggily to his feet and shouted, his voice echoing around the cavern.

"Free yourselves! Wake! Dalan! Lycon! All of you! Stir yourselves. Take arms!"

The company tore itself free of the nightmare visions and stood as one. Dalan held high his staff and it blazed, light reflected vividly from the swords around it. Somewhere deep down in the gulf, a thunderous roar of pain and frustration rolled upwards like a noxious cloud. Xumatoq's fury was palpable.

Elak turned and drove his rapier like a searing needle into the wooden wall and at once it smoked, glowing as the light from Dalan's staff, deflected to the sword, ignited the wood that had resisted fire since first it had come to the island. Others followed Elak's example, and soon a whole section of the wall was ablaze. From overhead, long, snaking tendrils unfurled, slick as tongues, as the island defended itself against the utter horror of flame. The writhing things slapped at the blaze, while Elak and Lycon led the assault on them, hacking at them as they would vines, severing great lengths, which fell, some igniting.

"Elak!" cried Dalan, his staff yet held high like a banner of light. "If we could open this cavern to the sunlight, we'd end this hellish god."

Elak understood. There was no time to discuss a strategy. Instead he grabbed one of the trailing vine-like things and, gripping his rapier in his teeth, nimble as any deep-sea pirate, swung upwards. Dalan and Lycon gasped, afraid for the safety of their king, but Elak used his strength to work his way up the strand as if he were shinning up a tall mast. He'd done it many times at sea, and often challenged any man to beat him at such a venture. Dalan frequently despaired of controlling the king, but for once he was glad of Elak's determination. The Druid watched as the king was swallowed by the darkness of the cavern's upper vaults, and silence closed in overhead.

6: Light and Fire

Elak wrapped his legs around the trailing growth, held on firmly with one hand, and used his free hand to wield his sword, cutting into the upper shadows overhead. He did this blindly, hoping to create an opening. It was dangerous work, swinging so high over the vault. A slip now would plummet him to almost certain doom. He thought of all that he and his warriors had been through in recent times, the furious battles they'd fought and the triumph at Zangarza. It made him more determined to break free of the god of this warped island. Small chunks of something fleshy fell around him as his weapon did its work, until at last, with the king on the point of exhaustion, a chink of light shone through from above.

He swapped hands and redoubled his effort, enlarging the opening he'd made to the outer world. Light bathed the edges of the hole, which began to smoulder, diffusing wisps of white smoke. Elak again gripped the sword in his teeth and eased himself downwards on the vine, his arms aching painfully, his muscles threatening to betray him. He almost lost his grip, one hand swinging free, but his legs were wrapped around the vine as tightly as a serpent's grip on a victim. More light spilled in, and the small fire spread quickly, as though fuelled by oil.

Almost upside down, Elak could see beneath him more clearly as light picked out details hidden by shadows until now. What he saw far down below made him gasp, again almost losing his grip. Whatever the god-thing, Xumatoq, was, its current shape was visible: a huge dome, like the cup of an enormous mushroom, its curved surface a bilious yellow, blotched with greens and scarlet veins. As the growing light struck it, it pulsed, its surface becoming increasingly transparent. For a moment those weird patterns resembled a giant's face, contorted with pain and fury. Elak gasped in horror as he realized what was happening to the monstrous being.

Under its thin skin, countless spores were heaving like an immense bed of maggots, writhing and frothing, stretching the skin of the god, threatening to rip it open and free themselves. If that happened, Elak knew, the danger to his world would be absolute. Desperately he lowered himself, more than once coming within an inch of losing his grip and plunging into the hellish things far beneath him.

Overhead the daylight streamed in, the sun at its zenith, and flames spread voraciously, widening the hole, exposing the great ship's beams that held up this twisted architectural nightmare. They, too, succumbed to the flames, whatever protection they had burned away, turning the beams to ash. The great structure creaked and groaned like a ship in a tropical storm.

Elak's companions reached out for him and pulled him to them. Many of the upper vines were falling like rain, incinerated.

Dalan's staff blazed on, too brilliant to look at, seemingly drawing the natural sunlight to it and deflecting it in numerous shafts around the gallery. The men used their blades to catch the light, their weapons no longer ineffective as they hewed and cut their way across the gallery and, with Elak and Lycon, chopped at the thicker strands that acted like mooring ropes for the god. They saw the fleshy dome lurch to one side as if wounded. Still its surface twisted and writhed, the spores yet contained, though the sunlight would surely burn through to them soon.

"We must go!" shouted Elak, knowing that a cloudburst of the creatures would likely be fatal. Quickly the company began the withdrawal, Dalan at their rear, though the work of his staff was done. Just as they reached the exit to the chamber, a roaring sound made them turn. They saw the skin of the mushroom-thing ripped asunder as a thick cloud of spores, miniature versions of the god, erupted upwards. The first wave was scorched by the sunlight, exploding like hot embers, but the cloud was so vast, thousands strong, that countless spores broke away.

Elak knew they would pursue him and his men. They ran as fast as they could back the way they had come. Behind them they heard another sound, a rush of air. Elak and Lycon, bringing up the rear of the company, heard the voice of Melshassar.

"Flee, flee!" it shrieked. "We will hold back the host as long as we can." The sounds intensified and became the maddened screams of a fierce wind, like the blasts of a hurricane across ocean waves.

The pathway ahead of the fleeing company had opened, falling downward towards the coast. Xumatoq's power was focused momentarily on the conflict inside the cavern. The weird terrain he had created in this outside world had fallen silent and stagnant, no longer resistant to the swords of the men rushing through it. They came to the place of the logs, where Melshassar had first appeared, but everything there had turned to dust, the jutting beams and fallen logs rotted away.

"To the ship!" cried Elak. He dare not spare time now to collect gourds and water.

Behind him there was a new sound. The horrors of the cavern, the howling, shrieking winds, had followed them, filled with menace, a new and terrifying threat.

7: The Ghost Storm

Dalan's voice rose above the roar of the aerial horrors. "Xumatoq has overcome Melshassar's resistance. He has forged them into a new, hostile force. See, the ghosts have swarmed into a cloud! Defend yourselves!" Once more his staff blazed, light spreading from it in shafts that seared the ghost-cloud, igniting sections of it. The warriors ducked as wave after wave of wraiths dived at them like huge hornets, buffeting and tearing at them, a force as powerful as a storm-swollen sea.

Elak and Lycon stood back-to-back, swords flashing,

though their weapons had almost no effect on thin air. Ironically, the ghosts were substantial as assailants and men began to fall, their heads torn, their bodies ripped by the claws of the flying monsters, whose faces were warped into screaming skulls, eyes ablaze with a madness from some other realm, a place of utter dread. Elak felt his mind invaded as the swarm of ghosts circled him, some from recent times, others from the remote past, and in their hunger, insanity threatened, offering a view of twisted futures yet to come for mankind, enslaved by the star-spawned gods of deepest space. Something buried far inside Elak would not be subdued, an intense, animal energy that revolted at this prospect of this alien domination. It welled up like molten lava and fuelled his resistance.

"Stand together!" he yelled, and his men closed ranks, forming a tight band around Dalan's central figure. The light from his staff bathed them and gave them a degree of protection. Around them the hurricane whirl of ghost shapes span faster, creating a vortex of power that threatened to drag every man into it and shred them. The sound of the ghost storm became louder, threatening to burst the eardrums of the crowded warriors.

Dalan swung his staff to and fro, all the time shouting out the words of ancient power, almost afraid to use their blasphemous phrases and couplets, some of which summoned up energies as dark and shunned as the things boiling in the air. Bolts of vivid light clashed with the ghost shapes, and thunder roared within their cloud. Where shapes were torn from it, dipping lower, Elak and Lycon struck at them with dramatic effect, shattering them explosively. The warriors, heartened by this success, redoubled their efforts and hit back.

For a long time the battle raged intensely, the men slowly feeling their energies drained, in danger of being sucked into that blanketing mass of demonic power.

"At least we'll die fighting," Elak shouted at Lycon, whose face was dripping with sweat, his chest heaving, close to exhaustion.

"Aye, by Ishtar! Better that than on a divan in Cyrena, surrounded by pompous Councillors who wouldn't know one end of a sword from another."

Elak laughed and forced himself to launch one more attack. As he did so, Dalan's staff dropped, its energy apparently failing. A dreadful silence closed in and the air became still. The ghost cloud remained, but its revolutions eased, slowly and more slowly, until they ceased. Faces, blurred and faint, stared down at the surviving warriors.

"What is it?" said Elak.

Dalan, dragging breath into his tortured lungs, almost sagged to his knees. "The sun," he gasped. "Up on the mountain, it has fully breached Xumatoq's chamber. The fires have consumed the upper dome. The god is no longer protected. Light has been his undoing. And as he falls, his links with the island melting away, so he perishes. Even the gods are vulnerable."

Elak watched the ghosts overhead. They were beginning to dissipate like mist, shrivelling up, the sunlight blazing through them, revealing cloudless azure skies beyond. Elak thought he caught a final glimpse of Melshassar, a last contorted grimace, that might have been a smile.

"Is it over?" said Lycon. "I can hardly lift my blade."

Dalan managed to straighten up. "Aye. They are gone. Let us get back to the fleet."

None of them needed any second bidding, and they wound their way to the riverbank and on to the shore, pausing there to draw breath. Half the company had died, and Elak cursed. He hated to lose a single man, and he'd known all of the warriors. It was, though, part of the unspoken pact they all made when they took up arms, part of the price they paid for adventuring.

A boat from one of the ships was pulling up on to the beach and the familiar figure of Balazaar stepped ashore. He studied the survivors, horrified by their dishevelled condition. He knew how many had been lost, but a glance from the king told him that whatever hell they had faced appeared to be over.

"I fear we have no fresh water with us," said Elak.

Balazaar indicated the men who had followed him ashore. "Shall I send these fellows to collect some?"

Dalan had recovered his poise, but his face was deeply troubled. "No!" he said. "I can feel the island beneath me. It moves like a great beast in pain. We must leave these seas with all haste!" No sooner had he spoken than a ripple of movement across the beach, like the shiver of a horse's flank, made every man there gasp. It was the only spur they needed to obey the Druid's instruction. They took to the boats with all haste, every man, including the exhausted survivors of the battle, using oars to good effect.

They quit the beach none too soon, for again it rippled, as if a minor quake shook it. Balazaar hailed the first of the ships, calling out for them to make ready to haul anchor. Elak and the company swarmed up on to the deck and with accustomed efficiency, *Windrider* turned for the open sea.

At its stern, Elak, Lycon and Dalan studied the island as it fell behind them. Its central mountain was smothered in dark smoke, as if volcanic ash had spewed out of it in a billowing, mile-high cloud.

"The seeds!" said Elak, a sudden flush of horror suffusing his face.

Dalan shook his head. "No more than embers now," he said. "See." He held out his hand. Something drifted down into it on the sea breeze, a grey flake. It was indeed an ember, a seed turned to cooling ash. "Xumatoq dies, and with him his spores from hell."

Epilogue

Elak and Lycon sprawled on the rough bedding in their cabin, *Windrider* well away from the dying strictures of the island. Sleep dragged at them and they had no will left to resist.

"When we wake, days from now, we'll be close to a friendlier shore," said Lycon. Somehow he'd managed to find a bottle of wine, most of which he'd imbibed in a single gulp, much to Elak's amusement. "Word of our success at Zangarza will surely have gone before us. Your new life awaits you, Elak. No more wild adventures. You will be waited on, hand and foot."

"And you'll have all the wine you can drink. You'll float in a barrel of it."

"I'd swap all that for the life of a pirate. Bring on another mad god."

"Well, perhaps. Not too soon, I pray."

There was a knock on the door. Elak frowned. He'd not expected to be disturbed again until they'd safely made port. But it was Dalan who eased the door open. For once he was smiling.

"There is something you should see on deck," said the Druid.

Elak guessed from his manner that it was not some new horror, sprung from the ocean deeps. The king rose, every bone protesting, Lycon likewise. Together they shuffled up on to the deck like a pair of old men.

Night had fallen, and by the ship's lanterns Elak and Lycon looked heavenwards and saw the falling rain, a steady drizzle. Already the crew were collecting as much of it as they could. Elak and Dalan opened their mouths and let the cool rain fill them. For once Lycon appreciated it as much as any wine.

"Our own gods favour us," said Dalan. "It bodes well for our return to Cyrena."

Lycon swung an arm around Elak's shoulders. "And you, my friend, will be crowned king of all Atlantis."

TOWER IN THE CRIMSON MIST

Elak's voyage northward along the eastern coast of the Atlantean continent was without major incident until he reached the dangerous waters off the northeastern headlands, the most treacherous of which was the notorious Cape of Blood, where ships had been known to flounder from time beyond memory. Myths and legends recorded that there were terrors in the waters far below the rocks far more terrible than the dreaded coast itself.

- Helvas Ravanniol

Annals of the Third Atlantean Empire

*

1: Dangerous Waters

Dalan the Druid had suffered a troubled sleep, some slithering force repeatedly nudging him awake throughout the deeps of the night. Finally, fully awake, he had come up on to the deck of the *Windrider*, the ship carrying Elak through the eastern ocean of Atlantis from its distant south to its eventual destination, the northern city of Epharra. There, Elak would be crowned king of all Atlantis, following his triumphant conflict in Zangarza, where the last independent states of the huge continent had sworn fealty to him and agreed to come under one banner. This journey north had not been without incident and already the warriors serving the young king had been tested in unexpected encounters along the way, and Elak himself had been pitched into situations that had Dalan fearing for his survival. The Druid told himself this was the reason for his own current acute nervousness.

He stood in the prow, studying the seas around the swiftly moving ship, its sails unfurled and billowing with a strong following wind which had given the rowers an opportunity to rest for the last two nights and days. These northern waters could be treacherous, Dalan knew from experience. He was long past middle age now, his former powers ebbing slowly, but he retained enough to be able to read the winds and the movement of the waves: they all whispered caution to him. The northern coast of Atlantis swept eastward towards a cape that curved around to the main eastern coast like a hooked claw, the cape known by many names. The Cyrenians called it the Cape of Blood, for there were many vessels that had foundered on its jagged, vicious rocks. Ships passing this way always gave it a significantly wide berth.

Dalan had instructed the pilot of the *Windrider* to keep well to the east of it, coming around the cape in a sweep that would take the ship into deep, but safe waters. Up ahead, in the total darkness, where the high waves could be heard rolling and unfurling, a sea mist spread across the horizon in a thin grey band like a cerement. A cry from the lookout, perched on the high point of the main mast, drew Dalan's attention. He climbed down to the deck from his own vantage point and hailed the lookout.

"There's something in the mist!" called the sailor from above. "I can't make it out. Could be ships. Could be –" His voice trailed off in a scream and both his hands went to his head as if something had taken it in a grip of steel. Presently, with another terrible shriek, the man toppled from his high place and crashed on to the deck. Dalan had been powerless to prevent disaster. The man's neck was broken, his head bloody and twisted at an outrageous angle, his frozen expression one of absolute horror.

The captain, Balazaar, was alongside Dalan at once, staring down at his fallen shipmate in horror. "What struck him? Karval was as able a climber as we have." Another sailor had sprung to the mast, shinning up it as lithely as an ape, but Balazaar shouted to him to beware. Others quickly bore the corpse of the fallen lookout away, shocked by the manner of his death.

"You must change course," Dalan told Balazaar. "I fear we are not as clear of the waters around the Cape of Blood as we thought. There are strange mists about us and almost certainly we have been drawn perilously close to the coast. You must head even further east and later, turn back to the north in order to round the cape."

"Aye, its winds and currents play tricks on the mind. Many a ship has been broken there." Balazaar turned to issue new orders to his pilot and crew.

Dalan again studied the waters ahead from the bow. He could hear fresh sounds far away in that curdling mist, sounds that disturbed him and kindled a fresh wave of dread. It was not so much the reefs and rocks of the coast he feared as much as the things waiting on it. Unnatural, hostile things.

His thoughts were interrupted as a tall figure edged up beside him and he turned to look into the bright face of the young king, Elak. Weather-beaten and with scarred muscles that attested to the rigors of too many battles for one so young, Elak was alert, his own eyes drinking in the heaving ocean and the far-off mists.

"The air is full of portents," he said, suddenly frowning. "I don't need your druidic skills to know that."

Dalan nodded. "Balazaar will steer us further east. The Cape of Blood reaches out its claw. You'd be well advised to rouse the men and have them ready."

"Pirates?"

"That would be preferable." Dalan knew Elak's warriors would be more than a match for any hunting pirates. "Since your rise to power, you have made many new enemies, you know that. Out here, you are vulnerable. I fear that the darkness you have disturbed will make a final play for you before we return to the haven of Epharra." The Druid carried with him his staff. It had been invaluable in their struggles against the horrors Dalan spoke of, but the Druid knew that its powers were not inexhaustible. There were rituals and rites that could restore them, but these were complex and would take time and the privacy of Epharra's sanctuary to perform adequately.

Elak's scowls turned once more into a grin. "Very well. Two weeks of lounging about this ship with nothing to shout at but the gulls has given me an appetite for action. I'll go and wake Lycon, though he'll complain that he never gets any proper sleep. There's no wine left aboard, so he'll be in a mean mood."

"Tell him we'll hang him over the side and use him to scare off the sharks," said Dalan, but his fears yet showed through his attempt at humour.

Elak could see this, but simply nodded and went below to where his constant companion was wrapped in blankets in his sea cot, snoring like a walrus, dead to the world. Cautiously Elak prodded at his partially exposed buttocks with his rapier point, and almost immediately the vast bulk burst upward, groping for his own weapon.

2: The Wall of Death

Lycon, now fully dressed and with his sword strapped

to his side, leaned on the ship's rail with Elak and glared at the increasingly heavy swell of the seas. Somewhere behind the *Windrider,* the remaining ships of the small fleet followed, their sails dipping and rising in the white banks of surf against a backdrop of pitch darkness.

"This is no ordinary storm," the big man growled. He was wide awake, alert to the worsening conditions about them. "The crew can smell something in the air, sorcery I don't doubt."

"We've made more than a few enemies since we began this quest for the crown of Atlantis," said Elak. "For every army we strike aside, a new power rises up. Balazaar is a worthy captain, yet something fights his attempts to steer this ship eastward. He dare not lower the sails and rely on the men to row, not in these seas. *Windrider* will break her back."

"By the Nine Hells! Give me a visible foe to strike at! We've been cooped up in this tub for too long! Where are these enemies? Let them show themselves! I'll give them a taste of steel."

Elak grinned and clapped his companion on the arm. "Patience, Lycon. There'll be enough of that ere long, I'm sure of it."

A shout from aloft sent the two men forward to join the captain at the prow. It dipped and rose, cutting into the foam, spraying the men with cold sheets of it, but through its salty curtain they could discern the sea mist, which had now become far more dense, rolling forward like a tidal wave. It would be impossible for the fleet to avoid it; the sea was like a live thing, dragging the ships into the embrace of the roiling murk. Instinctively Elak drew his blade, as did Lycon.

Although the ships continued to veer eastward in an attempt to stay parallel to the hidden coast, Elak knew they were slowly angling in towards it and now a new sound came to his ears. Surf breaking on rocks! The shore was far closer than they had realized. A collision was inevitable. Even as the grim thought beset the young king, the mists pulled apart, as if by mocking, demonic hands, and revealed what the men all dreaded: the fanged shore, with low cliffs that would pulverize the fleet when the waves tossed it effortlessly forward. Broken cloud banks allowed bright moonlight partially to flood the scene, where weird shadows danced and leapt.

"There!" cried Dalan, who had been leaning out from the point of the prow, desperate to find something in the maelstrom that might aid them.

Elak looked along the bleak coast to the east and saw a break in the rocks, a small bay, sandy but flat, a possible haven. With all speed and every last effort the ships were held on a course for the bay, and although several of them felt the grating of reefs under their keels, they forced themselves away from the wall of death and on to the sand. Waves pushed the vessels up and out of the heavy seas, tossing them forward like driftwood. The men gasped with relief, but Dalan turned to his companions.

"The elements are toying with us," he said. "We are not out of danger."

"What is this place?" said Elak. He was studying the small bay and its narrow beach, which looked as though it had been scooped out of the rocky terrain by the hand of a god. Its cliffs rose up vertically like glass, and topping them was another bank of mist or low cloud. Moonlight seeped through it, and in that sickly glow, shapes shifted, like mirror images of the thunderous surf, though on the heights all was silent, as if the storm blew elsewhere.

"We must be close to the Cape of Blood," said Balazaar.

"Secure the ships," said Elak, although Balazaar's seamen and those from the other vessels were already hard at work undertaking the work with ropes and stays.

"I'll climb up," said Lycon. "I need the exercise."

"Hold," Elak said, grinning. "Let the seamen take a look. It won't be an easy climb, even for them."

Lycon grunted with disappointment, but watched as several of the sailors came forward, ropes curled over their shoulders, and made their way upwards, like spiders on a flat wall. The gusting wind cuffed at them and more than once one of them almost lost his grip on the treacherous stone. However, they persisted and once they reached the top of the cliff, standing silhouetted briefly in the moonlight, they let down their ropes before giving a last wave and disappearing to investigate the high crags.

"We'll wait," said Elak, as others came forward to grab the ropes, eager to climb. "Let us hear their report." He'd seen the continuing look of unease on Dalan's face. The Druid feared something, a trap probably.

They did not have long to wait. Even though the cliff was a good hundred feet high, the sounds from up there were somehow not muffled by the elements, and came clearly down to the gathered company. Sounds – of terror! Screams, wild shrieks. Drawn out and nerve-shredding.

"By Ishtar!" Elak cursed, grasping a rope.

"No!" said Dalan. "Wait!"

The sounds quickly died away and the men all moved backwards, craning their necks to get a better view. There was only the mist, but now it was no longer milky. It had turned a shade of pink, intensifying as the horror-stricken company watched, becoming crimson, spread in a cloud around the rim of the bay. Again it pulsed with invisible shapes, though it gave forth not a sound, not a note.

3: Death in the Mist

Elak knew then what had happened to the sailors who

had climbed up onto the upper crags—he snarled in fury. Throughout the campaign he had recently fought and the tortured journey homeward he had felt the loss of every warrior keenly, incensed that men had to die fighting for him. It was clear from his manner that he desperately wanted to grasp a rope and haul himself upward as quickly as possible to confront whatever horrors were up there, but again Dalan interceded, holding him back.

"It is what they want of us. A trap in which we could not hope to survive," said the Druid. He held aloft his staff and by its light they could see the red mist boiling over the cliff tops, as if it would roll off them in a long bank and drop over the sailors below like a bloody net.

The light from Dalan's staff also threw the bay into better relief and it soon became alarmingly apparent that the tide was sweeping in, as several huge waves crashed over the sands and up against the beached ships.

"We cannot remain here!" shouted Elak above the sudden blast of the wind. "We'll be crushed against the walls if those waves reach higher. Dalan, we have to climb! We have to face whatever is in those red mists."

The two men faced one another, a silent mental struggle enacted between them while the sailors looked on, swords drawn, prepared to carry out whatever orders their king gave them. Another wave swirled around the narrow bay and again the ships rocked, shifting closer to the rocks.

A shout from further along the beach deflected the attention of the Druid and the king as one of the scouts came racing up. "Sire, a cave!" gasped the man, pointing behind him. "And a way up into the cliff."

Elak motioned the scout to lead them and quickly the entire party moved over the sand at the base of the cliffs to several buttresses of sharp rock, where between two of them a tall, narrow cleft revealed itself. Dalan again lifted his staff as a beacon and led the company inside. The cave was a huge split in the rocks, its sides sharp and festooned with weed, the smell almost overpowering. Deeper inside, Dalan made out the details of what the scout had found.

Lycon was beside him and his eyes bulged in surprise. "A stair!" he said. "Who could have cut such a thing?"

"Be careful," said Dalan. "It could yet be a trap."

Elak and Lycon insisted on leading the way, with Dalan behind them. The stairs were slick with more weed and it was clear that the highest tides reached far up the stairway. It was primitive and narrow, some of the steps crumbling, and progress upward into the darkness was slow. Elak paused to listen, but the only sounds were those made by the sea as it boiled further up the beach outside, its long fingers of surf reaching already for the cave mouth.

The company wound its way up the twisted stair, which in places was almost perpendicular, but there were chains set in the wall that aided the climb, though they were rusted and seemingly very ancient. It appeared that no one had used this stair for a long time. Eventually there was moonlight above, seeping through a vent, but at least it was a clean light, not tainted with crimson. Elak cautiously led his party up out of the great cleft and on to a flatter surface. They had reached the top of the cliff's wall.

Elak looked back along the wall towards the west, but barely a hundred yards away the banks of crimson mist pulsed, as if they would suddenly spill open like a huge cloud and swamp the cliff top. It was impossible to see anything clearly to seaward, for the night darkened unnaturally there, blotting out even a view of the beached ships. Elak could hear the pounding of the waves, striking against the rock wall now, shaking it like a maddened giant.

"The ships!" said Lycon. "Can they survive such a battering?"

"Balazaar will save them, if any man can," said Dalan.

Elak turned and looked along the cliffs to the west. There was more mist, but it was at least a mile away, and clean. The cliffs here were narrow and as he crossed them to look beyond, to the north, he realized he was standing on a man-made structure.

"Yes," said Dalan. "It is a sea wall, built millennia ago. I know not by whom. A pre-human society, possibly, or even a remnant of Valusia itself."

They had no time to study the blocks of flattened stone – another shout snared their attention. Elak went to the source of the cry and looked down at what had now been discovered on the wall. Corpses. The sailors who had first climbed up here. They had been drained of their blood, their flesh draped about their bones like cloth, thin and torn. As if to confirm the horrific manner of their deaths, the crimson mist shifted beyond them and again bulged with movement. Once more those blurred shapes moved within it, stretched faces, gaping mouths, vampiric and eager for more blood.

"Withdraw!" Elak cried and as one the party retreated back along the wall, the red mist inching forward as a huge cat would do, stalking its prey with calm but horrible confidence.

"What lies at the end of the wall?" Elak asked Dalan.

"Legend has it there is a tower. It is said to watch over the deeps, a beacon to warn off shipping from the talons of the reefs. If it is there, perhaps it will shelter us."

Elak watched the Druid's face. Something in those eyes hinted there was more to this mystery. Dalan had scented evil, another trap. Elak understood him too well to miss his doubts, and worse, his fear.

4: Into the Darkness

There were less than a hundred warriors on the wall,

following Elak, Lycon and Dalan along its broken surface, while behind them the curling clouds unfurled, shaped like crimson bludgeons. Beyond the sides of the wall, north and south, more clouds pressed in, creating a living corridor as the company closed ranks and headed for the far end of the wall. There were more clouds there, but these were lighter, banks of spume and surf thrown up by the raging seas below the cliffs. Here, where the northern waters boiled into those of the eastern ocean, the sound of the crashing waves blotted out even the roar of the winds. And through the salty, stinging spray, a lonely shape rose up, a grey, rounded tower, a squat construction that defied the blasts of the elements, its stonework slick with weed, eroded but not weakened, as though hewn from granite or a similar imperishable rock.

The company reached the tower, and in its base, facing the warriors, a single door was closed against them. Dalan considered it briefly, then swung his staff against its wooden surface. Light flared as the door caved in under the blow, and as it did so Dalan realized there was now limited power left in the staff. If there were to be evil magics contained within the tower, he would be able to do little to fend them off.

Elak kicked aside the remaining splinters of wood and stared into the half-light within the tower. It had no roof, and up above him, some fifty feet away, the circular opening revealed moonlit skies, and enough light filtered downwards to display the inside of the tower. It had been constructed over a circular hole in the floor, a wide opening. No light pierced its depths, but from far down below the sounds of water pounding on rock came upward. Around the rim of this well was a wide lip with enough room to accommodate the company. The men filed in swiftly, spreading out around the well's circumference.

Outside the tower the crimson clouds curled about the stone, wrapping it like huge shrouds, but though the doorway remained broken, none of that dreadful light entered, held back by whatever invisible forces were at work within. Dalan felt them, subtle as whispers: he studied the curving walls, up to their highest point, but the air was still and silent, the atmosphere of long disuse and decay, like that of a primitive mausoleum.

"What of the ships?" said Elak. "Will they survive the tide?" His fears were for Balazaar and the skeleton crews left to secure the vessels.

"I think the sea has served its purpose," said Dalan. "It forced us on to the wall. The ships are not the target of the powers in this place."

"We cannot remain here," said Lycon.

"You saw what the crimson mist did to those warriors," said Dalan. "The same fate awaits any of us who step back outside. I cannot protect us from that, not out there."

Several cries of alarm went up from the compressed company and Dalan looked up to see the night sky beyond the tower's rim. He cursed as he saw the veil of mist closing over the opening, mist that was pulsing with crimson life, an extension of the horror already enfolding them.

"Then we go down," said Elak, indicating the well. He leaned cautiously over its edge. There was barely enough light to see into it, but as his eyes grew accustomed to its gloom, he pointed. "There! Several feet down, there is a stair. Narrow and steep." He swung round to Dalan. "What lies below?"

"I can only sense it and its festering evil. It brought us here, herded us like cattle. If we go down, it will be as though we descend into the maw of a living entity."

Elak growled his anger. "If we stay here, we will slowly go insane. Or starve. If we are to die in this place, let's do so with fire in our belly! Confront whatever demons are below." He looked at his warriors. They were afraid, a natural thing in the face of sorcery, but they were with him.

He had fought beside them more than once. He was the king, and when he led the line, they would not waver.

"Let me go first," said Dalan, holding aloft his staff. He said nothing about its diminished power. The warriors needed encouragement.

Elak and Lycon let the Druid climb down to the top of the stairway and followed him as he began the cautious descent. Something flapped away down into the complete darkness, bats perhaps, though the sound of their calls was unearthly. Gradually the warriors dropped over the side of the pit, using the stair. It was no more than two feet wide, its uneven stones slippery, but the men formed a human chain. Some of them lost their footing, but they were quickly hauled back to safety.

Dalan's staff held enough power to light the way, and shadows danced back from its pale beams, revealing the curved walls, dripping with moisture, sheer and cut with extraordinary precision. Whoever had built this well had possessed great skills, however primitive they may have been. A sense of a long-lost era somehow pervaded the drop, as if the warriors were going backwards into prehistory, an age long past, an age, perhaps, when the old gods and terrible magics held sway, like dust waiting to rise up again if disturbed.

"What is that sound?" said Elak, his ears as sharp as those of any hunting hound.

Dalan had heard it, but merely shook his head. Again he masked his fears. Better, he thought, not to relay what he had heard, the sound of deep, stertorous breathing far below, as if the earth itself had come awake, and with it a hunger that craved satisfaction.

5: The Horror in the Tunnel

The descent was deceptively long and arduous,

twisting far down into the entrails of living rock, although the walls gleamed with a peculiar iridescence, minute organisms that suffused the surroundings with an ethereal, morbid light. As Elak stepped off the stair to the floor, his feet sank into wet, cloying sand and he gripped his sword the tighter, wary of any surprise attack. In this humid, fetid atmosphere, every shadow represented a foe. Dalan's staff retained its faint glow, reflected around the walls, where hidden eyes seemed to study the assembling company.

There was an opening in one section of the circular well, less tall than a man and several feet wide, a carefully constructed door to a tunnel, its stones set expertly in an arch that had withstood the pressure above it for millennia. Dalan studied the exit and led the way under the arch. Beyond, the tunnel opened upward and the company was able to pass down it, listening to the susurrations of distant water. Dalan had calculated that they must be far beneath the level of the seas at the foot of the cliffs, and knew that if a sudden tide did unfurl along this passage, they would all be swept away by it.

After a while the tunnel debouched into a wide chamber, its ceiling curved, low and dripping with minor stalactites, another reminder of the vast age of this place. The wall here was also curved around in a circle, and within it were set alcoves, plinths and small statues. Elak frowned at these, recognizing them as representations of gods and demi-gods from the ocean, hostile deities to Man, enemies he had faced before, and a threat to the rising power in Atlantis. In themselves they invoked in him no more than a basic apprehension, but it was the central statue that prompted a deeper emotion, a familiar dread. For here, twice as tall as a man, was a green-hued shape that was instantly familiar to the king, and to Dalan, and most of those present. Its arms were the appendages of a squid, its head long and bulbous, with a curved beak for a mouth, and in place of eyes it had two great jewels, crimson and shining unnaturally in the dim light of this place.

"Xeraph-Hizer," said Lycon softly.

"The Leviathan Lord," Elak added. "We may have smashed his cult followers in Zangarza, but they infest the eastern seaboard."

Dalan ushered his companions back from the statue. "Our journey from that city has been watched. This is why we are here. Xeraph-Hizer's followers have drawn us in and mean to finish his bloody work."

His words echoed from the opening at the opposite wall of the chamber, enhanced by other sounds as something moved in the darkness beyond it. The sounds were a mixture of shrieks and snarls, neither normal man nor beast, grating along human nerves, suggestive of something primitive and hostile. Presently the opening disgorged a mass of living things, crab-like, scuttling, with long, curling arms and claws, unknown creatures from the ocean deeps, their stench a solid miasma. In one sweeping movement they came forward, hurling themselves upon the intruders.

"This is one language I do speak!" cried Lycon, swinging his blade in an arc as he readied to meet the attack and beside him the king and his warriors likewise took their stand. Chaos broke out as the two forces collided, the Atlanteans roaring their defiance, relieved to be able to hurl themselves into action, the sea creatures apparently spurred on by an instinctive drive to kill, heedless of the cost. They were deadly, their claws slashing at the men, some of whom were cut down, ripped open and poisoned, but Elak's warriors were his elite troops and wrought utter havoc among their assailants, chopping them apart and clearing great swathes through them.

Elak and Lycon fought as always, shoulder to shoulder, their quick blades moving so fast they set up a mesh of steel the sea things could not break through. Dalan, usually paramount in these frightful contests, stood back, his staff little more than a heavy wooden pole, though he yet used it to dash out the brains of any of the creatures that attempted to drag him down. For a while the battle raged ferociously, but gradually the warriors pushed the sea things back, driving hard at them, sparing none as the floor of the chamber became a bloody, sodden carpet of broken creatures writhing in their death throes. The slaughter became too much for them and the survivors turned and slithered back into the tunnel from which they had emerged.

Elak's warriors had fought with him in similar battles and were veterans who knew their drill. Where inexperienced men would have raced after the enemy, intent on wiping them all out, these held back, knowing a trap may well be laid for them. Instead they turned to the king, awaiting his orders. He wiped sweat from his brow and praised them.

"We have to go on," he said. "But we do it with care. We have to find another way up to the surface. That, or a means to dissipate those banks of killing mist. My belief is, they are controlled from somewhere here."

Dalan was nodding.

No man demurred. They had a taste for battle now and were eager to follow up this skirmish.

Dalan listened at the tunnel mouth but heard nothing. The enemy had completely withdrawn. More septic light came from beyond, and in a moment the company moved on once more. The tunnel had become less of a construction, more like the burrowing of a large worm or similar denizen of the deep. Elak had experienced such things before and knew they could only lead to fresh peril. Nevertheless he forged ahead for some distance.

When he reached the next opening and saw what was beyond, his blood went cold and he felt his head swim dizzily as a new kind of terror threatened to well up.

6: The Land Beyond the World

Open skies curved overhead in cerulean splendour and another world spread out beyond the company, as though they had stepped through a dimensional gateway into this realm. Gone was the darkness, the walls of stone, the underground passageways and weed-choked seabed. Plants clustered either side of the wide path and distant trees shifted in a cool breeze. Beyond the measureless plain a city rose up, alien and unnatural, its towers and minarets gleaming pale pink in the sunlight, its walls sheer and giddy. And it was from this city that something emanated, a strange, unnameable force that brought such a chill to Elak and those about him. Instinctively the young king sensed that here was the embodiment of evil, the source of the powers that had entrapped him and his warriors.

He turned to speak to Dalan, whose expression of alarm compounded Elak's own fears. As he did so, Elak saw movement from either side of the wide pathway, and from out of the dark-hued jungle burst more of the creatures the warriors had fought back in the tunnel. There were countless scores of them, rushing forward in waves. In moments the battle began anew as swords rang and claws raked. There was no avoiding the conflict, for the gateway through which the company had entered had disappeared, to be replaced by a solid wall, its upper heights lost in the haze. The trap had indeed closed.

The assailants resembled crustaceans, their bodies armoured, their heads encased in shell, and it became more difficult to cleave them open. Elak knew that without respite or relief, he and his Atlanteans would die there on the perimeter of this mysterious land. They fought furiously, heaping up their slain opponents, but these were replaced as more and more of them poured out of the surrounding landscape.

"The skies! The skies!" someone shouted, and Elak spared a moment to look upward. To his horror he saw that new enemies were arriving to compound their predicament. Huge bird-like creatures were arriving in a dense cloud, diving down towards the battle. Elak's horror was magnified when he realized that these were not birds, but winged men, armed with swords, their lower legs shod with steel and claws that reached out as a hunting eagle reaches for its victims. Utter chaos ensued as these new assailants tore into the affray like missiles, but it was not the Atlanteans they attacked. Instead they ripped into the crustacean hordes, smiting them with their swords and ripping their shells apart with their metal-shod feet.

Elak and his companions, with their backs to the wall, watched in bemused amazement as the winged men, at least a hundred of them, flew over the crustaceans time and time again, wreaking havoc, avoiding any counter blows, swirling in an aerial ballet that almost defied the eyes. No one spoke, though Elak looked to Dalan for a comment. The Druid may have been relieved at the arrival of the bird men, but his expression remained one of deep unease.

Whatever drove the crustaceans to attack, whether a leader or their own blind, hunting instincts, was countered by their heavy losses as their dead heaped up in twitching, writhing mounds, their slaughter terrible to behold. They drew away and soon were in full retreat, back into the vast banks of undergrowth and cramped jungle paths that covered so much of the landscape. A few of the bird men hovered over them, watching their movements, ready to begin anew the attack. Otherwise the main force of the sky warriors dropped softly to the ground, forming into neat, disciplined ranks.

One of them strode forward and Elak realized just how tall these beings were, being at least a foot taller than him. They were slender, lightweight, and their armour clung to them like a second skin, cast in an unknown metal to Elak. They wore smooth helms, curving to a beak-like point over their noses and their swords were narrow and double-edged, unlike any weapons Elak had previously seen.

The man stood before him and bowed his head in a universal gesture. He removed his helmet to reveal a long face, its features pinched, its eyes very dark. When he spoke, it was in an accent unfamiliar to the king, but to Elak's surprise, he used the Atlantean language, and spoke it perfectly.

"I am Kai-Quetzar, Commander of the Queen's Guard. My people bid you welcome to our land."

Elak bowed. "I am Elak, king of Cyrena, soon to be monarch of Atlantis. My men and I owe you a great debt. Those creatures would have destroyed us."

Kai-Quetzar bowed once more, his features lit by an enigmatic smile. "It is our pleasure to clear away the shelled ones. Tell me, though, how did you come to be in our land? How did you break through the barriers our queen has set up to protect us from intrusion?"

"We were lured here," said Elak. "We sensed sorcery at work. We have enemies in our world who use it against us. They opened a gate and set the shelled ones against us."

"The gate is closed. In time we will have it re-opened so that you may return to your world. However, before that, my queen wishes to meet you and your companions. We have all been impressed by your fighting skills. There are men in our city of Utterzanek, but they are not warriors. Only my squadrons are trained for battle. Will you come with us to the city?"

Elak nodded and turned to Dalan. "We will accompany them."

Dalan spoke very softly so that only the king caught his words. "Be very alert, Elak. Our first impressions of the city were of danger. I cannot penetrate its aura, but there is a darkness about it, in spite of its beauty and the apparent friendship of these beings."

7: The City outside Time

The Atlanteans were taken by the winged men through the grassland at the edge of the matted jungles for a short distance before it sloped down to a broad river, where a small ship awaited them. It was crewed by other men, who were not winged and who were silent and went about their work doggedly and with sullen expressions, clearly slaves. The ship eased out into the current and wound along the waterway, while overhead the bird men acted as scouts, though the land here seemed remarkably tranquil, free of danger. Certainly the likelihood of another attack from the crustaceans appeared to be remote. Kai-Quetzar stood in the prow of the ship, arms folded as he studied the way ahead.

Elak, Lycon and Dalan were amidships, their men resting around them.

"These men," said Elak, indicating the morose sailors, "are as we are. Human. Kai-Quetzar and his fellows are not entirely so. Hybrids. There are old legends about such beings, though they are set far back in our histories."

Dalan nodded. "It's possible we've come through a veil of time. This place is like nothing known to our people. We should return to the place we entered and look for a way back. This is not a place to be stranded."

After a time the ship rounded a wide bend and the city of Utterzanek rose before them on the far bank. Its walls were spectacularly vast, over a hundred feet high, cut from immense blocks of the pinkish stone, engineered into place by a technology that must surely have been beyond anything known to the Atlanteans. The quay was long and wide, with several ships moored to it, although there was little activity around them. Elak assumed that the winged men had little use for this method of transport.

Kai-Quetzar and a select group of his warriors disembarked and led the Atlanteans across the quay to a small gateway, one of several. This Elak could see, served the humans that came and went into the city. There was no need for a larger, more ostentatious gate, as the winged men simply overflew the walls. The passageway was gloomy and cold, going directly beyond the thick wall, some hundred feet, to where the streets began. These were narrow, the buildings rising steeply. Elak felt like an ant squeezing itself between the cracks of immense stones.

The company went deeper into the city, beyond towers and structures that might have been temples or warehouses – there was nothing about their uniform stone to delineate them. There were no visible doors or windows, as though each colossal building might have been a mausoleum. Shadows deepened and Elak sensed that the winged men were uncomfortable so far from the skies, probably feeling vulnerable in the narrow confines of the alleys.

It was a vast city, for it was almost an hour before the company reached its destination. This was a huge square, opening out at probably the heart of the city, where there was more human activity. Men and women hurried to and fro across it, not pausing to study the group of outsiders. Were they afraid? Elak wondered. So controlled by the winged men that they kept their heads and eyes down and went directly about their directed tasks?

Rising from the centre of the square was an incalculably large domed building, set up above the floor on a sequence of wide steps. The architecture was remarkably smooth, as if the entire structure had been carved from a single block of stone, its joints were so precisely aligned. Several tall towers rose from around the dome, high into the azure skies, and at their highest points, flocks of the winged men could be seen, though from this distance they appeared no bigger than crows.

Kai-Quetzar took his charges up the steps, to be met by a company of winged men, guardians of the doorway to the building. This was huge, a great opening, its portals carved intricately, its columns topped with sculptures, beasts and quasi-humans that may have been adapted from legend. Elak studied them uneasily. He noted Dalan's expression, which could not completely hide his own discomfort. Whether the Druid recognized these things or not, Elak knew he had no liking for them.

Inside the great dome, the Atlanteans gazed up at the curved ceiling, a staggering architectural work, like a single gigantic shell, covering the entire building, the only columns holding it aloft at its perimeter. These were immense, and again seemed to have been shaped from single blocks, although surely only sorcery could have achieved such a thing. Light speared down from above, though its source was a mystery. It brightened the interior, even the spaces between the huge pillars. There were countless scores of armed warriors here, motionless as statues, their eyes fixed on the central area.

At the exact mid-point of the floor, a circular, low wall contained what seemed at first to be a pool, a dozen feet across. Elak was fascinated by its waters, if waters they were, for they gleamed and sparkled like liquid metal, giving off golden vapours that shifted over the surface.

Light suffused the pool, its source somewhere below those dazzling waters, and Elak had to tear his eyes away, fearing he'd be mesmerized if he watched for too long. Instead he looked beyond the pool to another set of steps, leading to a flat area and what must be the throne. It was carved from more unknown materials, brilliant blue rock, set with crimson jewels, rubies perhaps. On either side of it were smaller seats, also created from precious metals, their shapes moulded into the likenesses of legendary beasts, whose faces gazed regally at the men standing before them.

Elak's eyes, though, quickly passed over the lavish throne and seats and fixed instead on the figure which sat on the throne. Dressed in flowing silks from neck to toe, her arms woven with serpent-like golden charms, a similar brilliant torque hanging from her slender neck. Her figure was mostly hidden, but what was visible of her – her arms, neck and upper face – suggested youthfulness. Her nose and mouth were concealed in another silken band, but her eyes, a vivid green, pierced Elak's gaze haughtily. She may have been smiling, but somehow Elak felt a ripple of cold air around him, a warning.

"This is Araccneris, our queen," said Kai-Quetzar, bowing.

8: Ritual by Night

Her voice was as soft and soothing as silk. "You are most welcome, Elak of Atlantis. While you and your fellows are here, my kingdom and all it contains is yours to share. Though you are from a place far away, you are known. Your gods and our gods smile upon you."

Elak bowed politely, surprised that she spoke his language so comfortably, albeit in a strange accent unknown to him, for all his travels across the Atlantean continent. "My men and I are grateful for the help your warriors gave us."

The eyes of the queen were smiling, but Elak read in them something else, unspoken thoughts that made him wary. His exploits had sharpened his wits and the impulsive youth he had once been, not long since, had learned to step cautiously, especially in strange lands. And there was none stranger than those of Utterzanek.

Overhead, where light had streamed in, the glow suddenly changed, as if a vast shadow had crossed the skies outside and a sudden twilight began its brief reign. The queen looked up and her body gave a shiver, as though a draught had passed through the great chamber. "The night will soon be upon us. I have prepared chambers of rest for you, Elak. And refreshments. Go, and in the morning we will meet again and talk of the future, and many glories to come, for I have seen your destiny."

Elak started, barely able to refrain from asking more, but he sensed Dalan's discreet touch. There would be time to discuss this later. Elak bowed again to the queen, who rose, silent as a ghost, and took her leave of the chamber, her retinue behind her.

"Come," said Kai-Quetzar. "Let me take you to your quarters."

These proved to be lavish, sumptuously furnished and with several small pools where the warriors could soothe their wounds and bruises. Fresh fruit and lightly cooked meat was provided in abundance and Kai-Quetzar had several of the slave humans taste the food before anyone partook of it. None was harmed, but Elak thought the practice harsh on the slaves. Cyrena had long since done away with slavery. Servants in Elak's lands were employed in their own right, although some of the southern states, lately bonded to Elak's empire, still maintained the practice. These slaves acted like men and women drugged, eyes dull, movements sluggish.

Kai-Quetzar left the Atlanteans, and soon they were eating and drinking, and not long afterwards spreading out among the lavish sleeping areas. Nonetheless Lycon appointed several guards. He himself was soon asleep.

Elak stayed awake as long as he could, but dropped off to sleep as the light above faded and the lamps flickered faintly. When he was gently tugged awake, his hand went to his sword, until he saw it was Dalan looking over him.

"I have not slept," said the Druid. "Are you refreshed?"

"A little."

"Then come with me. There are things about this palace that disturb me deeply." He led the way through the sleepers, nodding to the alert guards, though they had nothing untoward to report. Elak followed Dalan further into the chamber, its far end becoming a small labyrinth of passageways, barely lit. Dalan was listening, his ear attuned to the silence, like a bat sensing movements and sounds beyond the walls. Elak knew the Druid possessed remarkable, unique powers of perception, fine-tuned by years of working his arts.

Dalan paused by a recess set into the wall. It was cloaked in shadow, but a sliver of light penetrated the darkness from beyond the wall, emitted through a crack in the ancient stone. Dalan put his eye to the crack and drew back at once, alarmed, his breath catching. He waved Elak forward and the young king peered through the crack. He, too, drew in his breath in horror.

Beyond was another tall chamber, lit by candles suspended in bowls from the distant ceiling. These were not the only objects hung from linked chains. A dozen or more shapes dangled down, the size of huge fruits, or cocoons. They were a dull white colour, and within them vague shapes had been encased, mummified like giant flies trapped by a spider. Elak watched, mesmerized, as voices drifted up from below. At the centre of the chamber a fat column rose up, stairs wound around it from the darkness far below. A single figure moved up this stair, its body wrapped around in layers of silk. Gold gleamed on bare arms. It was Araccneris.

She reached the flat top of the column and raised her arms. One of the cocoon-things began to lower on its rattling chains until it came within reach of the queen. She pulled it to her and with a few quick movements, pulled away the whitish wrappings. A human figure was revealed, naked save for a brief clout. Unlike the slaves in the city, this was a more muscular man who had the look of a seasoned warrior. He remained asleep, or drugged, his eyes firmly closed.

Elak's horror intensified as Araccneris lowered the silk covering her face. What was revealed was not human. The jaws were like mandibles, dripping with thick, green fluid. They fixed on the neck and upper chest of the man and by the revolting movements that followed, Elak understood that the queen was *feeding*. For a brief moment the man's eyes opened, filled with unspeakable horror, his mouth open as if he would scream, but his head sagged as if he were dead. Elak could not look away, continuing to watch as the queen let the man fall to the stone. She pulled her veil back in place. The man shuddered, then struggled to his feet. As his eyes opened again, he took on the sullen, docile expression of the other city slaves. His body had lost its vigour, slumped, with its muscles weakened.

Araccneris turned her back and began the descent insouciantly. The new slave plodded after her until both figures were swallowed by the lower darkness.

Elak turned to Dalan and described what he had seen, unable to keep from shuddering with revulsion.

"As I feared," said Dalan. "That is the fate she has

planned for us all. It is why we were brought here. The tower, the sea-things that attacked us – all part of the trap. My staff burns low and without it we have no protection against Araccneris's sorcery. Only your swords can win a way to freedom."

9: The Pool of Power

In the sleep chamber, Elak and Dalan were joined by Lycon, who for once could not sleep, and the three softly discussed plans with one another. Lycon was for an immediate break out, but Dalan warned that the place was very heavily guarded, and attempting to cut a way out through the city would be suicide.

"If we feign relaxation and compliance," said the Druid, "we may gain an advantage and strike when least expected."

It was the best they could come up with. Elak personally visited each of his warriors and explained the situation, making them ready. The company then spent a restless few hours, awaiting the dawn. Shortly after daylight washed the chamber from above, Kai-Quetzar arrived, and his slaves provided another light meal. After this he invited his guests to come before the queen once more. In her vast chamber, she sat astride the throne, still veiled, gazing at Elak and his men innocently, as though the horrific events of the night had been no more than the young king's wild nightmares.

"I trust you are rested, King Elak" she said in that sibilant, alien voice.

"Thank you, yes. We all slept most comfortably."

The answer seemed to please her. "The way back to your world can be safely opened for you, and I am happy to facilitate your return."

"We are indebted," said Elak.

"It is my pleasure, although there is one small gift I would be glad to accept from you, if you would agree."

Elak smiled, though he sensed this would be something far more sinister than the queen's gentle voice implied.

"That staff," she said, indicating Dalan's rod of power. "It fascinates me. Tell me of its history."

Dalan bowed. "This, o queen, is part of an ancient tree, fashioned from a branch cut from it in the first days of men, when sorcerers began to learn the secrets of the earth. When the cult of the Druids formed, such staffs were taken and used to band together the spells and the charms, and later the deeper powers. There are many legends about the staffs, some fanciful, others rooted in the truth. This staff, it is said, was once soaked in the blood of elementals, creatures of earth, wind and fire. It is bound to me, its well-spring of blood attuned to my own."

"And you alone can wield it?"

"In safety, yes. Others have tried to utilize it, but either it remains as lifeless as any normal branch, or, well, it can be dangerous, o queen."

"I am not without power myself," she replied. "Perhaps I could hold it and feel the rare beauty of its essence. I am a creature of the elements, human, but earth, sea, sky and fire are certainly in my veins."

Dalan stiffened. If he refused this request, the ranks of the winged men were all too close and were ready to enforce the queen's wishes. Elak had told his men to be ready at a word to draw swords and fight. For long moments the Druid stood motionlessly. Then he stepped forward and climbed the first few steps to the queen's seat. Guards pressed closer on either side of him, swords gleaming, but Dalan bowed and held out the staff. The queen took it in both hands.

"Yes," she said, her eyes reflecting light from the swords. "I feel its intensity. It is a marvel." She waved her men back and directed the staff at the low-walled pool in the centre of the chamber. "There is molten power there," she said. "Since I saw it I have thought it would be a joyous thing to summon and control."

Dalan and the Atlanteans had also stepped well aside. Elak spoke softly into the Druid's ear. "I trust the staff is impotent. You said its power had waned."

Dalan nodded. "She may feel it, but it will not ignite, even for me."

Without warning, the queen stood up and called out, as if summoning invisible powers, charging the staff to obey her commands. She directed its point at the pool and although no light sprang from it, the pool began to boil as if intense heat were being applied to it. Its surface heaved and steam rose from it in brownish clouds so the winged men near to it shifted well back. Light appeared below the surface, deep crimson and gold. Araccneris tried to pull back her arm, but she was held rigid as whatever force was in the pool reached out and snared the staff. The process of the delivery of power was being reversed.

"The staff is empty," said Dalan. "She sought to use its power to control the forces in the pool, but they are rising and will fill the staff."

Elak watched in fresh horror as the queen shook, her hands locked on the staff, though she tried to discard it. Power surged into it and it glowed like molten gold, the arms of the queen lit by a blinding light. Several of her guards realized she was in peril and rushed forward, using their blades in an attempt to sever the lines of energy as if they were thick ropes. But it was to no avail: the guards shook uncontrollably and to the king's utter horror they burst like ripe fruit. He and his Atlanteans moved further away from the chaos, swords drawn, although the winged men were too focused on the monstrous heaving of the pool – globules of heated lava were vomited forth, spreading quickly across the floor of the chamber.

Dalan suddenly rushed forward and up the steps. He grasped the staff and yanked it free of the queen's grasp and she toppled sideways, screaming as the fires licked hungrily at her silks. Molten arms from the pool groped for her and in a sudden explosion of light, everything became obscured. Dalan felt himself blasted backwards, striking the stone floor, the breath driven from his body.

10: The Face of the God

Elak dragged Dalan to his feet and his men rallied around. Chaos had broken out around the throne and for now the winged men were desperate to aid their fallen queen. Kai-Quetzar was trying to get her to her feet, but she was bathed in brilliant light, as if its fire would engulf her. Elak called to his men to cut through the remaining winged men and make for the doors. Their swords carved a path through the confused opposition, killing them with fierce abandon, releasing the bottled tension of the last few hours. Around the walls of the chamber, where the many servants stood like empty statues, more mayhem broke loose. The slaves appeared to be waking from a deep sleep, shaking themselves. Whatever powers the queen had used to shackle them were being dissolved in the fury of light.

Dalan felt the power surging in his staff. It was something new, possibly very dangerous, but its brilliant glow was anathema to the winged men, who tumbled aside in their haste to avoid its touch. A path to the doors was quickly opened enabling Elak and the company to reach them quickly. Behind them there were more explosions as energy burst up from the pool, a miniature volcano of golden lava.

Kai-Quetzar screamed in fury and made to rise into the air, but a hot blast from below him caught his wings and they were aflame in seconds, engulfing the warrior. Others fared no better and fire began to rage among them. The slaves were now awake and although unarmed, tore into the winged men like animals released from cages, their ferocity fuelled by long imprisonment. Elak broke out into the daylight, to see further chaos in the square and narrow streets beyond. It appeared that every slave in the city had joined in the rebellion.

Dalan led the way forward. "We must get to the river and find a ship."

Elak looked his last on the great domed building. Light speared upwards through it, almost too dazzling to see. But beyond it a huge shape had taken form in the swirling clouds, a hideous face that Elak recognized. It was Xeraph-Hizer, the Leviathan Lord, whom the winged people of Utterzanek worshiped. For a moment Elak thought the monstrous shape would rush forward like a storm and envelop him and his fleeing companions, but realized it was an image, a projection of the sea god's power. Its frustration boiled from it like waves of heat.

"We'll face that creature another day," Elak told Lycon. "Can you feel its mad desire to be avenged?"

Lycon growled an answer. Then they turned and went into the narrow street. It had become easier to escape now, with the people of the city either locked in individual battles, or crammed into the palace, sucked into the absolute carnage that ensued therein.

At the quay, the Atlanteans took possession of a fleet ship, crewed now by slaves who were freed of their drugged existence, men and women who also sought freedom beyond these lands. Dalan used his staff and its new power to infuse the waters of the river with churning power and the ship moved through them as if blown by a following storm wind. They were soon well away from Utterzanek, where vast black clouds had assembled over it, sculpted into yet another bizarre form of the Leviathan Lord. A wind roared out from them, bolts of lightning crackling around the ship, but nothing slowed it.

They reached the place where they had originally boarded the ship and alighted. In the deep undergrowth and sprawling jungles, massed creatures were about to surge forward in one last effort to drag the company into final conflict and almost certain death. As the hordes readied, a distant explosion rocked the land, Utterzanek being blown skyward as black power clashed with white. A huge cloud appeared on the horizon, rushing forward like the mightiest tide imaginable.

"We must leave this world!" shouted Dalan above the growing din. The explosion had rendered the massed crustaceans insensible. They collapsed, or slithered back into the undergrowth, their life powers sucked out of them.

At the rock wall, Dalan used the staff to summon up the gate. Mercifully it opened. The entire company, including the huge army of former slaves, poured through it. Behind them the landscape began to shake and break up as the first rolling clouds of destruction boiled forward. The gate closed like a massive stone door, and something thundered up against it.

In the tunnel, Elak stood on a tall rock and addressed the assembled company. "Those of you who were enslaved by Araccneris are now free. There will be a life for you in Cyrena, to which we are bound. Will you serve me, its king?"

There came a unified shout of acceptance.

"Then we climb back to the light." Elak dropped down beside Dalan, whose staff no longer glowed. The Druid looked exhausted, his face drained of colour, his body slumped. "And you, Dalan. Are you well?"

"The power the staff absorbed is not like that it formerly housed. I can control it, but at a price. I think we must take it back to Cyrena and entomb it. There are other staffs. The days are coming when clean steel will do the work of the sorcerers of old."

Epilogue

As the company wound its way upwards along the narrow, spiralling path inside the deep well, it could hear the sounds of raging waters far below in the darkness. The walls shook as water swirled and rose, bringing with them a curious light, the last energies, perhaps, of the fallen city of Utterzanek. It became a frantic race to get back to the surface as the sounds grew in volume and the waters rose rapidly.

Elak led the way back into the tower, he and Lycon urging warriors and former slaves alike through its circular shape to the outer doors, guarding their retreat, prepared to face anything that rose with the waters. In their weird lights, shapes swam, circling like finned predators, a last desperate attempt by the dark queen to claw back what had been lost. Dalan used his revived staff to shift aside the debris of the shattered door out on to the high wall and once he stepped out, he held it aloft. What remained of the shifting crimson mist had dissipated, as though it had lost its potency when the city fell. The Druid quickly waved the company outside and each one of its number sucked in the clean air in deep relief.

Elak was the last to emerge, just as the rising waters spewed over the lip of the circular well. Dalan was quick to rush forward, and with the staff he directed power at the waters. They roared upwards in a wide column, its light grey and mottled like the flesh of a leviathan, towering in the sky for long moments. The shapes within it seemed like creatures encased in ice or semi-transparent stone, their wide mouths gaping but rigid.

The company moved quickly along the wall until, some distance from the tower, every face turned to look back. The evil column crackled like a live thing and then, with no warning, collapsed in on itself and thundered back down into the tower, whose stones shook but remained intact. When the last of the column had disappeared, a pale yellow light seeped upward, a beacon, a new warning to ships passing around the Cape of Blood.

A shout from further along the wall drew Elak's attention and moments later he was reunited with Balazaar, the *Windrider's* captain.

"We thought we had lost you all!" he cried, setting formality aside and clapping the young king on the shoulder.

"I am so relieved to see you," Elak laughed, hugging the burly sailor. "What of the ships?"

"All made good, sire. When you disappeared into the cliffs, the storm abated and we've not been assailed since. The gods answered our prayers for your safety."

"We've a few more people to crew the ships. We'll give them a new life in Cyrena."

Balazaar frowned for a moment, but then started issuing instructions.

Lycon stood beside the king and smiled wearily. "Did I dream that, Elak? Was it something the Leviathan Lord sent to bemuse us all? It was an impracticable place in many ways."

"I think it was real enough."

"Strange that, for all the sustenance we took, there was no wine. Could such a place really exist?"

Elak laughed. "Well, you shall have your fill of it when

we get home. I will give you the keys to the royal cellars. You've earned that much."

Lycon joined him in his amusement, but he could see that something yet troubled his friend.

Elak said no more, but looked back at the glowing tower. Somewhere behind it, far down in the murky deeps of the eastern ocean, Xeraph-Hizer stirred, a monstrous power that yet had to be reckoned with.

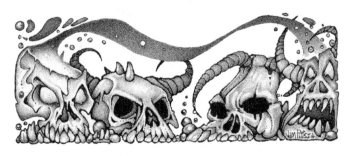

A DREAM OF LOST VALUSIA

Atlantis has a history that reaches back into the misty haze of time, epochs long since forgotten by men, knowledge of them restricted to legends or dusty grimoires locked away in the sacred vaults of libraries visited by few but the hardiest of scholars.

Ah, but what greater tales and secrets are hidden therein than those of once mighty Valusia, whose glories, it is said, were unrivalled and which may never be equalled. On his voyage home to Epharra, Elak was to face his sternest challenge when he had come closest to his capital.

- Helvas Ravanniol
Annals of the Third Atlantean Empire

*

1: Creatures of the Sea Storm

"We're veering well off course," said Dalan, standing beside the tall warrior at the ship's rail. "Something is pulling us north and east, well away from the coast. We should have been in sight of Cyrena's headlands by now."

"Is there a storm brewing?" said Elak, the young king, his keen eyes scanning the horizons. "The air seems calm

164

enough." Clouds drifted over the gently heaving ocean, but there was nothing in them to suggest a break in the weather for the worse.

Dalan scowled, and although he rarely smiled, Elak sensed there was more to his unease than he let on. The Druid's supernatural senses had forewarned the crew of *Windrider* more than once on this return journey from the far southern shores of the Atlantean continent. Not so many days before Elak and his sailors had averted disaster rounding the notorious Cape of Blood, encountering demonic forces that had almost destroyed them all. He'd hoped their tribulations lay behind them on their run back to Cyrena's capital, Epharra. Now Elak was not so sure.

"I cannot bring us about," said Dalan. "The currents of the ocean and its strange tides are too much for my powers. And there is something else, down in those vast depths, something that disturbs me." Elak thought of the creatures and entities that he and his crew had fought on the long voyage back from the city of Zangarza. Monstrous demi-gods, spawn of other worlds, and servants of old deities from beyond the dimensions of earthly time and space. Perhaps whatever drove these horrors, if such an omniscient power existed, may yet unleash its frustration and fury on the young king. Did it see his ascendancy to the Atlantean crown as a danger to its existence?

"Darkness yet seeks to draw us in," said Dalan. "We must prepare to defend ourselves."

He had hardly finished speaking when the lookout shouted from overhead. A sudden gust of wind swept his words away, but Elak and Dalan understood the shout as a cry of alarm. Dalan leaned out over the rail and studied the racing rise and fall of the waves as they grew increasingly powerful, lifting and dropping the ship more erratically by the minute. Elak's concern about a storm was even more well founded, it seemed. Dalan pointed.

"There!" he cried above another swirling gust of wind.

Elak craned his neck and thought he discerned something in the waves, a number of darting shapes, rising and falling like dolphins at play. Though these were no dolphins. They had faces, blurred in the foam and spray, semi-human faces.

"Water demons!" Dalan gasped.

Another man had come to the prow to stand beside them. It was Lycon, the king's stocky protector, his face clouded with deep unease. He drew his blade, glaring over the ship's dipping side. "They're all around us," he said. "Circling like underwater vultures."

Elak turned to the Druid. "What are they? Who has sent them? Could they be minions of Xeraph-Hizer?" he added, referring to the monstrous creature of the ocean deeps they'd thwarted at the Cape of Blood.

"I have not seen their like before," said Dalan. "Though there have been many sightings and legends of similar creatures. Some call them the ghosts of long sunken cities, or sailors drowned by the wild elements of the northern currents." He raised his staff – its tip glowed brilliantly before projecting a tightly focused lance of light out into the turgid seas. The circling creatures veered from the intense white glow, which revealed their astonishing numbers. They had formed a closely linked living shoal, surrounding the ship, beyond the range of arrows or javelins.

Balazaar, captain of the *Windrider*, joined the group. "Our lookout reports that we are completely surrounded by these horrors," he said. "We are at the centre of a whirlpool, and it's increasing in size."

Lycon growled with anger. "I can feel the ship turning steadily into its embrace! The creatures are churning the seas with their dark powers."

"Aye," said Balazaar, mirroring the growing fear of the others. "The crew are fighting hard against them, but are making no headway. See! There is a low point in the centre of the vortex and we are veering towards it."

"And the fleet?" said Elak. "I cannot see any of our other ships."

"We've been cut off from them," said Balazaar. "I fear whatever devils are at work here have singled us out. If this whirlpool deepens and grows even more powerful, we'll be sucked down into the ocean's depths."

"Use all the oars!" shouted Elak above the growing din. "Fight the pull! Dalan, can you conjure a wind to counter the waters?"

The Druid cursed and shook his head. "A greater force is at work here." Nevertheless, he raised his staff higher, calling out in a strange language that Elak and his companions had heard whenever Dalan invoked the extraordinary power of the staff, its magic from a remote, forgotten age. This time when light speared out at the tossing waves, the sea burst upwards in sprays of foam, as though shuddering against a line of reefs. Those uncanny, man-faced dolphins were tossed to and from among the flume like so many chunks of flotsam, but the turbulent swirl was not broken.

Balazaar had his oarsmen bent double with efforts to pull the *Windrider* from the centre of the whirlpool and by their superhuman efforts they reached its edge, where Elak saw the massed water beings swimming in a lightning blur along the crest of the swirling chaos. *Windrider* rose up, climbing a huge bank of water, and again Dalan flung bolts of light in an attempt to break through the encircling waters.

Yet it remained a hopeless task. The rowers struggled mightily but could not compete and the ship was drawn inexorably to the centre. Round and round the craft circled, and as it did so, the whirlpool opened its maw, its sides closing in, the circular well like a long gut running far down towards the invisible oceanic floor. Elak could only watch in impotent fury as the ship plunged into oblivion.

2: Into the Vortex

The roaring of the ocean grew almost deafening, and darkness welled up from below as the inner rim of the spinning water walls carried the *Windrider* swirling downwards. The waters resembled a huge column stretching towards distant daylight, filled with countless aquatic faces, quasi-human but contorted into bestial snarls, lamprey-like mouths gaping or snapping.

Elak and his companions drew back from the rail, though the creatures showed no sign of darting inwards and attacking. It was enough that they massed in the whirlpool's thundering sea.

"We'll be drowned!" shouted Lycon above the din, gripping his sword helplessly, frustrated at not having a physical enemy to assail.

"Whatever has brought us here," said Dalan, "has not done so to kill us, not in this vortex. We are being taken below for a reason."

"To be sacrificed, no doubt," retorted Lycon.

Elak laughed bitterly. "One thing is for sure, my friend – we're not being invited to a drinking festival!"

Darkness closed in overhead and the roar of the waters eased. The ship and its crew appeared to be encased in a bubble of air that preserved them from a watery doom. Under the hull, far below, the shadows were slowly dispersed by glittering emerald light.

"Which of the Nine Hells are we entering?" Lycon growled.

"There is no doubt that sorcery is at play," said Dalan.

"Terrible powers have been set loose." He used his staff's beacon-like light to probe the deeps, but as yet the ocean floor did not reveal itself. Giant shapes crossed below the ship as it twisted its way ever downwards, huge leviathans from a long-lost age of the world, denizens of the primeval oceans that seemed to be castaways in time. As the gloom thickened, the *Windrider's* swirling speed slowed, and its crew now massed around its rails, watching the deeps for any sign of the ocean bed. At last they had reached it and the ship settled, surprisingly gently, as if set in the layer of ooze by a god-like hand.

Elak looked up to see the waters closing in, sealing them into this weird underwater domain. And then, as though an invisible glass dome had been drawn over them, the sea pulled away like a receding tide. Lights flashed and throbbed, and the leering faces that had massed in the seas dissipated like ghosts. Slowly an intense silence gripped the sodden landscape that had been revealed. It was like no other that Elak or his companions had ever seen.

The seabed undulated, dipping and falling, rising into the distance. It was covered in high banks of coral and other more unusual growths, mostly green-hued or aquamarine, fronds of weed trailing in the air as if they yet danced in water. Dalan's staff provided immediate light, although the landscape was imbued with a bizarre illumination of its own, and by its eerie shades, shapes could be glimpsed, some small, some much larger, slithering or hopping away from the human intruders. The bed was primarily mud and ooze, though not deep, suggesting the ship had come to rest on an expanse of bedrock. Broken slabs led away from it like artificial paths in a zig-zag pattern.

Elak's company gathered around him, all of the men warily scanning the distance. They were the young king's most trusted warriors, sworn to serve him to the death if it came to it and more than once on this chaotic voyage they had proved their worth. Elak was about to comment, when a distant sound caught everyone's attention. It was a horn of some kind, possibly a sea conch, its one, long note rolling out mournfully over the broken plain.

"Something approaches," said Dalan, his mind attuned to the slightest intrusion in the atmosphere here.

The company formed a defensive wedge, backing on to the hull of the ship, every man armed. Lycon growled like an angry bear, eager to unleash his frustrations on something. A battle would be more than welcome. Elak gripped his arm, restraining his burly friend. Lycon could hardly suppress a grin: there had been a time when Elak would have been even more eager than him for conflict, and no one was more fearless and valorous in battle than the young king. But time was refining him, preparing him, if he survived, for a more subtle life.

From beyond the nearest ridge of undersea outcrops, a group of figures broke silently from the shadows. There were three of them, human in shape, wearing what first appeared to be long cloak-like garments, but as they drew near – apparently floating over the broken slabs – their upper garments could be seen to be thick masses of hair, or more accurately, weed. They were creatures of the sea, undoubtedly human to an extent, but with wide, rounded eyes and long arms with webbed fingers, possibly used for swimming. Indeed, the creatures gleamed as if they had stepped from water, probably being amphibious. They did not appear to be armed.

They came to within a dozen yards of the Atlanteans and hovered, their lower bodies hidden in more of the strange weed.

Dalan stepped forward, waiting. He felt a sudden buzzing inside his head, as if it had been entered, possibly probed. He gripped his staff more tightly.

There is no need to fear us, came a deep whisper in his mind. *We are alien to you, of course, and we sense your fear. But we mean you no harm.*

Dalan inclined his head in a gentle bow. "Who are you?" he said.

We are the last of those who ruled here. Our race is almost gone from this world. And this is our final retreat. We offer you a gift, a chance to survive the terror that comes.

3: The Palace of Wonders

Elak and the company followed the three strange shapes across the tumbled seabed, all of them alert and wary. Around them in the silence, small transparent organisms floated like snowflakes, singly or in clouds, hovering out of reach, as if drawn to them but too nervous to approach. Their bodies glowed, pulsing like organs, throwing an even more bizarre radiance over the underwater realm. Some distance from the *Windrider,* the three beings guiding them halted on a crest of bedrock, with a sweep of their hands indicating to Elak and his companions the dipping scene that was the grandeur below.

The young prince gasped as he studied the slope that fell away, a huge, curving dish-like depression. Its steep sides, seemingly sculpted out of the sea bottom by volcanic activity, were a giant undersea honeycomb, riddled with caves that gaped like vast windows. Deeper down in the dizzying chasm, partially obscured in shadows, there were unmistakable buildings, houses and larger structures that could only be a city, one that had once existed above the waves. Dalan lifted his staff and its now vivid light threw more areas of the city into perspective. Thick strands of weed partially covered many of the buildings and coral sculptures topped others, as if an aquatic god had lingered here, working his artistry. Shoals of multi-hued fish, drifted in and out of the buildings, although they swam in air, not water.

The whisper in Dalan's mind returned. *This is our last citadel.* The Druid imparted the words to Elak and the others. *Once it was a proud mistress of the northern shores of this realm, until at last the terrible magics of our enemies drove us into the deeps, where we have waited through the ages. We must hasten to the palace. Already the darkness gathers beyond our protective barriers.*

The words had hardly been uttered when Elak noticed movement outside the invisible force above them, where the blackness of the northern ocean's depths curdled, deep and infinite as the space between stars. Within it vast shapes shifted as if in preparation for an assault on the sanctuary, an unfurling of monstrous coils, about to wrap themselves around their victims, squeezing and pulping this eerie haven. However, the forces set in place by the inhabitants held and the party moved on into the first of the city streets. The walls loomed around it, huge fists of stone, many broken and collapsed, ruined beyond repair. Elak saw among them the shattered hulks of ships from the upper world that had come to grief here, wrecked and lost forever. He wondered what ghosts were trapped among their wooden bones.

The road into the city was partially choked with fallen masonry, once proud, soaring towers, architectural marvels to rival the glories of today's Atlantis, but long since overgrown. Here the sea life would inevitably drag the last of the edifices down and smooth them over, returning the remnants of human occupation to the levelled seabed, all trace of them obliterated, all memory of them dissipated. Elak felt a pang of melancholy as it occurred to him that his own world and its splendid cities would doubtless slide down the same road to oblivion eventually. He shook himself, annoyed at such grim thoughts.

At last they came to a wider area, possibly what had been a plaza. Its floor was sunken in places, its great slabs broken and jutting, so the party had to pick its way carefully through them until it reached a wide, low building, topped with a smooth dome. This gleamed as though sunlight reached down from the distant sky, and nothing grew upon it, its surface possessing a mystic quality that preserved it from the intrusion of aquatic life.

Elak and Lycon exchanged a knowing glance, and each murmured the word, sorcery, both keenly aware that it must lay behind this and all the other marvels they had seen in this sunken realm.

Shadows yet masked the face of the leader of the three guides, though his eyes gleamed therein. *Our palace, where our ruler sits in waiting.*

Dalan paused, taking a final look around him at the twisted buildings, with their clustered towers and minarets, their trailing growths and black, featureless windows. He nodded to Elak and the company climbed the wide steps. Crabs and other small creatures scuttled aside at their passing until they reached the columns on either side of the tall portal into the palace. The Atlanteans were well armed and made no attempt to sheath or hide their weapons, but their guides simply drifted on through the doorway into the interior.

Within, an amazing sight greeted Elak and his companions. The palace had somehow been preserved in all its splendour. The mosaic floor, depicting wonderful scenes of the city as it must once have been, stretched across the open area for many yards, and golden statues lined the walls, warriors and beasts intermingled, the workmanship of the artisans dazzling to the eye. On the walls themselves, rich tapestries and murals were spread like vast windows on a world of the past, scenes of battling armies, fiery chariots racing across sunlit skies. Where the ocean had been painted, the waters teemed with colour and life, strange beings rising up from waves that could almost have been real, so brilliantly had they been depicted.

There were great golden bowls, where hot coals burned, the scent of incense strong, wisps of smoke curling up into the vaulted dome like phantoms. Yet in all this sumptuous majesty, no one stirred. There were no soldiers, not even guards, no priests, no populace of any kind. It was though everyone had abruptly abandoned this wondrous place in a moment. Lycon was about to comment on this when something moved in the shadows to one side of the great chamber.

Slowly a new form materialized, a huge figure, very broad, with a massive head, wreathed in thick tangles of jet black hair. The man had no neck, his muscular girth that of three men, garbed in a white robe, woven with golden sigils. His eyes were sunken in that immense face, and they gazed upon the visitors eagerly, though the man's expression was emotionless, the edges of the man's mouth turned down, almost in a grimace, perhaps of some inner pain.

"You are welcome, Prince of Atlantis, who will be king hereafter. I am Amun Thuul, last sorcerer-king of Valusia. I have been waiting for you. You are the final hope of the world we know."

4: The Sorcerer-King Speaks

Amun Thuul moved from the shadows beneath the thick pillars of the palace as softly as a ghost, his long robe trailing behind him, hiding his vast lower body and legs, so that he seemed to glide, hardly disturbing the dust in his abandoned surroundings. There was a raised, wide throne close by and he sat upon it, his huge jaw resting on his chest as he looked down on the Atlanteans, a deep sadness etched on his features.

Elak bowed. "Well met, o king, although the circumstances are strange indeed. Was it your sorcery that brought us here?"

"What is left of it, yes. Once my people had immense power. I will show some of its past glories to you. Today that wondrous nation is gone, sucked into the ocean deeps, and all that is left of that power resides in me, waning with each passing moment." He raised a wide sleeve and a huge hand slid from within and indicated the nearest wall, on which one of the immense tapestries hung. Strangely it was immaculate, free of the dust of time, its colours vivid, its thick material perfectly preserved.

"Behold!" said Amun Thuul. "The wondrous golden city, where the greatest of Valusian kings ruled his empire under his tiger banner. From here his royal Slayers went forth and subjugated the lands around them, and even our fiercest rivals lived in awe of Valusian power!"

Elak and his companions studied the tapestry and its fabulous detail, which depicted a magnificent city, even more splendid and spectacular than Epharra. Its towers rose impossibly high, as if they could reach the very stars, its roofs gleamed with gold and precious stones, its temples and palaces spoke of incomparable power and beauty. Fabulous statues rose up in gigantic form, warriors, gods and creatures from the long-lost legends of the ages.

Dalan spoke softly to Elak. "This is a city from time on the very edge of living memory. A time of dreams, of forgotten mysteries."

"Atlantis was a majestic empire long before your own small continent rose to power," said Amun Thuul, as though he had heard Dalan's comment. "Yet man is proud and arrogant, and the gods are unforgiving, as you shall see."

The sorcerer-king waved his arm and as the Atlanteans watched the tapestry, it rippled, as though either disturbed by a strong breeze, or it had shifted like the surface of a lake, trembling so that crystal clear sounds could be heard from the myriad streets of the city, both near and far. Beyond its walls, the sea gleamed, sparkling and rising up. Elak could hear the sound of many voices, and beyond the city there was a roar, a surging sound, waves pounding. His men gasped in unison as the tapestry became a live window on the past, where momentous events were unfolding.

"In the eastern ocean, between the continent of Thuria and the Lemurian Islands, the terrible gods of the ocean, monstrous beings that had slept in their deep beds for millennia, woke and stretched their powers, powers that eclipsed those of man as man's eclipsed that of the lesser creatures of the world. The Old Powers fought each other, vying for dominion, and in their colossal struggles, the ocean boiled." Amun Thuul again pointed to the tapestry and beyond the city, which now seethed with thousands of citizens. Huge waves rose up, blotting out the sky, streamers of white foam flying from their crests like supernatural armies.

Elak and his companions watched in horror as the first wave exploded and cascaded over the great buildings of the city. Palaces and temples erupted, smitten by the almighty power of the wave and countless citizens were snatched up and swept away like so many ants in a flood. The noise had become deafening, the walls of Amun Thuul's palace echoing to that shuddering thunder. Another colossal wave rose and fell, crashing down upon the city, flooding every street, every passage, so that Elak and the others drew back, afraid that they, too, would be inundated.

"This was the Cataclysm," said Thuul, his deep voice rising above the boom of destruction. Yet the catastrophe was contained within the tapestry, where the picture soon changed, the water rising ever upwards, dragging down even the loftiest of the towers, levelling every last stone of the capital. "The whole of the Lemurian Islands in the east sank below the waves. Thuria tilted like an immense slab, Grondar in its east plunged into the deeps, lost like Lemuria. Valusia, too, was sucked below, as you can see. A few islands remained. And mighty Atlantis, the forerunner of your own, smaller continent, was inundated, reduced to a crippled, broken parody of its former glory. Far to the western ocean, the Pictish Isles were swamped, but not destroyed. The waters heaved them up and in time their people thrived anew.

"And as time slowly and inexorably re-shaped the world, Atlantis grew again, to what is has become today. Our kingdom, though, was lost. All that remained of our once mighty nation was a small brotherhood of sorcerers, barely able to sustain the survivors here in this forgotten aquatic realm. Now not one of my people remains, and what you see here are merely ghosts, pale shades of what they once were. There remains but a handful of my people, and we are changed, ghosts of what we were."

Dalan's face was grim, as though what he had witnessed on the tapestry had long since been a vision from his own personal nightmares. "Tell me, what of the gods that caused the Cataclysm?"

Amun Thuul's face was equally as distraught as Dalan's. "Their efforts cost them dear, and some were destroyed in the culmination of their undersea war. Time means nothing to them. They sleep for millennia, but it is no more than that – sleep, a pause between the renewed fury of their ambitions. And soon they will awaken once more.

Your Atlantis, and all its present world, will face their cosmic powers. They will not rest until they have dragged you all beneath the waves!"

5: Sorcery from Beyond Time

Amun Thuul sat back on his throne, arms resting on its sides, his manner one of deep sadness. The great mural was still once more, and its original picture had changed. Now it gave a view of unbroken ocean, waves frozen in movement across the horizon, static foam, dips and swells, but nothing floating there to suggest that a once proud city had been engulfed by the deluge, and no passing ships to observe the flood, or survive it.

"All that is left of this city's sorcery rests within me," said Amun Thuul. "Even the retainers I sent to fetch you were projections of my power. I am alone, but what I have is yours."

Dalan turned from the disturbing seascape. "We have faced the terrors of the deeps already. The sea god, Xeraph-Hizer, the Leviathan Lord, rose up and sought to destroy the southern kingdom of Zangarza. We prevailed. And we thwarted the ambitions of Araccneris, the evil queen of the undersea world, his servant."

"I know of these things. As I know of Xeraph-Hizer's fury. Even now he gathers a new army to send out against Atlantis and your lands of Cyrena. Epharra will suffer the watery fate that drowned my world unless you drive the horrors from the ocean back into oblivion. I have a gift that will help you, for I would see these evil gods wiped from this world, if it can be done."

Dalan felt the marbled floor beneath him shudder like the flank of an immense beast and he stepped back, lifting his staff. Its globular end began to glow as if in response to something within the ground as two slabs slid aside. From the revealed darkness, a stone menhir rose up like a stripped tree trunk, its surface completely covered in pictographic drawings, etched into the stone in what seemed to be a frenzied effort by whoever had sculpted it. The sigils and strange designs began to glow, pulsing, and Dalan could feel his staff humming in harmony with the risen stone. Presently light crackled between the two and Dalan jolted as fresh energies surged down his staff into his body.

The top of the stone, some eight feet from the ground, opened up like a flower, revealing a large jewel, a ruby the size of a watermelon, glowing a deep crimson, which also pulsed, like a living organ. More power swirled within its dazzling depths, a livid and disturbing essence, almost a live thing.

"All that I am, and all that I carry within me, the last magic of this city, is contained within that jewel," said Amun Thuul. "It is my heart. You must take it, Druid. Let your staff absorb it. When you have done that, you must hasten to the royal armoury. Elak and the warriors must arm themselves and each sword must be blessed with the ancient powers. Such weapons will give you all hope to defy the dark armies of Xeraph-Hizer and his dreadful brotherhood."

Dalan hesitated briefly, although he sensed through the transferred powers already running through his veins that Amun Thuul could be trusted. The sorcerer-king's fervid hatred of the dark ocean gods was a palpable thing, livid as pain. The Druid stepped forward and lifted his staff again, touching it to the surface of the crimson jewel. At once it crackled and blazed with bright light.

Elak gasped as Dalan was bathed in crimson, the king momentarily afraid that his companion was in grave danger of his life, but Dalan's face was resolved, his features curved into a mask of determination as he rode the storm of power.

On the great throne, the figure of Amun Thuul shuddered, the huge head flung back as the sorcerer-king gave vent to a loud shout, a cry of either exultation or agony. Then the shape slumped down.

Elak ran to him, but already the unleashed power of the stone had taken its frightful course. Not only was Amun Thuul beyond aid, but his corporeal form was shrinking, rapidly mummifying, as if its defiance of the ages was not only over but reversed. Soon the robe flattened out, covering little more than shrunken bones, and the great head had become a skull, crumbling as Elak watched in horror.

Dalan staggered back, breaking the contact with the crimson stone, which continued to glow, but with gradual declining energy. The Druid turned to Lycon. "Take the jewel. We must carry it with us and keep it safe."

Lycon sheathed his sword and clambered up the side of the menhir, using the chiselled glyphs to get footholds. Above him the jewel had contracted, now no bigger than an orange, its bright colour dimming. Lycon reached out cautiously and touched the jewel but felt only a subtle warmth. He snatched it up and slipped it inside his tunic, returning to Dalan's side. Elak also joined them.

"The armoury," said the king. "Where is it?"

Dalan seemed to use some sixth sense, like a hound searching for its prey. He pointed to one of the doorways out of the palace. "There," he said. "Follow the corridors."

The company did so, but as the Atlanteans made their way down a long, high passageway, lit by concealed torches, they could hear distant sounds, a roaring, like the renewed fury of the ocean, deep currents and tides pummelling the walls of this retreat, striving to shatter whatever magics Amun Thuul had set in place to preserve it. Time was running out quickly.

6: Crimson Steel

They reached an intersection, where several tunnels ran off from a circular chamber with a low ceiling, and for a moment the Atlanteans were nonplussed, unsure which of the corridors to take. As they stood close together, weapons drawn in expectation of conflict, they heard what sounded like the susurration of the tide, as if it were coming along the tunnels from the darkness beyond, a cold surf pushing forward to engulf them. If they were caught by it, they would be drowned like rats.

"There!" cried Elak, pointing with his rapier to one of the tunnels. Further down it shapes were coalescing like pale blue mist, vague and blurred but human-like, hunched warriors, distorted in the shifting glow. A pack of them were coming, the source of the tide-like sounds.

"We're trapped!" Elak said above the murmuring. "We stand and fight here."

Lycon, who had retained the globe of power, shook his head. "No." He pointed to one of the tunnels. "I can feel the globe being drawn that way – it leads to the armoury. It is unrestricted."

"Quickly," urged Dalan, and at once the company ran for the tunnel indicated by Lycon and moved down it swiftly. Behind them they heard the surge of movement as the other tunnels disgorged a horde of wraith-like beings, and the air became bitterly cold, as though the pursuers breathed clouds of misting ice. The tunnel ahead twisted this way and that until it eventually disgorged the Atlanteans into another tall chamber. Here there were many weapons, swords hung singly on the walls, javelins stacked in clusters, and there were shields, axes and maces, as well as other ancient Valusian weapons that Elak was not familiar with.

The last of the warriors turned to face the assault from

behind them as the blue tinted mist rolled forward. They slashed at the ghost-shapes with their blades, and for a while held them at bay, but it was already obvious that their Atlantean steel would have no physical effect on this enemy. One of the warriors was dragged into the winter-cold embrace of a wraith and his screams of agony echoed loudly round the chamber as his life was sucked from him.

"Pick a weapon from these!" Dalan shouted, and at once the Atlanteans complied. Elak took a long, slim blade, seemingly cast in silver, or an alloy containing it, on which numerous runes had been stamped. Lycon grabbed a long-handled axe, and it gleamed in the torchlight. Within moments everyone had taken a Valusian blade.

"Lycon – use the globe!" shouted Dalan as the wraith army shifted forward inexorably and another two Atlanteans went down in their death agonies.

Lycon held up the crimson globe and again it throbbed with power, an intense glow that bathed all of the warriors in its enigmatic light. At once the wraiths drew back. Crimson rays of light coruscated, darting outwards and striking each and every weapon the Atlanteans had chosen, until all of them also glowed a deep crimson, as though afire.

Elak uttered a war cry, rushed forward and struck the ranks of the churning wraiths. The first of them burst like spume on coastal rocks, exploding and falling back. The creatures were no match for the potent sorcery and it was not long before the Atlanteans were pressing the enemy back down the tunnel, carving them apart easily, the crimson light from their weapons like molten fire searing dried leaves. Elak felt a unique energy, as if he had tapped into something far beyond normal human endeavours. He laughed as he fought, an almost insane cry, and beside him Lycon smote mightily with the axe. In time it was the Druid who called a halt.

"Enough!" he roared above the savage cries of the

warriors, and as one they ceased. The wraith-things were scattered, dissolving where they had fallen, like fluid running back into the drains or bedrock. Soon the air was still, as if the beings had never materialized at all. Lycon had again wrapped the globe inside his tunic, but the swords and weapons of the Atlanteans yet glowed crimson, their steel and silver warm, making them like living things.

"The weapons of the royal Slayers, the elite guards of the ancient kings," said Dalan, as if he had peered back down the vistas of history, to the time before the great deluge. "These are Amun Thuul's gift, that will aid us in the coming onslaught from the sea gods."

"What now?" said Elak.

"We must get back to the ship and return to the surface. Put our trust in Amun Thuul. The sorcery of his city will protect us," said the Druid.

Elak nodded and at once led the company back along the tunnel. They went warily, but there were no further signs of an assault from the creatures they had fought in the armoury. The way through the palace was uncluttered and at its portal only the empty central square of the city remained to be crossed, and the streets beyond. They retraced their steps of earlier and came to the muddy sea bottom beyond the last of the crumbling edifices.

Elak led the way across the slick surface, but it did not hinder them. Some distance across the sea bottom, close to the rising sides of the dish-like depression, they halted briefly to look back for the final time at the forgotten bones of the last Valusian city. *Is this the fate of all great nations?* Elak asked himself. *Do all mighty empires crumble and fall? And is this to be the fate of my Atlantis, though I make of her a queen among empires, mistress of the world?*

There was no further time for reflection, for the sea bottom between the Atlanteans and the ruins was churning, in many places bursting as new shapes took form, creatures seemingly moulded from the mud and debris, twisted representations of men, lurching to stunted feet, staggering forward in a fresh wave of menace. A vast number of these horrific sea-things surged like a new tide, rough claws outstretched as Elak and his companions prepared to test their sorcerous blades anew.

7: Up from the Deeps

The first wave of the writhing mud beings crashed against the Atlantean warriors, whose weapons burned with renewed crimson light, searing their opponents, turning them to liquid mud where they struck. It was effective but exhausting work, like trying to hold back the sea itself. Lycon swung about him, releasing his anger and frustration in a roaring, howling fury, while Dalan used his staff to focus several beams of crimson light that sliced into the massed assailants, ripping them apart in a welter of mud and muck from the sea bottom. Elak shouted as he fought, calling out the names of his men who had already fallen, for he hated losing a single man, and on this seemingly cursed voyage he had lost too many.

So fierce was the warriors' defence that the mud creatures drew back like an ebbing tide, subsiding until the ocean bed was still. Far away there came the roaring, whirling sounds of the sea, a thunderous, whirling sound, and through the blanketing darkness Elak could vaguely make out wild movement, as of great waves swirling, threatening to crush whatever powers held this underground haven intact and pour into it.

"Quickly – to the ship!" the king called, and his companions needed no second bidding. As one, they turned and made their way as speedily as they could over the treacherous terrain. Behind them they heard the renewed amassing of the mud creatures, who prepared to launch a second offensive, this time in greater numbers. Beyond the crest of the ridge, the *Windrider* was yet settled on the seabed, and Balazaar waved to the oncoming warriors. The captain and the men who had remained aboard with him lowered a wide plank from the ship's side, so that the returning company was able to get aboard swiftly. Dalan, Lycon and Elak insisted on being the last to embark, ahead of the oncoming mud army. The first of the creatures slithered up the plank, but Dalan's staff spat fire at them, dissolving them, and the plank was withdrawn. Within moments the entire hull of the ship was surrounded by a surge of the creatures, their arms clawing at the timbers, their empty faces staring upwards like souls lost in hell, soundless mouths agape in pain.

"Set the globe at the masthead," Dalan said to Lycon, and the burly warrior did so, swinging up the mast with a dexterity that belied his bulk, and Elak laughed.

Once the globe of power was in place, its eerie light spread out around the ship and immediately the massed creatures around it drew back yet again. Dalan struck at them with his staff, adding to their discomfort, and abruptly the *Windrider* gave a shudder, its deck rolling. For a moment Elak thought the ship was foundering in the cloying mud, in danger of veering over and being sucked down into it, damning the company to its fate here in the ocean deeps. But it righted itself, heaved again, like a great beast ripping free of the seabed. An abrupt wave crashed alongside, part of it sluicing a vast mass of mud creatures aside like ants being washed down a drain. The *Windrider* was caught by the wave and lifted.

The roar of the waters increased until it became almost deafening, and the ship swung around, once again caught in a vortex, although this time it began to rise. Elak and his men could see upward where the churning whirlpool's sides gleamed and where the massed faces of the creatures of the ocean packed together in a solid wall, their dreadful faces pressed up against an invisible barrier, threatening to rip it aside and allow the waters to crash together and flood downwards, taking the ship to its grave. However, the vivid crimson light from the globe strengthened and bathed the racing waters in a counterbalancing energy, searing the water beings, many of whom fell back in horror.

"We're rising to the surface!" shouted Balazaar above the snarling spray. Around and around the vortex the ship raced, and the men gripped its rails, hanging on grimly. Elak studied their faces, seeing the steely determination, the refusal to give way to the endless nightmares that had beset them on this voyage. Every one of them was worthy of commanding a company of warriors, and it may well be that once they had returned to Epharra, they would have to assume that role, given the threat of war Amun Thuul had spoken of. *With men such as these*, Elak thought with a grim smile, *the darkness that is coming will yet be subdued*. The fate that had befallen ancient Valusia would not overtake his new Atlantis.

Beside him, Dalan studied him quietly, putting a hand on the young king's shoulder. "The worst is yet to come," said the Druid, a strange sadness in his eyes.

"We shall prevail!" Elak cried, holding aloft his rapier. "Come, Lycon, grip the rail before you're flung overboard!"

Lycon spat, almost slipping to his knees. "I enjoy a voyage, Elak, but I really do want to get ashore and sleep for a week. I feel as if every bone in my body has turned to mud."

Elak laughed again, watching the foaming waters of the vortex, the ship rising closer and closer to daylight. "I'm surprised you're not used to the sensation, Lycon. I mean, a few bottles of wine –"

"The effects of imbibing a small keg of wine would be infinitely preferable to this madness!"

Dalan shook his head, but even he smiled.

A few days later the *Windrider* rounded the last of the headlands that enclosed the wide bay where the city of Epharra awaited the returning king and his exhausted company. They had ridden out the whirlpool and at last entered the calmer waters of Epharra's Bay of Gold. Several smaller craft came out from the city to meet them, and the rejoicing began as word went back to the capital that Elak had returned.

8: Tide of Dread

It was long before dawn when Elak rose from his sumptuous bed, stretched, and walked over to the high balcony. Drenched in vivid moonlight, he leaned on the external parapet, rubbed the sleep from his eyes and gazed out over the bay of his capital. He breathed in the cool night air, which after his long voyage back from the far south of Atlantis was as heady as any perfume. He caught the scent of night plants that wound their way up the high walls of his citadel and heard overhead the snap of an owl's wings as it began its dive down into the shadowed gardens, in search of a late meal. It was a blessed calm, for although Elak loved nothing better than the excitement of a sea quest and pitting his wits and sword skills against the denizens of his world, his bones yet ached from the trials of the long journey up from Zangarza. For once, he would enjoy a rest and time spent in the otherwise dull confines of government.

Of course, there still the tricky problem of negotiating a royal marriage, for the City Council had made the union their priority, determined to wed the young king to one of the city's breathless beauties. Elak had no preference and remained stubbornly determined not to accede to pressure until he was ready for such a life-changing event. His adventuring away had given him a chance to set such things aside, but he knew he would come under renewed pressure now, especially from Zerrahydris, the Prime Councillor. Elak had to remind himself that Zerrahydris meant well, and had been a loyal servant of the kingdom, and whose his dependability had been invaluable after the debacle in which Elak had won the throne.

Elak studied the Bay of Gold. It had always been a beautiful sight, with its calm waters and on which floated countless ships of all sizes and persuasions. Even as a young child he had loved playing along its quays, dragging his indulgent guardians down there, where he engaged with the captains and sailors, who in turn regaled him with tales of the oceans and the countless mysteries to be found beyond the land.

He was about to return to his bed, but something about the stillness of the bay this night tugged at him, a faint bell of warning. He craned his neck. The bay was for the most part hidden in shadows, but Elak could see mud flats exposed near the harbour walls. As he studied them, he realized they stretched some distance across the bay, so that the tide must be at an unusually low ebb. Now that he looked closer, he saw that many boats and larger ships were beached, laying to one side on the mud. In the remote distance, out at sea, he heard a strange roaring sound, as though a storm boiled far away on the horizon.

His blood curdled, as he thought of the horrors he had seen in the drowned ruins of the ancient city. That undersea realm almost seemed like a dream now, but he knew it was not, having brought back the crimson globe and the weapons of the royal Slayers of the prediluvian Atlantean world. As he listened, he also understood that the moonlight flashing out in the bay was reflected back not from the sea, but from even wider mud. The tide had drawn out – even beyond the Bay of Gold! How was this possible!

Elak went back inside and threw open the door to his chamber. Immediately several guards were before him, weapons drawn to defend their king. "Fetch Dalan the Druid, and wake Zerrahydris, immediately. Bring them to me."

In a matter of minutes the Druid had materialized, a thick cloak wrapped around him. Elak took him to the balcony and pointed to the bay. "This is not a common thing," Elak said.

Dalan's expression betrayed his horror. "By Ishtar, you are right, Elak! This is what Amun Thuul warned us of. The creatures of the great deeps are at work."

Light footsteps behind them presaged the coming of the Prime Councillor, who rubbed sleep from his eyes and tried not to appear irritable at such an early summons. "What is amiss?"

Elak pointed. "We must prepare ourselves."

Zerrahydris stared out at the darkness until eventually he realized the truth. The Bay of Gold had emptied. "By the gods, this is unprecedented!" he gasped. "Where is the sea?"

"Gathering itself," said Dalan. "And when it returns, it will be no ordinary tide, nor slow. The city is in great danger."

Elak felt a wash of horror. He recalled all too vividly the living mural he had seen in the drowned palace below the ocean, the city in time depicted thereon and the terrible force of the unleashed ocean, the deluge and the ultimate immolation.

"The Cataclysm," said Dalan, as if seeing the same terrifying vision, the destruction of the city and almost the whole of Atlantean civilization.

"But that was millennia ago," said Zerrahydris.

"The evil gods that caused it have woken. What is coming to Epharra, and perhaps to all of today's Atlantis, is a second Cataclysm."

The Councillor would have dismissed Dalan's words as a fantasy, an exaggeration, but something about the manner of the Druid, and indeed of the young king, brought him sharply alert. "What must be done?"

"The entire populace must take to the hills above the city, to the highest points," said Dalan and Elak nodded. "And we must gather the warriors, all those from the voyage who carry the weapons we brought. We must form a barrier against what comes and link all the weapons. Elak – wake Lycon. Let him bear the globe once more. I will stand with him at the apex of our defence. There may not be much time. The waves will be upon us soon after dawn."

9: The Coming of the Death Tide

It was no easy matter to organize the people of Epharra and send them from the city, every man, woman and child. In the end it was panic and the sight of the waterless harbour that spurred them to leave their homes, mighty or humble, taking with them what few possessions they could carry, some in hand carts, mostly simply on foot. The hills under which most of Epharra had been built were thronging shortly before the first rays of dawn sunlight rose over the eastern cliffs. To the north, the skies remained dark, the clouds thick and thunderous, the noise of the coming storm already a loud promise of disaster. Boiling banks of sea fog churned ever closer to the city and the dawn light hardly registered in the gloom. Lightning flickered across the heavens and through the fog, crackling and fizzing as though unleashed through the direst sorcery.

Elak had deployed his defenders around the harbour and on the various small islands and islets at the ends of the bay, warriors who carried the weapons taken from the drowned city, so that they formed a crescent that could receive the incoming tide when its waves burst upon them. He, Dalan and Lycon had climbed the winding stairs up into the central lighthouse at the centre of the harbour, and Lycon set the gleaming crimson jewel at the apex of the building. It pulsed softly, like a slow beating heart, seemingly sensitive to the powers that were coalescing far out beyond the Bay of Gold.

Dalan held aloft his staff and Lycon gripped his weapon, a huge, double-edged sword that already had a soft, crimson glow. Elak had retained his rapier, but in his left hand he held an axe, heavy and gleaming, that took all his strength to wield effectively. The strange figures and sigils of its wide cutting edge danced in the crimson glow, as if the weapon contained live things eager to drink the blood of their enemies. Such an axe would have been used by the monarchs of the lost kingdom.

Elak tried not to think of the terrible deluge that had swept that wondrous place away, as revealed in the tapestry he'd seen – and heard. That crescendo of sound was echoed now as the northern ocean bulged forward, the horizon boiling, the sea racing back to cover the empty seabed it had revealed during the night. As if in response to the incoming tide, the crystal blazed up, lit by its inner fires, and Dalan's staff, bathed in the glow, also gleamed, too brightly to be looked upon. Both Elak and Lycon felt the weapons in their hands heating up, though not too fiercely for them to hold.

Abruptly beams of brilliant light shot out from the weapons, along the great arc of warriors set to guard the city harbour along the bay, linking them in a wall of crimson fire. Below them, on the mud flats, the light reflected, so the seabed seemed to be bathed in blood, right out towards the oncoming tide.

The first waves came racing in. These were not high, but they were fast, a sudden flood, so that the entire expanse of harbour bed was underwater in a matter of minutes. Large ships and smaller boats stirred and were re-floated, bobbing on the sudden swirls.

Dalan watched the rising water uneasily. So far it seemed to be no more than a common race, a flood tide that was often seen in the harbour. The huge waves, heaped up in the coming storm, still posed a colossal threat. Their unfolding darkness rolled to the very mouth of the great bay, the sound of their coming almost deafening.

"See!" shouted Lycon, pointing with his blade. Light speared forward from it and drove down into the waters now curling around the tower's base, and in its bloody glow, shapes gathered. Like small waves at first, they broke apart into individual things, formed apparently of seawater, hundreds of them. They remained blurred, but had assumed the rough forms of beings, sea creatures, the front line of an army, and their intention was clear as they raced forward as one.

Again the crimson crystal blazed, and its fiery light coursed into the weapons of the defenders, all along that curved line. Bolt after bolt tore down into the waters, and where they struck the sea close to the oncoming mass of invaders, it erupted in great gouts of spray. Countless sea-things were blown apart, but many reached the harbour walls, and rose up over them like an overlapping tide. The warriors used their crimson steel to drive them back, slicing into them, creating foam and spray, a bloody mist, as if flesh and bone were being cleaved asunder, rather than simple salt water.

The first wave of sea-things was quickly repulsed, but the tide disgorged a second wave, and again the defenders drove it back, the crimson light's power staggeringly effective.

"They are testing us," shouted Dalan in order to be heard above the raging din. "Those larger waves are closing in. They are the ones we have to repulse, or Epharra sinks forever."

Elak watched in horror as the first of the tidal waves pounded forward, sucking into it and pulping the first line of ships. It was as though these had been swallowed up by a great beast, mere morsels before the real feast it was about to enjoy. The crystal blazed anew and more light arced from it, forming a high defensive beam of ruby light. In the waters, the sea-things had gone, repulsed, and no sign of them – or their corpses – remained. Bolt after bolt of energy poured out into the bay, driving hard at the tidal wave. It had become enormous, well over a hundred feet high.

And in its puissant form, Elak saw faces, vast, gloating things, quasi-human and alien, mouths agape like wells into the Nine Hells. The sea gods, the ancient horrors, bitterest foes of humanity, gloated as they swept in for their merciless kill.

10: The Ghost Warriors

"Hold the line!" shouted Dalan above the furious din as the winds tore across the bay and around the Atlantean warriors, reaching near-hurricane force, battering the defenders, threatening to bring them to their knees. Yet they held aloft their Valusian steel. Dalan's staff glowed vividly, an eye-searing light that spread and linked into the blaze from the crimson jewel, and the dazzling beams spread at an even faster rate than the wind, igniting fresh powers in the many weapons, forming a tall barrier, like a gleaming, fiery curtain.

Elak felt his rapier and axe pulsing as if they would burst with the energies coursing through them. In the bay, the great wave towered higher, an enormous fist about to come down and obliterate everything beneath it. It advanced in a strange, slow curl, unfurling as if it moved in a different time stream, held in check, perhaps, by the numerous bolts of crimson light tearing into it, hurled by the defenders of the city. Light did explode within the wave, distorting the monstrous faces, some of which turned, open maws seared by the heat. The doom of Epharra looked inevitable, though, for nothing could withstand the full fury of the ocean, heaped up so massively.

"We cannot hold it!" Elak cried, feeling his every muscle tensing to the point beyond endurance. *Men against gods*, he thought. *We cannot restrain them.*

As the dark thoughts began to cloud his mind, something tore free from his weapons and he saw twin columns of crimson fire-red light rise up, larger than a man, but shaping themselves into the figures of warriors. With a jolt he recognized the armour and livery of the Valusian warriors in the great tapestry. The royal Red Slayers! Ghosts from the past, and now forming a whole line along the harbour, every weapon held by the Atlantean defenders giving life to one of the figures. They, too, held ghost-blades, and hundreds of them. In moments they swept upwards and across the mud flats in a crimson, dazzling tide of light.

"Our power alone has not been enough," said Dalan. "But with these and the old magics of Valusia, we may yet deal a telling blow!"

His words proved prophetic, for as the ghost-warriors raced forward, they clashed with the great wave, driving their swords and axes, spears and maces into it, as though cutting into living flesh. The winds howled and screamed and it sounded to Elak and his companions as if these were shrieks of pain, the hint of defeat. For long moments the colossal wall of water hung motionless, as though it belonged not here in the real world, but on a vast tapestry, a frozen panorama painted by an artist, every detail perfectly depicted.

In that long moment, the Atlantean world hung in the balance, powers locked, striving for dominion. Elak roared with anger, frustration, and a wild determination, and used his weapons to direct fresh bolts of crimson scarlet light at the great wave. All along the line of defenders, the warriors followed his example. And the wave trembled with new life as the combined power of the ghost-warriors and that of Elak's line smashed into it. Trembled – and began to collapse in on itself. The huge faces were torn apart in the churning waters, and the winds bent back upon themselves, increasing the onslaught of the defenders.

Elak laughed, the sound rising above the tumult as Lycon shouted with him, and in no time the cry was taken up by all the Atlanteans, a thunderous victory yell. It crashed upon the waters and the wave fell further back, as though the tide had suddenly sucked everything out beyond the bay. Ships bobbed and danced on the waters, no more than a few of them overturned or broken. The ghost-warriors followed, an army of clouds, their light blazing brighter with every league they covered.

Overhead the thunderheads of the storm evaporated, leaving a clear sky, lit by the rising sun, and the winds blew themselves out. In the Bay of Gold, the water gleamed, settling so that it was gently rising and falling, as if the threat of the tidal wave had been no more than a bad dream.

"Are they beaten?" said Lycon, glad to lower his arms and lean on the haft of his weapon. "I don't think I could hold on much longer. Every ounce of my strength has been sapped."

Elak gazed along the lines of warriors, waving to them. They all looked drained, but they yet managed a shout of triumph. "There's your answer," said the young king.

Dalan was gazing out to sea. His staff flickered, its light winking out, and above him, the crimson jewel likewise dimmed. "They have avenged their race," said the Druid. "I think their mighty king was with them. This is the last of their power. All that remains now lies among the ruins far down on the distant seabed."

"And the sea gods?" said Lycon. "Destroyed?"

"I think not," said Elak. "We have dealt them a telling blow. I would like to think we have set them back. They will lick their wounds, like so many beaten curs, and cringe away in their dark places. Yet their servants are still out there. We will need to be watchful, always."

"Then let us go back to the palace and drink to the health of those vanished shades, and honour their glorious passing."

Dalan, for once, approved. He masked his unease. Elak was right. The old gods of the night were not destroyed. *We may have bought time, possibly even a millennium,* he thought, *but they will rise again, and Atlantis must be ready to defy them, down through the long vistas of time.*

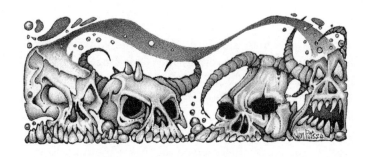

SAILING ON THE THIEVES' TIDE

With the unification of the Atlantean nations completed, Elak prepared for his coronation as the continent's Emperor. To honour his establishment of the Empire, he proposed to have the universally revered Dragon Throne, the sacred seat of kings that had survived countless millennia, removed from its place in the mountains of Cyrena to the recently renovated capital of Epharra.

- Helvas Ravanniol

Annals of the Third Atlantean Empire

*

1: When Old Friends Meet

Lycon was about to empty his tankard of ale, when someone gave him a hearty thump between the shoulder-blades that near knocked him off his seat and sent the tankard spinning from his grip. He held on to it and swung round, growling like a bear and ready to break the vessel over the cranium of the clumsy oaf who'd walloped him. Instead, seeing the grinning ghoul's face looming over him, he let out a yip of glee and gave the man a friendly punch, although the man staggered at the blow. When they'd finished hugging each other, they stood back, both now beaming imbecilically.

"I thought it was you, Lycon. Still as ugly as a mountain ape!" Not many men could have got away with the insult. Lycon was more than a little stout, square shouldered and stocky, but he was deceptively agile, and few could have bested him wrestling or with a blade.

"Mazzarond! By the stars! I thought you'd gone to a watery grave long since!"

The man laughed and signalled for more ale. "I've near been sent to the bottom twice this last year or so. Accursed pirates – aye, and worse! Won a bit of treasure, lost it, and almost my head with it." He held up a small bag, which rattled with loose coins. "This is the last of my worldly goods. And you?"

"I'm in service to the king. It's a long story."

"Elak? You serve Elak, the youngster who's blazing such a trail of glory among the Atlantean states? Gods, it's said he's uniting them, making an empire for himself. A man could serve a warrior king such as that."

"So what brings you to Epharra? Where have you been? Ishtar, I have a thousand questions for you. How many years has it been? A dozen? A score?"

Mazzarond laughed again, pushing a fresh tankard across the bar. "Who knows! I've spent most of my time in western waters. There are countless islands there, and many of them have hidden treasures from days long gone when an ancient empire thrived among them. A small continent that sank and left its peaks poking up from the deeps."

"I've heard the legends."

"And you? What is your place in the new kingdom?"

They spent an hour talking about their adventures. Lycon was a little guarded about his own position, sitting as he did at the right hand of the young king, careful not to let the free-flowing ale loosen his tongue too much. But Mazzarond and he had shared much together once, and owed each other their lives. Such bonds remained strong.

"Elak sits with his Councillors this night," Lycon said, stifling a burp. "You'd like him, Mazzarond. Fights like a tiger, drinks like a fish. Yet his new position has put a halter round his neck. We are still able to sail out and plunge into a battle or two, but royal duties are so demanding. Usually he would be here with me, but lately protocol has taken him away increasingly often."

"Is he planning a new campaign? I heard he has almost completed his union of Atlantis. He even has the Picts as allies! Such a thing would once never have seemed possible."

"Aye, I can vouch for that. For the moment Elak wants to bring the Dragon Throne down from its mountain fortress and set it up in Epharra. It will cement this city as the capital and all states will recognize it."

"The Dragon Throne! A thing of ancient wonder, I gather. Have you seen it?"

Lycon nodded. "It has resisted efforts to move it. There are many legends surrounding it and its powers. Strong magics protect it, sorcery from an age long before ours. Not a few Councillors and commanders are opposed to tampering with such a venerated seat of power. It would take a similar kind of sorcery to transport the throne. Dalan, the Druid who rules their Order, has searched many ancient texts to find a means, but without success."

Mazzarond was silent for a while. "I think the throne came from the western lands, probably that very continent I spoke of. It is said to be carved from the bones of ancient sea dragons, if such things existed. Is that not true?"

Lycon nodded. "Aye, that's one legend. What else do

you know?"

"Several of the western isles claim to have harboured great treasures and secrets. Pirates and other glory hunters have come to grief investigating such tales, as I can testify! The western islanders are a treacherous lot, but they survive by their wits! Who could blame them? I have heard of one island, though, that crops up time and again in their stories. Sea Fire. A place of ancient power where the Thieves' Tide runs."

Lycon grinned, a wolf at bay. "Really? You are as dazzled by yarns of treasure as any lusting pirate, my friend."

"Sea Fire Island is real enough."

"And what is this Thieves' Tide?"

Lycon had their tankards replenished, listening avidly to his companion's tale.

"Some call it the Death Tide," said Mazzarond, face creasing in a grimace that would have disturbed a bear. "They say it's a supernatural force, guarding the island and its incomparable treasures. For almost all of the year's seasons, Sea Fire's tides and whirlpools sweep around it, full in the winter and at their lowest in the summer, when more of the island is exposed. There is one tide a year, the lowest, which drops away and for a day reveals a deep chasm into the shoreline rocks and the stone portal at its heart. Doors that lead to, they say, a chamber where powers and riches beyond imagining are stored. Remnants of that civilization that flourished before the continent sank."

"I take it you have tried – and failed – to break into this place of wonders," said Lycon with a grin.

"Aye. Like all the others, I almost died in that mad sea race. But it was worth the attempt. If I could have won my way in and brought out at least the smallest of the dragon's bones, I'd have been made for life."

2: The Dragon Throne

"Dragon's bones?" echoed Lycon.

"I suspect that dragons are mythical beasts, but there was a time in the primordial past when huge sky creatures flew above Atlantis before men walked its lands. As time passed, they changed, mostly dying out, but some took to the earth, huge lizards, beasts that we are familiar with today, especially in the lost jungle lands. It's said that such things thrived in Lemuria of old."

"The Dragon Throne itself may well be linked to these stories," said Lycon. "Tell me more of the bones on Sea Fire."

"Things of power, Lycon. I have seen paintings of them, made by ancient tribesmen and their sorcerers. Carved with the runes of forgotten languages, used by a people once capable of ruling whole nations through their magic."

"Where are these paintings?"

"I saw them at a market on an island where pirates gather to trade and barter their gleanings. On parchments so old they were on the point of disintegration."

"You'd know these paintings if you saw them again?"

"Aye. I didn't understand them, but the style, the artistry, well, it was unique."

"Then, my friend, you need not worry about finding a roof over your head, for a while at least. There is something I want you to see."

*

The horses were stabled in the small stable block just beyond the high-walled entrance to the courtyard. Carved into the side of the mountain, high above the verdant jungles below, the temple looked to have been hewn by giants, its higher balconies and turrets a stunning tribute to the skills of the ancient masons who had created them. Lycon and Mazzarond walked across the courtyard, whose vast paving stones were free of weeds, kept tidy and as dust free as the servants of the temple could make them. A score of Atlantean warriors, all clad in the livery of Cyrena, Elak's prime state, watched the two figures. Lycon was known to them and their sergeant of the watch bowed to him as he took Mazzarond into the gaping darkness of the vast shrine.

Inside, numerous torches blazed in their cressets, throwing into sharp relief the walls and columns of the temple and the huge dragon emblem flags that were draped from them. There were more soldiers within, gathered about two other men.

"Permit me to introduce Mazzarond," Lycon said to them.

The erstwhile pirate bowed low.

"This is Elak, the king, and with him is Dalan of the Druidic Order."

Mazzarond rose slowly. The king was a young man in the prime of health. Tall, muscular but not stocky, almost willowy, though something in his mien suggested great strength. He was deeply bronzed, evidently a man who enjoyed an active life and not one shut away by the confines of his office. Mazzarond had heard yarns of how this man had led the field in many a battle and would spurn any suggestion of hiding behind his warriors. Elak had handsome, chiselled features, and eyes that sparkled with humour, even though in here his expression was serious.

"I am always glad to meet a man who lives for the sea," Elak said.

Mazzarond relaxed a little, although when he glanced at the Druid, he felt his unease returning. Dalan's gaze was almost fierce, probably, Mazzarond thought, probing his mind. He was tall, garbed in a grey robe, his long fingers pale, curled around the haft of a long staff like the claws of an eagle. His white hair and beard blended like snow about his shoulders and chest, his age unaccountable. These mystics were said to live for many generations. Mazzarond felt his scepticism waning under Dalan's scrutiny.

"Lycon has told us of the map you saw on a remote western isle," said Elak. "It may be the key to a secret I have been trying to unlock for some time." The youth turned and indicated the tall throne behind him.

Mazzarond gasped. The Dragon Throne was a thing of great beauty, just as the stories said. He could well believe it to have been hewn from the bones of a dragon. It reflected the light like a massive jewel, its intricate carvings and embossed workings almost alive. Its seat was shaped in such a fashion that it had been placed inside the wide, gaping jaws of a huge beast, whose many teeth lined its sides, a protective cave. For millennia it had rested here, the dazzling eyes of the sculpture witness to ceremonies since the birth of the Atlantean people.

"Go closer to it," said Dalan. "It will not harm you."

Mazzarond's fascination had rooted him, but Dalan's voice moved him forward. He studied the gorgeous workmanship, the exquisitely carved features. At the base of the throne, running along both sides were long slits in the bone, apparently carved there to take what could have been long rods or poles.

"We have tried to raise the throne," said Elak softly beside Mazzarond. "We have used the strongest wood, and then metal. Many men have toiled. But we have failed to move it. You see the writings?"

Mazzarond gasped. "Indeed, sire! It is the same!"

"As you saw on the map?"

"Yes. I'd know it anywhere."

Elak turned to Dalan with a smile that revealed to

Mazzarond a little more of this king's nature. Mischief, perhaps.

"Another piece of the puzzle," Elak said. "Tell me, Mazzarond – these paintings of the bones on which you saw this very writing – how did they depict the bones? What dimensions were they?"

"Long, sire, like rods."

"Long enough to slide into these slots?"

Mazzarond nodded.

Elak clapped him on the shoulders. "Then the riddle is answered. Dalan, Lycon, we must ready a ship! We must make all haste to Sea Fire."

Lycon groaned. "Yes, I thought you'd probably say that."

"Why so glum? This is wonderful news. Is there a problem?"

Lycon turned to Mazzarond. "Perhaps you'd like to explain to our impetuous king."

3: A Meeting by Night

"This is insane!"

Dalan thumped the arm of his seat, bristling like a cornered cat. His eyes blazed, fixed on the young king who sat beside him in the shadows of the ante-room to the king's chambers in Epharra, his capital city.

Elak was grinning. Beside him, Lycon looked away, refusing to be drawn into what was probably going to become a heated debate. Lycon was almost getting used to these exchanges between his king and the stoic Druid. The three men were closeted here, away from the ears of guards and administrators, for good reason.

"Time and time again you insist on doing this, Elak," said Dalan. "You are the king, and you cannot throw yourself at the mercy of fate, the whim of who knows what gods, on these mad ventures of yours. You've been fortunate thus far in your career. And now, with the unification of Atlantis almost complete, you want to sail off into a situation that piles peril upon peril!"

Elak smiled. He loved Dalan dearly and understood perfectly the Druid's concern for his welfare. "I think it's a good plan. It's worked well enough in the past."

"You've come through by the skin of your teeth. Picts, pirates, renegades, and all the rest. There will be one too many. There is no need for you to go in person. You have an army – several – why not select the pick of the sailors and let them bear the risk? They'd all gladly do it for you."

"I want the Dragon Throne raised here in Epharra. All Atlantis will rally to it. And the seas will be ruled by it. All men will prosper." Elak spoke proudly. He had been a buccaneer, a warrior in the field, a chaser after treasure in his young life so far, but he took his responsibility as ruler seriously, Lycon knew. Elak believed in fairness and justice. *It's just that he's headstrong and impetuous, and finds life at court unduly boring*, Lycon told himself. *And there's no doubt he'll always jump at a chance to sail off to a new escapade.*

"Sea Fire Island," said Dalan, "is the most treacherous place imaginable. That's one problem. Sailing on the Thieves' Tide is another. There is no other tide as unpredictable and as tortuous. It has wrecked countless ships on the rocks of Sea Fire, enough of them to form several entire fleets!"

"Which is why," said Elak, attempting to pour oil on Dalan's very troubled waters, "we need to send in the best ship and crew if we are to pass through the stone gates. The pirates of the west are the perfect crew. No one, not even our finest seamen, share the knowledge of those seas and tides and currents with them."

"Then let the pirates do the work. Reward them well!"

"And let them make off with whatever treasures they find? No."

"You trust this Mazzarond?" Dalan asked Lycon.

"Yes. He's a rogue, a privateer who'd normally put his own dreams of fortune well before anyone else's. But he and I go back a long way. There is a deep trust between us. He will select a crew to man the single ship."

"A crew comprised of the roughest, most violent vermin of the western seas!" cried Dalan.

"Even pirates have a code of honour. Without it, they could never operate. They'd all kill themselves within a year. They have to have a code."

"Then let them do the work!" Dalan persisted.

Lycon chose his words carefully. "Every man – and woman – who sails that ship will be under the protection of its captain. The ship's master's word is law. No one stands against it. If they mutinied, the others would gut them and cast them to the fish. The crew fights as one. Mazzarond's crew will be no exception."

"You think that the two of you can join that crew, disguised as sea rats from some western buccaneering port and be accepted, trusted and, above all, remain anonymous?"

Elak wanted to widen his smile, but he nodded soberly. "Certainly. We'll earn our keep on the ship. The others will be hard put to keep up with us."

Lycon swallowed. He was perfectly able to carry his burden as a seaman, but it was a hard, demanding life. "We'll fit in."

Elak nodded again. "Mazzarond will keep an eye on things. He has chosen a good portion of the crew, so he takes responsibility for us all. If anyone wants to fall out with me or Lycon, they'll have to deal with Mazzarond. It's the code."

Dalan threw up his hands in renewed frustration. "Gods of the Deeps! I am wasting my words."

"We'll be back before you know it," said Elak. "We leave in two days. Mazzarond's ship is already berthed in the harbour."

"And what, precisely, am I to tell the Council?"

Elak laughed gently. "Whatever you usually tell them, Dalan. Political intrigue, secret meetings with our agents, private treaties."

"Since I cannot prevail on you to eschew this mad adventure, I should accompany you –"

Elak shook his head. "I would rather you remained here. If the Councillors are persuaded by you that my absence is little more than a formality, and if you go about your duties calmly and in a relaxed manner –"

Dalan's gaze would have frozen most men. He rose, holding back his evident, boiling exasperation, and left the chamber.

"He means well," said Lycon.

Elak hugged him warmly. "Just as well he doesn't know the rest of it. This captain Mazzarond has chosen to lead the expedition – Scarletta. What do you know of her?"

Elak felt his companion shudder. "She gives a new meaning to the word terror," said Lycon. "There is no harsher mistress, or master, on all the oceans."

4: A Den of Thieves

The tavern was one of several down on the waterfront. Its doors opened onto a narrow quayside, while behind it the cliffs rose, sheer and daunting. The harbour, locked inside a small, curved bay was home to a score of ships, from smaller fishing vessels to the larger sea-going craft of merchantmen and pirates. Tredorric, this small port in the northwestern city state of Dumnor, was an uneasy haven for all comers, where the rivalries and enmities that existed out on the high seas of the measureless western ocean were set aside so that all seafarers could enjoy a respite. That and exchange information and secrets, without fear of being set upon or reported to higher authorities along the coast at Dumnor's capital, Polmarris.

Inside the tavern, the evening's revels were well under way, and at least threescore of the sea rovers were singing, shouting and generally raising havoc as they ate and drank their way through enough food and ale to supply a merchantman for a week. The air was thick with smoke, curling from the oil lamps and the men and women of several crews jostled and pushed each other for the most part good-naturedly, as they yelled out yarns about their latest escapades, or boasted of adventures to come. Among them was Mazzarond, laughing and carousing, although he privately held himself in check, keeping one eye on the doors. The moon was riding high above the harbour when he saw the two men enter.

Elak and Lycon, dressed in rough sailing clothes, looked little different from the teeming rabble around them. Both wore swords, Elak a rapier, and Lycon a more common short cutlass, as favoured by many of the pirates. Although the two newcomers were not known to anyone within, save Mazzarond, their entry was not opposed. It was common enough for new wanderers to sign up to a crew here in Tredorric.

Elak and his companion had been careful to slip into the port unseen. A royal ship had taken them from Epharra along the coast, where it had met with a privateer that also served the king, discreetly and exclusively. Its crew, loyal to Elak, took their part effectively, one of several such crews who spied for the king. Elak and Lycon were taken by rowing boat to the shore, cloaked in darkness, and reached Tredorric under its protective cover. They were confident as they pushed their way into the tavern that no one had seen them outside.

Mazzarond worked his way to them and the three men met, to all intents and purposes old sea rats reuniting, as was common enough here. After the hearty back-slapping and exchange of grinning pleasantries, the three men muscled their way to the bar where Mazzarond arranged for tankards of ale to be served up. Beside him a huge, black-bearded fellow with one ear almost removed in some maritime skirmish, stared at the two newcomers.

"Kazrak!" said Mazzarond, gripping the man's thick arm. "Here are two more fine seamen for our crew! This is Querrol," he grinned, indicating Elak. "And with him is Targat. These two have shared more than a few lively affairs with me. You'll not find many fighting men as reliable as these."

Kazrak, who had already drunk enough ale to content a gang, belched and roared a welcome. "If'n Mazzarond vouches for you, then you'm fine be me," he said. "Drink yer ale, lads. I'll get us more. We'll empty this den before the night's done."

After that, Elak and Lycon were able to enjoy the ribald humour and imbibing of the pirate mob, but were careful about how much they drank themselves. Both were well capable of holding their ale, especially Lycon, who, Elak knew, could drink most men to oblivion, but this night they needed to keep their wits about them. Mazzarond was able to give them a little more detail about the mission to the west and Sky Fire Island.

"We sail on the morning tide, on the *Tigress*, a fine vessel, built for speed and as seaworthy a ship as I've ever known. She'd be a match even for the king's fleetest. I chose the crew, for the most part. It wasn't easy negotiating with the captain, Scarletta. She's the harshest mistress this side of hell. Fears no one and is feared by all."

Elak hid his puzzlement, but asked, "How is it that you chose *her* ship and then picked the crew?"

"Scarletta's best men and women are a match for anyone. But I can bring as many worthies to this voyage again, and she knows it. I told her I'd commission the affair, and guarantee a tempting share of the spoils, if she'd split the crew. Her best and mine. She likes a challenge, so agreed, provided she captains the ship. She'll do that well enough. Once we're at sea, everyone pulls for each other."

There was a sudden roar among the press of bodies, which thinned back like a sudden tide and Elak saw a space open up in the centre of the inn, ringed by cheering pirates. The reason for the hullabaloo became obvious as two figures began to circle each other. One was a burly ruffian almost as large as Kazrak, his bare arms banded with muscle, tattooed with exotic sea beasts intertwined with sharp-toothed mermaids. Opposite him was a figure that could only be Scarletta, queen of the seas, as someone had called her. She was not tall, but was broader than most men, with wide shoulders and a vast girth. Her leather-clad thighs were twice any normal man's and her arms were no less muscled than those of the pirate she faced.

Scarletta was no beauty. Her face was marred by a long scar down her left cheek, and one eye had almost been put out by whatever weapon had cut her. Her red hair was cut short to her scalp, and her nose was flattened, as if it had been subjected to more than a few blows in any number of fist fights. Her teeth, surprisingly white, gleamed in a smile that would have frozen most opponents. With a yell that shook the rafters, she rushed the man before her, her body battering into him with the power of an enraged walrus.

5: Flying Fists

"Fight! Fight!" chanted the crowd as the two opponents wrestled each other, fists flying, heads butting and knees used to merciless effect. Scarletta was a human tornado, and the big man she was grappling with was almost brought to his knees.

Lycon grinned at the ferocity on display and beside him Mazzarond cheered as lustily as the others. "Isn't she magnificent!" he yelled in Lycon's ear. "No wonder she commands the toughest crew on the western seas."

Elak could hardly suppress a smile, though the atmosphere in the tavern had become rank with sweat and smoke, the air hardly breathable. At one point it looked as if the burly ruffian would swing Scarletta over a trestle table and bring her down, but she twisted unexpectedly, wrapped a massive arm around his neck and upper torso and heaved backwards. The man went down like a felled ox beneath her, hitting the table so hard it collapsed. A deafening cheer went up from the pirates as Scarletta reached for a huge tankard and drained most of its contents in one long gulp.

Mazzarond was about to shout something more into Lycon's ear when a large hand dug into his shoulder and spun him round.

"Mazzarond!" cried Scarletta. "We've not clashed heads for too long! Come, give me your best." She aimed a punch for his jaw, and it was only by a sudden duck of his head that he was spared a broken bone or two. Scarletta meant business.

Elak and Lycon drew back into the crowd, which was now at fever pitch. Mazzarond was already exchanging blows with his assailant, and Elak saw with horror that the two opponents were attempting to render each other senseless. Both landed punches that would have floored lesser men, but both staggered on. If Elak had thought Mazzarond was pulling his punches, head butts or kicks, so as not to inflict too much damage on the tenacious Scarletta, he soon realized it was all Mazzarond could do to prevent himself from being flattened.

The fight, however, looked to be coming to an end when Mazzarond got some sort of double arm lock on his opponent and began to squeeze the energy out of her. It appeared to be a successful tactic until Scarletta's head ducked and then shot back, crunching up against Mazzarond's forehead. It was like being hit with a mace, for the man's arms opened, Scarletta broke free and she turned, watching as Mazzarond sagged, shook his head dazedly and collapsed, out cold. The roar from the crowd almost took the roof off the building.

"By Ishtar!" Lycon growled beside Elak. "A blow like that would kill an ordinary man. Is Mazzarond still breathing?"

Scarletta, beaming idiotically, and streaming blood from several head wounds of her own, grabbed two near-full tankards of ale and dashed them into the unconscious Mazzarond's features. It took several more flagons of ale to revive him, but he was alive. He got to his knees, a bruise the size of a fist blackening his forehead.

"Get him up!" Scarletta shouted at the nearest pirates. "Mazzarond chose my crew, but only the strongest warriors are fit to serve under my flag! He's more than worthy!"

The shouting went on, but now the sailors were edging back, hoping Scarletta had enjoyed enough sport for one night. She, however, had other ideas, swinging round and gazing directly at Lycon. "One of our newcomers! Ho, Targat, how about it? Want to try your mettle?"

Lycon knew he dared not refuse. Slowly he handed his belt and scabbarded sword to Elak. "If she tries that head trick on me," he breathed, "I'll break her back."

Elak gripped his arm. "That would probably not be the wisest move. You may just have to take a fall." He knew it would be the last thing his burly companion would want to agree to, but if this expedition was to be a success, they would need the wild she-devil's help.

The contest began much as the others had, with much pulling and straining as the two opponents looked for an advantage and tested each other's strength. Lycon knew at once that, incredibly strong as Scarletta was, she'd worn herself down somewhat already, and the ale she'd guzzled had added to her gradual exhaustion. He himself had deliberately taken it easy on the ale, feigning slight drunkenness. Now, as they locked arms and wrestled, he was sure he had the edge physically. Their faces were nose to nose and her eyes, bloodshot though eager for another win, met his. In that brief gaze, she understood the situation. She had overreached herself. This man had her at a disadvantage. They both knew it.

Lycon was well versed in street brawling, and knew as many underhand tricks as any pit fighter. He knew also that Scarletta would not balk at using such tactics to get herself out of a hole. So when her knee shot up towards his groin, he was ready, twisting to one side, deflecting a blow that would have likely incapacitated him. He was also wary of the follow-up head butt, ducking his own head to meet Scarletta's, his forehead connecting with her right eye with a meaty smack. Dazed, she staggered back and Lycon got behind her and pinned her arms with his own. He knew she could not break his hold. The victory would be his.

He leaned forward and whispered something in her ear and the crowd to a man assumed he was taunting her with his success. However, in a blur of movement, the big woman gave one last gargantuan heave and swung Lycon over her shoulder, sending him crashing down onto the floor, where he gasped like a beached whale. Scarletta leaned over him, her bosom heaving, her face beaming.

"The win is mine, I think," she said, her breathing ragged, as she offered Lycon a fat paw.

He took it, nodding. "I concede," he said. "You're too much for me."

Elak, standing partly in shadows, breathed a deep sigh of relief.

6: Storm

Elak and Lycon leaned on the rail of the sleek *Tigress* as she ploughed her way through seas that grew heavier by the hour. A week out from Tredorric and all the signs were that a storm was bearing down on them from the north. If they were to make Sea Fire Island before it broke, they would be lucky. The one day they would have available to ride the Thieves' Tide was close, and if the storm fouled the seas on that day, the landing would almost certainly be compromised. Elak indicated the boiling darkness in the heavens.

"This is going to be a treacherous ride," he said.

Lycon grunted. "I've enough aches and pains to worry about. I'd almost welcome the buffetings of the storm. Scarletta is twice as violent as any storm."

Elak laughed and clapped his companion on a bruised shoulder, making him wince. "And how is the tempestuous mistress of the ship?"

Lycon shook his head. "Maybe I should not have let her throw me. She knows I had the beating of her. My discretion impressed her, but she's determined to keep me happy, as she puts it, in exchange for my silence. If I were to boast to the crew that I let her win, she'd have us both fed to the sharks. Gods, Elak, I don't need her close attention to keep me silent! It was easier to fight her than be tossed around in her bed!"

Elak laughed above the growing roar of the waves. "You should have Mazzarond stand in for you. It's obvious he carries a torch for her. He's furious to think you and Scarletta –" He broke off as a deafening clap of thunder rocked the heavens directly overhead. Lightning stabbed down in several blazing tongues and the sea boiled even more, the ship riding up and down frighteningly, seemingly about to plummet beneath the waves and down into the deeps. But the *Tigress* righted herself and ploughed on.

"How close are we?" said Lycon, peering ahead into the mountains of spray.

"By day's end, we'll sight Sea Fire. The Thieves' Tide rolls in and out just after dawn. But in this muck, it'll be like night. And no moon to guide us."

"We should abandon the venture," said Lycon. "We've as much chance of landing as snow in a furnace."

"That would mean another year's wait. I can't afford that."

There were other seamen around them now, watching the seas ahead, and battening down every last item on board, in preparation for the worst attentions of the storm. The winds gathered in strength, howling like swarms of banshees, and thunder boomed incessantly.

Mazzarond stood beside them. "We're going in," he yelled.

"It's suicide!" protested Lycon. "We'll be ripped open, torn to shreds."

"It's just a matter of timing. If we hit the running tide, it will steer us straight into the cove and the stone portals. The storm is chaotic, but at worst it will simply send us in at thrice the normal speed. Scarletta's helmsman, Jorgandir, is the best man alive for the task. He's a Northman. Born and swims in seas like these." Mazzarond went off to see to more of the preparations.

Elak and Lycon joined other crewmen as they began the last of the work. Scarletta stood at the prow, watching the tumultuous waves keenly, hoping to catch a glimpse of their island destination. Elak nudged Lycon. "Nothing will stop us now. Brace yourself."

"I've been doing that since we left port," Lycon muttered.

*

The last hours sped by in a furious sequence of waves, spume and boiling cloud as darkness dropped down like a palpable force, pierced every few minutes by shafts of lightning that slammed into the heaving seas. If one of those dazzling spears had hit the *Tigress*, she would have been blown to fragments. However, the helmsmen Jorgandir, guided his ship with amazing dexterity and skill. Numerous times it seemed that the race was lost, but he kept her afloat and driving on towards the shape that had now lifted itself above the near horizon. Sea Fire Island! A pitch-black stain above the waters against a backdrop of madness and mayhem, surrounded by all the mounting fury of the tempest.

"My only regret," shouted Lycon as the ship began its final run, "is that we two did not die fighting side by side."

"We're not dead yet!" yelled Elak, with a grin, but secretly he wondered if they had the remotest of chances of riding this nightmare out.

Already they had narrowed the distance to the island. It was a volcanic peak, its central core sheer, rising up through cliffs that looked to comprise of black glass, slippery and unscalable. Its rocky shores were row upon row of fanged rocks, the sea creaming round them as waves broke like giant hammers. No ship could land there. Jorgandir must know the land, though, for Elak saw how the huge helmsman swung the wheel this way and that, using the waves uncannily, as if they spoke to him. Just when it seemed the ship must be flung forward by a following wave the size of a small mountain, dashed to a million splinters on those forbidding rocks, an opening appeared in the shoreline, a high gash in the cliffs.

Elak gripped the rail, almost tossed overboard. He could feel the current beneath the ship, as if a god's hand had taken the craft and was propelling it forward. The Thieves' Tide! Or the Death Tide. Whichever, it flung the ship through the towering walls and into the cove beyond, where the waters swirled in a boiling cauldron of white spume and spray. Below the cliffs, two gigantic stone doors rose up. Closed, locked in place by the tide. The *Tigress* was going to fetch up, prow first on those portals, and all who sailed in her would be mangled and crushed.

7: Sea Fire Island

Elak was about to leap over the rail, dragging Lycon with him, when he saw the huge portals start to swing outwards, the tide striking them and dissipating like mist. Nothing could slow the terrific speed of the ship, even though the sea was dragged back like a rumpled carpet by the receding tide, exposing the dark sands of the cove's floor. The *Tigress* slid along the sand like a hurled javelin, its prow driven in between the doors and into the darkness beyond. The entire crew were flung to the deck as the ship raced on, out of the water altogether.

Inside the massive grotto, it shuddered to a halt and

behind it, mere moments after its stern had cleared the doors, they swung shut once more with a roar that drowned out the thunderclaps of the storm. Ragged light speared down from far overhead, where lightning continued to crackle. Rain poured in through the gaping oval, where the broken rocks poked inward like a ring of fangs, hung with sodden verdure.

"Move!" shouted Scarletta, her voice reverberating around the cavern. Already the sailors were unfurling rope ladders and dropping down to the sandy floor. Several flaming brands had been lit, throwing the bizarre terrain into relief. The rocks were twisted and contorted, worn into shape by endless tides and currents, but beyond them a crude stairway reached upwards into the heart of the island. Leaving a handful of seamen to look after the *Tigress*, Scarletta waved the crew on and a difficult climb began over the weed-strewn stairs.

Beside Elak and Lycon, Mazzarond pointed to vast arches that looked to have been hewn from the solid bedrock, supporting the high ceiling of the cavern. "The charts say there's a citadel up there, and a place where the treasures of the ancients are stored. Scarletta is here for the diamonds and other priceless jewels."

"She can take as much as she and the crew can carry away," said Elak. "As long as we find the dragon bones."

"That's the bargain I struck with her," said Mazzarond. "She's a dangerous enemy when roused, but she's as good as her word."

Lycon said nothing, but he knew Mazzarond was right. Lycon could have attested that Scarletta's dreams were of nothing but pearls and rubies and the like, given the number of times she had spoken in her sleep about them.

The company reached the top of the crumbling stairway and beheld an extraordinary sight, partially veiled by the slanting rain that fell from the huge orifice overhead. All around them, remnants of the city rose up. Most had been carved out of the naked rock of the island, natural blocks of stone from which windows and doors had been chiselled out, what must have been centuries before. Weed and coral and other sea growths festooned them, spilling from doors and windows, gleaming in the torch-glow. They were alive with half-glimpsed creatures, worms and molluscs and things that hopped and jumped, though none attacked the intruders. These great stone blocks were seemingly piled high, almost to the curved ceiling so far above, and many had fallen, smashing the constructions below them. Through the veil of rain, now falling in torrents as the storm outside reached its full strength, the city looked ethereal, cloaked like a dream, its images shivering and distorted.

Scarletta led them through streets that leaned, filled with dangerous cracks that could easily have swallowed the entire company. Weed and banks of knotted growths dripped, treacherous and teeming with invisible life. The sailors used their swords to cut through the worst of them, drawing back at the stench released. High above, the ringed hole that opened to the sky was directly above the company, and its rotting teeth could be seen more clearly in the pouring rain.

"You see why no one has ever entered from that direction," Mazzarond told his companions. "Too dangerous. Everything up there is crumbling. It overhangs and gives nothing on which to snag a line. Anyone foolhardy enough to attempt a descent would simply fall to their deaths." He indicated the wide carpet of sharp rocks and pointed stone where those falling would have landed and been pulped.

Elak nodded. "And none of us would stand a chance of

climbing up through the vent from here. You'd need wings to get out alive."

"Beneath the ruins," said Mazzarond, "are said to be tunnels and crypts, mostly broken and caved in. But in those that are passable, possibly to vents to the outer island, there are beings and creatures from another age that swarm and seethe like insects. They cling to the darkness but defend their vile realm ferociously. We dare not make our exit that way."

"So we go back through the portals?" said Elak.

"Really?" said Lycon. "You mean we have to locate and remove the treasures while the Thieves' Tide is out and before it runs back into the cove? Gods, that's no time at all. Unless you mean us to remain here until the next Thieves' Tide."

Elak shook his head. "Impossible – that would be a year from now." Mazzarond was about to respond, when a cry rang out from ahead, so loud it rose above the steady roar of falling rain. A unique central building had been discovered.

Scarletta stood atop one of the blocks, waving her sword, her face wet but beaming. "The temple, you dogs! Get ready to bend your backs!"

There was a unified roar of excitement as the company surged forward.

Elak glanced at Lycon. He had a feeling Scarletta had been here before. This had been all too easy so far. And the business of their exit from Sea Fire Island was by no means a certainty.

8: The Secret of the Temple

Elak and Lycon studied the stacked chests and mounds of precious stones here in the heart of the apparent temple. Everything had been abandoned, with no attempt made to secure it. Perhaps, Elak thought, the island itself had been thought to be defence enough against potential thieves. And certainly this squat rectangular building would once have had its windows and central door sealed against intrusion. Time had wrecked any such seals. Many of the chests were rotting, spilling golden ingots and blocks of silver. The sailors yelled with delight, rushing forward and burrowing into the hoard with reckless abandon.

Scarletta roared at them and slowly they became more organized. "Steady, you apes! We cannot possibly carry all of this away. Let each man take a sensible load. It will yet be fabulous for everyone. You'll need a dozen lifetimes to enjoy it all!"

While the company unslung the heavy sacks they had brought and began filling them with as much treasure as they could sensibly carry, Elak and Lycon picked their way through the piles of jewels and gleaming precious metal. There were several antechambers at the back of the temple, and in one of them they found what they were here for. A broken statue, cut from a single block of white bone, its top half lying in ruins beside its legs, rose up into the dripping shadows, as rain coated it in a sheen, its shroud. Running along beside the wide plinth were two lengths of bone, covered almost entirely in green weed. Lycon reached for the haft of one and tugged. Gently he slipped it free and held it up.

"That's it," said Elak, with a grin. He scraped off some of the weed with his knife. "The markings are clear." Lycon handed the bone over and went to the other, also freeing it. "Just as the charts promised."

Elak was nodding, but his grin had dissipated. Something had made him uneasy. "I tell you, old friend, this venture has become a little too simple. The landing was difficult, I'll give you that. But all this treasure, these bones

– just sitting here, waiting to be picked up."

"Let's just be thankful and get back off the island."

"How do we do that?"

A shadow in the doorway made both men wary, swords gripped in readiness. It was Mazzarond who stood there, a sack swung over one shoulder. "Have no fear," he called. "Jorgandir, our helmsman, knows the way. He has the chart. Although the great stone portals are opened when the Thieves' Tide recedes, they close when it returns, and cannot be opened *from the outside*. But there are mechanisms set into the inner chamber that allow the portals to be opened against the tide, no matter how fully it flows."

Lycon pointed upwards. "That storm has shown no signs of abating. It will give great strength to the waves when they shut us in. Can the mechanism defy their power?"

Mazzarond shrugged. "We'll simply wait the storm out." He turned and headed back out into the temple, where the crew had finished their scavenging.

Elak and Lycon joined them, each holding one of the long bones.

"Are those your prizes?" Scarletta called. "Ivory? Their value cannot match that of the jewels. Throw them away and grab a real treasure!"

Mazzarond laughed, trying to make it sound casual. "We have a special buyer for them. We're content to take them, and maybe a few of the jewels for good measure."

If Scarletta had been about to question them, she was interrupted by a howl of pain from the back of the ring of sailors. All heads turned, and Elak barely caught sight of sudden movement among the drenched coral. One of the crew was snared in something, grey coils that writhed and dragged the screaming man into a fat crevice. Immediately all swords were out and the seamen formed a defensive circle, their instincts taking over. All were prime fighting men and women and they were ready in an instant to defend themselves.

Elak spoke softly to Lycon. "I said it was too easy. That treasure was set there deliberately."

"A trap?"

"Aye. Bait. And we were foolish enough to take it. Look!" Elak pointed with his rapier to where a number of writhing creatures were emerging from the rocks. Huge, eyeless serpents, worms from the sea's depths, they ringed the company, affording no path of escape. One by one they opened their great gashes of mouths, revealing concentric circles of teeth and a scarlet maw, each creature eager to wriggle forward and snatch a victim. Already the first of them struck and the sailors had to hack at them furiously to avoid being sucked into the fleshy mouths. Three were dragged to their bloody deaths within moments.

There followed a deathly struggle as the circle of huge worm creatures closed, some of them cut to pieces, their dying bodies thrashing about in agony, their tails lashing, as much a danger as their blind, striking heads. The defenders fought with a terrible fury born out of terror, and they slew many of the worm-things, but for each of the beasts that fell, another rose up from its subterranean lair.

Lycon stepped back from delivering the death-blow to one of them and pointed. "Elak! There, someone is *directing* these monsters!"

Elak saw a figure higher up among the rocks, a squat, hunched being, apparently garbed in a wide cloak that glistened like weed. It held a staff, the point of which shimmered with eerie light. The being may have been a mutated man, its head a fat blob without a neck, eyeless like the worms, but with an open mouth. And as Lycon had said, it was driving the worms on, whipping them into a frenzy that would spell the destruction of every man and woman here.

9: Attack of the Death Worms

A furious battle ensued as the worm creatures struck again and again, the pirates cutting and slashing at them, the air a bloody mist of slaughter. Elak and Lycon fought side by side, almost brought to their knees among the rocks and hacked corpses of the slain monsters. Mazzarond stood beside Scarletta, as intent on protecting her as himself. Lycon, pausing briefly between killing, glanced at the two. Scarletta's blade was clean, and Lycon realized with surprise that she was not using it to strike at the worms. Instead she was focused on the hunched figure up in the rocks, though she made no attempt to fight her way towards it. But Elak had no time to puzzle over this mystery.

"We need to cut down that devil!" Lycon shouted to Elak, who nodded, redoubling his efforts to clear a path towards it. However, the treacherous terrain took his feet from under him and he slid sideways, barely diverting the snapping jaws of a huge worm. As he fell, he instinctively brought the dragon rod up and its point slid home into the flesh of the creature. Abruptly the whole rod glowed and Elak felt it vibrating like a live thing. He gripped it tightly as the explosion came, deep within the worm. Gobbets of its flesh burst asunder as the entire creature was ruptured, spattering Elak and Lycon. They both leapt clear. Elak's rod shone, a white beacon, though it felt only mildly warm where his fingers gripped it hard.

"Use yours!" Elak told Lycon, and the two of them began a renewed attack, both their rods flaring brilliantly, burning a path through the writhing creatures, some of which blew apart, others sliding away. In moments Elak stood below the rocks where the weird figure still used whatever powers it had over the worms to goad them on. It was aware of Elak's approach and moved back, trying to regain the shadows, but the young warrior leapt up and faced it. It was no human face Elak saw, a mockery, bloated and eyeless, with a fish-like mouth and several crimson tongues. Behind it another serpent-like worm rose up, preparing to dip its head and snatch Elak up in one swooping movement, but Elak swung the rod in a glittering arc, its brilliant power slicing through the fat neck of the monster, opening it up as if he were gutting a fish. Its blood gushed from the deep wound and the creature flopped sideways, shuddering in its death throes.

Before the mutant human could get away, Elak again swept the rod, striking at its head, which burst in a welter of gore and bone. As the thing collapsed, a sudden silence fell, broken only by the moans of wounded sailors. The worms drew back like a tide, abruptly slipping away into the dark places from which they had emerged. Elak swung round and surveyed the carnage beneath him.

A score of the pirates had been killed, as many wounded. Their bodies were littered among the still thrashing bodies of numerous worms, for the pirates had given an amazing account of themselves. Elak rejoined Lycon. Both of them were clotted with blood and ichor. Lycon snorted with disgust but gave Elak a wry smile.

"Who was the demon?" he said.

Elak shook his head. "Let's hope he was the only one of his kind. Master of this bloody island, perhaps." He led Lycon to where Scarletta had fallen. Mazzarond was holding her head up, his face creased in concern.

"When the sorcerer fell, she collapsed," he said. Around him the other pirates were gathering.

Mazzarond stroked Scarletta's face and after a moment, she opened her eyes and stared about her, apparently confused.

"What in all the hells –?" she began, sitting up. "Where

are we? Mazzarond, I know you. And Querrol, and Targat," she went on, indicating Elak and Lycon. She shook her head, as if to clear it of some dark vision.

"That thing was controlling you," said Elak. "The sorcerer, or whatever it was."

"The voice," Scarletta said softly. "Always in my head. Whispering to me."

Mazzarond looked baffled, but Lycon stepped in.

"This was a trap, and the treasure the bait. And we were the food for those underground horrors."

"I led you all here," said Scarletta, suddenly appalled. "It used sorcery to compel me." She stood up groggily. "It used me to bring food for its servant worms! Where is it! I'll slice it into as thousand pieces!"

"Destroyed," said Elak. "Whoever ruled this island, probably millennia ago, built a statue and these ivory poles of power were set into its base. It must have been the last place of resistance, protection against the things below the island. When their ruler released them, they inadvertently woke the power in the rods. They've dispersed for now, but we can't assume they won't attack us again."

Mazzarond could see the horror on Scarletta's face. "We've not lost everything," he said. "We have the treasure. Let's take as much as we can and make for the open sea."

Scarletta nodded slowly, her eyes turning to Elak and Lycon. She studied them for a moment, as if there was something about them she could not quite place.

Elak felt himself tensing. If she realized who he was, his situation, and Lycon's, would likely become untenable.

Scarletta's eyes dropped to the ivory poles and there was no disguising the avarice in her gaze.

Mazzarond saw it and gently pulled her back. "We struck a bargain," he told her. "They came for them. But we have a fortune in booty! Be satisfied, Scarletta."

Slowly she nodded, but Elak felt a fresh wave of unease.

10: The Gates of Doom

Jorgandir studied the ancient chart and looked up at the two huge portals that closed off the exit to the cove and open sea. There was nothing to indicate that the great storm that had battered the *Tigress* and the island had abated. The helmsman pointed to a set of steps rising from the shallow waters of the inner cove and up to a wide ledge cut in the bedrock. His fellow crewmen watched from the deck of the beached ship as he climbed. On the ledge he turned and shouted down.

"There's a mechanism here, just as the chart promises. It will allow the portals to open against all tides."

Mazzarond spoke beside Elak. "The doors can only be opened from the outside when the tide withdraws, once a year, as we know. But the ancient mechanism above powers forces that can open the doors from within. Long ago, it would have been a superb means of defence against enemies from the sea."

They waited as Jorgandir worked the mechanism. On the deck of the *Tigress*, numerous sacks of treasure had been stacked. Elak had been wondering how wise it was to allow a company of pirates, particularly one controlled by the fiery Scarletta, to carry off such a trove. Cyrena and the new Atlantean Empire had enemies who would profit hugely from such a haul, and he had no surety that Scarletta would come under the royal banner, given the opportunity.

"We're waiting!" she shouted, more like the wild Scarletta that had led them here. "Get the doors open, Jorgandir. The sooner we get off this accursed rock, the better!"

As she spoke, the twin portals groaned and the pirates saw them shudder, like two huge beasts struggling to move under a colossal load. Dust fell from above and there was a sound of grinding rock. A slim line of light ran down between the edges of the doors where they met, and the noise of the storm outside broke in. If anything, the tempest was raging even more terribly, and there came the distinct sound of mighty waves slapping against rock and cliff.

"It's too great a force," Jorgandir shouted. "The doors are designed to open outwards. The force of the storm is driving abnormally huge waves against them."

"It's no natural storm," said Lycon. "There is more sorcerous power in this island than we could have imagined."

"How long before it wanes?" said Mazzarond.

Lycon shrugged. "In human terms? Who knows. Centuries, perhaps."

Elak studied the portals. They quivered as the outer waves pummelled them but appeared to be unmovable. "Very well. Get Jorgandir and anyone else who is ashore back on board."

Scarletta would have questioned him giving any instruction to her crew, but something in his eyes kept her silent. She nodded, and soon everyone was on the *Tigress*. Elak led Lycon to the prow and the two men stood side by side.

"We broke the sorcery of the island's foul inhabitants," Elak said to his companion. "Now let's see if we can break the sorcery of the island itself." He lifted the dragon pole, and Lycon readied his. In unison, they pointed them at the doors, and waited. For long moments, nothing happened. It seemed that the power in the bone would only respond to the living threat of an enemy.

Outside, the thunder roared, blending with the crashing of the incessant waves. A spike of lightning crackled, its energy driven through the narrow fissure between the doors as it struck the points of both bone poles. These flared with almost blinding white light, but neither Elak nor Lycon were smitten or felt molten power coursing into their hands. The men shuddered, but held, and from the poles a unified bolt of light blew back at the doors.

There was a deafening eruption of stone and sea as the portals were torn apart, great fragments flung in all directions. As they disintegrated, the sea flooded in like an enraged animal, a great wall of water bearing down upon the *Tigress*. She rose up and was in danger of flipping right over, but somehow held. Jorgandir, now at the helm, used every vestige of his seafaring skill to right the ship and guide her through the crumbling jaws of the portal, dragged out by the tide as it pushed and pulled, churned crazily by the storm.

More than once the ship heeled and it looked as if she would be lost, but time and again she twisted and made her perilous way out beyond the reefs. Lightning danced overhead like an array of maddened gods, and the sea blazed as if on fire. Elak and Lycon held their dragon bone poles aloft, drawing to them bolt after bolt, absorbing them. It seemed an interminable contest, but eventually *Tigress* got out into slightly calmer waters, though the waves rose and fell as if they would sink her yet.

Lycon pointed back at the rapidly receding island, which was now bathed in an unholy glow, as if molten, the seas around it churning vividly, a sea of fire. "That island is well named," he called above the roar of the surf.

Mazzarond joined him and Elak at the prow. "Thank the gods," he muttered.

"How's your mistress?" said Elak. He'd seen Scarletta looking at him and Lycon from amidships, a frown creasing her face, as though she might be on the point of understanding something – their true identities, perhaps.

"Well enough," said Mazzarond. "As for your particular booty, I'd say you're welcome to it. Such power as lies within them is dangerous. There's usually a high price to pay for its ownership."

"Scarletta does not covet them?" said Elak.

"No. Whatever memories she has of being possessed are fading. And along with that, all memories of recent days."

"And hopefully nights," murmured Lycon.

"She'll have forgotten everything by dawn." Mazzarond went back amidships.

"There you are," Elak laughed. "She's forgotten everything."

Lycon gazed at the storm they had left behind. "By Ishtar, I wish I had."

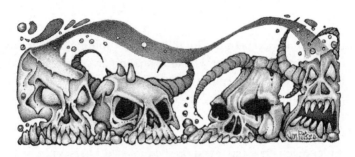

THE SINGERS IN THE STONES

And so the great Dragon Throne was brought down from the mountains and placed in Elak's palace at Epharra. Preparations were made for the king to be crowned as Emperor of all Atlantis, and although the many nations were content to unify and thus grow even stronger and more powerful under the dragon banner, there were those who chafed at the moving of the sacred throne, fearing that ancient rites and lore had been unwisely set aside. However, in Epharra, there was much rejoicing at the promise of a new era.

- Helvas Ravanniol

Annals of the Third Atlantean Empire

*

1: The Horror in the North

Waves curled, breaking and scattering in creamy white relays across the small bay. Three ships rode at anchor at the back of the surf. On each craft scores of tattooed Picts busied themselves loading and securing fresh water from the island, one of a small archipelago here in the northern waters far from the heavily populated islands and continent of the Atlantean people. Out in the bay, tumbling among the foaming combers, several naked warriors dived and sported like porpoises of warmer waters, alternatively laughing and cursing each other's antics. Some had acquired lengths of flotsam, narrow, broken trunks they used to propel themselves shoreward, driven by the waves. The more adventurous tried to stand on the makeshift logs, only to be flung off after they had been hurtled a few yards. More than once one of the men received a heavy clout, buffeted by the indifferent, rolling tide.

One of the men shouted: at first his companions roared with laughter at what appeared to be his capitulation to the sea's power. They realized, though, that something else had brought the cries for help. Two of the men swam across to him and at once realized what had caused the outcry. Something had come out of the waves, rushing headlong towards the shingle beach. Not another fallen trunk, but a series of several, lashed together to form a crude raft. And on it there was a lone figure, unconscious, possibly drowned.

The Picts guided the raft to the beach, dragging it away from the groping waters as they drew back, preparing for the next surge. Quickly the men attended to the figure, which had evidently tied itself to the makeshift raft. It was a man of middle years, thin and bronzed by exposure to the elements, his hair matted, his beard unkempt. They cut him loose and gently raised him, turning him and forcing a stream of sea water from his mouth. Coughing, the man opened his eyes, completely dazed. One of the Picts rushed off to find the pile of pelts and thick furs the swimmers had discarded before taking to the water, returning shortly, throwing several over the emaciated body. Slowly a little warmth came back into it and the man began to recover something of his wits.

He gazed at the completely unselfconscious naked

forms around him, too weak to react. "Am I alive or dead?" he gasped, his language a minor variation on the Pictish tongue, so they understood him. "Are you spirit creatures of the underworld?"

The Picts growled with laughter. "We're flesh and blood," said one. "As are you, who yet live. When did you last eat?"

"Too long ago to remember. Have you water?"

The men brought him a cupful and prepared a rough gruel for him, making him eat it slowly. They knew well enough the perils of being lost at sea, of the terrible thirst that could go with it, and the dangers of drinking too much too quickly once a man got back to land. Word was sent to the ships, and presently more Picts arrived, including the leader of the war band, Finn Mac Ruath. He was a swarthy, muscular man, whose grim expression was made grimmer by the tattoos that covered his face.

"Who are you, and what is your business in Borna's lands?" he said with little regard for the man's plight. He squatted, gripping his war club as if he would use it at any moment. One blow from that and the fallen sailor's head would be cracked open.

After the sailor had managed to take a few more mouthfuls of gruel, he leaned back on the pillow of furs the men had put behind his head. An expression of deep unease crossed his worn features, but it was not fear of these Picts that gripped him. In a moment he began his tale as a fire was kindled, its flames limning the warriors, who leaned in to hear the words, the revelation spoken at a feverish, urgent pace.

"My name is Quengamook, and my tribe dwells in the great ice wastes of the northernmost boundaries of the ocean. For years beyond number we have lived there, hunting between the ice packs and the bergs. Apart from the occasional skirmish between our tribes, there are no wars, and the people of the snows spend their days peacefully, worshiping our gods, enjoying the bounty of the sea, sharing our fortunes. We do not stray from our lands, and we are rarely visited by men of the south. When we are, we trade and make them welcome, for we have more than we need."

Finn Mac Ruath grunted. "Pictish sailors have been in the far north. We have many furs to show for it. Your tribe is probably known to us." Some of the fiery suspicion had gone from his eyes.

"A new darkness came to us. The darkness of death and despair. My people have been hunted by something from deep below the ice. A living god, they said. A voracious, all-consuming horror. It spreads like the most virulent of plagues, and no nation is safe."

As the afternoon began to wane, the sun falling to its bed in the western seas, Quengamook expanded his tale, the Picts around him listening, silent as ghosts, to the hoarse words as they tumbled like an ancient curse from cracked lips.

*

"My tribe dwelt on the southern shore of the northernmost lake, whose waters are deeper than anyone knows, reaching under the land and great ice sheet to the very ocean itself, so our shamans have always told us. We believe it, because from time to time a great current of saltwater runs into the lake and brings with it an abundance of fish that feeds the tribes throughout the bitterest of winters. However, not everything that swam in our inland waters brought good things to us.

"There have always been legends of gods and their strange servants, dwelling in the ice mountains of Vaarfrost,

234

a region few men have ever willingly visited. These gods are said to have come to the world from the stars, falling like meteors into the uttermost ice wastes, burrowing down into the cold places that are the very roots of Vaarfrost. They fled a cosmic war, banished by other gods, cursed for their use of extreme blasphemous powers and their cruel enslavement of other races among the stars. For centuries these gods, who my tribes have named the Orugllyr, have been content to exist in their subterranean caverns and the alien cities they have sculpted from rock and ice, so far below. They bred the slaves they brought with them, hybrid races akin to Man, and time drew a blanket over their isolation.

"The Orugllyr grew tired of their remote surroundings, and, having learned something of the races beyond their frozen realm, grew ever more hungry for expansion. Perhaps the gods that had harried them this far from their original home among the stars, and who had been content to allow them survival as prisoners of the ice deeps, had all but forgotten them, turning their faces away from our world to carry their wars to other places. The Orugllyr sent the first of their sorcerers upward to the sunlight, to where the outlying tribes lay unsuspectingly in their path.

"My tribe heard of the terror, the bloody harvest, as the Orugllyr's servants subjected the ice people to their laws, their control. They were forced to worship new gods, and many were sacrificed to appease the appetites of the invaders. Black sorcery was used, and powers that our peoples could not defy. Our shamans were viciously rooted out and devoured, or changed, made into other beings, things that flapped, or crawled, or hopped, no longer human, what little powers they had converted into the twisted magic from the stars.

"For an entire cycle of seasons this invasion has gone on, slowly driven across the ice lands, spearheaded by the priests of the Orugllyr and their sorcerers. One by one, the tribes fell, their people slaughtered, sacrificed on bloody altars, or forced into bestial slavery and capitulation. We fled, ever southward across the northern ice continent, our numbers dwindling, until we came to the last of the ice cliffs, the southernmost tip of the land. The enemy fell upon us there, and a few of us took to the ocean in a storm, a last despairing act, for the chaos of the ocean was hardly less dangerous than the fury of the sorcerers.

"Somehow we kept our small boat afloat, our strength waning day by day, our supplies and water dwindling. A dozen of us began the voyage south, three lost overboard during the first intense chaos of the storm. Others died, apparently from whatever curses our enemy had hurled after us. I am all that remains of that unfortunate crew, though I have seen death's shores bobbing on the horizon of my dreams constantly.

"I almost reached the island of Brae Calaadas, where I would have warned the people of its city, Tergarroc, but the sea itself was an ally of the things that pursued me, the elemental terrors that churned the skies and twisted the currents to their will. Instead of setting foot again on dry land, I was washed out across the wilderness of the ocean again, drifting towards oblivion."

Finn Mac Ruath had been listening intently to the stricken sailor's tale. "It is well you did not land on Brae Calaadas," he told him. "Some time ago the island was almost reclaimed by the ocean. A fleet of Pictish clans went there, under the banner of Borga, King of the Wolf Clan. Along with southern allies they clashed with an old sorcery there, and powers from the deeps."

Quengamook gasped. "Yes, the reach of the Orugllyr stretches beneath the waves. What happened on Brae Calaadas?"

"Its evil powers were turned, the city reduced to rubble, inundated by the sea."

"Then they would have slunk back to their masters in the north. It would have served only to have made the Orugllyr more determined to surge down into these waters, and beyond. Even Atlantis and all its powerful kingdoms will not be able to withstand the invasion."

"Borga must be told," said Finn Mac Ruath. "As must his southern ally, King Elak."

Quengamook gripped the Pict's powerful arm, his fingers like the talons of a sea hawk. "Elak! Even in our lands we have heard tales of this mighty warrior king. It is said he is building a great empire."

Finn Mac Ruath's fierce look masked his feelings in the matter. Not all Picts were in favour of the alliance struck between Borga and the southerners. For generations they had fought each other, and many Picts had died under Atlantean swords.

"Mankind needs to stand as one against the Orugllyr," said Quengamook, his fingers relaxing as he sank back. "It may be that all their united power can withstand the threat from beyond. That or sink beneath the oceans for all time."

2: The Gathering Darkness

The blind shaman, Cruath Morgas, stood on a raised stone, overlooking the throng of Pict warriors who had come together before the semi-circle of huge sarsens, the massive stones that rose from the earth like living beings on the crest of the wide hilltop. On either side of the hill the deep, rich verdure of the forests formed a whispering blanket, wrapping around the place, making of the sacred grove a unique sanctuary, a place where no man dared tread without being called by the shamans. Cruath, most powerful of them all, raised his gnarled arms to the night skies, where stars burned like fires, and an occasional streak of light marked the passage of one of them, gone beyond the distant ocean horizon in the blink of an eye. There were murmurs at such visions, for the superstitious warriors, though murderous fighting men, were never sure whether such omens were propitious or signs of coming disaster.

Behind and above Cruath Morgas, prime servant of the Pictish Lords of Midnight, their barbaric gods, the sarsens loomed, filling the sanctuary with their shimmering power, their stone flesh scarred with pictograms and runes that stood out like veins, pulsing with energy. Silence fell, broken only by the sighing of the distant waves below on the islands shore, far from the Pictish mainland. If the monstrous stones had eyes they would have seen the corpse laid out on another slab before them. It was the emaciated, naked form of Quengamook, who had died soon after he had passed on his message about the invaders in the remote north. Tonight he was being honoured by those he had tried to warn about the Great Darkness that had burgeoned into their world.

Cruath Morgas' voice came clear, speaking words of praise, commending the fallen sailor to the gods. He turned his blind eyes to the corpse, which had been carefully washed, its wounds gently bathed, its straggling hair tied neatly and pinned with gold. The northerner had no tattoos, but now his entire body was covered in painted signs and diagrams, in preparation for his final journey from this earth to the underworld, where he would join the spirits of the dead and be honoured by them. The shaman beckoned one of his fellows to him, and the man brought a torch that guttered and spat flames in the brisk wind. He set the torch to the heaped wood around the base of the slab and in moments it flared, the wood snapping and crackling, and Quengamook became a human furnace, his oiled flesh quickly succumbing to the blaze, its smoke curling upwards, drawn away into infinity by the stiffening breeze.

All heads bowed as the crowd quietly intoned their praise for the fallen, their eyes closed. Cruath Morgas lifted a long staff, from which small bones and knots of black feathers hung, and as he did so, light from the burning corpse reflected from the monoliths. Their pictograms and designs gleamed, shifting, coalescing, and the earth of the hill moved, trembling, so that men gasped, holding on to their reason with an effort.

"The gods hear us!" called the shaman. "They speak to us!"

As one, everyone fell to his knees, leaving only Cruath Morgas standing. There were mighty warriors among that throng, including Borga, King of the Wolf Clan, and Kurrach Mag Barrin of the Otter tribe, together with many other kings and highmost warriors of the Pictish nation. It was rare for so many of them to come together, but in these times of numerous dark omens, they did not refuse the call to this sacred place. When the shifting of the great hill subsided, the Picts waited, none daring to raise their eyes and regard the living stones.

"A Great Darkness is coming," said Cruath Morgas, and the Picts knew he was conveying the words of the gods, transmitted to him through the stones. "It has already manifested itself to us, and other peoples of our world. Many of you will recall the Crawling Death that was visited on our island of Skaafelda, which was rendered a place of death. It took a great coming together of our peoples and the aid of the southern king, Elak, to drive the horror back into the north. At Brae Calaadas an even greater blow was struck when the cursed city of Tergarroc was plunged into the ocean. More than a year has passed since then, but in that time, the Great Darkness has manifested itself once more. Quengamook, whose spirit goes now to the underworld, was the last of the far northern tribes. He gave his life to warn us."

The shaman's blind eyes turned inward on other visions, and as they were unveiled to him, he shared them through the power of the great stones with the warriors. Mainly they concerned the great Atlantean warrior and king, Elak, who was banding the many states of his continent into an empire. Once a bitter enemy of the Picts, the Atlanteans, through Borna, had sworn to aid each other again in time of need.

"Since he fought alongside us at Brae Calaadas, Elak has visited many lands in the Atlantean continent, and has seen the veracity of the Great Darkness and its powers. The Crow God, Muthraan, sends us word of these exploits through his black-winged messengers. In the far south of Atlantis, in the city of Zangarza, Elak first encountered the threat of the Leviathan Lord, Xeraph-Hizer, and thwarted his designs before restoring order, and an alliance with the city state.

"On the island of the Death Seeds, Elak and his followers defeated Xumatoq, a god-like creature from the stars, destroying it and the seeds that could have blighted our world. Just as the Orugllyr in the north begin their invasion, so does the monstrous sea dweller in the east, Xeraph-Hizer, thirst again for human victims and the destruction of all our nations. Twice since the god was repulsed at Zangarza has he again attempted to bring the Atlanteans down, but the powerful Druid, Dalan, right arm of the king, drew upon ancient powers to help the king defy him.

"Yet now an alliance between the northern threat of the Orugllyr and Xeraph-Hizer, together with other deep dwellers in the far western ocean, will bring far worse down on us all."

Thus the great stones had spoken, and there was not a man among that fierce company that did not feel the cold wind of coming doom and hear the laughter of mad stars.

*

"It's magnificent!"

A group of men stood before the steps leading to the throne, the heavy, extraordinarily decorated Dragon Throne that had taken a month to haul across the wilds of northern Atlantis, through the passes of Cyrena's low border mountains to its new location here in the capital, Epharra.

The voice of Zerrahydris, Prime Councillor, rang out in the great hall and behind him a hundred fellow Councillors, officials and dignitaries of the city roared approval. Beside Zerrahydris, Elak and Dalan exchanged smiles, relieved that the mighty throne had at last completed its hazardous transition from its previous western location. It had taken more than physical effort to get it here to the royal palace, not least through the use of the bone-carved rods taken from Sea Fire Island in the young king's perilous voyage there.

"Once the last of the treaties are signed with our allies," Dalan said softly to Elak, "you can sit upon the Dragon Throne and be crowned king of all Atlantis. It will be the first time in generations that the continent will come under the sway of a single ruler."

Elak nodded. The thought both excited and worried him. It would be a heavy burden for one man, but he knew he had reliable people around him to help him govern, in Councillors, priests and warriors who obeyed him unquestioningly, reliable and loyal. Elak's voyages over recent times may have frequently infuriated the Council, notably Zerrahydris, but they had secured the love of the army and navy. Men willingly swore fealty to a king who had proven himself in battle and been first to lead the way against the throne's enemies.

Once the hubbub had died down and people went back to the duties of state, Dalan took Elak to one side, where

Lycon was waiting for them. Elak noted the sour look on his sword companion's face. "Not cheering our success?" said the king, laughing.

Lycon smiled, though ruefully, but before he could comment, Dalan motioned both men aside and led them through a low doorway to private rooms where they would not be interrupted. Elak turned to them, aware that something disturbed them. "So, is our happy day to be soured?"

Dalan grunted. "There is word from the Picts. A flight of crows, servants of their Crow God, Muthraan. From Borna himself."

Elak could see from the Druid's expression the news could not be good. "What's happened?"

Dalan spoke solemnly. "A new terror has birthed itself in the farthermost northern ice lands. Whole tribes have been slaughtered, sacrificed in the Vaarfrost region."

"Who is responsible? Have the creatures we defeated at Brae Calaadas returned/"

"Aye. They have darker masters now. Beings the Picts have named the Orugllyr. The Old Gods from times lost in misty oblivion. The Crawling Death they sent was merely the beginning. Their ambitions are clear. Invasion. And worse, Borna's shaman predict that these Orugllyr will seek a union with the deep-sea powers in the eastern oceans."

"Xeraph-Hizer?" said Elak, face clouding as he spoke the hated name.

"We have always known they would come," said Lycon. "Perhaps not so soon, but this is no false alarm."

Elak cursed softly. Epharra had not long recovered from the devastating conflict with the servants of the Death Tide, with much rebuilding and reorganizing of the city's defences against threats from the sea. "How soon can we expect this invasion?"

"Borna has asked for a meeting, in the islands east of his kingdom. He wants men of Atlantis to stand beside him as they did at Brae Calaadas."

"Of course," said Elak, without hesitation. "I will organize a small fleet."

Dalan scowled. He was well used to the young king's impetuosity, and knew he'd insist on accompanying the fleet to meet Borna. "It is a delicate matter, Elak. More so than ever."

"Gods, Dalan, you mean the Councillors! They want to sit me on the throne and not move from it. A statue can do that, but not me! Borna is our ally now. We cannot afford to slight the Picts, and we'll need their help if we're to be attacked by these northern invaders."

"Within a few days you are to be made king of all Atlantis," said Dalan. "You would postpone that?"

"The occasion must not be rushed. Everything must be conducted with all due regard to protocol and to the satisfaction of the nations of Atlantis."

Dalan smiled. It was ironic to hear the young man make such a statement, given the headlong pursuits of his life so far. Was he beginning to understand the rudiments of statecraft already?

"We must visit Borna first and then have the coronation on our return. In fact, I would hope to bring the Pictish king back here as a representative of all his nation. They may not consider themselves part of the new Empire, but it would cement the alliance to have his support on the great day."

Dalan looked at Lycon, who was now grinning with genuine pleasure. "Spoken like a king," Dalan laughed.

3: In the King's Absence

Vannadas coughed, a dry, retching sound that shook

his rapidly aging body. The Councillors who had gathered for this private meeting watched him with deep unease. Slumped in the seat, it was more evident than ever that his health had taken an abrupt turn for the worse: he was declining far more rapidly than previously. In the last few months the king's cousin had been improving, relieved of the burden of regency when Elak had returned from his voyages and taken up the mantle of office. Whatever illness wracked Vannadas seemed to have subsided and the court physicians were hopeful that he would make a full recovery. Now, however, he was grey-faced, hunched, and lined with premature age. The timing of the illness' return could not have been more inconvenient.

"I am not fit to be regent, even for a short while," he said, coughing again. "Epharra needs a much stronger man in command while Elak visits our Pictish allies."

Eupherites, another of the elder Councillors, nodded calmly, although his glances at his colleagues implied he was anything but inwardly calm. "Zerrahydris has done his utmost to persuade the king not to leave the city until he has set the crown of all Atlantis on his brow."

"And failed," grunted Munnaster, like Eupherites, an elder with much experience of governance. "Much as I love our young king, his stubbornness frequently exasperates me. There will always be threats from beyond the borders of empire, and a dozen reasons to sail off and meet them. I for one have never been completely at ease with this Pictish alliance. Gods, but we've been killing each other since men first walked!"

Eupherites nodded again. "Nevertheless, Elak will sail to meet Borna. He takes this threat from the ice wastes of the north seriously. As does Dalan. You, Vannadas, will be regent. Elak will not hear of anyone else taking the role."

Vannadas grimaced. "He knows I am unwell, but says it is his Council who have the real power. I would be a mere figurehead. Anyone else, Elak says, might be tempted to overreach himself as regent and exercise power too freely. Elak knows I would not do that."

Bardoc, a younger, more hard-line Councillor, said coldly, "I take it you refer to your brother, Scuvular? A blind man could see that man's ambition. He'd like nothing more than to take the regency."

"And from there it would be a short step to taking the throne itself," said Eupherites.

Vannadas shook his head. "You are too hard on my brother. You forget it was Scuvular who rooted out the plot to assassinate Elak. Thanks to him the traitors were brought to justice. Scuvular, you remember, was injured for his pains. Elak could do worse than to make him regent."

The Councillors exchanged glances in silence, none prepared to speak their minds to Vannadas, who was clearly set in his own thoughts.

"Since I am to bear the burden of regency," he said, "I will do so. But you know my health is not good. I will lean on you heavily."

"We are united in our support," said Eupherites and the others bowed in confirmation.

Once Vannadas had left them, Eupherites emitted a deep sigh of exasperation. "We'll have to be very wary of Scuvular. There have been promotions in both the army and navy, favouring his supporters. He's exercised his influence over Vannadas more than once. The regent just doesn't see it."

"You fear a coup?" said Bardoc.

"Scuvular will be at his most dangerous while Elak is away."

"Why not have him removed?" said Bardoc, his meaning obvious.

Eupherites shook his head "Much as I'd like to

sanction such action, it would be impossible. Scuvular's back is too well defended. He knows well enough we'd have him killed if the chance arose. And we cannot bring him to court. He covers his tracks far too well. We'll just have to be doubly vigilant."

*

The subject of the three Councillors' discussion sat in another chamber, two others with him, and all drank glasses of the finest Atlantean wine. Scuvular was corpulent, his face pale, testament to a life spent out of the sun and away from affairs of state that might have placed him in the line of battle. He had always ensured his services to the crown required him to be at court, embroiled in diplomatic issues, an apparent willing tool of the Council. It was behaviour that had won him the trust of Vannadas, and through that the king, though others remained sceptical.

With him were Theorron, a former sea captain who had performed numerous shadowy enterprises for him, a man of middle age, battle-hardened and now enjoying the rank of commander of a small fleet of Atlantean warships, operating mainly along the continent's western seaboard. It was a coast that he knew well, having run numerous underhand dealings with pirates and other private bands for years. The third member of the company was Rannadal, a younger man, distantly related to Scuvular, also promoted to commander, ruthless and eager to win further favour, ready to do whatever instructed in Scuvular's power games.

"Word has it," said Theorron, "your brother is about to take up the regency for a further tenure." He was a weather-beaten, coarse man, far happier on the swaying deck of a ship than at court, where he came as infrequently as possible. He preferred the rough badinage of his crewmen and the taste of ale, rather than this tart wine Scuvular was so fond of.

"Indeed," said Scuvular. "But it will not be for long. Once Elak sails, and that'll be very soon, Vannadas will take over."

"We all know," said Rannadal, sipping his own wine thoughtfully, savouring its rich flavour, "his health falters." He was as lean as a war hound, his eyes reflecting the cold inner drive, his pinched features drawn into a smile that those who knew him were wary of.

Scuvular laughed softly. "Dalan's physicians did well to restore my brother's vigour, once the king returned from his eastern escapades. But they grow complacent. Vannadas has been an easier target of late. The poisons that have been introduced into him will do their work subtly. It will not be long after Elak has sailed that Vannadas will die. His last wish will be that I succeed him as regent. Many of the Council will protest, but enough of them will respect Vannadas' authority."

"So you'll have your opponents removed," said Theorron grimly, drawing a hand across his throat and releasing a great belch of laughter.

Scuvular ignored the man's ignorance. He was too valuable to reprimand. "This will not be an open war. There'll be a time for that. You'll get a chance to flex your muscles, Theorron. Keep your men fit."

"None fitter! You've only to say the word."

Scuvular glanced at Rannadal, who smiled at Theorron's bombast. "We are well prepared," the young man said with confidence.

*

Elak gripped the rail at the prow of the royal flagship,

the *Wavecutter*, leaning forward, letting the cool northern breeze rifle his hair and the flecks of spray dampen his features as he studied the seas ahead. In his fleet, dozens of Atlantean ships skimmed smoothly through the waves, each of them filled with armed men, as large a company as had been assembled for many a year, for Borna's message from the north had been taken seriously. Elak could scent the lure of battle on the wind. How much more he enjoyed this situation than the cloying chambers of the palace. He knew how important it was for him to rule from the newly set Dragon Throne, in the heart of Epharra and the new empire, to be present and to exercise his hard-won power from there, but oh, how he ever longed to be at sea, pitting his life and that of his men against its endless perils. *Maybe when I'm an old man*, he thought, *if I reach such an age, I will be ready to sit back in the halls, and be content to relive my adventures. But I must undertake them first!* He laughed and turned to meet the broad grin of Lycon.

"Something is amusing you?" said the latter.

"The sea, Lycon. Would that I could live my entire life upon it. I love my homeland dearly, and we've all given much to secure its future, but this is where I come alive!"

Lycon laughed. "You and I will always be torn. We've had our fun on land. Too many adventures perhaps, but that's behind us now. Once you've taken the crown of empire, well, you will need to settle. Find a wife –"

"Gods, let's not discuss that now. We've more than enough to contend with in Borna's lands."

Lycon grunted. "If he's right, war is coming." *And you, my king, will relish it. You'll be the first to fling yourself into the melee.*

*

In Epharra, below the palace in a private chamber where only members of the Council were ever allowed to set foot, Zerrahydris greeted three of his colleagues and waited for the guards to leave them.

Eupherites spoke softly, though no sounds escaped this sacred place. "Elak would not be turned?"

Zerrahydris snorted angrily. "He told me again that he knows we can manipulate Vannadas, so is confident we have control over Atlantis. It's a mock regency."

"But if Vannadas dies?" said Munnaster.

"That's a real concern. The serpent, Scuvular, has far more allies than it first seemed. If Vannadas dies, he will make his move, and he'll do so with steel at his back."

"He'll take the regency by force?" said Eupherites.

"There are those on the Council who think he's right. They've never approved of Elak's rash adventuring and suspect it'll never end. Worse, some of my colleagues are violently opposed to any treaties with the Picts, as I was since my father was killed fighting them years ago. Since Borga and Elak fought side by side on Brae Calaadas, my attitude towards them has softened. Yet Scuvular has played on the prejudices of many of our colleagues, creating a rift between sections of the Council. When he does make his move, it will be with a strong backing. I've made my own feelings clear, to you and to the king. I would have him here, in Epharra. I'd have him crowned, and I'd have him wed. But although he insists on dealing with half of the problems of empire by standing in the prow of a ship, I will not deny him my support. There is no finer man to rule us."

"Well said," agreed Eupherites. "He's exasperating, but well loved by his people."

"And he has the respect of many of Atlantis' lands and kings. Scuvular could not command such support," said Bardoc.

"Yes, many ships have sailed with Elak to Borna's islands with armed forces from places such as Sarhaddon, Poseidonis and Kiriath," said Munnaster.

Zerrahydris looked thoughtful. "Scuvular most know Elak's power is very great. If he truly wants to bring Elak to battle over the throne, as it seems he might, he knows he would be opposing a united Atlantis. One he could not possibly hope to overthrow."

"Yet we all know his ambitions," said Eupherites.

"It poses the question, what allies does Scuvular have? Who would support his apparently insane intentions?"

Zerrahydris' words sent a chill through the three Councillors.

"Is it possible," said Eupherites, "that Scuvular would seek an alliance with Elak's enemies? Servants of the powers that are said to be rising *against* Atlantis?"

Zerrahydris stared into the shadows of the chamber, as if seeing some dark vista there, an unsettling vision. "You have given voice to my worst fears," he said softly.

4: The Thing Beneath the Waves

Lycon tossed and turned in his bunk, fending off dreams that had him mumbling in his sleep until he rose from their darkness to full wakefulness. He was in a small cabin adjacent to Elak's. The gentle roll of the *Wavecutter* had done its best to lull him to even a partial night's rest, but the churning of his mind had won out. He was not going to be able to drop back to sleep. He swung off the narrow bunk and pulled on his boots, opening the door quietly. Lycon nodded to the guards outside, squeezing his not inconsiderable bulk past.

"Need some air," he told them, and they grinned. He was a popular leader among them and had won his place

250

beside the king through his deceptively energetic skills with sword and axe.

Up on the deck of the sleek war galley, Lycon made his way across the moonlit boards to the rail, looking eastwards to where swells of grey sea rose and fell rhythmically, flecked with the white mane of occasional breaking waves. These northern waters were reputedly prone to violent storms, but since leaving Epharra several days previously, the ocean had been sluggish, the passage of the fleet across it comfortable. Elak was due to meet up with Borna two days from now.

A few more guards acknowledged Lycon, keeping their distance, knowing he and the king and their other companion, Dalan the Druid, were rarely away from the ship's rail for long, their stares fixed on the waters, always intrigued by them.

Lycon's dreams had not been disturbing, but the coming meeting with the Picts brought back glimpses of his past. His mother had been of Pictish blood, the daughter of a marriage between a roving Pict warrior and the woman he had abducted from one of the outer islands of Atlantis, on one of many raids at the time. Lycon's blood father had been killed in the raid, and Lycon had been brought up among the Picts until he was of an age when he was able to fight. During a peaceful period between the Picts and Atlantis, Lycon had been sent with others to serve among the ships of Cyrena. In time he broke all ties with his mother's captors and thought of himself as a citizen of Epharra.

For many years he had nurtured a secret vow to bring as many of the Picts to their doom as he could, given the opportunity. His mother had long since died, and although she had known happiness with her new husband, Lycon's grudge against his nation ever burned within him. Now, leaning on the ship's rail, his mind ran over the events of his last visit to these Pictish waters, when he, Elak and Dalan had fought shoulder to shoulder with Borga, and brought down a far more dangerous enemy. They must do so again. The Atlanteans must reaffirm their allegiance to Borga.

Lycon had never said much to Elak about his upbringing, keeping his feelings about the Picts under control. The king was too diplomatic to pry.

The *Wavecutter* moved with the grace and speed of a creature of the seas, leading the line of other vessels, crewed by men of several Atlantean nations, all serving under the new banners of empire. Their warriors would want to blood themselves in battle against whatever was coming from the northern ice wastes, eager to show themselves worthy to Elak before he sat upon the Dragon Throne and formalized his stewardship of them all.

As he watched, Lycon became conscious of movements in the dark shadows of waves slapping the ship's side, something more tangible than the sea. His first thoughts were of seals, which populated these waters in great numbers, colonizing many of the smaller islands. There were porpoises here, too, often accompanying a ship on its voyage, rising out of the seas and plunging back into them like children enjoying freedom. Something below the waves snapped Lycon out of such calm thoughts. This was no playful sea beast, flirting with the ship's passage.

To confirm his sudden unease, a long, whip-like tentacle lashed the side of the craft and attached itself to it, followed by more. Lycon's mouth dried and for a moment he was unable to cry out in alarm. He watched, bewildered, as several shapes squirmed up the tentacles, using them like cables to swarm towards the rail. Lycon went to draw out his sword, but realized he had left it in the cabin. He had only his bare fists with which to defend himself. He did manage to force a cry from salt-crusted lips but a sudden gust of wind tore it away. One look over his shoulder told him he was alone at this section of rail. The other sailors were looking out to westward, unaware of the intruders.

Before Lycon could break away, more of the shapes came upwards, crawling on to the deck like twisted spiders, quasi-human, with long, raking talons, spawn of some deep domain, far from the homes of men. Lycon rushed the first of them, shouting now, his bunched fists driving at the horrors, their sea stench almost overpowering. His knuckles drove into wet, scaled flesh, battering them aside, but a dozen swung over the rail, lithe as apes and slippery as eels. Several guards had at last realized what was occurring and rushed over the deck, swords gleaming in the moonlight. They cut into the sea beasts, but Lycon was surrounded, dragged to the rail.

No one fought more ferociously than him in a such circumstances, and he smashed several of his assailants aside. Yet he may as well have resisted a heavy tide, trying forlornly to beat back its rolling waves. For all his strength, Lycon was gripped and pulled over the rail. By the time the guards had cut through to him, leaving the deck strewn with bloody corpses, Lycon had been torn from the rail and over the ship's side. His body tumbled into the sea, and as it did, the last of the creatures dived back into the ocean and the thing that had attached itself to the *Wavecutter* freed itself and slid below the water.

The sailors raised further shouts of alarm, though none of them dared to take the plunge after the fallen Lycon, all filled with terror by the sight of the thing that had disappeared. In the ensuing furore, more men came to the rail, including Elak and Dalan.

"It's Lycon, sire," said one of the guards. "they dragged him overboard."

"What!" roared Elak, at once preparing to mount the

rail and dive off it.

Dalan gripped his arm and restrained him, though it was no easy task. "Wait, Elak. It's a trap."

"I can't let him drown!"

"No. But he won't drown."

Elak swung round to look into Dalan's troubled gaze. The Druid had stretched out an arm towards the sea, as if he could feel the waters, or read them. "They've taken him below, but not to drown him. He lives. I can feel his heart."

"We must follow," Elak insisted. "Turn the ship! We'll set a new course."

"It's what they want."

"Who? Who has done this?" Elak's panic threatened to overwhelm him, and only Dalan's reassurance prevented him from issuing immediate orders to turn the *Wavecutter*.

"Servants of the Orugllyr. They've abducted Lycon for a reason."

*

Lycon fought his way back from unconsciousness, hands clawing at the air like a drowning man coming to the surface of a swirling sea. He struggled to his knees, looking around him. His immediate thought was that he was in a large cave, thrown by his captives on to a rocky floor. His captives – yes, he recalled them. Men who were not men, aquatic beings whose strong arms and talons had locked on him, dragging him beneath the waves, bearing him down into unconsciousness and the sure knowledge that he must drown. Then there had been silence and darkness.

He studied his situation. He had been left almost naked, stripped of his robe and sandals. Around him the floor of the cavern dipped away on all sides and by a shimmering light overhead he saw he was on a rocky outcrop, a tiny islet, surrounded by flat, grey water. A sea cave? Some distance above him, the ceiling appeared to be made from glass or crystal, a large, curving dome through which the light of day, as he assumed, gleamed. Outside the glass countless shapes swam to and fro like huge birds, and he understood it was the sea beyond the dome.

Swinging round he looked for signs of his abductors, but there were none. The cavern was closed in by impenetrable shadows. If he wanted to investigate beyond the surrounding waters, he would have to plunge into them and swim across. He went to the shoreline of the islet and looked down. Although the waters were flat and very still, his senses warned him something stirred within them, and further out he was certain he had seen something turn just below the surface, something large and coiled. Beside him there were a few broken chunks of rock; he lifted one and threw it as far as he could out into the pool. It splashed noisily on entry and a frantic surge of waters followed as whatever lurked beneath investigated.

Lycon swore softly. He was a prisoner. For a while he watched the aerial display high above. Shoals of fish passed, followed by the unmistakable silhouettes of larger, unrecognizable creatures, and beyond, at the edge of the light, much larger shapes moved like great vessels, disturbing as leviathans. A sound behind him made him turn. Something had been pushed up from below the islet's surface. It was a small plinth, made from polished marble, and on it rested a pitcher and a platter, with bread and meat. His hunger spurred him to it, but before he tasted the food or set the pitcher of water to his lips, he paused. It wouldn't be poisoned: his captors would not have gone to the trouble of bringing him here to poison him. Drugged? It was a dilemma, but after a while his hunger forced him to try the meat. It tasted good and the water seemed pure.

When he had finished, he saw a light across the water, a bobbing lantern, and a flat craft being poled across towards him by a hunched figure. Standing in the boat was a tall, robed being, leaning on a long spear. Its head was covered, but its eyes gleamed with an emerald fire, unnatural and malevolent. Lycon went to the water's edge cautiously. The boat stopped and remained away from the shore as the robed figure watched him as if studying a specimen in a cage.

"Who are you?" Lycon growled.

The figure remained silent. For answer it lowered the spear, though not hinting at throwing it. Instead it pointed the weapon at Lycon, and a sudden crackle of light lanced from the spear's tip, crossing the space and splashing on Lycon's chest like a hot blast of air. Lycon stumbled backwards and saw a second beam of light rise up from where the first had struck him and fly, true as an arrow, up through the air and then the crystal dome, out into the sea beyond. As it left him, he felt something inside him, some vital force, drawn out of him and mingled with the light. The strange sensation lasted for no more than a few moments, and then darkness descended once more, and he blacked out.

Later, when he came to, the flat boat was gone. On the plinth there was more food and drink, and beside it, his clothes and sandals. No weapons, of course. He dressed sullenly, knowing all he could do now was wait.

5: Shadows beneath Epharra

Elak paced impatiently, pausing now and then to turn to Dalan. The Druid, however, remained as fixed and unmoving as a statue, gazing out over the small bay and beyond to the vast expanse of northern ocean. Since Lycon's abduction, the fleet had been anchored here for most of the day. It had taken all Dalan's persuasive arts and common sense to prevail upon the king not to sail blind into the mists of the eastern waters in immediate pursuit of his friend.

"Whoever has taken Lycon, they have done this for a single purpose – to goad you into following," Dalan had said as Elak fumed and initially had made ready to turn the fleet away from the Pictish isles.

"Every moment we delay puts his life at risk!" cried Elak. "I will not abandon him."

"Would you jeopardize the entire fleet? Lycon has not been snatched simply so that he can be killed and tossed aside like a gnawed bone. He would be of no value to our enemies dead."

Dalan's powerful argument won out and as there were a number of small islands close by, they had swiftly sailed there and anchored the ships. Dalan, Elak and a small company of guards had climbed the highest point of the eastern isle, from where the Druid studied the seas. At last he stirred, lifting his staff, watching the waves and – light. A beam of it skimmed across the choppy waters, its target the island. Elak saw it as it rose and speared in, striking Dalan's staff.

"What is it?" Elak cried, gripping the Druid's arm as he staggered from the impact. For long moments he was bathed in a soft hue, his eyes closed as if he were reading something in the air.

"If it is a language, it is not one I know. Yet it tells me one thing," replied the Druid as the light abruptly winked out, its work done. "Lycon is alive. His abductors have told me that much."

"Why have they abducted him?"

Dalan scowled. "I can only assume it is for one reason. He is bait. They want us to go to them. They want you, Elak."

"How far away are they?"

"Fifty sea miles eastward, no more."

"Borna cannot be far to our west. He'll know these waters. And he'll provide our fleet with ships of his own. When he does, we will sail eastward." Elak's words had a finality about them that Dalan recognized only too well. Once the young king had determined a course of action, there was little if anything that could be done to change his mind.

*

Borna's fleet was closer to the Atlanteans than they realized and by evening its messengers reached the island and the bay where Elak's ships were anchored. Dalan and Elak met the Picts on the beach, so eager was Elak to speak to them and prepare for action. It was Kaa Mag Borga, son of the Pictish king, who stood before him, a grim smile on his fierce features. He was taller than most Picts, a muscular man, his torso tattooed and oiled, elaborately painted, a war club at his side. His warriors were likewise equipped, but their hostility was reserved for other intruders in their waters.

Elak and Kaa Mag Borga gripped arms in friendship. They had once fought a bloody battle together and it bound them fiercely in blood ties. Elak quickly explained to the Pict what had befallen Lycon.

"What lands lie in the east?" Elak asked.

"The ocean is empty for hundreds of miles. There is no island known to us there."

Elak turned to Dalan. "Fifty miles," said the Druid. "Something is there now. Either risen from the deeps, or below them."

"Our shaman, Cruath Morgas, may know," said Kaa

Mag Borna. "He is with my father on the island of Grunfelda, awaiting your coming."

Elak nodded slowly, but his frustration at another delay was plain to see on his face. "How many Pictish ships have come?"

"At Grunfelda there are a score of our war craft. Further west the main body of our fleet, prepared for war, lies at anchor on our eastern island boundary. Should you and my father decide to attack the Orugllyr, we are ready."

Dalan met Elak's anxious stare. "Then we must go to Borna at once. Certainly we should sail east, but we must be fully prepared for whatever lies there."

"A trap, you say," said Kaa Mag Borna. "How large a force awaits us?"

"It is shrouded in mystery," said Dalan. "It is well hidden from my eyes. Perhaps if your shaman and I combine our powers, as we have done before, we can unfurl the shadows cloaking it."

*

Scuvular came to the wide bed in the chamber of shadows, where a single lamp burned, throwing the figure on the bed into relief. The face of Vannadas was a sickly white smear, the eyes closed in sleep. There was very little rise and fall of his chest beneath a thin sheet. One of the physicians standing behind him looked across at Scuvular, slowly shaking his head.

"I thought he was beginning to recover," Scuvular whispered.

"He's taken a turn for the worse. We fear he will have passed by the morning. We have tried everything, but cannot reverse the sickness."

Scuvular glared at the other physicians, controlling

what appeared to be a mixture of anger and sadness. Slowly he withdrew. Outside in the corridor, his face became a blank mask. One of the soldiers stepped forward, a man who had become an almost constant companion to Scuvular. This was Azarvis, a dark-haired commander, his face like stone, obedient as a trained hound, a man who had risen quickly from the ranks in devout service to his master.

"He'll not see the dawn out," Scuvular told him.

"There is a message," said Azarvis. "From below."

They left the chambers of the regent, escorted by a small group of Azarvis's men and made their way down into the lower passages of the palace, discreetly bypassing the busiest areas and keeping as much to the shadows as they could. Night had a firm grip on these corridors, where few lamps burned. Far beyond the palace's corridors, in places generally shunned they went. Eventually, when they reached a certain door, Azarvis ensured they were not followed or seen. With a heavy, ancient key, he opened the door, posting two of his guardsmen outside it while he, Scuvular and the others passed within and began a long climb down a stair into the uttermost bowels of the earth. A faint glow rose up from the deeps, barely limning each narrow step and the air was pungent with a reptilian stench.

For a long time the small party descended, the stairwell twisting and turning like a monstrous burrow into the earth, its walls slick with moisture, dappled with fungus and blobs of lichen. The air was clammy and the men pulled scarves around their lower faces. When the party came to the floor at the foot of the stair, it was uneven, its incalculably ancient flat stones broken and cracked. Whoever had set them here, it had been done untold centuries ago, testament to an age long forgotten.

There were numerous tunnels off the main run, holes into utter darkness and silence. Scuvular and Azarvis reached another door and again Azarvis used a key to open it. It swung on oiled hinges into a low chamber, lit by several glowing candles. By their insipid light a number of figures stood around the far wall of the chamber, hunched and hooded, larger than men, but whose features were invisible, their arms cloaked in dark robes. In the centre of the room a lone figure waited, its face also covered, a hood covering the head so that only a gleam of reflected light shone from the eyes within.

Scuvular inclined his head. "I received your message, Yssargur."

The voice that issued from the invisible lips of the figure was soft and sibilant, almost a hiss, as if the being was unused to using the human tongue. "My master holds himself in readiness. All is prepared, as you asked. For your allegiance, my master will aid you in your ambitions and reward you when the time is ripe. What news do you have for me to take back to him?"

"The ancient poison you provided for me has almost done its work. Vannadas will be dead by dawn, if not soon after."

"And the Council will make you regent?"

"They have no other choice. Some may dissent, but my rights should not be questioned."

The eyes within the hood blazed for a moment like the coals of a fire. "My master will be satisfied. Once your place is secured, you have only to call upon us. Epharra will fall while its king is embroiled in the cold north. When he returns, assuming he survives, with what little he has of his fleet, he will not be strong enough to reclaim the city. When my master sits on the Dragon Throne, this kingdom will be his."

*

Grunfelda was a small island, low, but with an excellent sheltered harbour. Elak, Dalan, Borna and men of both their forces gathered on the central hill in an area that had been cleared to form an amphitheatre, in the centre of which stood a ring of low stones, each of them carved with ancient writings and pictograms representing the waves of the ocean and some of its creatures. Dalan whispered to Elak that these were very ancient demi-gods of the Picts and this was a highly sacred place, one which few, if any, Atlanteans had ever been allowed to visit previously. It was also, said the Druid, a place of human sacrifice, and the earth here had once been soaked in the blood of offerings to the Pictish gods, the fearful Lords of Midnight.

Borna came to them and set a spear in the earth before Elak. "My people are grateful for your renewal of our alliance, Elak. As we fought before, and shed blood for each other, so we must again. The Orugllyr will soon be upon us. My son tells me that the great warrior, Lycon, has been abducted by the enemy. They hold him somewhere in the east."

"What lies there?" said Dalan.

Borna shook his head. "It is a vast expanse of open ocean. There are no islands. But there are legends of lands beneath the seas. In such places the Orugllyr may have gathered in preparation for war."

Beside the Pictish king, his primary shaman, the blind Cruath Morgas, had his head turned seaward, his senses tuned to it, as if he could see with an inner eye the rolling ocean and whatever secrets it harboured. "Lycon is alive," he said. "Just as Dalan has told you."

Elak, whose handsome features for once looked strained, his expression one of anguish, spoke quickly and emotionally. "A trap, we believe. Our enemy wants us to rush in and attempt to free Lycon. And I will not abandon him. The Orugllyr must be made to understand that Atlantis and her allies are not to be mocked."

Borna smiled, though it was a cold, disturbing smile. "They bring war. Whether we wait for them to come to us and fight them on our islands and in our seas, or whether we sail to them and fight them in the eastern waters, or below it if we must, it is all one."

"Then we will answer their challenge?" said Elak.

Borna pulled his spear from the earth and held it up for his company of warriors to see. "We do! Let the gods in the stones speak to us this night." He swung round to the low stones in the centre of the amphitheatre. "Summon them, Cruath Morgas! Call upon their ancient powers and make ready our blood, and that of our allies. War is upon us."

6: The Voice of the Stone

Low in the skies east of Atlantis, the sun began to spread its vivid dawn rays, the ocean coming to life in a blaze of colour. In Epharra, the city had awoken to tragedy, for the king's regent, Vannadas, beloved by many of the capital's citizens, was dead: the unknown disease had done its work, reducing him to a shadow of himself, a withered corpse, dry and parched as a mummy. Already preparations were under way to carry him from the royal chambers to a brief place of rest before he could be set upon his funeral pyre and offered to the gods. While all of Epharra mourned, the City Council gathered in its chambers.

Zerrahydris sat at the high table, central to it, with all the prominent Councillors on either side of him, preparing to address the company seated in the echoing hall. Among the others assembled were Scuvular and his immediate guards. They waited in silence, carved like statues, whatever personal thoughts running through their heads concealed.

There was a long moment of prayer and reflection in respect to the deceased Vannadas, before Eupherites stood and made a speech about the worthiness of the former regent, and of the benefits his life of service had brought to Cyrena and latterly the expanding Atlantean empire. When he had finished his address, Eupherites sat and Zerrahydris rose.

"Our ruler, Elak, will not be able to return to us until matters are concluded in the north," he said, his words sharp and clear. "As always, the king has responded to a threat to our nation. It has never been in his nature to sit while others ride or sail to war to protect us. Knowing his present voyage might demand months of his time, he gave the Council clear instructions about the governing of his new empire."

Scuvular watched the Councillors openly, though not one of them met his gaze. He knew he was not popular, but he had the right of succession. Tradition was with him. They had to bestow the regency on him until Elak returned.

Zerrahydris held up a roll of parchment. "Here are the express wishes of the king. In the event of the regent, Vannadas, being taken ill, or otherwise becoming unable to fulfil his royal duties, it is necessary to provide an alternative regency. Thus, with a heavy heart, we acknowledge the death of our regent and friend, Vannadas, and apply the wishes of the king in his absence. The duties of the regency are to be divided between the primary members of the Council."

Zerrahydris read on, giving comprehensive details of how the Council was to operate in Elak's absence, but Scuvular did not hear. His fury boiled inside him, though his features remained fixed, his expression revealing nothing of his raging anger. He would have risen and roared out his objections to this betrayal, this rejection of his rights, but he knew this was not the place to make a scene. He did have followers, and far more of them than the Council might have known, but they did nothing without his express command. He knew he must continue the game of being loyal to Elak and his wishes, a seemingly dependable servant, a man who would put Atlantis before his own ambitions.

When the meeting adjourned, Scuvular was sent for. He subdued his anger and donned the calm face that had kept him in high office, entering the private chamber of the senior Councillors and bowing to them.

Zerrahydris waved him to a seat. "We realize you will be disappointed by Elak's decision. Your service to the crown is appreciated and respected, Scuvular. However, we are bound by the king's commands." He held out the parchment from which he had read the announcement. "You will note the royal seal."

Scuvular gave it a cursory glance. "As always, I will obey the king's instructions. And those of the Council. I am at your disposal, and my men are yours to command." He handed back the parchment. "Although this is a break with protocol. There is a line of succession. I trust that the tradition of history remains unbroken."

"This is a temporary matter, outside of our rules of succession. I suggest we address such matters as and when we need to."

Scuvular bowed with apparent good grace, and a few further pleasantries were exchanged before he quit the chamber. In his quarters he sat with Azarvis and others close to him, men of war who owed their status to him and who would stop at little to promote his interests. Scuvular's anger finally got the better of him and he released a stream of invective, hurling his empty wine beaker across the chamber.

"Maybe it's time some of these accursed Councillors disappeared," said Azarvis. "Like Vannadas."

"No! No more poison. I'm sure some of them already suspect the manner of his death. They won't know the source of the poison, but if we repeat the dose among Councillors, Dalan's Druids will sniff it out."

One of the others, Theorron, a former sea captain with a very dubious reputation as a collaborator with pirates, now a commander, tapped his sword hilt. "A swift strike in the night, then. It's been done before."

Scuvular cursed again. "All fingers will point at me, if I am not careful. But you are right. We need to reduce the Council. I need time to think about this."

"What about Yssargur and his master?" said Azarvis. "Does their support not depend on your becoming regent?"

Scuvular did not need reminding, and swore again. "There is time, as long as the king is embroiled in the northern war. We will pick our moment. What is coming to Atlantis in inevitable."

*

Elak and his companions stood alongside Borna and other Pictish chieftains and watched as Cruath Morgas approached the circle of stones at the heart of the island, raising his arms and intoning words of ancient sorceries and invocations of his gods. The shaman's blind eyes seemed to be focused on the stones as if they could see them clearly, and his spear, wreathed in black crow feathers and tiny bones, reached out to indicate each individual stone. Overhead the darkness churned like an aerial whirlpool, the stars blurring. A wind roared like the voice of a god and beneath the watchers the ground trembled as though something vast moved beneath it. For a moment Elak thought an earthquake would shake the island, but when he saw the stones lifting, collapsing to one side, he knew this was no natural disturbance. The heart of the circle split open, and gouts of soil and smaller stones burst aside as something emerged from the ground, something far larger than the stones ringing it.

A deep, resonant sound rose from below, a chorus of voices that was far too low on the scale to be human, and as it rose, so the huge monolith became an immense finger poking at the swirling heavens, drawing the power of the elements into it, surging with the energy. It was as smooth as glass, and opaque, so that the shapes within it, vaguely glimpsed, were like figures, though grossly distorted. They were squat, far too wide to be human, with heads sat upon shoulders without necks, their features altogether indistinguishable, and their bloated arms hung down, their lower bodies hidden in shadow. Their mouths, ovoid darkness, were the source of the deep, unearthly singing.

Elak and his companions drew back as the monolith ceased rising, now twenty feet high, the sound emerging from it blotting out all other sounds other than a sudden cry from Cruath Morgas. "The Lords of Midnight have answered our call." The shaman turned to the company. "Step aside!"

Immediately both the Atlanteans and the Picts did as bidden, moving quickly to either edge of the clearing. As they watched, all mesmerized by the spectacle of the monolith, it dragged its hidden roots from the soil like some arboreal giant of the forest and moved, wreathed in shadows. Slowly its shape and solidity began to fade, consumed by a darkness that welled up like a tide from the ground around it, until it became no more than a pulsing, black cloud. Only the deep, throbbing chorus of sound remained as the darkness rolled like an immense boulder down through the clearing and into the trees beyond, making for the bay below, where it quickly sank into the hungry embrace of the waves. The watchers fell back further, brushed aside by huge forces they neither controlled nor understood.

Elak shook himself as if waking from a dream, staring into the wide-eyed expression of Dalan, who gripped his arm. "It has passed," said the Druid.

"Ishtar, but what sorcery drove it!" Elak gasped, his voice low.

"Our gods are far from here, Elak. These are not lands they know. What dwells in the deeps belongs to an antiquity that makes the birth of Atlantis a recent event in the affairs of our world."

"Where is that thing?" Elak was peering down into the night towards the sea far below them. Remarkably there was nothing among the trees to mark the passage of the stone, as though it had moved like a wraith through them.

Borna stood beside him, no less dazed. "It will sink far beneath the waves to the ocean floor," he said. "And on other islands in these waters, more will do the same. The Singers have been woken. They will cross the bottom of the sea and find the sunken realm of our enemies."

*

Lycon feigned sleep, his attention fixed on the place where the plinth rose from time to time with food and drink for him. He had suffered no ill effects from eating and drinking it. Once he'd had his meals, the plinth withdrew, slotting back into the surface of the island, a neat seal. In the waters surrounding him dark shapes continued to coil and uncoil like serpents, a constant reminder there was no way off the islet by swimming. Instead he concentrated on the plinth.

After a long while it hummed upward, the usual plate

of bread and meat and small pitcher of water waiting to be consumed. He snatched at the meat and started chewing it, then gripped the edges of the plinth with both hands and tugged. Initially he couldn't move it or twist it. He gave a harder wrench and heard something crack, like a bone being broken. Encouraged, he twisted more and used every ounce of his strength to force the plinth to one side, like trying to snap tree roots and work it from its bed. The sweat stood out on his face as he renewed his efforts, until he gradually pulled the plinth and its base from the ground, again using all his physical power to work it loose. He tossed it to one side, and dropping to his knees, pulled the small slabs surrounding the hole aside. He scooped out soil and more stones until the hole widened, revealing a darkened space. He thrust his head and shoulders into it, but could see no more than a few inches.

He gave a brief prayer to his gods and gripped the sides of the hole, swinging himself down into the utter dark, then let himself fall.

7: They Met in Darkness

Elak stood at the prow of the *Wavecutter*, studying every swell ahead of the sleek craft. The skies were thick with dark grey clouds, crushed together by the fierce northeastern winds, and the seas raced, the waves growing increasingly powerful. Alongside the flagship, other craft rushed eastward as the combined fleets of the Atlanteans and Picts knifed through the foam, each ship with its lookouts, watching for any sign of the place they sought, the promised island that Cruath Morgas had described.

"I have seen it on my inner eye," he had said. "It has risen from the deeps through sorcery and wild storm, the workings of old magic beyond the memory of Man, from a time when other creatures ruled the oceans."

"Lycon is there?" Elak had asked him. "You are certain?"

"Yes. Deep inside its black heart."

"Then we sail at once. No more delays."

Dalan nodded. He knew there would be no point in trying to hold the king back any longer, and it was clear that Borna was eager to join the hunt. The Picts had scores to settle with whatever had crawled up from the sea deeps. Somewhere down in its darkest places, on a seabed thick with weed and rucked up by constant shifts in its crust, the monoliths moved, like creatures of the ocean, invisible but real, their targets fixed.

Elak ignored the blasts of wind, the cold splash of salty spume. He thought only of Lycon, the man who had been an almost constant companion to him since his teen years. He recalled their first meeting as though it had been a few days since. Elak had been one of a group of young blades, sons of the nobility and hotheads who thought they could prowl the night streets of Epharra and enjoy its dark side like any others of their age. They had slipped from the royal palace, ignoring the commands of their seniors, and temporarily eschewing their own royalty, and its infuriating restrictions, a barrier to enjoying life. More than once the group got itself into a scrap and there were injuries and narrow escapes from a nasty end for some of them, but they had always proved effective enough as a fighting unit to be able to drag themselves out of potential disaster and sneak back to the palace before dawn betrayed them.

There came a time, however, when their escapades led them, and Elak in particular, into a desperate situation. They had chosen to visit the most insalubrious of the city's harbour quarters, alehouses where the worst of the visiting pirates gathered, men and women who swore fealty to

Epharra and who had fought for its kings, but who also carried on their secretive trade. For a dare, Elak and a few of his closest friends went into the wharf-side's most notorious drinking den, posing as seamen, but fooling no one. Typically trouble broke out and blades were drawn.

Outside, in a narrow alleyway, Elak found himself cut off from his companions and at the mercy of several burly sailors. They were clearly intent on beating him to a pulp, and in all likelihood would kill him before tossing him into the harbour. Elak and his fellows had made a pact – none of them would ever reveal their identities and use them as a means to get out of trouble, not unless they wanted to invoke the scorn of their fellows. Elak knew if he could convince these thugs he was the brother of Orander, they would not dare to finish him. They were coming at him from both ends of the alley, and although he was skilful and fast with his rapier, the odds against him were too great.

As they closed in, a loud voice roared in the night, coming from one end of the alley, beyond the men. It cursed them roundly and the insults that rolled from its lips made Elak grin in spite of his predicament. Moments later all hell broke loose as the newcomer launched himself into the first of the pirates, lashing out with a sword that shattered the lighter blades and cracked a few skulls. This was Lycon, and it was the first time Elak had set eyes on him. He was a muscular fellow, several years Elak's senior, and what he lacked in speed, he more than made up for in the strength and ferocity of his attack.

By the time Lycon had shouldered his way to Elak's side, half of the pirates were down, nursing bloody heads or broken arms, crawling away, cursing every bit as furiously as Lycon, and Elak marvelled at the inventiveness of the profanities that soured the night air. Between them, Lycon and Elak saw off the remaining pirates, who may have been more dangerous opponents had they not been drinking heavily for most of the night.

"I owe you my life," Elak said, offering his hand.

The bulky warrior gripped it and almost crushed it. "I am Lycon, and you, sire, call yourself Elak on these night rovings, though you are Zeulas, Orander's brother. I recognized you, though these idiots did not. Why did you not tell them?"

"I'll not hide behind my position."

"Too proud, eh?"

"They called you a Pict. There are likenesses in you to that nation, but no more."

"My mother was a Pict. So it's in my blood. In the Pictish islands no one gives much room to anyone not of the pure blood, so I came to Atlantis, seeking a better life. I found a place among the soldiery, but it's a lowly one. My imperfect blood holds me back here, too, it seems."

"Atlantis needs good fighting men, and you, Lycon, are as good a fighter as I've yet seen."

"We were lucky. Now I think it would be best if you quickly made your way back to the palace. You'll not be safe here tonight."

"I have a better idea. Why don't we find somewhere less turbulent and sink a jug or two of wine?"

Lycon scowled, but then laughed, a deep, warm sound. "You'd drink with me?"

"Who better to share wine with than a man who saved me from a watery death? And afterwards, you will come to the palace. I'll find work for you, I promise you."

Now, as Elak watched the passing ocean, he remembered the words as if he had just spoken them. He smiled. It had been a beginning, and by the gods, the times he and Lycon had enjoyed since!

*

Lycon fell a short distance, his feet striking a flat, hard surface; he used his hands to steady himself in the darkness. A few rays of light seeped down from the hole he had made overhead, barely enough to see by. He was on a table or dais, from which a small, curious wooden construction rose up towards the hole. Part of this was composed of wheels and chains and Lycon understood it was the mechanism that had raised and lowered the food and drink that had been sent to him. It leaned to one side, some of its workings dangling like torn ligaments, and he grinned, recognizing the damage he had done to it.

Cautiously he shuffled to the edge of the table and swung down, feet touching the stone floor below. By the weak light he saw he was in a small chamber, the table the only thing it contained. The roughly circular walls were stone, slick with weed and dripping, broken by a single doorway, a low portal that led into complete darkness. He stood beside this, listening intently. He could hear running water somewhere beyond and other murmurings that could have been low voices, though in such a confined space sound was contorted. He went back to the table and tore a short length of wood from the crippled mechanism: it would serve as a rough club.

Satisfied no one was coming from beyond the door, he went through it and darkness swallowed him, cold and clammy. He kept one hand on the wall beside him, though it was unpleasant to touch, its growths slippery, redolent with the smell of deep water weed. Tiny shapes shifted within the knotted mass, and he was glad of the dark. The floor sloped downwards, and he assumed he was passing under the water surrounding the islet. Presently he stepped into what he thought must be a puddle, but it extended down the tunnel, getting deeper as he went on, rising to his knees. The water was cold and stank of weed, though there was none here.

He was about to go back when he felt the floor beginning to rise and moments later he was in shallower water and then broke from it. He must be beyond the pool surrounding the islet. Ahead of him he felt something solid blocking his path. It was either a dead end or a door. He slid his hands over the soaking surface. Wood! Then it must be a door. He explored more of it but was unable to move it. Locked. Then he must wait. Someone would have been replenishing his food and drink, and they must have come through here.

There was enough space in the cramped tunnel for him to get to one side of the door. There he had to endure a seemingly endless vigil. He felt the cold slowly biting into his flesh and bone, trying to exercise his arms and legs. By the Nine Hells, he could do with a flagon of ale to ease his misery! The numbness was slowly threatening him with unconsciousness when there was a loud crack from the darkness in front of him. A key was turning in the lock.

The door swung outwards, creaking on fat hinges, and light from an oil lamp spilled out. Lycon used the door to shield himself. Presently a single figure emerged, holding up the lamp, and by its light Lycon saw she was a young woman, her single garment muddied, her hair long and tangled. She attached the lamp to a hook on the wall and brought a tray with food and drink from beyond the door, setting it down in a niche in the wall while she prepared to close and re-lock the door.

Lycon pushed the door shut and gripped her, one hand across her mouth. She was surprisingly strong and wriggled like an eel, but she was no match for his strength.

"Keep still and you'll not be harmed. Lock the door."

She understood him and did as asked, but still

struggled, her eyes glaring at him in anger. He took his hand from her mouth. "You're the prisoner," she gasped. "How did you get free?"

"Who are you, and who do you serve?"

"I am Arnuell, from the Pictish islands. My chieftain is Janndrak. I am a prisoner here, too."

"Of who?"

"They don't say. My tribe was overwhelmed, most of them killed. Those who are left are made to do menial work here."

"Where exactly are we?"

She shook her head. "This place is not known to us. Some say it heaved itself up from the ocean floor. The creatures who live here are not human. They belong in the sea, far down in places remote from our kind. You are human. Where are you from?" She spoke without fear, her expression one of challenge, but also with hope in her eyes.

"Atlantis," he said and at once her face lit up. "From the city of Epharra, where Elak is king."

She seemed amazed. "Elak! We have heard of him."

"I have to get off this island. Can you and your tribesmen help me?"

"Gladly, although there's no hope of escape. We are far under the surface, and even if by some miracle we got up there, we'd never evade our captors. Their numbers are many. It is only a matter of time before they kill the rest of us, or feed us to their sea beasts."

8: Island of the Orugllyr

Dalan had settled himself near to the prow of the *Wavecutter* and sat with his legs crossed, statuesque and motionless in a way Elak recognized, that of a savant deep in a trance, utilizing all his energy and mystical powers in an effort to read the very elements around him. In these deep waters where storms eddied and swirled in skies as restless as the waves below, the elements came alive like gods, powers clashing, mocking the efforts of humanity, always threatening to overturn any fleet, no matter how large. Dalan's eyes were closed, but all his attention was focused on the chaos around him, sifting it slowly, seeking knowledge and understanding. He had been aware for a while that something vast and puissant had risen in the east, and in his mind he saw the island that had thrust itself up from the fathomless deeps, an island raised not by the fiery unrest of the seabed, but by a sorcery of a magnitude beyond human endeavour. Whatever was behind this incursion into the world of humanity had not originated in this world.

As the *Wavecutter* sailed eastwards. Dalan pictured the island, its vast mass towering above the waves that pounded its shores impotently. Its rocks were contorted and twisted like massed banks of coral, a dark, sinister green, rising like cliffs, studded with caves and openings, long high channels that cut into them, filled with boiling, foaming waters. The sea crashed inwards, vainly attempting to bring the towering walls down. Hanging from the uppermost reaches down to the milling waters, thick tresses of weed draped over the rocks, torn and twisted in the gales that constantly beset them, but they prevailed. Beyond the walls, the island rose up in tiers and tower-like growths, bloated fingers that reached for the heavens, gnarled and grasping, like gigantic hands frozen in time. Beyond the uppermost of them, where clouds lowered like impossibly large vessels, black-winged shapes swooped and eddied with the currents of tempestuous air, great beaks snapping at the elements, talons extended as if in readiness for conflict, and in their wild, crimson eyes, a glittering malevolence shone like coals.

Dalan's vision opened up the inner island, its alien city,

grown out of the monstrous coral outcrops, its dizzy flights of enormous stairways that burrowed far down into the entrails of the city, passageways from which the leviathans of the ocean could surge upwards to the garish light. And in those depths, huge shapes stirred, beings from beyond this world eager to break free from the hold and release themselves into the ocean beyond the island. Other parts of the island were fused together like immense buildings, with black windows, lightless and seemingly uninhabited, although the entire conglomerate construction throbbed and pulsed with living energies and the promise of seething, teeming life.

As he studied the architectural nightmare, Dalan felt his resolve to go further weakening, his nerves subjected to the cold, crawling terror that suffused every inch of his visions. It was a supernatural aura, he knew that, suffused by the tormented workings of the sorcerers who ruled in that blasphemous city, the same sorcerers who had been defeated at Brae Calaadas, when the city of Tergarroc had been sent crashing down in ultimate ruin. They had come here from their remote northern lair in the wastes of Vaarfrost and raised this hellish island up from the depths. Now they had saturated it with their spawn and they had summoned from beyond the world the unthinkable army they would use in their lust for conquest.

Memories of the dreadful conflict on Xumatoq's island brought Dalan back to a sudden awareness of his surroundings, the heaving deck, the snarling wind, and Elak standing close to him, a look of deep concern on his face. Dalan, like the young king, had looked into the past, when Xumatoq, the thing from the stars, had rooted in this world and released the death seeds that had come close to spreading their murderous plague.

"The island is close," Dalan said, his voice barely above

the wind. "I have seen it, Elak."

"And Lycon?"

"He is there somewhere. You realize what the sorcerers want?"

Elak nodded. "They have chosen their battleground. They want to lure us to it. It is not how I would have fought them."

"Borna and the Picts favour a direct invasion of the island. They prefer to fight on land rather than at sea, but that island is full of traps and is shaped from corals and growths that are hostile to men. Climbing across its terrain and storming its coral city will be as much a battle as any fought with its creatures."

"How would you fight this war?"

"At sea. We have to draw them out."

Elak scowled. "How would that be possible?"

"We have to play them at their own game. First, we must free Lycon. But to do so would take a miracle, several of them, I suspect. And it would not be enough. We have to lure the enemy to us, here among the waves. It will take power, dark sorcery maybe. And of a dangerous nature. We must call upon gods whose price for aid would not be easy to meet. Cruath Morgas knows this. He would invoke the Lords of Midnight, and bring them to earthly form. I fear the consequences, Elak. Our world is no place for such as them, and the things that serve them."

*

Lycon was led by the woman, Arnuell, along several winding tunnels, barely lit, until they came to a chamber where other people were busy at tasks set them by masters as yet unseen by Lycon. Some were cooking, others burnishing arms, others fashioning crude armour. In all there were some two dozen of Arnell's people, apparently all that remained of her tribe. Arnuell managed to secrete Lycon in a smaller room, away from prying eyes, warning him that some of her companions might be prepared to betray him in an attempt to win favour.

"They'll kill us all when we've outlived our usefulness," she told him.

"Is there a way out of this maze? To the outside?"

"Since they brought us down here, none of us have ever been beyond the main portal upward and returned. It's heavily guarded by creatures we cannot defy. They are too powerful and too well armed."

"Is there another way out?"

"Possibly, but it's dangerous. Below us there is a cave, fed by the tide coming in through several low tunnels. When it recedes, the tunnels would allow us to swim beyond, but to what? The waters are never still, always beating at the rocks. And the sea beyond is like an angry god. Anyone swimming through the tunnels would simply be pulped."

Lycon grunted. His exploits at sea had made a good sailor of him, but he knew he was no champion swimmer. "Are the tunnels guarded on the other side?"

"It's unlikely. Even the sea creatures keep clear of the pounding of the waves. Do you mean to try that way?" Her eyes widened at the suggestion.

"I have to get away. I have to find a way back to my people. The king must be warned about this place. What about you and your people? Are you content to remain, knowing you'll be killed?"

"We are not cowards!" she snapped.

He grinned, pleased that his barb had sunk home. "I am sure you are not. But this is an opportunity to defy the creatures. If there is any chance of escape, you have to take it."

She seemed about to retort, but then nodded. "Some would take the risk. Nagrak, my man, and two of his companions, Stratha and Morthog. If they know I am prepared to swim for it, they'd be shamed into joining us. They wouldn't betray you."

"Go to your man. Tell him."

Lycon waited while she slipped back into the main chamber. He was praying the young men would prefer a gamble for freedom, albeit a perilous one, to handing him over to their jailers in the hope of winning favour. Time dragged as Lycon waited, almost on the point of slipping away. A movement in the shadows made him stiffen, crude club held at the ready. Arnuell had returned with two young men. They had the muscular frames of the Picts, arms and chests covered in vivid tattoos: their weather-beaten faces glared at him suspiciously.

"You're from Atlantis?" said the one Arnuell called Nagrak.

"Yes. I am the king's man."

"You mean to swim through the tunnels and risk being turned to bloody surf?"

"I told you, I'm an Atlantean. We practically live in the sea."

Nagrak's glare intensified, as if he had been insulted. Then suddenly he was laughing, his bright teeth white in the shadows. "Well, we are of the Sea Otter tribe. A ducking in a rough tide is second nature to us. What have we got to be afraid of?" He clapped Lycon on the shoulders.

Lycon joined the laughter. "Good. Show me these tunnels."

Cautiously the small company made its way around the chamber via another dark corridor until they came to a sloping ramp into a gaping maw in the coral. The sounds of distant water echoed up from it, and as they went downward, these intensified and became recognisable as waves crashing against the foundations of the island like the fists of a giant. There was light here, the phosphorescent glow of tiny creatures embedded in the rock, and it shimmered, creating an other-worldly effect, eerie and disconcerting.

9: Among Prisoners

Secreted away far inside one of the island's larger towers, in a chamber where natural daylight never reached, a gathering of robed figures spread around a circular table, cut from stone, their pale faces limned by the glow from the walls, ghost-like and sickly, only the sea-green eyes vibrant with life. The seven sorcerers of the north waited in silence broken only by the occasional roar of the remote skies, or the subterranean thunder of the sea. Their shapes were cloaked in dark garments, thick folds that concealed the nature of these beings, though they had the arms and legs of humans and when they moved, it was in a way that mimicked human movement, though it seemed awkward, a little foreign to them. When they spoke it was in low voices, a batrachian croaking, using a language few men would have recognized or understood.

"Our enemies have responded as we had hoped," said the central figure. "Their great fleet is anchored like a bow across the west and south of the island. It can only be a matter of time before the arrogant king from the south hurls his force at us. We will crush it as we would crush a crab without a shell. We will strew the ocean with the wreckage and sail through it as we swoop down upon Atlantis and replace its human vermin with our destroying legions. And then we will bring the masters up from the depths to begin their new reign."

The others would have voiced their pleasure, but for a

disturbance at the door. From it emerged a stooped being, also cloaked in dark robes, who scuttled into the room, apologizing for its intrusion. It was un-hooded, its face devoid of hair, the flesh scaly, the eyes bulging, testament to its aquatic nature.

"Masters," it said, grovelling for fear of retribution for its intrusion, "the man, Lycon, is missing. We sought to have him brought up into the tower as you ordered. He is no longer on the islet."

The central sorcerer's eyes widened, the half-seen features of his face pulled into a grimace of anger. "He attempted to swim away from it? If so, he will have been devoured. It's no matter, though. He has served his purpose. The Atlanteans and their allies have come. Elak will not know his friend has perished. And even if he does, his anger will drive him to attack us."

"We don't think the man Lycon is dead," said the hunched messenger. He described the damaged food plinth and the hole down into the corridors below the islet. "We have guards searching the place and questioning the human slaves incarcerated there. None so far admit to having seen the man Lycon, but four of their number are missing, a girl and three men."

"*Missing?*" the sorcerer hissed. "How is it possible to be missing on this island?"

Another of the sorcerers rose quietly and crossed to a section of the wall where a number of niches had been scalloped out of the rock. In each of them was set a glass ball, perfectly circular and as wide in diameter as a man's chest. The sorcerer lifted it with ease and set it down upon the table. "This eye looks upon the tunnels around the slaves' quarters." He passed his elongated, webbed fingers over the globe and in its misty interior, shapes moved, focusing sharply. "This occurred a short time ago."

Each of the sorcerers bent forward to watch the events in the globe unfolding. Five humans were creeping along the shadowed tunnels, heading downwards to where the bruising tide rushed inwards, blocking off the tunnel, defying any attempt to swim through its lower end. The sorcerer controlling the globe again made a pass over it and the picture changed to show an empty tunnel with the edge of the sea licking at its slope.

"This is as it is now. The humans have gone."

"To where?" snapped the central sorcerer.

"Into the waters."

"Then they will be ground to pulp."

"Not yet," said the sorcerer by the globe. "The sea smothers them from view, but they are yet alive."

"Then wake the sea guardians! Let us waste no more time on these individuals. Send them their doom! In the meantime we will raise up the ocean swarms and begin the destruction of the fleets."

*

Far below the sorcerers' tower, Lycon and his four companions had taken to the water, using the movement of the tide to shape their flight. As the waves dragged back, they dived into them and wriggled like sea creatures underwater for as long as their lungs would allow. Breaking surface, they were yet in the tunnel, with a few feet of air above them, under its curved ceiling. Again they weighed the movement of the tide and dived, progressing further down the tunnel. They did this three times, their lungs straining at the effort, their muscles protesting against the coldness of the sea and the strength of its flow. As they rose for the last time, breaking surface, they came up into daylight in a circular cove of brilliant green rocks that towered over them, slick and glass-like, impossible to climb. The seas churned around them, spinning them in a vortex that threatened to drag them back under.

"There's a way out!" Lycon shouted above the roar of the waters, pointing to a narrow gash in the gleaming rock face. Daylight beckoned beyond it, possibly the open sea. As the four of them kicked out for the long crevice, they all felt fresh movement below them as something swam there. Whatever invisible things these were, they were attempting to wrap themselves around the legs of the swimmers. Lycon kicked out brutally and felt his heels smack into something pulpy, which withdrew long enough for him to propel himself closer to the crack in the wall. The others similarly kicked out or used their hands to claw at the things that sought them. Stratha's head suddenly disappeared beneath the surface.

Lycon reached the glassy wall, and his fingers gripped the edge of the crevice. He hauled himself up on to a ledge as a long tendril swung out of the sea at him and tried to whip him from his perch, but he again kicked out at it and it fell back. He bent down to help Arnuell up beside him, and in a moment Nagrak was also with them. They saw Morthog looking around him, his head barely above the swirling waves.

"Quickly! This way!" Nagrak shouted at him.

"Where's Stratha?" Morthog replied.

"He won't abandon him," said Nagrak. He was right, for Morthog dived and the three figures on the ledge waited anxiously for another sighting of him or Stratha. The waters boiled, rising up and threatening to sweep Lycon and his companions from the ledge, but they clung on in desperation, their fingers numb and bloody. There was no more time to wait and they squeezed their way into the fissure just as a wave slapped at them. Lycon struggled to get further into the great crack, the rock surface on both sides tearing at his clothes, ripping them. Arnuell and Nagrak fared better, the girl being slender and Nagrak carrying less weight. Behind them the water rushed into the chamber, but not strong enough to drag them back into its embrace.

Gradually they made their way to the outer wall and found themselves on a ledge overlooking a cove into which more waves were streaming in constant procession, battering at the cliffs and foaming furiously, the sound deafening. Overhead sea birds whirled and flocked, some of them diving down to investigate, their hooked beaks snapping as if intent on assaulting the three humans.

Nagrak looked back into the crevice, shaking his head in despair. "No sign of them," he said.

Arnuell gripped his arm. "We've lost them," she said. "We dare not go back."

He cursed, but nodded, knowing she was right. Instead they turned to Lycon.

"The gods alone know how we're going to get off this rock!" he shouted above the din of the waves. "Even if we had a boat, it would be battered to pieces in no time. And if we swim, where do we go?"

"We're facing south," said Nagrak. "If we can get around the shore towards the eastern coast, to the lee of the island, the sea may be less fierce. In the waters below us here, there will be other guardians, and certainly more terrible than anything we've yet encountered."

And we need fire, thought Lycon. *Otherwise when night falls, we'll freeze to death.*

*

Scuvular sat in the small chamber with Theorron and

Rannadal, deep under the palace corridors of Epharra where their conversation could not be listened to through the sorcery of the Druids or other Council lackeys.

"They suspect Vannadas was poisoned, though they don't know what was introduced into his food to kill him," said Scuvular. "If they continue their accursed investigations, they may get to the truth."

"Then they must be stopped," said Theorron. "It's time to tighten the noose, Scuvular. Strike first. Who's leading the investigations?"

"Munnaster. He is ambitious. I sense a desire in him to rise and replace Zerrahydris as Prime Councillor," said Scuvular.

Rannadal smiled, the smile of a sea predator. "Let me deal with him. I have enough discreet followers who could remove him. I assure you, his body would never be found. With Munnaster out of the way, any inquiries would drop away, surely."

"Too dangerous," said Scuvular. "But I have an idea. We must use Munnaster's ambition to net him. Pretend to support him. Encourage him to seek the high office. Once we've won his trust, we can expose him to the Council. Expose *him* as the one responsible for Vannadas's death."

Theorron laughed coldly. "Of course. The Council will execute him. And you, Scuvular, will again be seen to have demonstrated your loyalty to the throne."

Scuvular's eyes gleamed as he contemplated the plot. "I'll visit Munnaster on the pretext of having information for him. The first strands of the web will be set in place."

*

Later, in chambers closer to the royal halls of the palace, Scuvular waited in silence in an ante-room of Munnaster's offices. He had been granted a private audience with the Councillor. Eventually the door to the main chambers opened and Scuvular was ushered in by Munnaster's servants.

"I trust this is urgent, Scuvular," said Munnaster. "My days are filled with Council business."

"I appreciate that, of course," said Scuvular, bowing. "It is well known that no one works harder than you for the good of the crown. It is why I have chosen to speak to you, and you alone."

Munnaster eyed him sceptically. Scuvular's deviousness was recognized by more than a few of his colleagues. "So what is this matter?"

Scuvular turned to look at the guards by the door. "It is of the utmost privacy."

Munnaster waved the men away and they retreated, closing the door. "We're alone," said Munnaster. "Speak freely."

"I know you have your suspicions about the death of Vannadas, and that his death may not have been an illness."

Munnaster fixed him with a cool stare, but said nothing.

"You could be forgiven for thinking *I* was behind some plot to remove him. After all, did I not expect to become regent after his death? An obvious conclusion, but a wrong one."

"Go on."

"If someone else was responsible, it begs the question, who? Who else would stand to gain by the death of Vannadas? In fact, who *has* gained by his death? Not me. I've been pushed aside."

"The Council act as a body. No single one is regent."

"Quite so. But your leader wields more power than any of you. The longer Elak is absent, the more Zerrahydris strengthens his grip. I am certain he would remove me if he could. Am I to be the one who next tastes whatever poison it was that killed Vannadas?"

Munnaster stiffened. "Poison? How could you know that?"

Scuvular snorted. "Come, Munnaster, there are few secrets in these corridors. The walls listen and whisper in the ears of those who pay close enough attention. You are investigating a poisoning. Admit it."

Munnaster remained motionless.

"I only mention it because I stand to be accused! You are looking in the wrong direction for Vannadas' killer. All I ask is that you let me help you unmask him."

10: Flight into Terror

Lycon, Nagrak and Arnuell had made their way like spiders around the gleaming coral cliffs, battered by the wind and occasionally soaked by waves that exploded upwards from the white cauldron of the sea, a hundred feet below. They paused occasionally to shelter from the buffeting, barely keeping their fingers from going numb, as the afternoon sun was swallowed by banks of lowering cloud, black and bruised with imminent rain. Premature darkness smothered them. They were about to find enough shelter to hole up for the night, when Nagrak pointed. Some distance below, further along the jagged coast, there were lights.

"Is it a harbour?" shouted Lycon above the roar of the tumultuous seas.

"Yes."

"If there are boats there, we'll take one. No matter how dangerous these seas are, it's the only way off this island. We dare not remain."

Nagrak nodded. "We'll be sought. The Orugllyr won't rest until they've recovered us."

For a long and painful time, the three figures clawed their way along and down, hands bleeding with effort, teeth chattering in the vicious cold swipe of the winds, but each of them harboured a fierce determination to reach their goal. Eventually they came to a coral buttress that directly overlooked a small bay scooped out of the coral, and around this the natural growths had been cut and sculpted into strange shapes the three watchers realized were buildings, piled one on top of another, reaching up the huge cliff face in a dizzying parody of a village. Some of these contorted houses had lights in their oblong windows, glimmering, eerie fires, throwing a glow over the place that created an even more alien effect.

"There!" said Nagrak, again pointing. In one small cove, with what looked vaguely like a crumpled jetty, several shapes bobbed up and down like leaves on the boiling waters. They were craft of some kind. Daylight was being snuffed out, thick darkness rolling in. Only the bizarre lights of the cliff village enabled the watchers to see anything.

"Shall we wait till dawn?" said Nagrak to Lycon.

Lycon looked at Arnuell, whose lips were blue, her face white. "I doubt if any of us will survive the night's cold," he said. "We need one of those boats. That place will be hostile."

As if his words had been heard in the twisted buildings, a number of shapes emerged from what they had taken to be windows, huge crab-like creatures, with elongated claws and numerous chitinous legs. They paused, raising their claws as if using them to test the air, and the watchers ducked behind the coral. When they dared to look again, the horrors were gone, either back into their burrows or down into the foaming sea.

Lycon urged his companions on and they found a narrow passage that took them to the edge of the cliff village.

Cautiously they wormed their way down to the jetty, getting to within yards of the first of the boats. They were curiously shaped, narrow but with deep holds, several long oars shipped inside them. There was no mast and Lycon knew that sailing these seas would be hard enough for war galleys, impossible for smaller craft. As for rowing out beyond the island's edges, that was not what these fragile boats had been designed for. Nevertheless, they would have to take one out.

They scuttled across the jetty to the first boat's side. It was heaving up and down with the wild tide, held fast by two lengths of rope wrapped around great knots of coral that served effectively as capstans.

Nagrak pointed to the first. "Untie these. Arnuell—go aboard and keep watch. If you see anything, shout to us."

She scowled, as if annoyed not to be included in the work, but she was at the point of exhaustion, so did as he asked. Nagrak and Lycon gripped the fat rope and heaved, but it resisted their efforts. They waited until the sea shifted the boat, giving them a little slack, and then put their backs into the work, As they freed it and let its end drop over the jetty, Arnuell gave a cry. A figure had emerged from the lower buildings and was coming towards them. The darkness made it difficult to make out and gave it the peculiar look of something wrapped in weed.

Lycon had put down his makeshift club, which he had brought with him from the chamber under the islet, and now Arnuell leapt from the boat and snatched it up. "Hurry!" she yelled at the two men. Instinctively they rushed to the second rope and began working to loosen it. As they did, Arnuell confronted the figure, which groped for her, using arms that looked more appropriate for a crustacean than a human. Without hesitation Arnuell drove the club down at them, smashing one into splinters, following up with a shattering blow to the dark blob of a head. Cartilage cracked and the figure dropped to its knees before the girl brought the club across the side of its head and sent the creature tumbling. Others were coming out of the shadows.

Lycon and Nagrak were almost spent, unable to free the rope. Arnuell ran to them, shoving the club into her belt, one eye on the approaching figures. There were a score of them, their intent clear. Lycon was on the point of despair when the boat swung round, thumped by a great wave, the rope pulled taut as a bowstring. Some of its threads snapped and Lycon realized what was about to happen.

"Get aboard!" he roared above the din. The others had no time to deliberate and leapt over the boat's side into the hold. They clawed their way on to the narrow deck. Beyond them the jetty was filling with the murky figures, who looked as though they had been dredged up from the bottom of the harbour. Several were gripping the rope, trying to prevent the boat from breaking free. Lycon watched in horror as dozens of them got hold of it. Over his shoulder, up in the heavens, a great boom of thunder rolled across them, and with it came a gust of wind that swept the sea back and with it the boat, yanking at the rope as if a sea leviathan had pulled it. It shredded and the creatures hanging on to it were flung in all directions. Within seconds the boat had been snatched by another massive wave and swung out into the bay.

"The gods are with us!" shouted Nagrak, putting his arm around Arnuell and she laughed, pumping her fist. Lycon almost toppled into the hold, hanging on to the rail. He was not sure if Ishtar or any other of his own gods had effected this unbelievable escape, but if the Pictish gods had a hand in this, well, so be it.

However, once tossed out of the bay like a leaf in a gale, they knew their safety was not assured. The boat rose and fell dangerously, and already the chances of being scuppered were huge. Lycon would have dragged the oars up from below, but he understood well enough that they would be of no use in this mighty swell, and would likely snap. He and the others were completely at the mercy of the storm, swiftly heading for the open ocean, where the waves would become mountainous and the boat would stand no chance at all of staying afloat. And these waters were cold, far more so than those around the island. Lycon shuddered and death grinned at him from a dozen places in the fuming clouds.

*

Elak studied Dalan's face. The Druid had been motionless despite the fierce winds and huge swell of the ocean. "What is it?" said Elak.

Dalan was alert now, looking out keenly at the waters ahead of them, vast rolling white waves that the ship ploughed through, shuddering at every impact. "Lycon! He's there. No longer on the island!"

"How is that possible? A boat?"

"Somehow he has found one."

"How close can we get to the island? I want to take the *Wavecutter* in."

"The storm surrounding the island is monstrous, the vile work of the Orugllyr sorcerers. To penetrate it would court annihilation."

"We must go closer. If Lycon is coming this way, we must shorten his voyage."

Dalan nodded, knowing the irrepressible young king would not be turned from his efforts to save Lycon. "I'll have the fleets signalled. They must hold their positions until we are ready to attack."

"We sail on alone," said Elak. "We find Lycon."

As his orders were carried out and the sleek war galley tore through the waves, Dalan felt a renewed onset of deep unease. He gripped Elak's shoulder. "This is far more perilous than I knew. It is not just the storm that we have to navigate."

"What is wrong?" Elak knew Dalan well enough to read his fears, and this was beyond all he had revealed to this point in their reckless pursuits.

"The Orugllyr have summoned something from the deeps. Guardians of their island, a swarm of them. And with these horrors comes the cold, the freezing cold from the Vaarfrost that will turn the ocean to ice and snare us all in a grip of iron."

*

High above the towers and uppermost tiers of Epharra, washed in vivid moonlight, a single figure clung to the shadows, clinging to the stonework like a lizard, working its way deeper into shadow and the clutches of the moon. Its tight-fitting black garb made it difficult for any guard to see, even close up, so well did the figure blend with the night. There was no more skilled a thief in all Cyrena than Castobar, and there was no one more daring, no task too daunting to him. When Scuvular had offered him work, Castobar's pride had swelled. Of course, he knew that to refuse such an eminent person as the king's cousin would be courting certain death, but that was irrelevant. He thrived on such adventures as this.

It took him longer than usual to descend the lofty tower, as he knew he could not take the slightest risk of being discovered. That, too, would mean execution, for this tower and its near companions were part of the chambers reserved for the Councillor, Munnaster. Castobar reached the roofs and crawled along the first of them, following the route given to him by Scuvular. There was a narrow window, as promised, and Castobar swung down and through it, lithe as a cat. Although he found himself in almost total darkness, his night vision was superb, unnaturally so, one of the reasons he had taken up his particular calling.

He had been told there would be guards here, but this was a time of peace in Cyrena, and Epharra had become more than a little relaxed in its vigilance. True, the king was away on what rumours reported to be a possible fresh war, but that was far from here. Epharra slept soundly, and what few guards were in Munnaster's quarters were just as likely to be dozing.

Among the tools of his trade, Castobar had many keys, specially made to open any lock. Certain sorcerers, the Druids among them, used locks that could deny Castobar, but Munnaster's locks were not among them. He found the store he sought, unguarded, and was inside at a turn of the hand. He permitted himself to light a spill, and by its flickering light selected a small cabinet that looked as though it may have been ignored for some time, as attested by its layers of dust. Careful not to disturb them, the thief opened its lid.

There were old manuscripts and documents within, and it was the work of a moment for Castobar to insert between them a small vial of blue liquid. Powerful poison, they'd said. It had been enough to kill the regent.

11: Ice Storm

Lycon stood in the stern of the rolling boat, legs braced, his crude club clenched in a fist as he glared at the thunderous seas. Both Nagrak and Arnuell were exerting every muscle to keep the boat heading seaward, using the oars with deft skill, knowing that the slightest misjudgement would snap them or even plunge the boat into the waves and sink it. Beside them there were two other oars, which Nagrak had broken over his knee to form rough weapons. Lycon smiled grimly. If they were to be attacked, they were ill provided for, but whatever happened they'd sell their lives dearly. *Amazingly*, he thought, *I'll draw my last breath fighting alongside Picts!*

As the boat rose and fell in huge dips and swells, Lycon saw through the clouds of spray shapes thrusting up from the waters behind them in the distance, closing like immense claws reaching for a victim. White and gleaming in the strange light, these burst through the surf, and Lycon realized with a shock they were formed of solid ice, glacial tongues. *Sorcery!* His mind shouted. The Orugllyr must be responsible for this; by now they had discovered his escape and were set on recovering him. There was no avoiding the ice as it rushed onward, unnaturally fast, mocking the normal movement of a glacier. The white walls began to rear up.

"Brace yourselves!" Lycon roared above the din of the sea, and his companions gaped in horror at the oncoming ice, putting down their oars and lifting their makeshift weapons, although they knew they'd be totally ineffective against this supernatural terror. "We may have to take to the water!" Lycon added, but he knew they were deathly cold.

"No!" yelled Arnuell. "We'd be frozen instantly. We must get on to the ice."

Lycon would have replied, but the first of the floes bobbed up yards from the stern, some fifty feet high, making any attempt to jump or clamber on to it impossible. As Lycon watched, the seas boiled even more furiously and something broke surface so that for a moment he thought a huge sea creature had risen between boat and ice. Then he realized it was no whale or similar beast, but something comprised of smooth rock, a great stone that had shot up from the deeps as if hurled by a god. In utter amazement Lycon watched it tower over the ice floe and drop down on to it with a shattering crash, smashing the ice like glass into a million shards.

Fifty yards on either side of the boat, more great stones heaved upwards like leviathans coming up for air; they rose and fell on to the ice, crunching into it so that it exploded in a glittering rain. There were other such massive stones further away, all of them rising and falling with the same devastating effect. The front of the ice flow was completely broken up, allowing the sea to cuff the boat further away.

"What in all the gods –" began Lycon, stunned by the chaos.

"The Pictish gods are with us!" shouted Nagrak. "This is the work of the Lords of Midnight. These are their monoliths, come from the islands."

Lycon swung round to stare at him incredulously. "What?"

"Sorcery against sorcery!" called Nagrak. "The Orugllyr have used their dark arts and in so doing have disturbed and angered the guardians of the islands. Hear their voices!"

Lycon listened and at once caught the sounds in the storm, countless mingled voices raised against it, a deep chorus, sonorous and booming, like the voice of the ocean, a power to make a man shudder. Darkness had smothered the heavens, as if it, too, poured power down into the stones. All around the boat there were chunks of ice, tiny bergs ripped from the massive front, and Nagrak and Arnuell used their oars to propel them away. Behind them the darkness descended from above, blotting from view the incredible conflict between the raised monoliths and the ice pack, though not its tumultuous sounds, a song of confusion and death.

Another shout from Nagrak made Lycon turn to see something looming out of the waters ahead, the prow of a warship, its lines wreathed in shadow, the billowing sails behind it painted black by the roaring darkness. This time there were no rising stones to protect them and in moments the ship would either plough right through them, or its crew would scoop them up and snare them where the ice floe had failed.

*

Zerrahydris sat at the head of the curved table, a number of his fellow Councillors on either side of him, arranged in a semi-circle, raised on a dais above the audience hall. With him were Eupherites and Bardoc, but the seat usually reserved for Munnaster was empty. He, in fact, stood below them, the subject of their interrogation.

"I understand," said Zerrahydris, his face cold, his gaze accusing, "your investigation into the death of Vannadas has led you to make some surprising accusations, Munnaster. Would you care to speak openly about them?"

Munnaster looked confused. If this was an act, it was a clever one. He had been unexpectedly roused from sleep and brought to this chamber, amazed to find an almost full Council meeting in session. "I don't understand," he said. "What has happened?"

"As you well know," cut in Bardoc, "you made claims, albeit privately, that Zerrahydris and possibly others, were the ones responsible for the death of Vannadas, by poison. Part of a coup to put them in power."

"That's preposterous!" gasped Munnaster. "I made no such claim. Who told you this lie!"

"Not everyone you confided in was disloyal to the Council," said Zerrahydris. "Some were sensible enough to report your words to us."

Munnaster swung round to study the audience, where lesser Councillors and many of the royal house, priests and leading military men looked back at him. Among them was Scuvular, whose expression was bland, unreadable.

"Lies or misunderstandings," said Zerrahydris, "we take such things very seriously. Consequently I insisted all my apartments be searched, together with those of my colleagues."

"Searched? For what?"

"Whatever poison was used on Vannadas. Clearly it was something previously unknown to us. Brought in from an outside source."

"I never asked for such actions to be taken. But I have had my suspicions."

"Oh?" said Zerrahydris. "You did not think to share them with me, or my fellow Councillors?"

Munnaster gaped. Of course, he dare not say what he had been told by Scuvular. "I was looking for absolute proof."

Bardoc spoke again. "No one here had anything to conceal." He pulled something from his robe and set it down on the table so that it was clearly visible to most people in the hall. It was a small vial of bluish liquid. "But we did find this. You recognize it, of course."

Munnaster stared at the vial. "Why should I?"

"Well," Bardoc snorted. "It was found in your apartments, hidden among some old documents."

Munnaster felt his mouth drying up. Gradually he was beginning to see the trap that had been set for him. He wanted to shout out in protest, but a sudden terror held his teeth clenched against speaking. Scuvular! He was behind this.

"A clever deceit," said Zerrahydris. "No doubt you were seeking an opportunity to secrete the poison in *my* chambers. If you'd done that, it would be me facing execution."

Munnaster finally opened his mouth. "Execution! But this is a trick. The real enemy –"

His words were drowned out as several members of the audience shouted out, calling for Munnaster to be removed and beheaded forthwith. Had anyone made an attempt to identify these angry protesters, they would have recognized men who were principal supporters of Scuvular. He, however, remained silent.

Zerrahydris stood and silence fell. "The senior Councillors will deliberate. Munnaster will be confined to a cell. The meeting is dismissed."

On his way out, Scuvular brushed shoulders with Azarvis, speaking to him discreetly. "That went rather well. By nightfall there will be one less Councillor in our way. So—what of the thief?"

"Castobar is already on Theorron's ship, bound for Poseidonis. He'll find work to keep him far from Cyrena until we need him again."

*

Elak leaned over the rail, studying the churning foam below the *Wavecutter's* prow. He could hear the roar of something close by, waves crashing, possibly on to rocks, and the violent groans of ice. Small bergs were bobbing on the sea's surface, and the last thing Elak wanted was to run into something bigger.

Beside him, Dalan pointed with his staff. "There!"

Elak squinted into a fresh blast of wind, and caught sight of something rising and falling. A boat! Three figures in it, hunched down against the freezing wind. Gradually the boat was tossed forward until it reached the *Wavecutter's* keel. Suddenly Elak was laughing, staring down at the three drenched people, fixing his attention on the bedraggled and unmistakable shape of Lycon. He and his companions stood, legs braced against the storm, each of them holding a ridiculously inadequate wooden weapon.

"Ho, sea dogs!" shouted Elak. "What treasure are you in search of?"

Lycon's face lit up. "Elak! By the Nine Hells! Is it you or a sea ghost?"

Already Elak's men were tossing ropes over the side. "I'm real enough. Are you strong enough to haul yourselves up to the deck?"

Nagrak and Arnuell needed no second bidding and scrambled like rats up the lines, helped aboard by the Atlantean sailors. Lycon followed, less speedily, his club gripped in his teeth.

Elak laughed, swinging him aboard. "What is that, some powerful relic?"

"A memento of my stay on that hell island," said Lycon. "Something for my grandchildren."

"Gods," said Elak, his smile widening. "You mean to settle down and start a family?"

"Rather that than come back to these waters. I've never known such cold. My bones are ice, my guts frozen. Please don't tell me there is no wine aboard."

"On a fighting ship, Lycon? Come, let's get below to warmth." Elak motioned for Nagrak and Arnuell to join him, and Dalan went aft to supervise the voyage back to the fleet.

In his cabin, Elak listened to an abbreviated summary of Lycon's abduction and escape from the Orugllyr, also listening patiently to the words of Arnuell and Nagrak.

"What about your people?" said the king. "They are trapped."

"They are used as slaves," said Arnuell. "As long as they perform their duties, they'll be ignored. The sorcerers are too preoccupied with their plans to consider them. You must not risk your ships in an attempt to save my people." Nagrak nodded in silence, typically stoic.

Elak turned back to Lycon, who had dried off and wrapped himself in a thick robe, though his teeth were still chattering. "You say the stones rose from the deeps?"

"But for them, we would have been snatched by the ice and taken back to the Orugllyr," said Lycon.

"We heard the voices of the Lords of Midnight," said Nagrak.

"Where are the monoliths now?" said Elak.

Dalan had joined them. "I had a message from Borna. He has decided against attacking the island. Instead he wants us all to form a wide semi-circle, falling back on the outer Pictish isles. The stones will return to them and form a barrier against the Orugllyr invasion. He seeks a council of war."

Elak nodded. "Agreed."

While Lycon and his companions enjoyed piping hot bowls of stew, Dalan took Elak to one side. "Borna wants to hold the Council on the island of Skaafelda. You recall it?"

"Of course. It is where the Crawling Death wreaked so much havoc. It's a dead place now."

"Aye, but it has its ghosts. I am not so certain it is a good omen for us. So much dark magic is gathering about us. No one fully controls it or the things it can release."

12: A Sentence of Death

Zerrahydris stood once more before the Council and dignitaries of Epharra. When he rose a hush fell over the gathering. "Let it be known that the appointed Councillors have considered the matter of Munnaster's involvement in the death of the regent, Vannadas, and find him guilty of murder by poisoning. Consequently Munnaster is hereby stripped of his robes of office and will be executed later today. In respect of his former position on the Council, the execution will be a conducted privately."

Munnaster, shackled at the wrists, stood before the Councillors, flanked by two armed guards. He hung his head, all resistance and anger apparently drained from him.

"Take the prisoner to the assigned chambers," Zerrahydris instructed the guards, who immediately gripped Munnaster's arms and led him away. "The meeting is dismissed," Zerrahydris added with finality, and the assembly quickly began to dissolve, Scuvular among them.

When he reached the door, one of Zerrahydris' aides met him. "Sire, the Councillors would like you to attend the execution, since Munnaster made accusations against you."

"Accusations which have subsequently been shown to be a pack of lies."

The aide bowed. "Indeed, sire. Please follow me."

Scuvular did as bidden, a number of his private guards automatically stepping into line behind him, among them their commander, Azarvis. Presently the company reached a corridor leading to a short stairway into one of the towers set aside for the Council's confidential business. Scuvular nodded to Azarvis; he and his guards stationed themselves outside the doors, where another company of Council guards were also standing stiffly to attention.

Inside, Scuvular looked around expressionlessly. The chamber was circular, devoid of furniture, apart from a bench and a few wooden seats. One high window admitted light, and there were no decorations. It might have been a prison cell, which was why, Scuvular assumed, it had been chosen. Presumably Munnaster was to be executed here. Zerrahydris, Eupherites and Bardoc were waiting, together with a handful of armed guards who stood round the periphery of the chamber.

"This is a sorry day," said Scuvular. "My brother Vannadas deserved a better fate."

"He did," said Zerrahydris. "No one served Cyrena better, nor was more loyal."

Another small door opened and two guards entered, accompanying Munnaster. They had removed the shackles from his wrists. He was completely calm, regarding Scuvular coolly.

Behind him another soldier entered, carrying a wide basket. Zerrahydris nodded to him and the man went to Scuvular and opened the basket so that its contents could be clearly seen. Scuvular gasped and drew back in horror. There were two grisly trophies in the basket, heads soaked in blood.

"I'm sure you recognize these men," Zerrahydris said.

"What is the meaning of this!" Scuvular cried, reaching inside his robe for his sword, which he pulled free. He stood in alarm, as if expecting to be attacked.

"They were taken before they could board their ship. Captain Theorron, a man personally bound to you, and a notorious thief, Castobar."

"Theorron was my man, yes, but I know nothing of this thief."

Munnaster spoke calmly. "That's not what he told us. He confessed he had been paid handsomely to secrete the poison phial in my chamber. Paid, Scuvular, by you."

"That's ridiculous!"

Munnaster shook his head. "There are others who will implicate you in your brother's death. And, of course, there's my own testimony of how you sought to deceive me.

The Council have been given full details."

Scuvular pointed with his sword at Zerrahydris. "You have pronounced the death sentence on Munnaster. You are bound by law to carry it out!"

Zerrahydris nodded. "And all of Cyrena will think the execution completed when we announce it. In reality we will secure Munnaster in a private retreat while we conduct the business of revealing the truth of these vile machinations against the crown. As far as the kingdom is concerned, Munnaster will be dead, his cremated remains tossed over some remote seas." He turned to the guards. "Relieve this traitor of his sword."

Scuvular moved surprisingly quickly for a big man, He dashed forward, making for the nearest of the Councillors, Bardoc. Munnaster's two guards pulled him back out of the way, weapons raised to protect him, and both Zerrahydris and Eupherites stepped back to where other guards protected them. Scuvular grabbed Bardoc's robe and thrust his blade close to his neck.

"Any attempt on my life will result in Bardoc's death," Scuvular hissed. He stepped back carefully towards the door, reaching for the bolt, and swinging it slowly open. "Azarvis! To me!"

There were shouts and the sudden clash of steel without, and when Scuvular dragged Bardoc through the door, it was to plunge into a melee, swordsmen fighting in a confined space. Guards from within the chamber followed Scuvular, but were mindful of Bardoc's plight, unable to attack. Bardoc felt himself crushed against Scuvular for a moment and used it to strike out at him. Scuvular ducked, the blow slamming into his shoulder. He worked his sword arm free and drove the blade up under Bardoc's ribs. The Councillor slid to ground.

"Cover me!" Scuvular shouted and his guards ringed

him until he was able to tear free and struggle down the corridor to another set of stairs, leading back down into the lower tower. Azarvis was close behind him, ready to protect his back. Frantically, almost toppling more than once, Scuvular went down the circular stair, the sounds of the fighting slowly diminishing.

"We must get to the tunnels," Scuvular told Azarvis. "We must flee Epharra. Munnaster and the others have condemned us. We must throw ourselves on the mercy of our allies under the earth."

Azarvis, a hardened warrior and seasoned fighting man, shuddered. He knew that only death awaited them once the Councillors caught up with them. And yet the thought of going to Yssargur, the creature that was only partly human, and the monstrous being whom he served, filled him with cold fear.

*

Skaafelda, the principal easternmost of the Pictish isles and home of two important ports that specifically served the eastern ocean, had become an almost bare rock, after the dreadful incursion of the Crawling Death. With the repulsion of the horror from the sea and the creatures that spread it, Skaafelda was beginning to sprout the first signs of renewed life, and the least damaged buildings of the ports were being restored by the Picts. The harbours had been cleared, making it possible to use the island as a new base. When the *Wavecutter* rejoined the main fleet after scooping Lycon and his companions out of the sea, the king and Borna of the Picts agreed to fall back along the line of eastern Pictish islands, where they could await the invasion of the Orugllyr hordes on land and sea, for they were certain they would come.

Ashore on Skaafelda, Elak, Dalan and Lycon joined Borna, with countless warriors and sailors lined along the low eastern cliffs of the old port's bay. They expected to see something out on the horizon, signs of the Orugllyr, sending out their ice packs and their own ships, filled with ice warriors from Vaarfrost. There was a long curtain of mist spreading along that horizon, white as milk, though nothing stirred within it.

Beyond the shallow bay, among the tossing waves, the sea boiled, the waters flung from something that disturbed the rhythm of the foaming tide, as if beneath it some invisible and monstrous force was at work. Among the warriors, other shaman waited, and only by their efforts did they prevent the massed Picts – and consequently the Atlanteans – from panicking.

"What is that?" said Elak, suspecting the sorcery of the Orugllyr.

"Behold!" cried Cruath Morgas, and the waves near the shore parted to reveal a great stone, a monolith from another of the isles. Water cascaded from it as it rolled up the beach and swung itself upright, like some impossible swimmer from the deeps. As one, the Picts fell to their knees, bowing down in worship, and around them many of the Atlanteans knelt in respect, or fear.

"The stones have returned from the ice packs at the Orugllyr island," said Cruath Morgas. "They will form a semi-circle along the eastern defences. Their power will be a strong deterrent to the Vaarfrost invaders." As though in confirmation of his words, the heavens thundered and lightning seared downwards, striking the great monolith, and others that had come ashore along the eastern seaboard, standing now like sentinels.

"The Lords of Midnight are with us!" shouted Cruath Morgas.

Dalan turned his troubled glance upon Elak, silently affirming his unease with Pictish magic and the demonic gods who wielded it. Yet in this coming conflict, the strength of the Atlantean navy and its sailors, coupled with what powers Dalan could bring would not be enough to repulse the Orugllyr, and both men knew it. The risk of courting darkness had to be taken.

Elak gripped the Druid's arm in understanding. "I will always trust in your judgement," he said and Dalan nodded, his face solemn.

Not long after the coming of the great stones, fresh movements were seen on the distant horizon, where the white mist was shredding, to be replaced by what looked like the enormous prows of ships carved from solid ice. Scores of them chopped their way through the waves in a long, curving line, and as they swept ever closer, their icy decks could be seen to house countless thousands of Vaarfrost warriors, and the noise of their war cries came across the bay like a fierce wind. The monolith before Elak and his companions began to shudder like a live thing, and soon its heat burned fiercely, radiating outwards across the waves, which steamed at the passage of power over it.

All along the tide line on Skaafelda and the other islands close to it, the seas suddenly spewed forth another threat, a crawling, slithering tide of creatures dredged up from the ocean depths by the Orugllyr, their ocean swarms. Elak gasped, recognizing something similar to the ghastly things he had fought in the south, servants of Xeraph-Hizer, the Leviathan Lord. There was no time to deliberate – the massed Picts and Atlantean defenders rushed across the sand to meet them and as at the celebrated battle on Brae Calaadas, old rivalries and hatreds were forgotten as the company tore into the sea beings, wreaking havoc and striking about them with the fury of demons.

Out at sea, sorcery clashed with sorcery as the energy from the stones struck that of the oncoming ice ships, great bergs that shuddered on impact but which were not halted. Their swarming warriors readied to come ashore and stand with the seething things from below, accelerating what would become the bloodiest of conflicts. Elak and Lycon stood shoulder to shoulder with Borna, whose face cracked in a grim smile as they began their own merciless contribution to the mayhem.

*

Zerrahydris picked his way carefully along the broken tunnel, its sides slick, its floor scattered with loosened bricks. The stench down here was appalling. The Councillor, put a hand to his mouth, in mind of a snake pit. Ahead of him two guards bore torches, and behind him Munnaster and other guards stepped forward equally as uncertainly. The leading guard turned, lifting high his torch.

"They came this way, sire. Their footprints are clear. But the way beyond is blocked." The light of the flames struck a solid wall of debris, an impenetrable jumble of rubble.

Zerrahydris had initially balked at the idea of entering the vile smelling passages Scuvular and Azarvis, had taken in their frantic rush to escape the Council's justice. However, once told there was no longer any danger, he had come with Munnaster to see for himself the impossibility of giving further chase. He studied the wall before him, which the traitorous Scuvular had evidently brought down in desperate defiance of pursuit.

"Where does this disgusting tunnel lead? It is like a great drain," said the Councillor.

The captain nodded. "There are a number of such tunnels, sire. Long since disused. They are old beyond memory and appear to go deep down and under the mountains beyond Epharra. Unstable and very dangerous. Scuvular and the man with him will be fortunate to survive."

"There are other such tunnels?"

"All had doors fitted long ago, sire. Securely sealed."

"Then bring down the ceilings. If there is anything below the city, these routes must be closed to whatever it is." He turned to Munnaster. "It appals me to think Scuvular has evaded us, but there will be nowhere safe in Epharra for him now."

"We'll have word sent out to all of Cyrena. I will attend to it personally."

"Offer a reward. As much as the treasury can afford. That odious swine must never be permitted to see the light of day again."

Epilogue

As the Atlantean and Pictish armies clashed headlong with the oncoming swarms of ice warriors, the great stones emitted an even more grotesque chorus of sound as the singers within them, the voices of the Lords of Midnight, increased in volume until it became a solid wall. Like a series of great waves, the sounds bellowed outwards into the bay, to be met by the shields of the enemy and the sorcery that bound them, raised by the Orugllyr, who had come forth from their lair at last and stood at the prows of several vessels. These had burst out of the ice, tall and black, shimmering with evil light, their masts threaded with skin-like web, as if woven by a monstrous spider at the heart of each ship.

In all their remarkable voyaging, Elak, Lycon and Dalan had not felt such supernatural energies before, not pitched as such a level. Overhead the skies were in utter turmoil, clouds shredding in a wind like the breath of furious gods, malign faces leering out of them, and winds tearing this way and that like elementals in search of victims. The din was frightful, and as the two armies smashed into each other, the shattering of steel on steel, blade on shield and weapons cutting into flesh and bone rose to a crescendo that almost drowned out the sonorous singing of the great stones. Elak more than once deflected a death-blow from both Dalan and Borna, and they did the same for him, Borna with his blood-soaked axe and Dalan with the blazing staff, its end set with the great stone of Valusian power. None of them were prepared to stand back and watch the battle unfold, and it was all Dalan and Lycon could do to protect their king, while the blind shaman, Cruath Morgas stood with Borna, his staff ablaze with fire in which strange and terrible shapes writhed and hissed like creatures of the darkest night.

On Skaafelda, the central point of the battle, the defenders had ranged themselves in a long semi-circle around the eastern coast, leaping over sand and rock to cut into the swarming ice warriors. The fighting was desperate, no quarter asked or given, bodies cut down on either side. In the air above the ferocious contest, power crackled and fizzed as the stones sent out their unwavering song, a deep battle roar that formed the rocks of defiance upon which the lightning bolts of the Orugllyr broke. For an endless time, these forces clashed and cancelled each other, rocking the island, allowing the forces on the beach to surge back and forth, the outcome undecided. Still the things from the deep surged up from water turned to crimson, where the bodies of the slain were heaped up in mounds.

Behind the ice warriors, fingers of ice thickened and ground forward, groping for human flesh, and many defenders were forced back off the beach, re-grouping. Dalan and Cruath Morgas used their rods of power and other Pictish shaman also combined their efforts to strike at the oncoming ice, melting it and stalling its progress, though it could not last. Beyond Skaafelda, on other islands, the battles also raged, but in each case the ice moved inexorably forward and the Orugllyr began the crush that, if not halted, would see them victorious.

Elak shouted to Dalan above the din. "We will have to fall back, otherwise our armies will be engulfed. There'll be nothing between us and Atlantis to protect it."

Dalan's face was a mask of fury, his determination not to bow to these invaders burning like molten lava. His dread of the supernatural powers of the Lords of Midnight was overcome by the thought of defeat. "Then we will raise another army!" he cried. He looked up at the nearest of the great monoliths and spoke to it in the strange tongue of the Druids, using speech other men were not familiar with. From the monolith a new sound burst forth in response to Dalan's speech, an even deeper song that shook those who heard it and made them cover their ears. All across the bay and beyond to the other islands, this new song surged. It caused the attacking ice warriors to pause, and for a long moment the battle ceased and the only movement was the crawling of maimed men and sea creatures, damaged as cracked crabs, to relative safety.

"The Crawling Death killed many a Pict on these islands," said Dalan, and Borna nodded grimly. Beside him, Cruath Morgas gasped, turning his blind eyes inland as if he could see what was there, and drew back in alarm at the thought of it. Up from the dust-white rocks and sterile surroundings, small clouds wafted from the ground, as if a slow dust storm, a white blizzard was beginning. Yet this was not snow. Human shapes emerged, bone white,

311

seemingly carved from malleable chalk.

"The fallen!" said Elak. "Returned."

"The ghosts of all those who died on Skaafelda!" cried Borna.

As one this new force flowed across the rock and sand and poured down the beach to the ice warriors' front ranks. A new contest began, even more violent than the first, and as it did so, the voices of the stones rose up anew like thunder, powerful as god-like fists, and struck at the enemy. Out in the bay one of the black ships rose up and exploded as if it had struck something volcanic, and all around it the ice warriors were flung into the sea, where the waves had abruptly formed themselves into elemental creatures with the power to tear and rend. The sea churned, a foaming red.

Elak and Borna's forces took renewed heart from this injection of crushing sorcery and again ran forward, beating aside the wavering ranks of ice warriors. More of the great black ships were ripped apart by explosions, as black-winged entities from the skies reached down for them. The forces of the Orugllyr were slaughtered, ripped and torn, forced to retreat, though in the chaos of trying to re-board their ships they hindered themselves, falling easy prey to creatures from land and sea alike. Other horrors from the depths, things under the sway of the Pictish gods, fed on the sea creatures of the Orugllyr, which began their retreat.

The white ghosts stalked the beaches, smothering and choking the ice warriors, who could make no impact on the spectre army. They, too, turned and fled, though they struggled in the waves, where both the dead and the crumbling ice ships hindered them. A false night had spread over the bloody spectacle as Elak and Borna stood their ground, surveying the carnage. It was impossible to count the losses, but rarely had such huge numbers fallen in a single battle. Elak wiped blood and gore from his face and turned to Borna. "Is it over?"

"It took darker arts than men have called upon for long centuries," said the Pict, himself covered with the blood of his slain enemies. "But the Orugllyr are beaten. See, their remaining ships, crippled as they are, are sliding back into the retreating ice. They will go back to their island, and it will sink. The Lords of Midnight will drown it!"

Elak turned to Dalan and Lycon. "Are they done?"

Dalan shrugged. "For a long time. They risked all on this, thinking they had us at their mercy. We've won the day, but neither Atlantean nor Pict can rest until Xeraph-Hizer is expunged from the earth." *And we have unleashed dreadful powers on this island,* he thought. *What price will the Lords of Midnight exact for that?*

"Ishtar!" groaned Lycon. "Can that wait until another day? I need a bath."

"You surprise me," said Dalan. "You usually demand wine above anything else."

"I do," Lycon said with a typical grin. "And I do now – it's what I will fill the bath with."

*

In Epharra, two weeks after the devastating battle at Skaafelda, Elak, Dalan and Lycon came together with the city's Council, making the last preparations for the coronation of Elak, now recognized and accepted as the king of Cyrena and all Atlantis. Kings and queens of all the city states, large and small, that comprised the new empire, attended the coronation, swearing fealty to Elak, and Borna of the Picts, with his son, Kaa Mag Borna, also present. Both were praised and honoured for their part in the brief but brutal war with the Orugllyr and their supernatural agents, and a new age of peace between Atlantis and the Pictish Isles began. Now in the central court one of the great

Pictish monoliths stood, silent, but a testament to the union of the nations and the bloody battles that had fused them. Frozen upon its polished stone, images of the servants of the Lords of Midnight danced and barred their teeth, together with the chalk white spirits of the dead of Skaafelda. In the great armoury of the city the ancient weapons of Valusia had been locked in a vault, ready for the day when they might be used against the enemies of Atlantis once more, and with them resided the great staff of Dalan the High Druid, who took a lesser rod of power to serve him.

Even deeper beneath the city, the ancient tunnels and all those found to be linked with them were blocked up and sealed, ancient words of power used in the ritual. Of the traitor, Scuvular, there was no sign, and those who had supported him were quick to denounce him and bow to the mercy of the new ruler. Most of them did so with good grace and were accepted. Others were less amenable, but their days of rebellion against the king and Council were over. Zerrahydris enjoyed a new level of authority and served his king loyally and dependably.

A new age of prosperity beckoned, although Dalan, the High Druid, the most watchful and sceptical of men, knew that the darkness was never far from Atlantean shores, and complacency was a potential new enemy.

- Helvas Ravanniol,
Annals of the Third Atlantean Empire

ALSO AVAILABLE *from*
PARALLEL UNIVERSE PUBLICATIONS

Carl Barker: *Parlour Tricks*
Charles Black: *Black Ceremonies*
Benjamin Blake: *Standing on the Threshold of Madness*
Mike Chinn: *Radix Omnium Malum*
Ezeiyoke Chukwunonso: *The Haunted Grave & Other Stories*
Irvin S. Cobb: *Fishhead: The Darker Tales of Irvin S. Cobb*
Adrian Cole: *Tough Guys*
Andrew Darlington: *A Saucerful of Secrets*
Kate Farrell: *And Nobody Lived Happily Ever After*
Craig Herbertson: *The Heaven Maker & Other Gruesome Tales*
Craig Herbertson: *Christmas in the Workhouse*
Erik Hofstatter: *The Crabian Heart*
Andrew Jennings: *Into the Dark*
Samantha Lee: *Childe Rolande*
David Ludford: *A Place of Skulls & Other Tales*
Samantha Lee: *Childe Rolande*
Jessica Palmer: *Other Visions of Heaven and Hell*
Jessica Palmer: *Fractious Fairy Tales*
Jim Pitts: *The Fantastical Art of Jim Pitts*
Jim Pitts: *The Ever More Fantastical Art of Jim Pitts*
David A. Riley: *Goblin Mire*
David A. Riley: *Their Cramped Dark World & Other Tales*
David A. Riley: *His Own Mad Demons*
David A. Riley: *Moloch's Children*
David A. Riley: *After Nightfall & Other Weird Tales*
David A. Riley: *A Grim God's Revenge: Dark Tales of Fantasy*
David A. Riley: *Lucilla – a novella*
Joseph Rubas: *Shades: Dark Tales of Supernatural Horror*
Eric Ian Steele: *Nightscape*
David Williamson: *The Chameleon Man & Other Terrors*

www.paralleluniversepublications.blogspot.com

Childe Rolande
The Myth and the Legend

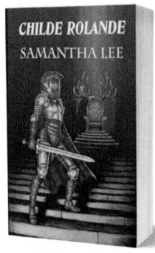 

Childe Rolande, Hermaphrodite and Freak, is born into the fiercely matriarchal society of Alba at a time when the fabric of the nation is crumbling.

Rolande fulfils all the technical requirements of an ancient Prophesy which promises that one day a 'Redeemer' will arise who will be 'the one and the both', and who will sweep away the age-old tyranny of Alba's female rulers to 'bind the nation together in peace'.

The hopes and dreams of Alba's downtrodden males are centred on this mystical being, whose eyes hold the wisdom of the ages and who can reputedly change into an eagle at will.

Can Rolande live up to their expectations, wrest the antlered throne from the Warlord of the Clans, drive the evil Sorceress, Fergael from her stronghold in the Dark Tower, and unite the polarised Kingdom?

Published as a paperback and kindle eBook

by

PARALLEL UNIVERSE PUBLICATIONS

GOBLIN MIRE
David A. Riley

Many years have passed since Elves defeated and killed the last Goblin king. Now the Goblins are growing stronger in their mire, and Mickle Gorestab, one of the few remaining veterans of that war, is determined they will fight once more, this time aided by a renegade Elf who has delved into forbidden sorcery and hates his kind even more than his Goblin allies. Murder, treachery and the darkest of all magics follow in a maelstrom of blood, violence and unexpected alliances. Facing up to the cold cruelty of the Elves, Mickle Gorestab stands out as the epitome of grim, barbaric heroism, determined to see the wrongs of his race avenged and a restoration of the Goblin King.
A savage blend of High Fantasy and sword and sorcery.

"A well written fantasy novel not for the faint hearted. The author created an interesting world and great characters. I recommend it to those who enjoy their fantasy with lots of violence and bloodshed."
(amazon review)

Published as a paperback and kindle eBook

by

PARALLEL UNIVERSE PUBLICATIONS

Tough Guys contains three previously unpublished novellas and a short. Based on the
title theme, these four works are completely different in subject matter and tone. There
is, of course, A Nick Nightmare story herein, *Wait for the Ricochet*, in which the gumshoe
is entrusted to convey a message about "The Malleus Tenebrarum", a book that names
the properties and powers of dark and light, to the Mechanic, one Oil-Gun Eddy... His
adversary is the sinister Lucien de Sangreville, plus assorted non-human denizens of
the murky lower levels, and his sidekick the sword-wielding business-woman Ariadne
Carnadine. In contrast, in *If You Don't Eat Your Meat* the reader enters a post-
apocalyptic world where the very unsavoury Ryan relates his story of rival families
and cannibalism. It is gruesome and unflinching horror. In *A Smell of Burning* a hospital
patient finds he is having out-of-the-body experiences. On his astral journeys he visits
a man recalling his abused childhood and this leads to a shocking revelation... Finally,
Not If You Want to Live explores the fate of Razorjack, who is a Redeemer, a dead man
used by a shady organisation to bring back others from death. An intriguing and
engrossing story of love between Razorjack (aka Jack Krane) and mobster's moll
Rebecca Fellini, with science fictional and satanic elements.

Published as a paperback and kindle eBook

by

PARALLEL UNIVERSE PUBLICATIONS

Printed in Great Britain
by Amazon